THE
MEPHISTO
THREAT

D1414091

E V SEYMOUR

THE MEPHISTO THREAT

MIRA

All the characters in this book have no existence outside the imagination
of the author, and have no relation whatsoever to anyone bearing the
same name or names. They are not even distantly inspired by any
individual known or unknown to the author, and all the incidents are
pure invention.

Published in Great Britain 2009.
MIRA Books, Eton House, 18-24 Paradise Road,
Richmond, Surrey, TW9 1SR

© Eve Seymour 2009

ISBN 978 0 7783 0295 7

58-0909

MIRA's policy is to use papers that are natural, renewable and
recyclable products and made from wood grown in sustainable
forests. The logging and manufacturing processes conform to the
legal environmental regulations of the country of origin.

Printed and bound in Spain
by Litografia Rosés S.A., Barcelona

ACKNOWLEDGEMENTS

I couldn't have written this book without the generous help of others. It's been a long time since I last visited Turkey so I'd like to thank Brian and Margaret Fox for bringing me up to date and for giving me such a personal insight into a country they clearly love. Special thanks also to Keeley Gartland, Media and Communications West Midlands Police, and to Detective Sergeant Maria Cook who shared her knowledge of the workings of the Organised Crime Division. It must be stated that the opinions and attitudes expressed in the story are my take and not a reflection of the views expressed by the officers with whom I spoke.

Selwyn Raab's excellent book, *Five Families*, provided the starting point for the novel. For inside knowledge of gangs and organised crime, I highly recommend all books written by Tony Thompson on the subject. Likewise, Peter Jenkins's book on Advanced Surveillance helped to give Tallis the edge in a number of tricky situations.

I'm not sure I'd have been able to write about Billy's injuries had it not been for my visits to the Acquired Brain Injury Education Service, Evesham College. The staff and clients there are truly inspiring, and big thanks to all for making me feel so welcome.

Lastly and by no means least, thanks to my agent, Broo Doherty, and to Catherine Burke and the team at MIRA. I couldn't have done this without you.

For Bex, Milly, Katy, Olly and Tim
My Famous Five

1

HEAT was killing him. Blades of light skewered his skin. Without air, the soaring temperature suffocated, halting time and muffling his senses so that he couldn't focus on the narrow streets, sprawling stalls and brightly coloured bougainvillaea, couldn't smell the spice and fenugreek, honey and dried beef, couldn't taste his apple tea or hear the blare of car horns signalling another mad couple's leap into matrimony. In all of his thirty-three years Tallis had never known weather like it, not even when he'd fought in the first Gulf War. It was as if the whole of Istanbul was being microwaved.

He changed position, slowly, lethargically. He would have preferred a café nearer to the university. Students were always attracted to the best hangouts, but Garry had insisted they meet close to the Spice Bazaar, or Misir Carsisi, to give it its Turkish name, a cavernous, L-shaped market within sight of the New Mosque. He didn't know the reason for Garry's choice of venue, or whether it held significance.

Tallis reran the conversation he'd had with Morello at

the airport. They'd literally bumped into each other, a surprise for both of them.

'Fuck me, Paul, what are you doing here?'

'Could ask you the same question.'

Garry tapped the side of his nose. 'Work.'

Tallis copied his friend, taking the piss. 'Holiday.'

'Lucky sod.' Oh, if only you knew, Tallis thought. 'How long for?'

'Three weeks, maybe more.'

'Good. I'll be back from the UK by then. Actually,' Garry said, 'there's something I'd like to bounce off you, something I'm following up.'

'I'm a bit out of the game, man.'

'Once a cop always a cop.' Tallis flashed a smile. Garry had no idea that, since he'd left West Midlands police, he'd become involved in working for the Security Services. Oblivious, Garry returned the smile then his look turned shifty. 'I'll explain more next time we meet. Give me your number and I'll give you a call soon as I'm back in Istanbul.'

Tallis had hesitated, felt tempted to give him the brush-off. He was working undercover and *off the books* for MI5. Asim, his contact, had been privy to a limited amount of chatter, which he wanted Tallis to verify. There was no huge expectation because the word on the ground was embryonic, no specific threats, no timing, no hard targets, but there remained a major fear that terrorist organisations were dreaming up a new kind of campaign, involving different methods of destruction, different tiers of people, hinting at an involvement with British organised crime. In among the white noise, the city of Birmingham was hinted at. A meeting with Garry could horribly complicate things but, apart from the insistence in Garry's manner, he owed the man.

As a freelance crime correspondent, Morello had covered the botched firearms incident in Birmingham for which Tallis, then a member of an elite, undercover firearms team, felt responsibility, even though he had officially been cleared. Unlike many, Morello wrote a balanced account, sympathetic almost, along the lines of a firearms officer's job was not a happy one. Tallis had phoned him afterwards to thank him and they'd hit it off. He'd stayed in touch ever since, even having several dinners with him and Morello's wife, Gayle, at their home in Notting Hill. When Garry was in Birmingham, he made a point of calling Tallis so they could hook up. Friends like that were hard to come by so, in spite of the risk, Tallis had given Garry his new mobile number with a smile. And Garry had got in touch.

Tallis adjusted his sunglasses. He was looking and listening, his senses attuned for anything out of kilter. He'd already closely considered his surroundings: five tables arranged outside on what passed for a pavement, all of them occupied, one by a group of middle-aged Turks smoking and playing backgammon, another by a young British couple. Some dodgy-looking Russians were eating mezes to his left. The furthest table away was taken by a single male, early thirties, nationality unidentifiable. For some time he'd been mucking about with a mobile phone. As Tallis glanced at him the man smiled with hooded eyes, black, same colour as prunes, then put away the phone and turned to his *Newsweek*.

Tallis continued to sip his tea, a beverage more suited to regulating body temperature than beer. Not that he was drinking alcohol—unprofessional to consume booze on the job.

He looked out onto a street crackling with latent heat, sky a screaming shade of blue. There was a small commotion as a street trader ambling past, his cart filled with plump bulbs of garlic, narrowly missed a taxi, the moustachioed cab driver displaying his displeasure by placing his hand flat on the horn and gesticulating wildly. Tallis smiled. When it came to driving in Turkey, you took your life in your own hands, the high road accident rate evidence that it was never wise to assume right of way. Just one of those many little things he'd discovered in the short time spent travelling in this strange, beguiling nation, a magical blend of ancient and modern, fast-paced and fast-changing and full of contradictions.

Take its government, Tallis thought. It desperately wanted to be accepted into the European Union but did the very things that made it unacceptable; it was an open secret that Turkey's human rights record continued to raise concern. By the same token, its people were friendly, generous and full of good humour. Especially the blokes. When a Turk declared himself your friend, an *arkadas*, he genuinely meant it, and it amused Tallis that while every Turk honoured the female of the species, every Turk also reckoned himself irresistible to women. While fathers could allow their daughters to enjoy certain freedoms, many saw no contradiction in offering them for sale, particularly to well-heeled Englishmen.

But this was all extraneous stuff, Tallis reminded himself. His brief concerned the criminal and political. Turkey might be a secular society, but there was enough pull from a variety of religious quarters to make it extremely vulnerable to conflict—that and its geographical position. Lying midway between Europe, Asia and the Middle East, the country was a gateway, a melting pot for culture and ideas on the one hand, terrorists and organised crime on the other. No accident that many unsuspecting girls were trafficked through its borders. More worrying still the significant trend for criminal organisations specialising in arms smuggling and extortion, with all their consequent violent sidelines, to get themselves involved in religious fundamentalism. An explosive mix.

Tallis checked his watch: after noon. Garry was late. He refocused his gaze on the Russian contingent. A popular holiday destination for many Russians, Istanbul was a particular favourite, though Tallis decided from a snatch of overheard conversation that tourism was not uppermost in the Muscovites' minds. He idly wondered whether these hefty-looking guys with flat, sawn-off features were Mafiya, a breed who favoured no room for error killing—cut throats, crushed lungs and bashed-in skulls. Job done.

'Paul, good to see you,' Garry Morello said, slumping down in the chair next to him. A heavyset man with dark features that spoke of Italian blood, he took out a handkerchief and mopped his profusely sweating brow. 'Christ, this heat is insane.'

Tallis agreed. For the past hour, perspiration had been consistently leaking from his hairline and plastering his short dark hair to his brow.

'Good holiday?' Garry said.

'Most enjoyable.' After bumping into Garry at Dalaman Airport, he'd travelled by taxi on a blood-pressure-raising journey through the mountains to Fethiye, a working town with a Crusader castle. There he'd treated himself to a Turkish bath, full hot and cold and slapped flesh, and, as a means to build up his cover, joined a *gulet*, a traditional Turkish wooden sailing vessel. Apart from the four-man crew, there were six others on board—four Brits, two Australians. The destination was Kalkan, originally a fishing village with winding, paved streets, recently transformed into a cosmopolitan marina of sophisticated but unspoilt charm. Apart from swimming and fishing off the boat, he'd spent the first week zombied out in what felt like a narcotic-induced sleep. He guessed it was his body and mind's way of recovering. He'd experienced something similar after engaging in battle. There was a particular type of lethargy that set in with exhaustion, especially when the fight was so unequal, when your enemy were half-starved boys and old men. But his most recent battle had involved neither guns nor grenades. His battle had been with grief and sorrow. He still felt raw from losing Belle. When it had finally sunk in that he would never see her again, he hadn't really believed that he'd ever recover.

'Drink?' Tallis smiled.

'Beer, thanks.'

Tallis ordered the locally brewed Efes Pilsen, leant back in his chair, waited for Garry to set the pace. There was a restlessness about him, Tallis thought. The Russians paid their bill and left the table, noisily scraping back the chairs as they went. Tallis briefly wondered if they were the reason Garry had chosen the venue. He inclined his head towards the departing diners. Garry followed his gaze. 'Mafiya,' he said neutrally. 'Wrote a book on the subject last year.'

Yesterday's news, then, Tallis thought.

The beer arrived. Garry took a long draught then glanced over his shoulder. His expression was uncertain. To help him out, Tallis kept his mouth shut. Most people couldn't bear silences. Garry was no exception. He craned forward. Tallis wasn't certain whether it was to block out the din from the neighbouring streets or because he wished to speak in confidence. 'Know a guy called Kevin Napier?'

'Not "nearly took out one of his own side" Napier?' Tallis said dryly.

'Care to enlighten me?'

'*If* we're talking about the same guy…'

'Suspect we are. Napier was a tank commander during the first Gulf War and left to join the police same time as you.'

Tallis pushed his sunglasses onto the bridge of his nose. After leaving school at sixteen, he'd joined the army and served with the First Battalion, the Staffordshire Regiment. Eight years later he'd joined West Midlands police.

'Am I right?' Garry said.

'Napier served with the 7th Armoured Brigade.'

Garry flashed him another expectant look.

'He shot at one of our vehicles by mistake,' Tallis said, 'and doused the occupants with machine-gun fire, injuring a couple of British officers.'

'Not a very smart move.'

'Proved no obstacle to his career path.' Tallis shrugged. It had rightly caused an almighty stink at the time, he remembered. The Brits were used to the Americans accidentally firing on them but not one of their own.

'Did you know he's with the Serious and Organised Crime Agency?'

Tallis resisted the temptation to react. 'I'd heard along the grapevine he'd applied.' So the bastard got in, he thought. Possibly not the smartest move. It was reputed that SOCA, with its high ideal of taking on the Mr Bigs, had fallen rather short of its remit. Experienced officers were leaving in droves either to retire or return to policing. Word on the ground implied SOCA was hamstrung by an unwieldy and top-heavy management system, crammed with analysts, but with no clear brief or expertise in processing data and intelligence. He wondered how Garry knew about Napier. 'What about him?'

'I'll come to that in a moment. Thing is, Birmingham's your patch, right?'

'Used to be.' It was almost two years since he'd worked as a firearms officer. After handing in his notice, he'd temporarily worked as a security guard in a warehouse before being recruited to work off the books for MI5. It hadn't been one of those 'apply, endure a host of interviews under the gaze of humourless experts, we'll get back to you' type appointments. His was more 'we want you, we need you, you've got the job' arrangement.

'But you still know the movers and shakers in the criminal world?'

'Not exactly up to date.' This time Tallis had to lean forward. The noise from the street had suddenly grown in intensity and penetrated the thickened atmospherics. Sounded like the Dolphin Police, a rapid response motorcycle unit, but when he glanced round, trying to source the din, he saw a Ducati hacking down the narrow street, zipping in and out, driver and pillion passenger clobbered up in leathers and helmets. They must be cooking, Tallis thought.

'Reason I ask…'

But Tallis wasn't listening. He'd turned back. Something was off. Couldn't quite work it out, but his sixth sense was suddenly on full alert. The air throbbed. Street hawkers continued to ply their wares but the chatter of conversation receded like someone had turned down the volume control. He felt that nip in the pit of his stomach, part fear, almost sexual, like when he'd been going into a firearms incident. Everything that happened next followed in slow motion. The driver ground to a halt, one foot resting on the pavement, bike tilting at an angle, the engine still running and revving. Garry glanced to his right but, unperturbed, continued to talk. Too late, Tallis saw the pillion passenger reach into his jacket. Fuck, too late, he saw the gun, the outer reaches of his mind processing that the weapon was a Walther PPK. Tallis shouted out, and dived for cover as three shots rang out and hit Garry in the chest.

Chaos broke out. Someone shouted. Everyone hit the deck. Tables overturned. Glass and crockery smashed. The British girl was screaming her lungs out, as were several passers-by. Blood was pumping out of Garry's chest like an open faucet and although Tallis ripped off his shirt and tried to staunch the flow, it was no use, no fucking use at all. Blood. Blood everywhere.

'*Bir ambulans cagrin! Polis cagrin!*' the café owner screamed. *Get an ambulance. Call the police.*

'Report,' Garry rasped, his face fast draining of colour, becoming pale as old snow.

'Take it easy, mate,' Tallis said, applying as much pressure as he could to the wound, appalled at the speed with which Garry's body was going into shock.

'*Report,*' Garry said again, his breath laboured, expression contorted, life-blood filling his mouth and spurting out between his teeth.

'Don't speak. It's all right,' Tallis murmured, watching with dismay as Garry's body twitched and juddered. 'Everything will be all right.'

But it wasn't. Two minutes later, Garry was dead.

Tallis leapt to his feet and ran. The imagined sound of the speeding motorbike drum-rolled like a heavy-metal soundtrack in his head. He guessed the killers had headed off in the direction of Galata Bridge, a bridge spanning the mouth of the greatest natural harbour in the world, the

Golden Horn, and providing the vital connection to the dense interior of the city. Although they had more than a head start, would have probably ditched their bike by now, stripped off their leathers and jumped into a car or cab, even though pursuit was entirely fruitless, Tallis gave chase. It didn't matter that he was a stranger and this was their terrain. Didn't matter that the traffic, which the police systematically failed to control, was clogging every turning. Some bastard had just callously killed his friend. Bloodied, tense with anger, oblivious to the baffled stares of Turks and tourists, he continued for almost a full kilometre, through streets dense with a tapestry of colour and life until, lungs exploding, he stopped, pitched his six-foot-two-inch frame forward and gasped for breath. Several lungfuls of fetid air later, he walked back to the café defeated.

At the sight of the police, Tallis took another big, deep breath. He'd only ever had one encounter with them and that had been the customs guys. He and his fellow sailing companions were drifting dreamily through navy-streaked and turquoise-coloured seas alongside Patara beach when a high-powered launch suddenly disturbed the calm and roared towards them. Two officers lashed their boat to the *gulet*, climbed on board and aggressively demanded to see everyone's passports and papers, their disappointment at finding everything in order palpable. Tallis was used to aggro, but his fellow travellers found it a deeply unsettling experience.

The police had clearly moved with impressive speed, he thought, looking around him. The café, no longer a place of entertainment, was cordoned off as a crime scene. Someone had draped a tablecloth over Garry's body, though nothing could conceal the vast amount of blood that slicked the ground. Several security police officers in uniform were talking to witnesses. Traffic police, distinguished from the others by their white caps, were trying, and failing, to disperse the gathering crowd of onlookers. Out of them all, one man stood out. He was short and trim. Educated guess, Tallis thought, a man in his forties. Clean-shaven, with a shock of dark hair, the officer's nose was wide, mouth full and mobile and his teeth were spectacularly white. He wore navy trousers and a pale blue, short-sleeved shirt, open-necked. He was speaking in rapid Turkish, ordering his men to ensure that witnesses remained where they were, that nobody was to leave without his say-so. Might prove tough, Tallis observed. The single man who'd been sitting alone, playing with his mobile phone, was noticeably absent.

At Tallis's approach, the man in charge turned, introduced himself as Captain Ertas.

'You must be the Englishman.' Dark eyes that appeared to miss nothing fastened onto Tallis. He suddenly realised the state he was in. In any other circumstances he'd have felt a prime suspect. 'Why did you run away?' Ertas said.

'I didn't. I gave chase,' Tallis said evenly.

'Lying dog,' one of the uniformed officers said. Tallis understood every word, but resisted the temptation to either look at him or answer back. More valuable for them to believe he couldn't speak the language.

'I understand you were with the dead man,' Ertas said, inclining his head towards Garry's fallen form. Tallis noticed that Ertas spoke excellent English with an American accent. Probably one of the new, modern, ambitious brands of Turkish police officer that choose to study at the University of North Texas and get a criminology degree.

'Yes,' Tallis confirmed.

Ertas stroked his jaw, said nothing for a moment. 'Friend?' Ertas enquired.

'Acquaintance.'

'He has a name?'

'Garry Morello.'

Ertas nodded again. He already knew, Tallis thought, just checking to see whether we're singing from the same hymn sheet. He'd probably checked Morello's pockets straight away and found his passport. Since a spate of terrorist attacks, aimed mostly at the police, it was obligatory to carry some form of identification, particularly in the city. 'And you are?'

'David Miller,' Tallis said.

'Passport?'

Tallis unzipped the pocket of his trousers and handed it, freshly forged care of the British Security Service, to Ertas. Not that they needed to have gone to so much trouble. From what he'd heard it was pretty easy to fool the Identity and Passport Service. All you needed was a change of name by deed poll.

'Your business here?'

'Tourist,' Tallis replied.

'And what do you do when not a tourist?'

'I'm an IT consultant.'

Ertas said nothing.

'I sell technology systems to the hotel and leisure industry,' Tallis said smoothly.

Ertas raised his eyebrow as if technology was a dirty word. This wasn't quite going according to plan, Tallis thought. Everything he said seemed to rattle Ertas's cage. Was it personal or had Ertas rowed with his wife that morning? Historically, the cops were poorly paid, lacked proper facilities and received contempt from the rest of the population. Tallis had thought this a thing of the past. Perhaps he was wrong.

Ertas glanced at Tallis's passport and read through the bogus list of destinations to which Tallis had ostensibly travelled. Tallis mentally ticked them off—Spain, Germany, Czech Republic, United States of America.

'Look, I could really do with cleaning up.'

'Of course,' Ertas said, handing back the passport. 'I will instruct one of my officers to fetch you clean clothes. You may use the facilities at the station. You have no objection to accompanying us, Mr Miller?'

'None at all.'

'Your relationship with Mr Morello…'

'A passing one.' Christ, Tallis thought, this could get tricky. 'We'd briefly met in London. Mr Morello is, *was*,' he corrected himself, 'a journalist.'

'A crime correspondent,' Ertas said with a penetrating look.

Ertas didn't get that off the passport, Tallis thought. 'I believe so.'

'So your friendship with him had no professional basis.'

'None.'

'Affedersiniz.' Excuse me. It was the uniformed officer who'd made the jibe about Tallis being a lying dog. He was stick thin with the same sweating, sallow features Tallis had observed on smackheads. He was instantly reminded of a conversation he'd had with Asim, his current contact in MI5 and the guy he directly reported to. It was suspected that many Turkish drug gangs were protected by official-dom. Same old: heroin and money. Tons of it.

'Evet?' *Yes?* Ertas said impatiently.

'The café owner.'

'What about him?'

'He says he saw everything.'

'Ve?' And?

'He says the bullet was meant for the Englishman,' the police officer said. Eyes narrowed to slits, he looked straight at Tallis.

2

WHY the hell would he say that? Tallis wanted to demand. Fortunately, Ertas asked the same question.

'The dead man often frequented the café,' the uniformed officer replied. 'He was well known, respected.'

'Even respected men are killed,' Ertas said, with irritation. 'Besides, if Morello routinely visited the café, he was an easy target.'

'He says,' the officer said, jerking his head in the direction of the café owner, 'that Miller's reaction was so swift, he must have known the bullet was meant for him.'

Balls, Tallis thought contemptuously as he was hustled into a waiting police car. He simply possessed excellent reflexes and training. But he could hardly mention that to the police.

The Grand Bazaar nearby had its own mosque, bank and police station, but Tallis was taken to Istanbul Police Headquarters. Tallis hoped it wasn't the next target for a suicide bomber. Not that long ago, police stations had become a terrorist's dream location.

If there was air-conditioning, it wasn't switched on. The overwhelming noise came from a flurry of flies buzzing around, either copulating or beating the shit out of each other. It was so hot inside, Tallis thought the concrete walls might crack and explode. At first he was forced to wade his way through several impenetrable layers of administration, lots of hanging around, lots of giving the same information, lots of meeting the tired gaze of disinterested clerks who smoked like troopers. He noticed that his fellow witnesses were detained elsewhere. Lucky them, he thought.

In bureaucratic limbo, he had ample time to consider his position. As traumatic as the sudden turn of events was, it didn't need to jeopardise his cover. To come clean would only confuse and complicate the issue. Besides, he really didn't want Asim alerted to the mess he was in. Wouldn't look very suave on a first outing with his new handler, especially as it might be construed as treading on the Secret Intelligence Service.

As for the café owner's remark, he reckoned the man had it all wrong. Tallis had witnessed the hit for himself, seen it coming. At no time had he been afraid for his own personal safety. It had been more a diffuse fear of being caught in someone else's crossfire. Which brought him back to Morello. Who would want him killed? Sure, as a crime correspondent Garry mixed in muddy circles, but he was British, for God's sake, and British journalists didn't usually get themselves slotted—unlike their Russian and Turkish counterparts. So, whomever he'd pissed off, or whatever it was he'd stumbled across that meant his life was worth extinguishing, it had to be big.

Ertas turned up an hour and a half after Tallis's arrival. 'So sorry to keep you. Much to do,' he said, rolling his eyes.

'Have you contacted Mr Morello's wife?' Tallis said, his stomach lurching. It was a second marriage for Gayle. She'd lost her first husband in a car accident. What a lousy hand of cards she'd been dealt, Tallis thought grimly.

'Next of kin have been informed,' Ertas said in business-like fashion. 'Everything to your satisfaction?' he added, eyeing the clean shirt Tallis was wearing. It wasn't. The shirt was a half collar size too small.

'Fine.'

Ertas suggested coffee, an invitation which Tallis grate-fully accepted. After giving the order to a junior officer, Ertas took Tallis down the corridor and into an area the size of a doctor's consulting room. It was cooler in here. The fan actually seemed to work, rather than simply rearrang-ing warm air. There were two chairs either side of a large desk upon which rested a telephone and a number of buff manila folders. In the corner were several filing cabinets.

Closing the door behind them, Ertas indicated for Tallis to sit down. Tallis noticed that Ertas was wearing a ring, a thick gold band inlaid with tiny precious stones. Although jewellery, particularly gold, was sold in abundance at the Grand Bazaar, with only a tiny charge for craftsmanship, it seemed like a strange affectation for such a seemingly precise and ordered man.

'Before we begin,' Tallis said, 'I'd like some legal representation.' He might know the form in Britain but here he was boxing in the dark.

'Not necessary, I assure you.'

'Then I'd like to contact my embassy.'

'We can arrange this for you.' Ertas smiled politely. He picked up a phone and, with a flourish, asked to be put through to the British Consulate. Tallis listened in as Ertas explained the situation. As far as he could deduce from Ertas's side of the conversation, someone was on their way.

The coffee arrived in traditional Turkish coffee cups. Both men took their time stirring in sugar. Tasted good, Tallis thought, taking a sip. Black and strong, it was a hell of an improvement on West Midlands cop coffee. Ertas spent several seconds surveying Tallis and Tallis spent several seconds looking at him. 'For a man who has suffered a terrible experience, you seem very relaxed, Mr Miller.'

'Probably shock. I haven't had time to process it.' Which was true. He'd witnessed men die in battle, seen the grotesque dance of bodies hit by machine-gun fire. He'd coldly observed the messy aftermath of suicide by shotgun, and the remains of turf wars played out on busy Birmingham streets, yet Garry's death fell into none of those categories. Unexpected, cruel and apparently without motive, it felt strangely and horribly similar to Belle's. The only difference: Garry had been a friend, Belle a lover. Tallis gave an involuntary shudder. He should be falling apart, he guessed, but he was too empty to feel anything right now.

'And do you normally play Rambo?' Ertas enquired.

Cheeky bastard, Tallis thought. About time Ertas got up to speed on current American heroes. At least he could have chosen someone nearer his age. Sly must be almost double it. He gave a lazy shrug. 'Can't say I've ever been put in that position before.'

Ertas leaned back in his seat. 'We are trying to establish Mr Morello's movements before he went to the Byzantine.'

'I wouldn't know.'

'He said nothing?'

'We'd hardly had time to exchange much more than a greeting,' Tallis said.

'You don't think he was followed?'

'And the hit team tipped off?'

Ertas smiled. 'You use dramatic language.'

'Killers, then.' Tallis briefly returned the smile. 'If he was, I know nothing about it. He certainly didn't suggest to me that he was being followed.' Garry probably wouldn't have known. He had been too preoccupied, Tallis remembered.

'And how did he seem?'

Restless. 'Hot.'

'Troubled?'

'By the heat, yes.' He was playing hardball with the guy. He knew it. Ertas knew it. But, then, Ertas knew a lot more than he was letting on, Tallis sensed. We're both playing masters in the art of deception.

'We have witnesses who appear to think that you were the intended victim.'

'Bullshit.'

Ertas smiled again. 'You are very direct, Mr Miller.'

'My apologies.'

'Not at all. I like a man who is straight with me.'

Ditto, Tallis thought, meeting Ertas's smile with one of his own.

'So you really think the other witnesses were mistaken?' Ertas pressed.

'Others?' He'd thought only the café owner had expressed a view. Careful, he reminded himself, you're not supposed to understand the language.

'Does it make a difference how many?'

'Not particularly. Like I said, they're wrong. In the heat of the moment, it's quite easy to draw flawed conclusions.' Tallis could have given Ertas a lecture on perceptual distortion, the firearms officer's nightmare. What the brain couldn't process, it made up. Wasn't lying, simply the mind's natural inclination to join the dots and fill in the blanks. It often explained discrepancies in witness accounts.

'I'd like you to run through everything that happened,' Ertas stated, 'from the time you were seated in the café to the final tragic event.'

Tallis did. Ertas listened. He interrupted only once. 'You say the gun was a Walther. How do you know?'

Damn, Tallis thought. No way could he bluff this one. Only way to go: tell Ertas the truth. 'It has a very distinctive finger-extension on the bottom of the magazine, giving a better grip for the hand.'

'I didn't know IT consultants were so well versed in firearms.' Ertas's dark eyes lasered into Tallis's.

'I served in the British army as a youngster.' It wasn't a very compelling explanation. The most he'd learned in the army about weapons had been directly connected to theatres of war—SA80s, 30 mm Rarden cannon and 7.62 mm Hughes chain guns—but Ertas gave the impression of accepting his account.

'And the motorcyclists—did you see their faces?'

'No.'

'Think they were men?'

Tallis hesitated. The individual riding the bike had certainly seemed too big and broad to be a woman, but judging by half the female population of the United Kingdom you simply never knew. The pillion passenger had been much smaller and could have been of either sex. He told Ertas this. Then something else flashed through his brain. Maybe he was mistaken. Maybe he imagined it. Surely not, he thought.

'And which way did they go?' Ertas said, breaking into Tallis's thoughts.

'Heading for the bridge.'

Ertas asked Tallis to repeat the conversation he'd shared with Morello. Tallis gave an edited account. He wasn't going to mention Kevin Napier or the Serious and Organised Crime Agency. As far as Ertas was concerned, he and Morello had been two Brits who'd happened to run into each other, chums passing the time of day. Happened all the time.

'Did Mr Morello have any enemies?'

'I wouldn't know but, I guess, in his line of work you can't rule anything out.' Tallis remembered the meze-eating Russians. Garry had written a book. Had he pissed someone off? He floated the idea. Ertas seemed to file the information away. Again, Tallis had the sensation that Ertas knew something he didn't.

'Whose idea was it to meet at the Byzantine?'

'Mr Morello's.'

'Did you know it's a hangout for the criminal fraternity?'

'I didn't, no.' So that was it, Tallis thought. Made perfect sense. The cops had already got a line going there. Probably explained why Ertas was so suspicious of him and how the police had got there so quickly. 'Perhaps there lies your answer.'

Ertas gave him a slow-eyed response. 'A line of enquiry to follow, certainly. I noticed from your passport that you have spent almost three weeks here.'

'That's correct.'

'In Istanbul?'

'No.' Tallis told Ertas about his sailing trip on the *gulet* and then his week of resort-hopping via taxi to Marmaris and Bodrum and finally the coach ride to Ephesus, one of the greatest ruined cities in the Western world. Images of colonnaded marble streets, intense heat and dust, the three-floored library with its secret passage to the brothel, and the Gate of Hercules, which formed the entrance to Curetes Street, flashed through Tallis's mind. Everywhere

there'd been reminders of Ephesus's past. It was reputed
that if the city's torches were not lit, Ephesus was in peril.

'And when are you planning to return?'

When I've got what I came for, Tallis thought. 'Not
made my mind up yet.'

There was a knock at the door.

'*Bir saniye lutfen.*' *Just a moment, please,* Ertas said,
getting up. 'So you say you've been in the city here for the
past week?'

He was really labouring the time factor, Tallis thought.
He guessed Ertas appreciated accuracy so he gave it to him.

'Five days.'

'Five days,' Ertas repeated. 'Where are you staying?'
Ertas asked, opening the door.

'The Celal Sultan Hotel.'

The skinny police officer with the sallow, sweating
features was standing on the threshold. He handed Ertas a
note. Ertas took it, thanked the man, closed the door and,
thoughtfulness in his expression, sat back down. 'We will
not be releasing the details of this afternoon's incident,' he
told Tallis. What he meant, Tallis thought, was that they
would not be releasing the identity of the victim. If it was
suspected that Garry had been the wrong target, the police
didn't want the killers coming back for a second crack at
it. Probably a sensible precaution, or...

Something inside him buckled. What if he was wrong?
What if someone *had* got it in for him? He immediately
discounted his current connection with Asim, his MI5
handler, as a factor—all he'd done was keep his ear to the

ground, visit certain places, clock faces, all low-key. He was playing the original grey man—most intelligence gathering was mundane, quiet and unassuming. He'd done nothing to stir up that kind of violent response, but it was perfectly conceivable that others from his past might bear him a grudge.

'Are you all right, Mr Miller?'

'What? Oh sure,' Tallis replied.

The phone rang. Ertas picked up. 'Right,' Ertas said, standing up.

'That it?' Tallis said, making a move.

'For now, but, please, no need to get up. I understand there is someone from the embassy to see you.'

Jeremy Cardew was not Tallis's idea of an official from the consulate. From the name alone, he'd expected a louche-looking middle-aged individual, dressed in creased linen, with an expanded belly and public-school accent. This bloke was probably not much older than Tallis, whippet-thin and, as it turned out, originally from Newcastle, which explained the Geordie accent. He had pale, penetrating eyes that assured Tallis he was a man given to action. After the swift exchange of names, and handshakes, Tallis explained his situation. Cardew's expression became one of growing concern. He'd barely finished before Cardew started quizzing him as effectively as Ertas then, like a rabid trade-union official of the old school, launched into a low-down on procedure, outlining what he as an embassy official was empowered to do—help with issuing replacement passports, providing local information, assisting individuals with mental illness, helping British victims of crime and, more relevantly Tallis thought, 'doing all we can should you be detained'.

The list of what they couldn't do was shorter but of more consequence. 'Can't give you legal advice, I'm afraid,' Cardew pointed out. 'Neither can we help with getting you out of prison, prevent the local authorities from deporting you after sentence or interfere with criminal proceedings.'

Tallis folded his arms. 'Looks like I fall outside all the categories.'

'They're not keeping you, then?' Cardew's expression was not one of disappointment exactly, more surprise.

'I'm free to go,' Tallis assured him.

'And you had no problems with the police?'

'None at all.'

'You've given a statement?'

It felt like several. 'Yes.'

'You've clearly been through a most traumatic experience,' Cardew said, with what felt like genuine concern, 'but, from what you're saying, it looks as though you have the situation under control.'

Hardly, Tallis thought. He was having a hard time coming to terms with Garry's violent death. Inside, he was churning with emotions.

'Just thought you should be made aware of my circumstances. For my own protection,' Tallis added.

Cardew's features fell into a quizzical frown. 'Turkey's moved on a lot since *Midnight Express*.'

A film about an American student arrested in Turkey for carrying hashish, Tallis remembered. The scenes of prison brutality were chilling. 'I'm sure it has, but—'

'When the police have finished with you, my advice would be to get the next flight back.'

Tallis met the other man's eye. 'I don't want to.'

'Then I suggest, Mr Miller,' Cardew said slowly, his voice tight and strained, 'stay out of trouble.'

'Right,' Tallis said, meeting Cardew's steely gaze. 'I'll try to remember that.'

3

TALLIS returned to the Celal Sultan, a pretty, traditional town house in the old city centre, not far from the Blue Mosque and Topkapi Palace. He took a circuitous route, as he'd done since his arrival, variously taking a cab one way, tram back the other, and finally walking to check for and shake off any possible tail. His fully air-conditioned room, Moroccan in style, was a familiar and welcome relief. Now that he was in the privacy of his own space, he seriously felt in need of a drink. Garry's death had left him stunned. But, in his heart, he knew that alcohol, far from further deadening his senses, would only bring his emotions roaring to the fore. He couldn't take that risk. Stripping off, he shaved then took a long, cool shower and considered the day's events.

He still clung to the thought that, horrible though it was, Garry had been the target rather than himself. Tallis couldn't think of anyone offhand who bore him a grudge and, even if they did, he believed that if someone were going to kill him, they'd attempt it back in the homeland, not here in Turkey. Why go to the trouble? Only one major spike in that theory: the killers were British.

He turned the shower to cold, feeling a pleasurable cascade of water across his skin, and tested out his theory on the ethnicity of the killers. That shout he'd heard amidst the chaos was as captured in his mind as the memory of Belle's smile. As sure as he could be, he'd heard the words '…fuckin' out of here'. Not Turkish, not any other nationality, Anglo-Saxon, pure and simple. At least one of those guys was definitely British.

As far as his current activities were concerned, he was simply maintaining a watching brief. Since the new man, a former grammar-school boy, had taken over MI5, there had been a significant change in direction, which meant that people like him could play a role. Some called it privatisation of the security services, and something to be feared and resisted. All he knew was it gave him gainful employment. He wasn't officially on the books, never would be. He was more mercenary than spook, a necessary evil and, he had no illusions, expendable. He tilted his face up towards the showerhead, opening his eyes wide, thinking about the brief and exploring the suspected link between terrorism and British organised crime. The hardcore terrorist relied more on the spoken word to transmit information than the written, and it was generally carried out person to person rather than via an easily traceable phone line or computer. So far he thought he'd stumbled across nothing significant, but the killing at the café changed everything. Ertas, by his manner, had given the game away.

Tallis turned off the shower, ran a hand through his hair

and reached for a towel. He rubbed himself dry, caught sight of his lean, deeply tanned and muscular reflection in the mirror. He was probably in better physical shape than he'd been for a couple of years thanks to some fairly serious working out. Mentally, he still pushed all the buttons. Only the slightly haunted look in his dark eyes spoke of a man who'd lost the very person he needed to live for. Belle, he thought, what I wouldn't give to see you again, to hear your voice, to hold you. Christ, it's so damn lonely here on my own.

Dressed again, he took out a hunting knife from underneath the clothes in the bottom of the wardrobe. He'd bought it from a trader, no questions asked, after a memorable visit to Gemiler Island where, long ago, legend spoke of an albino queen who'd lived there. To protect her from the blistering sun, the islanders had built a walkway, hewing out the solid rock so that she could walk freely from the temple at the top of the island down to the sea. Tallis had followed the trail, chipped and crumbling now from the tread of many pairs of feet, and marvelled at such devotion. Tombs embedded on either side gave it a spooky feel.

Back on the *gulet* once more and only a few metres out to sea, he'd heard the familiar put-put sound of one of the many little boats trading everything from sweet and savoury pancakes and ice cream to rugs and painstakingly embroidered scarves or *oyali*, and neckerchiefs. Except this boat and its wares were different. The woman, sure enough, was selling legitimate goods. Her gypsy-looking colleague, however, after some minor probing, was in the market for what he called ancient ornamental weapons. Four inches long, with a wide stainless-steel blade ground to a deadly point, the knife was neither ancient nor ornamental but it was more than enough to frighten, maim or kill. Not that Tallis harboured malign intent. Just wanted back-up. He flicked the blade open and closed it again with lightning speed, one-handed. The knife felt solid in his grip yet light to carry. Perfect. With the same minimum of fuss as when he'd made the purchase, he slipped it into the pocket of his chinos, and went down to the dining room where he ate a delicious dinner of *karniyarik*, stuffed aubergines, followed by grilled trout, and headed back out onto the street.

It was steamy as hell outside, the Turkish night asphalt black and starless. Street lamps lighting his way, he headed away from the main tourist area of Sultanahmet towards Constantine's Column. From there he took a tram out to the massive covered Grand Bazaar with its painted vaults, and streets studded with booths and shopkeepers as pushy and relentless as any City trader. Here, all manner of commercial human activity was at work. He felt as if he was at the centre of a large ant nest, lots of rushing about, even though most of the actual manufacturing and trading was carried out in the *hans* or storage depots, tucked away behind gated entrances, shaded and concealed. Finding it hard to get his bearings in spite of the profusion of signposts, he allowed himself to be carried along with the flow, through Feraceciler Sok, passing cafés and restaurants with local diners, and ancient copper and marble fountains dispensing fresh water. He skirted the oldest part of the bazaar, veering left and coming to an Oriental kiosk, which had been built as a coffee house in the seventeenth century but now served as a jewellery shop. Left again, he cruised down a street of carpet and textile shops. Overhead, Turkish flags hung with the familiar crescent moon and stars, a reminder and symbol of national pride. After pushing through a scrum of bargain-hunters, he eventually found himself at the entrance to the largest *han* in Istanbul, the Valide Hani. Beyond lay the Spice Bazaar, inside this the café and last place he'd seen Garry Morello alive.

By returning to the scene of crime, he didn't really expect to discover anything, the trip more a means to jog his memory and get things straight in his head. Voyeurs and the naturally curious had gathered outside the spot. Someone, he noticed, had laid flowers at the perimeter. Sealed off by white crime-scene tape, a single bored-looking policeman on duty outside, the café was over-run by Turkish Scenes of Crime Officers, their distinctive forensic suits declaring that they were part of an international club. Christ, he thought, guts turning to water, why did he feel so lashed by memories? Before joining the Forensic Science Unit, Belle had once been a SOCO. It was partly the reason he'd elicited her help in a previous case, that and the fact he hadn't been able to live without her. He felt a spasm of regret and grief shoot through his body. Perhaps, if he hadn't involved her, he thought blindly, she'd still be alive.

Tallis turned away, partly to shield his face from an embarrassing tear in his right eye, partly to maintain a low profile. At once, he spotted a familiar countenance. Dark eyes met. *You*, Tallis thought, watching as the stranger unlocked his gaze and walked purposefully away. Tallis observed the smaller man's retreating form, waited, counted to ten and dropped into casual step behind him. Only two reasons he could think of to explain why the man who'd left the café so abruptly had suddenly turned up on the scene: curiosity or involvement. Or—Tallis felt something flicker inside—it boiled down to the curved ball theory. He, like Tallis, was simply caught up in someone else's game. Happened all the time.

They were heading west along Cami Meydani Sok, running parallel to Galata Bridge before breaking off into the sort of quiet and narrow streets where you might get your throat cut. Tallis could tell from the way the man was walking that he knew full well he was being tailed. He seemed to be moving in no specific direction, crossing, recrossing and doubling back, all classic anti-surveillance tactics. The law of averages dictated that he had the advantage. Single tails always carried a high risk of exposure.

The man suddenly leapt onto a tram. Thinking he might be heading for Sirkeci station, Tallis clambered into the next car after him. Like all trams, it was clean and fully air-conditioned, a triumph of Turkish engineering and the speediest method to get around in a city like Istanbul. Tallis paid the driver and sat down, keeping his eyes pinned, and rearranged his thinking—thinking that was based on many years' experience of bad guys. He didn't doubt that the stranger in the tramcar was probably one of them, up to no good, sure, but not necessarily connected to the hit in the café. So he was taking one hell of a risk by reinserting himself at the scene. He'd have been better off lying low. Tallis smiled to himself. *So you are involved somehow, somewhere.* More obliquely, he wondered whether this man was also the very type of person he'd come to spy on, one of the many faceless Islamic terrorists, the masterminds, the ghosts, those who had no profile on any security service database.

The tram passed the stop for the station and was continuing in the direction of the Celal Sultan Hotel. Either by accident or design, Tallis felt as if he was coming full circle. Had it been light he would have seen more clearly the painted wooden houses lining the street. As it was, he saw nothing but the glint and glow from sitting rooms and lighted cigarettes. Then the motion of the tram began to change. It was slowing. Sixth sense told him that his man would make a move. Tallis held back, watching and waiting for signs of his quarry. Sure enough, he slipped out and darted through a hole in a hedge and into the outer grounds of Topkapi Palace. Tallis followed him, catching his shirt on a wooded thicket. Cursing as he ripped himself free, he discovered he was standing alone in what looked to be an old rose garden. Shaded by overgrown bushes and plants, the place had a neglected air, making it a perfect rendezvous for lovers or thieves. That he was walking into a trap became a distinct possibility. He looked around him, listened. Pale moonlight sifted down through a sky of banked cloud and suppressed heat, lighting his way.

Then he saw him. No more than twenty metres in front, his man was moving at a slow trot along a designated walkway, towards the palace. Time to change the dynamics, Tallis thought. *'Merhaba!'* Hello, he called out. The man quickened his step, broke into a run. Tallis kicked off the back foot and sprinted after him, ducking and weaving to avoid being lashed in the face by several overhanging branches. Shorter, the man darted with a quick zip of speed, off the main path and across another piece of woodland, feet pounding the uneven ground, but he didn't have the staying power, something at which Tallis excelled. He called out again, shouted a reassurance, he only wanted to talk. Still the bloke kept running, jinking through the wooded grounds, giving the strong impression that he knew the place well, that he was heading for a rat run. Then, without warning, he ran back onto the main path, across a square, screeching to a halt, and turned, his face and form illuminated by a shaft of light from a tremulous moon. Hand reaching, face cold as antique marble, lips drawn back in a pale snarl.

Tallis made a rapid calculation. The bloke was carrying. And he was prepared to open fire. Automatically, twisting to one side, Tallis drew out the knife, simultaneously flicking it open, just as the tell-tale glint of gunmetal swung and homed in on him.

His attacker stood no chance. Before he'd even got off a shot, he was falling. The blade had flown through the air, sliced into and stuck fast in his throat.

4

THE man's death rattle was mercifully short but noisy and terrifying. Tallis glanced around, checking first that he was alone—*yes*—then searched the body for identification, picking out both a wallet and passport that identified his victim as a Turk by the name of Mehmet Kurt, born in 1977. Next, Tallis looked for a place to conceal the body. He didn't have great options. All he could do was buy time. Ironically, several metres away lay the Executioner's Fountain, the place where, long ago, the executioner washed his hands and sword after a public beheading.

Tallis briefly wondered whether he could just ditch the body and run, make the kill look like the bloke was a victim of some assassin with a macabre sense of history. Beyond, there was open ground and the entrance to the Palace. Not a great welcome for the tourists in the morning, Tallis thought, brain spinning like three rows in a fruit machine. That left the Rose Garden, his firm favourite for a shallow grave but too far to cart a body. He gave an urgent glance to his left. There wasn't much more than a triangle of trees, but it was the best place. The only place.

Dead men were heavy, but Tallis picked the stiff up with relative ease. There was little blood due to the trajectory of the blade—Tallis took care not to disturb or remove it—and though acutely conscious of Lockard's principle—every contact left a trace—he knew that his DNA was unlikely to be stored on a Turkish database. The British system stood head and shoulders above anything in Europe, which was why fast-track plans to automatically share information were already in place, but that did not include countries bordering the Middle East.

Dumping the body where the trees grew more thickly, Tallis wiped the shaft of the blade. That only left the weapon, which was of professional interest to him. Russian, slim for easy concealment, it was a simple blowback pistol, the PSM, reputed to have remarkable penetrative powers, particularly against body armour. Intended for Russian security forces, it had resurfaced and become available on the black market in Central Europe. Tallis picked it up with a handkerchief and put it next to its owner.

Hugging the side of the path, he retraced his steps back the way he'd come. Once, just once, he felt a shiver of fear that there was someone else in the shadows. He neither stopped, nor looked, but kept on walking. Out onto the street again, he thought about taking a detour to the Cemberlitas Baths near Constantine's Column. There he could have the equivalent of a steam clean, the best way to rid himself of the odour of death, but it was already fast approaching midnight, the time the baths closed. Adrenalin flooding his nervous system, he strode back the short distance to the hotel.

Back in his room, he ripped off his clothes, threw them into a carrier bag and chucked them into his suitcase. He'd get rid of them in the morning. He showered until his skin stung and put on a clean pair of trousers. After a quick exploration of the mini-bar and coming up empty, he picked up a phone and ordered a bottle of raki, a jug of water, and a *pide*, a flatbread with salami and cheese. Room service wasn't part of the package. It was only a three-star hotel. But, in reality, money bought anything.

The food arrived. Tallis offered enough notes to ensure both the porter's discretion and gratitude. After he'd closed and locked the door, he ate and drank slowly, without pleasure, food and alcohol the best cure for the terrible nausea that followed the taking of a life. While he chewed and drank, his mind brimmed with questions, ranging from burning curiosity about the man he'd killed to how long it would take before the body was discovered. He came to no firm conclusions.

After a fitful night's sleep, partly as the result of the incredibly high temperature, partly because he was still coming down from his adrenalin fix, Tallis got up, packed up some things and left the hotel shortly before eight in the morning, the carrier bag containing the contaminated clothes swinging idly from his hand.

A saffron-coloured sun beat down hard upon him. Within minutes, his shirt was stuck to his back and perspiration was oozing in a constant trickle from his brow. Heat was doing funny things to his vision. Colours seemed more vivid, shapes less defined. Pavement, buildings, cars looked as though they might burst into flames.

His destination was Eminonu, a port bustling with traders keen to sell goods or offer trips up the Bosphorus. A cooling breeze usually blew in off the water but not today. A small podgy individual with down-turned eyes caught Tallis's attention. For some reason he had no takers even though the small boat he was chartering looked sturdy enough. Expecting to haggle, Tallis spoke in English and asked how much for a two-hour trip. Predictably, Podgy named his price, which was eye-wateringly high. Tallis immediately offered half. Podgy looked insulted. Tallis shrugged. Podgy broke into a grin, a sign that he considered Tallis a worthy adversary, and offered him a cold drink. Tallis accepted with a gracious smile. All part of the game. He discovered that the little man was called Kerim. 'Look, Kerim,' Tallis said, feeling the delicious chill of ice-cold water at the back of his throat, 'no need to do the full trip. How about you take me as far as the Fortress of Europe and I'll get the bus back?'

Kerim clutched a hand to his chest as though he was having a heart attack, shook his head, his expression dolorous. 'Not good. I have expensive wife.' His Turkish accent was as thick as the coffee.

Tallis let out a laugh. 'More fool you.'

'And many, many children,' Kerim said, face forlorn.

Christ, the bloke could win a BAFTA, Tallis thought. 'All right,' he said, feigning sympathy. 'Full trip, there and back with a twenty-minute stop at the Fortress.'

'Is better,' Kerim said, significantly brightening up.

'And something else,' Tallis said, lowering his voice.

'I very quiet,' Kerim said, pointing to his mouth. 'I say nothing.'

You'd better not, pal, Tallis thought, jaw grinding at the terrible yet calculated risk he was about to take. Kerim leant in close, allowing Tallis to explain what he wanted the little man to do, that there would be a great deal of money paid if he looked after something he was about to give him, but dire consequences, not only for him but for his family, should he default, then he offered a little more than his original sum for the trip, which, like the good businessman Kerim was, he accepted with a small bow.

Rumeli Hisari was a maze of steep, narrow cobblestone streets leading to tranquil Muslim cemeteries in a fortress setting. Everywhere were reminders of its fifteenth-century past, and the grand plans of Mehmet the Conqueror in his quest to take Constantinople. Much as Tallis adored history, he couldn't have been less interested. He was looking for a suitable place to get rid of his carrier bag full of clothes. In a little less than ten minutes, he found it. Although most hotel and restaurant lavatories were of the modern flush design, public conveniences remained stubbornly old-fashioned, of the squat-over-the-slot variety. Setting aside any squeamishness, he took out his belongings and thrust them deep into the bowels of the latrine. Nobody in their right mind would try to retrieve them. Ten minutes later, he was back on the boat, allowing his offending arm to trail in the deep and narrow waters of the Bosphorus.

After checking and booking a KLM flight out of Ataturk to Spain, part of a set of precautionary measures following the killing and the previous night's excitement, he spent the rest of the day lying low, eating a simple meal in the hotel restaurant before retiring to bed early. Deeply asleep, he was suddenly alerted to someone hammering on his door. 'All right, all right,' he said, dragging on a pair of boxers, instantly awake. 'Who is it?'

'*Polis!*'

Tallis glanced at his watch. It said two-twenty in the morning. 'You got ID?' he called out.

More banging.

He took a deep breath, opened the door a crack, clocking two men in plain clothes flanked by two police officers with firearms. Shit. He opened his mouth to say something. The door burst open. An outstretched fist shot out. Connecting.

Next stop darkness.

5

TALLIS came round feeling muzzy. Half-naked, feet bare, handcuffed, he was lying flat on his back on a piece of thin cardboard. His mouth was dry, as if it were laminated, and his temple throbbed with a viciousness he'd only experienced once before in his life after getting legless, at the age of seventeen, on a bottle of rum. He gingerly ran his cuffed fingers over his body. No broken bones, only bruises.

He looked around. Low-wattage light swinging from the ceiling throwing a nicotine glow on walls the colour of British cement. A hole in the ground signalling a convenience, the malodorous smell and dark cloud of flies buzzing round the entrance further confirmation. A dodgy-looking stain, the colour of dried pig's blood, on the floor to his right. A steel door, with a slot in it for those outside to see in, remained resolutely shut. So much for Turkish hospitality, he thought dryly. There was no sound of far-away traffic, no human voice, no birdsong, so he guessed he was deep in the bowels of a building. The size of the cell, for that's what it was, was the human equivalent of a battery hen's coop. And, Christ, it was hot. His lungs felt as if they were sticking to his ribs. Might as well shove him in an oven, turn it to 200 degrees and roast him.

He staggered to his feet, tried to get his bearings, *tried* to focus. His watch was missing from his wrist so he had no idea of time. Without natural light he couldn't even make an estimate. Wherever he'd been taken, he doubted that it was a police station. That worried him.

He retreated to the corner of his cell. Best he could do was conserve his energy, stay upbeat. There was absolutely nothing to connect him to the dead man so it was pointless to speculate about the reason he'd been brought and banged up there—wherever *there* was. Fear of the unknown was his greatest enemy. He refused to entertain the notion of detention centres and secret police, of places where men were detained without charge or trial, or of ghost prisoners held in legal limbo. He had a high pain threshold, but even seasoned soldiers knew that the mental anticipation and anguish was often worse than the horror itself. As soon as his captors came for him, he decided to play the role of outraged tourist. No heroics. No trying to beat the system. But plain old browned-off from Britain. Oh, and act frightened, he thought. Remember, he repeated to himself, you're David Miller, boring, lowly IT consultant.

At last, he heard some movement and the scraping sound of metal against metal. The slot in the door drew back. A face with midnight eyes peered in, expressionless, followed by another face, which Tallis immediately recognised. On seeing Ertas, he got up. 'Captain,' he began, hope briefly rising. 'So glad—' Before he could complete his sentence, the slot slammed shut. Irritated, Tallis hunkered back down on the cardboard. At least he wouldn't freeze to death.

Hours seemed to pass. He was getting seriously dehydrated, his thinking lacking clarity, becoming muddled. Who was Ertas? Was he part of the administrative police keeping track of foreigners, the judicial police investigating crimes or the dreaded political police who combatted subversives of any denomination? Bound to be crossovers, Tallis thought foggily, or maybe Ertas belonged to none of these groups.

He must have fallen asleep. He woke up with a yell. A guard standing over him had thrown a bucket of ice-cold water over his head. Tallis stuck his tongue out, eager to catch a few precious drops. Two other guards were pulling him up, banging his knees along the concrete, dragging him towards the open door. God, he thought, what next? He'd heard about enhanced interrogation techniques. He'd heard they weren't very nice.

He managed to get up onto his feet. They were taking him at a fast trot down a dingy corridor. He could hear voices now. Men shouting. A gut-wrenching cry of pain tore through the fetid air. Barked orders.

Stairs ahead. One of the guards led the way, the other behind threatening him with a Taser stun gun should he try anything clever. Not that Tallis had any intention of risking 50,000 volts and total muscle paralysis. The noise was growing louder now. More desperate. The unmistakable clamour of violence. In spite of the heat, Tallis felt a chill as cold as a desert night creep deep into his soul.

The corridor opened out. Overhead strip lighting flickered with enough of a strobe effect to induce a fit in an epileptic. Doors off on either side, some of the metal grilles open, sounds of excessive use of force crashing around his ears. He hoped it was staged. If it wasn't, poor sods, he thought.

They were walking three abreast, Tallis stumbling slightly, not used to walking in bare feet, and feeling off balance with his hands tied together. Finally they came to the end and to what looked like the type of lift you saw in a car park. One of the guards pressed a security keypad and the metal doors drew apart. Tallis was butted through into another corridor, more stairs, more fancy codes and security panels, more shouts of protest. For a brief moment, he thought he heard the strains of classical music and the sound of dripping water. Must be the product of a vivid imagination. Either that, or he was hallucinating. And then all his birthdays came at once. He was standing in an open space, like an atrium, natural light flooding through the barred windows in the ceiling. So delighted by the sight of the sun crashing down on blue, he hardly noticed Ertas, but he did clock the man standing next to him. Deeply tanned, strong-jawed, and sturdy with eyes that were too close together so that it was impossible to detect who or what he was looking at. The man dismissed the two guards with a short command. At once, Tallis could tell that, fluent though the man's Turkish was, it wasn't his first language.

'This way, please,' Ertas said, coldly remote, indicating that Tallis follow.

Despite feeling a twat, standing there in his underwear, Tallis stood his ground. 'This how you normally treat visitors to your country?' he fumed. 'I demand to know where you are holding me and why. I also insist that I have full legal representation. I want to see Mr Cardew at once.'

'You make many demands, Mr Miller,' Ertas said quietly, with disdain.

Thank God for that, Tallis thought. At least his true identity hadn't been revealed. Could only make things complicated. A quick visual of the building told him that escape was probably out of the question. The atrium appeared to be the highest point of the structure. There were no other windows, only doors off with a staircase leading down at the opposite end. A man in boxer shorts, even in these soaring temperatures, wasn't exactly likely to go far. 'Who's your friend?' he said, bolshie.

Ertas answered. 'You may call him Koroglu.'

Strange, why can't he speak for himself? Tallis thought, eyeing the man suspiciously.

'Come,' Ertas said, pivoting on his heel.

Tallis let out a belligerent sigh. He felt less fear now, his outrage building and genuine. Shown into a room not too dissimilar to the one at the police station, he asked first for water then to be untied. Both requests were ignored.

Ertas pulled up a chair for himself. Koroglu took a position behind Tallis. Ertas asked Tallis to sit down.

'I pro—' Two firm hands grabbed his shoulders, fingers

digging deep into his nerves. Tallis gasped with shock and slumped down, arms half paralysed. He wondered what rank Koroglu held, from which department he hailed. Bastard division, he concluded.

Ertas, who was sitting opposite, showed no emotion. 'After you left the station, what did you do?' His voice was soft, coaxing.

Fucking predictable, Tallis thought, straight out of the hard-guy, soft-guy school of police interrogation. Ertas had probably picked that up in the States, too.

'Not sure exactly when that was,' Tallis said, leaning forward slightly, wishing he could rub his arms and get the circulation going. A stolen glance at Ertas's watch told him it was four in the afternoon.

'Two days ago.'

Right, Tallis thought so now he knew exactly how long he'd been held, which wasn't very long at all. Just felt that way. 'I went back to the hotel. I can tell you what I had to eat if you insis—'

The blow came from the left, flat-handed, medium-strength, precision-aimed. Tallis's ear rang. He felt temporarily deafened.

'I will ask the questions,' Ertas said softly. 'You will answer.'

Tallis nodded, raised his tied hands, rubbed at his ear and did his best to look stricken. Inside he boiled with rage. In two fluid movements, he could throw his head back against the goon standing behind him, swing his hands round and punch Ertas in the throat, smashing the hyoid bone.

'And after dinner, what did you do then?' Ertas continued elegantly.

'I went for a stroll.'

'Where?'

'Not sure I re—'

Another clout on the other side ensured that he did. He told Ertas what he wanted to hear. No point in denying it. These guys already knew where he'd been.

Ertas leant forward with a tight smile. 'You were observed, Mr Miller, following a man who is of interest to us.'

'I don't know wha—' Tallis flinched, expecting another blow. But it was Ertas who raised his hand in a restraining gesture. Tallis heard Koroglu grunt with frustration at being denied another chance to use him like a punchbag.

'You deny it?' Ertas's expression was hard.

Tallis smiled. 'Since when was following someone a criminal offence?'

'So you *were* following him.'

Checkmate, Tallis thought. Those blows to his head must have addled his thinking.

'The man in question,' Ertas continued smoothly, 'is a Moroccan known to have links with al-Qaeda.' A *Moroccan*? Tallis thought, surprised. According to his victim's passport, he had been a Turk—unless it was false, like his own. 'He was deported by your own government two years ago,' Ertas continued, 'and is of interest to the United States.'

Shit. Tallis baulked. Who the hell did they think he was? More to the point, who were they? In his mind, the

USA was synonymous with extraordinary rendition and secret detention centres. Could this be one of them? From what he'd heard, they were more likely to be found in Poland and Romania, but the closed prisons there were reputed to be full and so the States had outsourced and turned their attention to the Horn of Africa. What all this definitely pointed to: Garry Morello *had* been onto something, and *he* was deep in the shit. He remained stubborn. 'I don't see what this has to do with me.'

'Because you were the last person to see him alive,' Ertas said, down-turned eyes meeting Tallis's.

'You mean he's dead,' Tallis said, sounding aghast.

Ertas picked up the phone, ordered a jug of water and two glasses. Nobody said a word. Tallis was trying to work out what they wanted from him, confession or revelation? The water arrived. Ertas poured out, unlocked Tallis's cuffs and handed the glass to Tallis who drank it down in one. 'Thank you.'

'So, Mr Miller,' Ertas said. 'Would you like to explain exactly what you were doing?'

'All right,' Tallis said with a heavy sigh. 'I admit I followed him. I recognised him from when I was in the café with Mr Morello.'

'Our Moroccan friend was at the Byzantium?' Something in Ertas's expression led Tallis to believe that he already knew the answer to the question.

'Yes.'

'Then why didn't you mention this when we spoke at the station? Why was this not in your statement?'

'Because I didn't think it relevant.'

'But you thought it relevant later.' There was a cynical note in Ertas's tone.

'No, you don't understand.' Tallis allowed his voice to notch up a register to simulate frustration. 'It was only because I saw the guy there in the evening.'

'When you went back to the café,' Ertas said, scratching his head.

'Foolish, I know, but I was hoping to find something important that might help with your inquiry.'

Ertas flashed another tight, disbelieving smile. 'And then what?'

'I followed him.'

'Where?'

'To the gardens at Topkapi. Then I lost him.'

Ertas glanced up at Koroglu. 'Ask him what he was planning to do,' Koroglu ordered in Turkish. Ertas nodded. Obedient, he put the question.

'I don't know.' Tallis shrugged. 'Talk.'

'To a stranger, in the middle of the night, in a foreign land? Wasn't that reckless of you?'

'I suppose it was. I wasn't thinking.' But he was now; he was thinking that the guy standing behind him wasn't what he seemed at all. He'd assumed Ertas was calling the shots. He was wrong.

'Did you know he was armed?' Ertas said, watching Tallis like a crow observed carrion.

'Certainly not.'

Koroglu spoke again. 'Tell him that we know he

intended to meet the Moroccan. Tell him that he had already contacted him in Britain. Stress that he has already lied and to lie further will only make things worse.'

Tallis did his best not to jump in, to shout and protest his innocence. Ertas, meanwhile, cleared his throat and repeated word for word what Koroglu had said.

'This is ridiculous. I never met the guy before coming to Turkey. I don't even know his name.'

'And your name is?'

Neat move. Tallis didn't flinch. 'David Miller. Look, is this a case of mistaken identity or something?' he said, twisting round. Mistake. Koroglu whipped a ringed hand across his mouth. Tallis registered the distinctive taste of metal and sand as blood dribbled down his chin.

'Point out that we can keep him here indefinitely if we have to,' Koroglu said savagely.

Ertas did.

'I'm a British citizen, for God's sake. You have no jurisdiction to keep me here.'

'Tell him to shut up. Ask him about his business interests,' Koroglu commanded.

Ertas again complied.

'What? I told you, I'm an IT consultant.'

'You work from home?'

'No, I—'

'Where is home?'

'Birmingham, West Midlands, UK.'

Ertas glanced up at Koroglu with a significance that made Tallis realise he was sunk.

'What is your religion, Mr Miller?' Ertas said, inclining towards him.

'My religion?'

Koroglu bent over him and with one swift movement grabbed him by the balls.

'You understand the term?' Ertas said, scathing.

'I was brought up a Catholic,' Tallis gasped, eyes watering. That was true. His Croatian grandmother had insisted on it.

'And now?'

Once a Catholic, always a Catholic. 'I'm lapsed,' Tallis grunted. The pain was searing.

Ertas frowned incomprehensibly. Koroglu explained in Turkish then let Tallis go with a final squeeze of his genitals.

Ertas turned his eyes to Tallis. 'You have not converted to Islam?'

Jesus, now Tallis knew exactly what they were driving at. After the London bombing of 7/7, many nations, the USA in particular, were critical of Britain for spawning its very own breed of homegrown suicide bombers. Originally termed 'clean skins' by the British security services, it had since been revealed that the culprits had already come to the attention of MI5 and were associates of those later convicted of a fertiliser plot that amongst other targets would have had the Bluewater Shopping Centre in Kent blown to smithereens. As much as the British Government was viewed as an important ally, its citizens were regarded with a great deal of suspicion. Tallis had just fallen under that particular cloak of distrust.

'Look, guys, I already explained. You have this all…'
Tallis shot out of the chair, threw his head back, heard the
sickening crunch as it connected with Koroglu then made
a grab for Ertas. Knocking the captain to the ground, he
made a dive for the door, tore it open and ran.

The level was approximately three hundred metres long
with a metal staircase leading down. Tallis ran the full
length, took and charged down the steps. Christ knew
where he was heading. All he knew was that if he wanted
to breathe air again, see the sun, he had to get out. He'd
heard too much about places where only the people
holding you knew you were there.

The building opened onto another level: gangway to the
left; railings on the right. Below was a long row of open-
barred cells with men tightly caged together. An alarm
sounded, the noise triggering them into action. Immediately, they started shouting abuse, rattling against the bars
of their prison, jeering as a group of armed officers speeded
past. Tallis kept running, muscles in his legs knotted, bare
feet pounding, oblivious to the sound of shouts and clattering feet behind him as he leapt down the next staircase.
On hitting the bottom, a guard, younger than the rest,
raised his weapon, but Tallis twisted away, the ensuing shot
missing him by a whisker.

More men now. More shouts. Tallis zigzagged as much
as he could in the confined space, eyes to the front, focused
on the end set of doors, wondering how he was going to
get through, how to operate the security lock, how…

The doors snapped open. Koroglu stepped out, black-eyed, mean and moody. Didn't look like a man to bargain with. Tallis put both his hands up in a defensive gesture. 'All right, let's be cool about this,' he said.

'Shut the fuck up,' Koroglu snarled before delivering a knockout blow.

6

THE cell in which Tallis surfaced was no improvement on the original. Concussed by the second serious blow to his head in less than twenty-four hours, he still, mercifully, retained a sense of direction. If the previous guest suite was located on the third floor down, he guessed his current quarters were four floors. It stank of human excrement and despair. The single light hanging from the ceiling only further illuminated the hopelessness of his situation. Same old squat hole. Same lack of water. Thin layer of cardboard replaced by a stone plinth for reasons that soon became obvious—his cellmates were a small family of rats. The way his stomach was growling from lack of food, the best thing he could do was kill and eat them. Welcome to the Turkish Hilton, Tallis thought, taking immediate advantage of his new bed.

Resting back, hands tucked behind his head, he replayed Koroglu's last words. *Shut the fuck up!* Pure Brooklyn. CIA or FBI, Tallis wondered, or some other covert organisation that the world knew nothing about? He didn't like to consider the political implications, but he had to. Surely the Americans weren't conducting their war on terror from the bowels of a Turkish detention centre? He couldn't envisage the Turkish government allowing it. Yet stranger things had happened. Governments the world over passed off dodgy or ambiguous dealing with regimes not to their taste with phrases like *in the national interest, real politic*, or the more recently popular *in the interests of national security*.

Any of the above usually involved obscene heaps of money, sometimes armaments, often the granting of power and influence. Poor old Turkey had been stonewalled by the Europeans for so long, why be surprised if they looked to America to win them some grace and favour? That the Americans used their considerable funds to oil the wheels of various intelligence services throughout the world, Pakistan being one of them, was common knowledge. Like Pakistan, Turkey was also open season to religious fundamentalism. Lately, the political situation had grown considerably worse.

He let out a knackered sigh. And where did all this leave him, apart from being stuck in this rodent-infested gulag? They, whoever they were, obviously thought he was someone he wasn't, which was true, but not the someone they thought he was. He very much doubted his cover was shot. If so, they'd have come out and said so. What worried him far more was their mistaken intelligence about his connection to the dead Moroccan. They clearly didn't think he'd killed him. If the bloke had been that serious a threat, and they suspected him of being involved in his death, why not treat him like an ordinary criminal, or even someone who'd done them a favour? No, they had him down for an associate.

He rolled over, tried to get comfortable, finding it virtually impossible. The skin on his back felt sandpapered from being dragged unceremoniously along the concrete floor. Escape seemed less possible now. His only hope was that when they took him away to do God knew what, he'd be presented with another opportunity. He wasn't overly optimistic. In the absence of having any better ideas, he decided to try and sleep.

Napier, Morello, Ertas, Koroglu, all puppets and players in his dreams, clamoured for his attention, each morphing into another in such a cacophony of sound and vision he wasn't sure whether his waking thoughts were part of his subconscious or the here and now. Gingerly opening one eye, he swore the walls were shaking. A deep rumbling sound appeared to be coming from the centre of the earth. He sat bolt upright. The light above his head flashed, jittered and cut out. Then followed a thunderous noise, which shook the entire cell, followed by popping, not like gunfire, but as if the planet was splitting. Tallis threw himself under the bed. The rats had the same idea. The walls were really shaking now, the earth shuddering. Lights flashed back on, as if a generator was kicking in. Before his eyes he could see the floor near the makeshift latrine begin to lift and tear, then open.

The cell resembled a house of moving floors like he'd seen at a fairground when he'd been a kid.

No doubt about it, this was an earthquake. Gripping the side of the stone plinth, he hung on, determined not to be lost to Mother Earth, his greatest fear being buried alive. Nothing felt fixed and what little there was in the cell was moving. Everything that had seemed quiet was dancing with noise. Shouts and screams rent the air. Tallis rolled himself into a ball, mute, every sinew in his body tensed for action. When the wall nearest the door started to yaw, crumble and disintegrate, he seized the opportunity and lunged through the gap.

Out into the corridor, Tallis saw a vision of chaos. Two officers were lying on the ground, their heads mashed in by fallen masonry. Tallis checked their pulses. Both dead. Either a bomb had gone off or, as he'd originally suspected, there'd been an earthquake. If the latter, it seemed to have lessened in potency. Aftershocks, however, could prove as powerful and devastating to already weakened structures. He needed to get out. Now. Problem was he knew he wouldn't escape without a credible disguise.

He turned to the largest of the two dead men, stripped off the man's uniform, put it on then dragged off socks and boots from the feet of the other dead officer, who looked to be nearer his size, and put those on too. A quick search yielded a cap. Tallis dusted it down on his sleeve and slapped it on his head, pulling it down hard over his eyes, then headed for the remains of the staircase. Badly damaged, there was a yawning gap, revealing a vault three feet wide.

He suddenly realised the significance of the sound of

running water. He must be near the Basilica Cistern, a popular and most unusual tourist spot. A vast underground water cistern dating back to 532, the roof held up by three hundred and thirty-six columns, each over eight metres high, only two-thirds of the original structure was visible, the rest bricked up in the nineteenth century, but had it remained so? What if it had been redeveloped? Where better to hide something as sinister as this place than right under the noses of the general public?

Tallis backtracked six steps, took the staircase at a run, leapt high and sure, adrenalin aiding his flight. His next obstacle was the automatic security door, which was shut. Not knowing the code, he banged on it, praying he'd be heard and hoping that in the mayhem protocol would be relaxed. Sure enough, the door drew open, a guard appearing. He was young, probably no more than twenty. He had frightened eyes.

'Thanks, mate,' Tallis said in Turkish, touching the young man's arm in gratitude.

'No problem. You all right?'

'Sure, but don't go back that way,' Tallis said, gesturing vaguely behind him. 'It's completely annihilated. Was it a bomb, or what?'

'Earthquake,' the guard confirmed, eyes wet with terror. 'Rezul came this way. Did you see him?'

'*Cok uzgunum.' Sorry.*

'You mean?' The guard's eyes widened.

'There's nothing you can do for him now.'

The young man looked stunned. He looked as if he

might breach the gap, investigate for himself. Tallis had to stop him at all costs. 'What's it like up there?' he said, inclining his head, drawing the man's attention away.

'It's bad. Many have been killed. Some of the prisoners have already escaped.'

Good, Tallis thought. 'Come, we must get out.'

'But Rezul,' the guard said plaintively, trying to look past Tallis. 'My brother.'

Tallis clamped a hand on his shoulder. 'He has already gone to Allah.'

Tallis quickly discovered that his rescuer's name was Hikmet. Above was exactly as Hikmet described: death and destruction. As always, the Grim Reaper had made no distinction. Bodies of prisoners and officers alike lay where they'd been crushed. The wounded, most of them beyond help, moaned where they fell. Tallis blocked out the sound of screams and the cries of those alive beneath the rubble.

He fell into step beside Hikmet, two buddies together, as far as anyone who counted was concerned. The guts of the building had been devastated. Structures twisted. Columns shattered. Water poured in. Electrics flashing. Still some tilt and sway with aftershocks. Both of them headed for the remains of a metal staircase, the only way, Hikmet assured him, of reaching safety. But they were not the only ones intent on saving their skins. Prisoners desperate for freedom, some of them armed, were massing in large numbers. As Tallis surged forwards, a fight broke out behind him. He quickened his pace, keen not to get caught up in the brawl, and saw Koroglu up ahead. Barking orders, he was trying to stem the tide of rising panic in the small number of officers at his side. Christ, is that how many survived? Tallis silently asked himself until it dawned on him that, rather than signifying the strength of the quake, the actual number of guards was probably very small, a classic schematic in detention centres. The fewer the people who knew what was going on, the less chance of word getting out.

Thick and dusty air coated his mouth. Shouts and yells bounced off and reverberated around the walls. Tallis could feel the tide of humanity threatening to crush and over-whelm him. It felt as if he was in the middle of a football crowd on the rampage. People were jostling on all sides, desperate to get onto the rickety staircase, which he feared would collapse underneath the volume of men. He and Hikmet leapt on together, steaming up the stairs, brutally punching away those who tried to obstruct them, glad to get to the next level.

They were in a vault. Light was limited, the air filled with ancient dirt. Tallis covered his mouth, trying not to breathe in the choking atmosphere, but what he could see through narrowed eyes was quite beautiful in its design. Gazing at the most exquisitely engraved columns of stone, he remembered that for a century, after the Ottoman conquest, the victors had known nothing of the original cistern's existence. Perhaps this was a part of the old struc-ture. Sound for thousands of years, would it hold up in the wake of an onslaught by Mother Nature? As if she'd heard and wished to remind them of her power, another tremor shook the ground. Tallis and the others stood stock-still, breath held, listening in terror as the walls around them crunched and crackled. Without warning, there was a terrible noise of tearing metal followed by the far worse sound of men screaming and falling to their deaths. As Tallis glanced behind him, he saw that the stairs, the only route to freedom, were gone.

They were moving urgently forwards again. Ahead, an archway and the entrance to a stone staircase like those seen in ancient castles. It led up. Koroglu had stepped aside as if counting his men in. Tallis fell in behind Hikmet, adjusted the cap he'd stolen so that it fell down a little more over his face and shuffled forwards. In line with Koroglu, near enough to smell his breath, the earth shook once more. Hikmet and the others threw themselves forwards, surging ahead, bounding up the stone steps as if it were their last snatch at freedom. Tallis followed. He didn't look back to see whether Koroglu had joined the flight. Up and up, they went, until at last, dizzy and disorientated, they were disgorged into a stinking alleyway.

Tallis took a deep breath of dusty air, thinking it had never felt so good. Looking up to a sulphurous-looking sun, he estimated it was roughly around five-thirty in the morning, maybe earlier. He'd never seen the city look so busy at that time before. Everywhere were people out of their homes and shops, staring nervously at the sky, as if it, too, were about to fall in on them. He guessed men had been doing the same since time began. You didn't have to be religious to require an explanation for a sudden act of God. Bang on cue, he heard the haunting call of the clerics to the faithful, encouraging the devout to attend the first of the prayer times as laid out in the Koran. Not all Turkish Muslims were quite so dutiful, but Tallis reckoned today the mosques would be full.

He turned at the sudden sight of a man wandering past, the shirt torn from off his back exposing burns to his skin. Tallis didn't know if he was a local resident or one of the prisoners. Glancing furtively around him, he saw Koroglu striding away. Probably heading for the American embassy, or a safe house. Tallis didn't care. He had no intention of following him. Hikmet turned and thanked him.

'For what?' Tallis said, perplexed.

'For witnessing my brother's passing.'

Tallis hung his head, feeling terribly ashamed. Didn't Hikmet realise that he was wearing the clothes of the dead? 'I'm truly sorry,' was all he could manage.

'I must go and find my family,' Hikmet said simply.

Both men hugged each other as strangers did when thrown together in extraordinary times. Tallis wished him well.

While others also went in search of loved ones, Tallis set about finding his way onto a street he could recognise. Quick examination of his pockets yielded Rezul's wallet. Tallis opened it. Inside he found an ID card, a photograph of Rezul's girl and money. He was tempted to run after Hikmet, but it would be too dangerous to explain. Besides, he needed the loot.

At last, he found himself walking down a main

thoroughfare, heading towards Sirkeci station. Most buildings there looked unaffected. Those that had collapsed had been of inferior build and situated in narrow alleys. As usual the poor and less well off copped for it. Many were standing around, some blank-faced. Others, more sanguine, sat outside in the open, drinking coffee. Word on the street was that an even bigger quake was on its way. A police car crawled slowly past, an officer hanging out of the passenger side with a loudhailer to his mouth, instructing people in both Turkish and English to head for an open area. Many were heading for Gulhane Park. Tallis didn't join them. He'd learnt his lesson. Never revisit the scene of a crime. In fact, he knew exactly where he was destined. And it wasn't the station. He only hoped that Kerim would be there.

7

THERE were no more tremors. By six-thirty, Tallis had bathed, bought shorts and shirt, dumped the guard's uniform and purchased a rucksack. Two days of not shaving ensured a growth of stubble. The swelling around his mouth had gone down a little. Any visible wounds he could blame on the quake. At least it made him look less recognisable.

He'd already been to the ferry terminal at Eminonu. Kerim's boat was there but of Kerim there was no sign. Tallis was not unduly worried. Yet. His flight from the airport didn't leave until 2.35 p.m. By then, he hoped that air travel would be operating normally, though he realised there might be congestion and long delays because of the ground conditions. He was also acutely aware that once Koroglu had recovered his equilibrium, he'd be issuing strict orders for his arrest. Tallis smiled. Koroglu would be looking for David Miller. He'd also be searching the flight manifests for passengers heading for Britain, not Spain.

Tallis took advantage of the Turk's natural inclination to make the most of every commercial opportunity. Enterprising young men selling cans of Coke and bottled water, stuffed vegetables, mezes and Turkish bread were milling about, doing their bit to feed the city in its hour of need. Tallis paid top dollar. Worth every luscious mouthful, he thought. It had been over twenty-four hours since he'd last eaten.

An hour later, he'd bought enough convincing clutter to stuff in his rucksack to trick the most astute customs officer. Half an hour after that, Tallis's patience was rewarded. Kerim, his podgy frame distinct amongst the crowds, went over to his boat and jumped aboard. Tallis jumped in after him. At first Kerim's face expressed alarm, but as his mind made the connections he broke into a beaming smile. 'Friend,' he said, clapping Tallis on the back. 'You come. You are safe. Praise Allah!'

Good, Tallis thought, Kerim wants his money. 'And you,' Tallis said, reciprocating with a hearty slap that made Kerim cough, 'your family is also safe, all those children?'

'Indeed. All is good. Very good,' Kerim said expectantly, drawing the small parcel from the pocket of his trousers. 'I brought as you said. I bring every day in case you come.'

'Good man,' Tallis said, taking the package and opening it. Inside was the Turkish equivalent of five hundred pounds in sterling. He gave two hundred to Kerim, keeping the rest for extra expenditure. Of more interest was the passport he'd secreted inside. It belonged to none other than Paul Tallis.

Using up the bulk of Rezul's money, he took an expensive cab ride to Ataturk Airport. Spacious and modern, the arrivals hall was crawling with people. There he made his way straight to the international terminal. He went to the desk for reserved tickets, showed his passport. After brief enquiry, he discovered that his KLM flight was delayed, predicted to leave at 4.30 p.m. Tallis tried not to look too disconsolate. With a stopover, he wouldn't arrive until 2.30 a.m. Pocketing his economy-class airline ticket, he glanced at the clock in the airport lounge. He had almost four hours to kill.

He spent the intervening time trying to stay out of trouble. He bought a stash of magazines and newspapers, including the *Turkish News*, and topped up his calories. Whenever he saw a police officer, he resisted the temptation to either turn away or run. Instead, he tuned out, acted the part of tourist, just another traveller bumming his way round the Med.

At the earliest opportunity, he went to the check-in counter, joining the queue displaying the hand luggage sign. It was extremely busy. When it came to Tallis's turn, the looks were stony, but he was cleared and given the appropriate accreditation.

Approaching 3.30 p.m., Tallis found himself anxiously watching the terminal's clock. Still his flight had not been called. A curdled feeling slopped about in the pit of his stomach. What if Koroglu turned up? What if he arrived with a bevy of armed police? What if CIA operatives stalking the airport already had him staked out and in their cross-hairs? What if...?

There was some disturbance down the far end of the

lounge. Several armed police officers were on the move. They were making for the departure lounge for British Airways flights. Oh, Jesus, Tallis thought. Koroglu was striding along behind them. Then came an announcement:

'KLM, flight number 082, originally due to depart at 14.35 hours and departing now at 16.30 hours, will be leaving from terminal…'

Tallis was on his feet, jaw grinding, walking with as controlled a step as he could. He handed his passport and ticket over to a young Dutch woman with milk-white skin and almond-green eyes. He met her steady gaze with a relaxed smile and watched her cheeks flush pale pink. She handed back his belongings. 'Have a safe journey, Mr Tallis.' She smiled back.

Amen to that, he thought.

He wasn't happy until the plane had taken off. Even then he spent the first couple of hours fretting. Only when they finally touched down at Madrid did he start to breathe easily.

The next flight to London left at 7.10 via Iberian Airways. The ticket desk was closed. Already well past midnight, he decided to sit it out at the airport. By the time the desk was open, the flight had already left. Pissed off and exhausted, he eventually caught a flight that arrived at Heathrow, terminal 2, shortly after three in the afternoon. He fully expected to be stopped and searched at Customs, but was waved through, mainly, he suspected, because it was choking with people as a result of delayed flights, understaffing and a lack of screening machines. From

Heathrow, he took the tube to Kensington and booked into the Kensington Close Hotel, where he was escorted immediately to the room already allocated to him. Inside, he found a wardrobe of clothes his size. He also found the safe. Entering the code, the door clicked open, yielding one thousand pounds in used notes and a mobile phone. Tallis pocketed the money and punched in the number given to him by Asim. He waited while the call was routed. Asim answered straight away.

'Paul,' he said, warmth in his voice. 'How are you?'

'Apart from surviving an earthquake, having a gun pulled on me by an a-Q operative and escaping from the clutches of some CIA bastard who took a fancy to my balls, I'm good, thanks.'

8

WHEN Tallis finished, Asim said, 'Welcome to the club.'

Tallis pointed out dryly that he wasn't part of anyone's club.

'Is that the reason you didn't reveal your true ID?'

'What is this? Phone a friend?' More to the point, whom should he have called? Tallis wondered. As far as MI5 were concerned, he wasn't officially working for them. He was, without doubt, one of many freelancers, paid for his expertise, yet utterly deniable if he screwed up, a spook of sorts but without formalised backing. Strangely, it didn't bother him, perhaps because he had nobody to worry about and nobody to worry about him. The attraction for the security services was obvious: expendability.

Asim's voice trickled with laughter. 'Wasn't a criticism. You did the right thing by keeping schtum.'

'What I want to know is why they thought I had connections to the Moroccan.'

'They mention the guy's name?'

'No, but shouldn't be too difficult to find out.'

'True.' Asim paused. 'Sounds to me as though they had

limited intelligence, you burst into the picture, they decided to add three and three together and made fifteen.'

'*They* being?'

'Not entirely certain.'

Bet you have some idea, Tallis thought. 'And Morello?'

'A side-show.'

Tallis didn't agree.

'You said at least one of the hit team was British,' Asim said.

'Yup.' He remembered the words: '*...fuckin' out of here*'.

'That may be significant as far as the hunt for the people behind Morello's murder are concerned.'

More than significant, Tallis believed. He thought it was their first cock-up. All he had to do was find the next.

'And this guy, Koroglu—an American you say?'

'No doubt about it.'

Another pause. Tallis decided to go the direct route. 'Are the Yanks outsourcing their detention centres to Turkey?'

'The Turks are under pressure from extremists, too. They might see it as being to their advantage.'

'Are they, or aren't they?' Tallis said, stubbornly pushing his luck.

'I don't know,' Asim said smoothly.

'Oh, come on,' Tallis said. 'You must have some idea. We're all supposed to be best buddies.'

This time Asim's laugh was hard. 'Notwithstanding the change of head honcho across the water, a political event that takes time to download to the game on the ground, the

Americans are no longer happy to play when it comes to intelligence concerning potential a-Q suspects.'

'Because our government decided to voice opposition to Guantanamo Bay, and reduce our forces in Iraq?'

Asim concurred. 'We've reached a fairly dire situation. If we want to know something from a suspect held in American custody, we're no longer able to fly out and talk to them. We have to put the question to the American operative who will ask on our behalf.'

How very Russian, Tallis thought, remembering the Litvinenko investigation in which Scotland Yard officers were denied direct access to suspects.

'It signals a grave lack of trust,' Asim continued, 'something that needs to be restored and quickly, which is why the head man is so hell-bent on getting Five, the Secret Intelligence Service and all the other British law enforcement agencies to bond together in the fight against terrorism.'

And they needed to, Tallis thought. It was reputed that at any given time there were two thousand terrorists and two hundred plots aimed against British citizens. No longer was it a case of *if* there would be an attack but *when*. In response to the threat, MI5 had launched a hip recruitment campaign aimed at young Brits, including Muslims, doubled its size, regarded languages for its operatives as crucial and had adopted a policy of international and national co-operation right across the board.

'They ever thought about using organised crime?'

'What?' Asim said, baffled.

'Use a thief to catch a thief.' Asim gave a snort of

ridicule. But Tallis wasn't going to be deflected. 'The CIA recruited Mafiosi to kill Castro.'

'One man,' Asim pointed out. 'We're up against entire legions, people from every walk of life, who think nothing of exploiting each single easy route into our country.' Tallis thought of the Middle Eastern doctors who'd taken advantage of a shortage in the NHS to blag their way in and initiate a reign of terror in Scotland. 'Who, in case you've forgotten,' Asim continued pointedly, 'are rumoured to have links with organised crime, which is what we're investigating.'

'I was wondering when you'd come back to that,' Tallis said briskly. 'Well, this is how I read the runes. I think the two incidents are connected. Morello discovered something. The fact he chose the Byzantium, a known criminal hangout, for a meeting is significant. Whatever he knew, someone wanted to shut him up. Somewhere our Moroccan is involved. You mention the purported links between British organised crime and terrorism. Well, I think I just stumbled across them.'

'You're making some fairly big assumptions.'

'It's the only picture that fits.'

'In this line of work there are usually several pictures that fit, Paul, and the obvious one is usually a blind.'

Ouch, this was the nearest Asim, who it had to be said he didn't know that well, had come to a rebuke. 'Point taken,' Tallis said with as much humility as he could muster.

'Going back to the hit. Are you really sure it was meant for Morello?'

Tallis let out a sigh. He'd been over and over it. 'Yes.'

'Reason?'

'Something Morello said before he died. He kept repeating the word "report".'

'What kind of report?'

'I don't know.'

'You're sure that's what he said?'

'Quite certain.'

'And you think this is what got him killed?'

'Possibly. Not sure, could be a blind,' Tallis said, a smile in his voice. Asim let out an appreciative laugh. 'And there was something else,' Tallis said. 'Morello asked if I'd ever come across a guy called Kevin Napier.'

'And have you?'

'He fought in the first Gulf War same time as me and, like me, left to become a police officer, only his route took him to the dizzy heights of the Serious and Organised Crime Agency.'

'Go on,' Asim said, voice sharpening.

'That's it. I confirmed I knew the guy.'

'And Morello didn't state the reason for his interest?'

'Didn't get the chance.'

There was a brief silence. 'SOCA is the UK arm of Interpol,' Asim said, as if thinking aloud. 'It also maintains a large network of overseas officers.'

'So Napier might have been posted to Turkey?'

'It's possible.'

Another little piece in the jigsaw, or simply a meaningless piece of detritus? Tallis thought.

'You've done really well,' Asim congratulated him. 'Shame about the screw-up with Morello, could have done without it, but you handled everything superbly. I'll see what I can find out from my contacts and get back to you. In the meantime, I suggest you go back home, get some rest, forget about it for a bit.'

Forget about it? And poor Garry relegated to nothing more than a gross inconvenience. Tallis sadly shook his head. He really felt like a most reluctant spook.

He didn't go back home. He stayed the night in London. The hotel was overrun with American kids doing a sight-seeing tour. As he went down to breakfast the next morning, an anarchic help-yourself affair, he stood in line behind a youth wearing a T-shirt that announced he wanted to shoot all the fucking jackasses. Couldn't agree more, Tallis thought drolly.

The earthquake in Turkey featured well inside most newspapers' covers, sometimes not making it until the 'World News' section. Loss of life was reported as minimal, a couple of dozen deaths scattered over Istanbul, many more injured. Tellingly, there was no mention of those crushed deep within its city streets.

Outside heralded a fine September day, warm and sunny, with puffs of light cloud. After a quick wander around Kensington Palace Gardens to take some air, he returned to the hotel, checking out shortly after ten. From there, he took a tube to Ladbroke Grove.

Gayle Morello lived in the heart of Notting Hill in a

handsome loft apartment arranged on two floors. The visit was a flyer. There was a strong possibility that she might already have left for Turkey. If she was at home, he knew that, whatever came up in the conversation, he couldn't admit to being with Garry in his final moments. The police were bound to have mentioned David Miller, the man Garry had met at the café. No way was he confessing to being the same man.

Getting out at the station, he walked past a range of local shops, including a number that had a culinary theme. Outside the Morellos', he stood for a full minute, gazing up at huge arched windows, black wrought-iron balcony, red brick, freshly painted white rendering. He was wondering how the hell he was going to talk to a woman who'd lost not only her first husband in sudden circumstances but her second husband, too. But he had to. Gayle deserved no less. As for Garry, it was Tallis's way of honouring his old friend's memory.

With a heavy heart, he trudged up the four steps to the painted black front door and pressed the entry-phone. After a few moments, Gayle answered. 'Yes?' Her voice sounded tired.

'Gayle, it's Paul Tallis.'

'Paul?' she said, sounding confused then, as if it suddenly dawned on her who he was, she let out a small cry. 'Come on up,' she said, pressing the buzzer to let him in.

Tallis ascended two flights of narrow stairs. Must have been a bugger moving the furniture in, he thought, his frame constrained by the architecture. The front door to the apartment was already open, Gayle standing there. She was wearing dark glasses. Her skin was ashen. Although a tall, statuesque woman, she seemed to have shrunk since the last time he saw her. Stooped shoulders, long blonde hair unwashed, clothes thrown on anyhow. That's grief, he thought, wondering if he too, perhaps more subtly, had morphed since Belle's death. A sudden image of her dying in his arms flashed into his mind. She'd been shot. The man responsible for the order was Belle's husband, Dan, a bent copper and wife-beater, the act perpetrated not out of jealousy, but as a means to get back at Tallis, Dan being Tallis's morally disconnected older brother.

Tallis put his arms around Gayle, gave her a hug. A memory of Hikmet flashed through his mind. Was he becoming a magnet for the bereaved?

Gayle began to cry. 'How could somebody do that to him? How could they? I keep going over and over it, imagining, wondering what it must have been like.'

Tallis murmured softly, letting her weep, feeling her tears soak into his shirt. Eventually she calmed down a bit, pulled away from him.

'They said he died instantly, that he didn't feel pain, so I suppose that makes it more bearable.'

'Yes,' he said, unflinching.

She nodded, attempted a smile. 'You look well,' she said. 'Been on holiday?'

'Sicily,' he said, seizing on the first place he could think of.

'Come on,' she said, taking him by the hand, 'can't

stand here all day, bawling.' He admired her spirit. She seemed to be holding it together better than he'd done.

They went through to the kitchen. Hand-painted, hand-crafted, and of traditional design, it made a refreshing change from the pathology-suite-themed cooking environment. Tallis sat down at the kitchen table and watched as Gayle made coffee with an amazing contraption that hissed and blew like an old steam train. The result was amazing, the real deal.

'How did you find out?' Gayle said at last, raising the cup to her lips.

He was prepared. 'One of Garry's mates. He works on *The Independent*.'

'Typical journo. Always have their ears to the ground.'

'And you?'

'Police in Turkey traced me through Garry's passport details, contacted our boys here. I received the proverbial knock at the door.' She grimaced, putting the cup back down, clattering it against the saucer. 'Two officers: one male; one female. I knew it was bad soon as I clapped eyes on them. Remembered from last time. I can tell you,' she said, 'having been through this once before doesn't make it any easier.' She reached for a box of tissues, blew her nose fiercely.

'Sorry, I didn't mean…'

'No, it's all right, Paul. I'm all right. It's just…' Her voice faded away.

Tallis snatched at his coffee. Maybe he shouldn't have come so soon. 'You here on your own?'

'Of course.' She looked taken aback.

'Should you be?' Tallis smiled. 'Haven't you got family, friends?'

'You're beginning to sound like my family liaison officer,' Gayle snorted. 'Like I already explained to her, my mother wasn't that keen on my marriage to Garry, my sister lives in Canada and most of my friends are hard out at work.'

Now that she'd reminded him, Tallis remembered Gayle once talking about her mother's opposition to the marriage. 'You shouldn't be alone,' he said, thinking, What do I know about such things? After Belle's death the thought of spending time with people had quietly appalled him. Still did.

'I'm not. I get regular visits from the police.'

'Are they keeping you informed?'

'They've been brilliant.'

'You're not flying out?'

'I don't need to. Someone from the MET's gone on my behalf.'

'But surely…' Tallis began.

'Unfortunately, my passport's expired.'

'I'm sure, in the circumstances, someone could rush one through.'

Gayle gave a morbid shrug. 'What difference will it make? Garry's gone. Doesn't matter whether I see him here or in Turkey.'

Neither of them spoke for a moment. Tallis was first to break. 'Do the police have a line on the killers?'

Gayle took another sip of coffee. 'To be honest, it all sounds fairly confused. A bike matching the description was found in a back street.'

'They say where exactly?' Tallis chipped in. 'I visited Istanbul a few years ago. Know it pretty well.'

Gayle frowned. 'Strange-sounding name, Beyoglu.' North of the Golden Horn, Tallis remembered. 'According to the Turkish police, they want to trace a man Garry was having coffee with before he was killed. Ever heard Garry mention David Miller?'

Tallis frowned, stroked his jaw, shook his head. 'Doesn't ring a bell.'

'With me neither. They seem to be fairly worked up about him, mainly because he's disappeared.'

'Disappeared?'

'Gone missing, although I suppose it's possible he could have been injured in the earthquake.'

'Or killed,' Tallis said, warming to the idea. Gayle asked if he'd like a refill.

'That would be great,' he said, watching as Gayle went through the coffee routine once more. 'You don't think the police are connecting this Miller guy with Garry's murder, do you?'

'I don't think so. I mean, it's got to be some mad Turkish nutter, hasn't it?'

'You reckon? The guy or guys who ordered the contract could be any nationality at all.' Like British, for instance.

'You think so?'

She looked a bit perturbed, he thought. 'Gayle, I know

this is an obvious question, but do you know of anyone who'd want Garry dead?'

She let out a mournful sigh. 'Honestly?'

'Sure,' he replied.

'In Garry's line of work he was always being threatened. He didn't speak much about it because he knew it frightened me, but it stands to reason that you can't rattle cages as much as Garry did and always expect to get away with it.'

So whose cage had he rattled this time? 'Anyone threaten him recently?'

'Not specifically.'

Tallis arched an eyebrow.

'He got a bit roughed up the third time he went to Turkey, had his wallet stolen.'

'Did he report it?'

'Are you kidding?'

Tallis threw her another quizzical look.

'Ever spent any time in a Turkish police station? They take hours simply to fill out a form.'

Yeah, he remembered. 'Did he speak to you about what he was currently working on?'

Gayle glanced away. 'Not really.'

Tallis leant towards her, adopting his most persuasive tone. 'Gayle, this is me you're talking to.'

She looked up, swallowed. 'Like I said, I knew nothing of specifics but the general theme of the book he'd mapped out was an exploration of links between organised crime and terrorism.'

Right. Tallis felt something snatch inside. Now they were getting somewhere.

Gayle was still speaking. 'He was very preoccupied. It was his fourth trip to Turkey this year. Every time he came back, he seemed more distant.'

'Do you remember when he went exactly?'

'Easy enough to find out,' she said, twisting round, reaching up and swiping a calendar from the wall behind. 'Here,' she said, showing it to Tallis, pointing with a finger. 'January 13th for a week, back in April, 17th to the 28th, then more recently early August and then this last final time.' She folded the calendar over, hooked it back onto the wall, let out a deep sigh.

'Mind if I take a look in his study?' Tallis already knew that Garry had used the spare bedroom as his base. It doubled as a guest room. Tallis had slept in it when he'd last visited.

'Help yourself. Warn you, police have already been through it with a fine-tooth comb.'

'Take much away?'

'Garry's diary, containing an audit trail of contacts, his files and computer.'

'Find anything?'

'If they have, they haven't told me.'

Probably a waste of time, but he thought he'd take a peek anyway.

The room was neater than he remembered. It had recently received a fresh coat of paint. Sofa bed up against one wall, Garry's desk, an IKEA self-assembly job, against

the other. It looked sad and pathetic with only the keyboard
lying there on its own. A rummage through the drawers
yielded nothing of startling import, mainly because the
police had probably already removed anything of significance. He found a couple of building-society books, one
in Gayle's old married name, which he quickly flicked
through, pausing over one of the entries before moving on
to a sheaf of receipts that proved Garry had recently visited
Birmingham. Tallis looked up, a snatch of conversation
whistling through his head. It felt as if Garry was in the
room right next to him.

'Thing is, Birmingham's your patch, right?'

'Used to be.'

*'But you still know the movers and shakers in the
criminal world?'*

Tallis closed the drawer, aware that Gayle was standing
in the doorway. He didn't know for how long. 'Find
anything?'

'No.' Tallis thanked her, said he ought to be making a
move. 'All right if I use your loo before I head off?'

'You know where it is.' She flashed a sudden, tight smile.
Probably thinking of happier times, Tallis thought as he
went into the main bathroom to take a leak. Afterwards,
glancing in the mirror over the washbasin, an offbeat
thought hovered and began to take flight in the outer
reaches of his mind. He blinked, grabbed a towel, drying
his hands, and ambled back towards the lavatory, staring
out of the open window for a few seconds then squashing
the offending idea dead before it had a chance to fly.

Gayle was waiting for him outside. She'd removed her sunglasses. The skin around her grey-blue eyes looked dark and tired. 'Thanks for coming.'

'You'll take care?'

'Sure.'

'Remember what I said.' He squeezed her arm. 'Don't be alone.'

9

HE TOOK the train from Marylebone to Birmingham, Snow Hill. The closer to home, the more his thoughts centred on family, or what was left of it. His father, with whom he had an appalling relationship, was dying of cancer. Dan, his elder brother, was banged up in jail and would remain so for many years to come. How his mum continued with such courage and good humour was a source of constant inspiration to him. And then there was Hannah, his much younger sister, falling in love with a geography teacher when still in her teens, married, two kids, happy and settled. She rarely returned home.

Tallis idly looked out of the window. They were pulling into Solihull. A middle-aged man carrying a large suitcase was walking towards a woman of similar age, the look of delight on both their faces the most uplifting sight. As soon as they were within arm's length of each other, the man put his case down in the same momentous way an explorer marks his triumph by sticking a flag in the ground, and took the woman in his arms. Tallis watched enchanted, glad that life continued joyously for the vast majority of people, while also feeling an overwhelming sense of something precious lost.

From Snow Hill, he took a cab to Quinton, getting out at the end of the avenue so that the driver couldn't see where he lived, his motivation nothing to do with security, everything to do with embarrassment. Young, cool guys didn't live in bungalows. Unless bequeathed. Although grateful for his Croatian grandmother's generosity—it put a free roof over his head after all—it didn't quite square with the image. He'd thought many times of selling and buying something more suitable, yet every time he got as far as phoning an estate agent he bottled it. The bungalow and what it represented was part of his history, something that couldn't be overestimated. Without history, he felt sunk.

The sun was less intense, more cloud in the blue. As Tallis lowered his vision, he saw the familiar figure of his next-door neighbour's son shambling along the pavement, sidestepping the dog shit. *Jimmy*, as Tallis insisted on calling him after the great guitarist Jimmy Page, seemed to have grown several inches in the past three weeks, legs absurdly sticking out of three-quarter-length trousers, manly hairs sticking out of his legs. He was wearing scuffed top-of-the-range trainers, no socks and a black T-shirt touting some group Tallis had never heard of. His thick fringe made him seem as if he was peeking out from a foxhole. Although studiously listening to an iPod, he gave Tallis a goofy grunt as he walked past. Relations had improved beyond recognition since Tallis's computer had blown up one morning. Not fully realising how terminal things were, he'd gone round next door and appealed for help. Jimmy, for once not manacled to his electric guitar, loped round, fingers whizzing over the keyboard as though he were Elton John then bluntly announced that it was fucked.

'What you need is an Apple Mac, a proper computer, not some crappy old PC,' he told Tallis.

Whenever people offered that type of advice, Tallis knew it meant only one thing: forking out. 'It'll cost a bit,' Jimmy said, shrewdly reading his expression, 'but worth it. And you get ever such good back-up if things go wrong.'

'You on commission, or what?' Tallis grinned.

'Nah, just got taste.' To prove the point, Jimmy invited him round to examine his own machine.

'Your mum in?' Tallis said warily. Jimmy's mum had a bit of thing for him. Well, a bit of thing for any man with a pulse, if he was honest.

'Nah, gone to the social club.'

Twenty minutes on, Tallis was sold. Two days later, he was the proud owner of a flat-screen seventeen-inch iMac with web cam and full Internet connection.

The bungalow looked the same: elderly. In the carport, his Rover stood mute and accusing. He presumed nobody thought it worth nicking.

Inside there was a musty and neglected smell. After dumping his stuff in the bedroom, he set about opening all the windows and, ignoring the phone winking with messages, stepped out into the garden. Since losing interest in home DIY, he spent more time outdoors. Not that his efforts proved much of an improvement. The grass had grown with a speed that was only rivalled by weeds, his half-hearted attempts to nurture some plants whose names escaped him a resounding failure. Still, there were always the birds. He had a bit of a theory about them. In the criminal sphere, he reckoned the sparrows and robins were bobbies on the beat, wagtails private investigators, rooks and crows hit men, buzzards and sparrow hawks the Mr Bigs. The blackbirds, clever little bastards, were CID on account of setting up their own early warning cat alarm. Every time next door's moggy appeared in his garden, there would be the most terrific racket, giving him enough time to turn the hose on the feline intruder. He thought the bloody thing would have got the message by now, but it kept coming back, strutting its stuff as only cats could. Maybe they were the real Mr Bigs, he thought idly, his thoughts turning to Garry Morello once more, and the potential people he'd crossed.

Back inside, Tallis made himself a cup of coffee, black, with sugar to make up for not having any milk. Finding a pen and a piece of paper, he steeled himself to play back his messages. Only one message was urgent. It was from his mother. His father had died.

'Where have you been? We've been trying to get hold of you.' It was Hannah, his sister.

'I've been away.'

'Well, we know that,' she said accusingly. 'Why didn't you tell anyone?'

'It was a spur-of-the-moment thing. Look, when did he pass away?'

'Over a week ago.'

Tallis closed his eyes. Perhaps they'd already buried him. *Please*.

'We've been waiting for you to get back so we can have the funeral.'

Oh, God. He muttered apologies, his sister admonitions. 'How's Mum?' he said.

At the mention of their mother, some of the heat went out of Hannah's voice. 'A little better than she was. Hard to say.' She paused. 'Look, I know you and Dad never got on, but now he's dead, you might feel…'

Nothing, he thought coldly. 'Hannah, let's concentrate on Mum, make sure she's looked after.'

'Of course, but—'

'Mum must come first,' he said firmly. This was not the time for an examination of his feelings towards the man who'd done his best to break him. And yet the man *had* been his father and, as his son, Tallis felt it wrong to harbour such animosity towards him. He'd often wondered what it would feel like when his dad died. If he was honest, there had been times in his life when he'd wished for it. Now that his father was dead, his emotions were less easy to pin down.

The silence throbbed with hurt and disappointment. Then he heard his mother saying something in the background.

'Hold on,' Hannah said, strained. 'Mum wants to talk to you.'

'Hello, Paul.'

'Mum, how are you?' Stupid bloody question. And then she took him completely by surprise.

'You of all my children know how I feel.'

It was the first time she'd openly acknowledged his grief for Belle. She must be feeling pretty dreadful, he thought. 'Mum, what do you want me to do?'

'Come home.'

'I'll be right there.'

She waited a beat. 'But could you to do something for me first?'

'Anything.'

'I want you to get Dan out of Belmarsh.'

Something in his stomach squelched. 'Mum, I really don't—'

'Please. I know what he did, but it was your father's dying wish for Dan to be at his funeral.'

Always Dan, even to the last, he thought bitterly. The compassionate part of his nature was having a difficult time shining through, yet even he realised that Dan needed to be there as much as his old man had desired it. How the hell he was going to manage it was another story. Dan was in no ordinary prison for any ordinary offence. His only hope was Asim. 'I'm not making any promises, but I'll see if I can pull some strings.'

'Thank you.'

They talked a little more. Now that he was home, they planned to go ahead with the funeral in five days' time. To his surprise, his father was going to be cremated. Somehow

Tallis had envisaged a full Catholic funeral, all bells and whistles. He had to remind himself that his mother was the religious one. His father never had much time for it. So much he hadn't had time for.

'You'll let me know,' she said, 'about Dan.'

'Soon as I can.'

Asim got to him first. Tallis was halfway down a bottle of fine malt whisky, all peat and bog, the taste suiting his mood, when Asim called. 'The Moroccan was a guy known as Faraj Tardarti,' Asim told him. 'He'd trained at camps in Pakistan, was not considered to be a main player, although known to have contacts to those who were.'

'Looks as though the Americans have a different take on him.'

'He was on their watch list. Of more interest as far as Morello's concerned,' Asim continued, 'two British men flew out of Heathrow to Istanbul and back again in the very twenty-four-hour period in which Morello was shot. Customs cottoned onto them because they were travelling light, and alerted the embassy.'

That prat Cardew, Tallis thought. Damn him and his blasted procedure. Either he didn't make the connection or he was bought. 'Names?'

'Toby Beaufort and Tennyson Makepeace.'

What sort of names were those? 'Having a laugh, were they?'

'They were indeed.'

Forged passports.

'Looks like they might be good for Morello's murder,' Asim said. 'Must have picked up their gear the Turkish end.'

'I'd say so. Still think there's no connection between Morello and our Moroccan?' Tallis couldn't disguise the playful note in his voice.

'Go on,' Asim said, humouring him.

'I went to visit Morello's widow. She told me that Garry was working on a book exploring the link between organised crime and terrorism.'

'Historically, there's always been a link. Only have to look at the IRA.'

Asim could be so infuriating. 'I don't believe it was in a general sense,' Tallis persisted. 'Garry wanted to pick my brains, ask me about my patch, Birmingham, who the movers and shakers were. My take is that he was talking about current events. Gives more credence to what we already suspect.'

'Birmingham, you say?'

'Yes.'

Asim remained silent. Tallis assumed this to be a good sign. What he said was being taken seriously. 'Maybe we should have left you at home.'

'And deny me my two-night stay in a Turkish gulag?' Tallis cracked.

'Still got your contacts within the police?'

'Some.'

'Then maybe you should check out those movers and shakers.'

Tallis cut the call. It was only afterwards he remembered that he hadn't asked Asim about Dan.

10

TALLIS had never been able to lie to his mother. 'I simply don't think it's possible.'

He was back at home in Herefordshire. They'd spent the morning sitting in the little room they called the snug, going through the funeral arrangements. Hannah was forced to return home to Bristol for the kids. Her husband, a nice enough bloke in Tallis's opinion, wasn't a very hands-on dad. She promised to return with the rest of the family for the big send-off.

'Take care of each other,' Hannah said, tipping up on her toes to kiss them both. She didn't really look like either of her parents. Small, with chestnut hair, she resembled more the photographs he'd seen of his grandmother as a young woman. As soon as Hannah left, his mother collared him.

'Did you try?' Her blue-grey eyes looked up into his brown.

'Not yet.' Shame made his neck flush. She'd been through so much, watching his father's slow and lingering death. Then there'd been Dan and Belle. He didn't want to let her down. And what was he really afraid of? That Dan would be allowed to come? That Dan would act *in loco parentis*? That all the fear and intimidation his father had visited on him would be transmitted through his evil elder brother? Or was he more frightened of his own reaction to seeing Dan again? He patted her hand gently. 'But I will.'

After they'd eaten, she insisted on washing up the dishes immediately. He offered to help.

'No need. Won't take more than a few minutes.'

And so he went out into his mother's garden, walked along the carefully created paths with the little bridge over the lily pond and, crossing to the far end, took out his mobile phone. As he looked back at the house, he remembered summer evenings watching the bats burst out, as in a hail of machine-gun fire, from underneath the eaves, dozens and dozens of baby horseshoes and pipistrelles.

Asim was sympathetic but not hopeful.

'I'm not asking for me, but for my mum,' Tallis pleaded. 'You're the only person who can swing it.'

Asim sounded doubtful about that, too. 'When's the funeral?'

'Friday.'

'I'll get back to you,' Asim promised.

Tallis spent the rest of the day with his mum. They talked of old times, laughing a little, avoiding the bad, which was easy. When two people remembered an event they generally viewed it in the context of their own personal narrative and prejudice. Staying the night was more taxing. He slept in the old room he'd shared with his brother, the same room in which he'd received taunts and beatings from his dad.

The next morning his mother announced that she wanted to go into town. Tallis offered to drive but she declined. 'Time you went home.'

'But I've only just arrived.'

'Don't you have work to go to?' His parents had always had a strong work ethic, something they'd imbued into their kids. Tallis had led her to believe that he was some kind of private investigator, an occupation of which she disapproved. 'I'll be fine,' she insisted.

'But, Mum…'

She broke into a radiant smile, almost girlish. 'I'd actually like to be alone.'

Hannah wouldn't approve, he thought, standing there like a dumb animal.

'Go,' she said, giving him a gentle push in the middle of his chest.

Tallis looked into her face and found her impossible to read. He'd always worried that she'd go under when his father died, but he saw something else emergent, something strong. He thought it was hope, and envied her.

After picking up some basic supplies, Tallis got back home around noon. Jimmy next-door was still asleep. Apart from the fact the lad's bedroom curtains were closed, neither property was being pulverised by sound.

Once inside, he picked up his mail, chucked it on a side table for later, stowed milk in the fridge, bread in the bread

bin and made himself a pot of coffee. After that, he called
Stu. They'd worked together as part of an elite group of
undercover firearms officers. Stu had stayed on with the
force after Tallis left, but after hitting the bottle had been
returned to basic duties. Last time they'd spoken Stu had
been in the process of kicking his addiction. He wasn't
finding it easy.

'Hi, Stu, how are you doing?'

'One hundred and twenty-one days and counting,' Stu
said morosely, his Glaswegian accent less pronounced
since he'd packed in the booze.

'That's terrific.'

'Fucking boring.'

Tallis let out a laugh. 'You'll just have to find some
other addiction to float your boat.'

'Yeah, but will it be legal?'

This was better. Even if everything was tits up, he could
always rely on his mates to get him through. A sense of
humour was essential to survival—especially in their line
of work. 'So what's new on the old bush telegraph?'

'Same old. Why?'

'Ever have any contacts with the Serious and Organised
Crime Agency?'

'Must be joking. Wouldn't sully themselves with the
likes of us.'

'So you've never come across a guy called Kevin
Napier?'

'Can't say I have. Is he with SOCA?'

'Recently promoted.'

'No, it's the Organised Crime lot SOCA have most contact with and even that's carried out in darkened corridors.'

'What do you mean?'

'SOCA is extremely secretive. Have to be. They're working against organised crime at the highest level. Most of us wouldn't be able to get beyond a phone call to their press office.'

'But I thought they worked closely with police on intelligence and operations at local level.'

'They do. Every so often one of their officers swoop on Organised Crime, mix it up a bit then swoop back out again. We call them the free-range chickens of law enforcement agencies.' Stu gave a low chuckle. 'As you might imagine, their input isn't always appreciated.'

An age-old problem, Tallis thought. Oh, he knew how it worked in theory: counter-terrorism was an amalgamation of police and security services, working side by side in a spirit of joint co-operation against a common foe, sharing intelligence, indivisible, one for all and all for one. However, the powers that be took little or no account of the frailty of human nature. When push came to shove, everyone ruthlessly guarded his or her own patch.

Stu was still banging on. 'SOCA works at national level. They have the big picture. They know best, allegedly, patronising bastards.'

Add to that too many newly formed government agencies, too many new initiatives, way too many analysts, and nobody knowing what the hell they were doing, Tallis thought. More cynically, Tallis suspected the constant round of name changes was entirely deliberate. It was impossible to pinpoint who was running what. 'So it's a one-way street. SOCA gives the benefit of their expertise and fuck off. That right?'

Stu let out a raucous laugh. Tallis had no doubt that he'd pass that one on to a receptive ear. 'I don't suppose SOCA see it that way,' Stu said, serious again. 'I think they genuinely feel they're doing their bit. In spite of some recent bad press, they are trying to get their act together. Problem was they were disadvantaged from the start.'

'Because everyone had such high expectations?' Tallis said.

'That and because it takes time to build up intelligence. To be fair, they don't openly trumpet success, but bearing in mind any local Organised Crime division knows its patch, exactly what's going on, who's doing what and where, it tends to have a bit of a pissing-off effect when the so-called elite muscle in.'

'I don't suppose you'd have a friendly contact whose ear I could bend?'

'In Organised Crime?'

'Yeah.'

'Nick Oxslade,' Stu said without a moment's hesitation. 'Great bloke. Came from the other side of the tracks same as me so I've got a lot of time for him. Can I ask why?'

'You can ask,' Tallis said enigmatically.

Stu gave another snort of mirth. 'If they ever give that bloke playing Jason Bourne the chop...'

'Matt Damon?'

'That's the one,' Stu said. 'I reckon you'd be a great re-placement. After myself, of course.'

Tallis phoned the Proactive Crime Unit via the main number and then asked for an eight-digit extension. It had once been possible to contact an Organised Crime Officer direct via Lloyd House, the West Midlands Police Head-quarters, but, since a number had received threatening phone calls from imprisoned villains they'd help put away, certain security measures had been put in place. Organised Crime Officers were no longer based there but at a number of secret addresses. Although Tallis wouldn't be able to talk to Oxslade directly, he could leave a message for him to call back. On getting through, he was told that the entire department were busy on a major operation. He left a message anyway and then, undeterred, called another number, got straight through.

'Bloody hell, the walking dead!' There followed a cloudburst of coughing.

'Waking dead,' he corrected her, 'and isn't it time you packed in smoking?' He imagined Crow sneaking out of her office, heading for a secret space not yet comman-deered by the fag police. Their paths had crossed in his last investigation. Based in Camden, Detective Inspector Michelle Crow had proved an invaluable if slightly uncon-ventional ally. She was big, butch looking and ballsy. She also had electric thinking.

'And do what exactly?' she scoffed, regaining her com-posure.

'Breathe more easily?'

'You sound like an advert for cough sweets. Look, you should be grateful. Once our merry little band have been exterminated, they'll be turning the full spotlight on booze next…'

'They already have. Don't you read the newspapers?'

'Try not to,' she fired back, and returned to her main theme. 'Then they'll be banning sex.'

Tallis blinked. That D.I. Michelle Crow had sex with anyone had never occurred to him. Time to move on swiftly. 'Reason I'm calling, Micky…'

'Is because, unable to resist my womanly charms, you want to ask me out.'

'I'd love to, darling.' He cringed. 'And next time I'm in London I will, but—'

'You want to use me.' She dropped her voice to a lascivious growl. Christ, what was she on? Tallis wondered, deeply regretting making the call. 'Wish I could see your face.' She burst out laughing. 'So what can I really do you for?'

Tallis ignored the double entendre and ploughed on. 'I need to know if two guys have sneaked within your radar. They go by the names of Toby Beaufort and Tennyson Makepeace.'

'What did they do, steal someone's poems?'

'Killed a British journalist in Turkey.'

'Straight up?' A wily note had crept into Crow's voice. Tallis imagined her chair creaking under the weight of her sizable rear.

'Evidence pointing that way.'

'Ah-hah,' Crow said knowingly.

'Obviously, this is all off the record.'

'You need absolute discretion.'

'Absolute.'

'Strictly *entre nous*.'

Sod, that playful streak had crept back into her voice. 'Yes.'

'It will cost.'

He had been very much afraid of that. 'I'm sure we can come to some agreement,' he said neutrally.

'I still haven't forgotten being locked in your bloody toilet.' It had been the only way to prevent her from getting involved in the action, he remembered.

'I'm sure you haven't,' he said, closing his eyes. When he'd finally let her out, she'd charged at him like a wounded rhino.

'Right, then,' she said, businesslike. 'I'll see what I can turn up.'

The phone call from Oxslade, the Organised Crime Officer for whom he'd left a message, came through shortly before four in the afternoon. Tallis explained his contact with Stu. The mention of his old mate's name worked like a magic charm. 'I'm at the Forensic Science Service, waiting for a statement,' Oxslade said, 'but I could meet you later.' He sounded bright and enthusiastic. How refreshing, Tallis thought. Oxslade suggested they meet at the Tarnished Halo on Ludgate Hill. Tallis knew that it was a popular haunt with the Fraud Squad so he proposed the White Swan in Harborne instead. This agreed, they arranged to meet at six that evening.

'I'll be wearing a brown leather jacket, jeans,' Oxslade added, 'and I've got short red hair.'

The rest of the afternoon was spent tackling the savannah outside and cutting it to more manageable proportions. Plants past rescue Tallis dug up and chucked onto an ever-increasing compost heap, the rest he weeded and fed with something out of a bottle that smelt mildly of antiseptic. By five, he was having his second shave of the day followed by a shower.

Instead of taking the car, he walked and caught a bus. It wasn't far. He was still smarting from the earthquake and, though this minuscule change in lifestyle wouldn't matter a damn in the great scheme of things, it made him feel more comfortable with himself.

The pub was already buzzing with early diners. Oxslade greeted him with an open expression. He was indeed red-haired and pink-faced and probably older than he looked. Already a third of the way down a pint, he asked Tallis what he was drinking. Tallis viewed the ales on tap and plumped for a pint of Banks. Eventually, they found a corner table far enough away from the clamour to hear but not be overheard. Tallis took a pull of his pint. Oxslade did the same and viewed Tallis with an expression bordering on awe.

'Stu explained you once worked together.'

Stu would. 'That's right.'

Oxlade beamed. 'I've often been asked if I thought my job was dangerous, you know when we take the big guys down? Know what my standard response is?'

Tallis didn't. He shook his head.

'I tell them we send the firearms officers in first to do the dirty stuff. We only waltz in once the offenders are trussed up like chickens.'

Tallis smiled, remembering.

'Anyway,' Oxslade said, 'gather you want to talk about SOCA.'

'Amongst other things.'

Oxslade grinned, leant forward conspiratorially. 'We think of them as the blokes who write jokes for comedians.'

'Yeah?' Tallis grinned back.

'They never receive the applause or the laughs.'

Different take to Stu, Tallis thought, sharing the joke. If Oxslade was right, he wouldn't have thought Napier was that well suited to the job.

Oxslade took another drink. 'Can I ask why the interest?'

'I want to track someone I fought with during the first Gulf War.' He asked if Oxslade knew Napier.

'In passing. Not well.'

'Was he advising on a particular operation?'

Oxslade smiled an apology.

'It's all right. Shouldn't have asked.' Tallis smiled back. He looked around the pub. Stylish interior. Good, friendly atmosphere. 'Look, I'll be straight with you, Nick.' Tallis turned to him. 'Since I left the force, I've gone into private investigation.'

Oxslade frowned. Tallis knew how Oxslade felt. PIs aroused the same high level of suspicion as journalists. 'This connected to the reason you want to trace Napier?'

'No, that's entirely personal,' Tallis lied. 'My interest lies in the very people you referred to, the people I used to take down.'

'Not sure I follow.'

Tallis flashed his best smile. Oxslade was privy to the massive database detailing all the active Mr Nastys. Of course he followed. 'I remember there was this bloke in Wolverhampton. He had four different addresses, four different women, no meaningful employment and a great lifestyle. He was eventually tripped up through extensive examination of his business and financial transactions.'

'The way we get a lot of these blokes now,' Oxslade concurred.

'I appreciate you can't tell me who's still in the game, but how about we play I Spy.'

'You mean you name and I nod yes or no?'

'Yup.'

Oxslade rolled his eyes. 'You have to be joking.'

'It's not as though you're telling me anything I don't already know.'

'Things have moved on.' Yeah, Tallis knew. Road-traffic accidents were now referred to as collisions or incidents. Even the word 'force' had been substituted for 'service'. However, some things never changed. 'It's much tighter,' Oxslade said categorically. 'I can't tell you stuff like that.'

'You're not telling me anything, just agreeing or disagreeing. Come on, we're on the same side here.'

'But I don—'

Tallis stood up. 'You think about it,' he said decisively. 'I'll get in the next round of drinks.'

Think, think, think! If he were in Oxslade's shoes, he'd have walked by now. Somehow he had to say something that would connect and bring Oxslade on side. Prove that his desire to know who the main players were was justified.

From the look on Oxslade's face when Tallis sat back down, he had a mountain to climb. He really didn't like what he was about to do. It was gross exploitation, but he needed Oxslade's help. 'I have a client who's worried sick about her son. Usual story. Rebellious youth. Broken family. Dad pissed off. Son fell in with a bad lot and got himself involved in drugs and gun running. Lately, he's started kicking around with bigger fish.' Tallis took a sip of beer, watched Oxslade's face; saw how his pitch was going down. A lot of the shine had gone out of Oxslade's bright and bushy expression. 'His mum's all messed up,' Tallis continued. 'Reckons that, with the right encouragement, right motivation, her lad could make something of his life.' Bit like you, Tallis thought. 'I've got some names.' Tallis reeled them off from memory. They were probably two years out of date but these individuals would probably still be on the scene—if they were still alive. Oxslade's pale features fell into a frown. The freckles on his face seemed to blur together to form one single skin tone. Tallis thought he'd blown it. 'Only small fry, I know,' he added.

'Your information's out of date. Wayne Jennings is in Featherstone,' Oxslade said, cool eyes meeting Tallis's.

'Alrick Hughes was found dead after a drugs overdose last summer. I suspect Stu was your source regarding myself.'

Shit, Tallis thought. 'Don't blame Stu. It was a chance remark.'

'Which you took and ran with,' Oxslade said, cold. 'The other bloke you mentioned skipped the country, used to work for Johnny Kennedy, lately resident of Her Majesty's Prison Birmingham.'

The name was hauntingly familiar to Tallis. Maybe he was simply getting it confused with a long-deceased American President. 'Is Kennedy still in the game?'

Oxslade's face broke into a thin smile. 'Nice try. Sorry to disappoint, but he's gone straight.'

Tallis hiked a dark, disbelieving eyebrow. 'You think?' These men were genetically primed for criminal activity. 'What did he serve time for?'

'Money-laundering.'

'That the full extent of his operation?'

'Not really but it was the only thing we could nail him for.'

Like Al Capone, Tallis thought. He'd been done for tax evasion, not murder or extortion. Forensic accounting had also been responsible for tripping up a number of Mafia dons.

Oxslade was continuing to speak, presumably because Kennedy was old news and he felt he could. 'He used to be involved in the construction business, property development. I gather since he got out of prison he runs an online company supplying building materials to trade.'

'And he's legit?'

'Absolutely. It is possible for men to reform,' Oxslade said with a small, reproving smile.

Tallis nodded, giving the impression he was conceding the point. In his experience, small-time crooks indeed saw the light either because a significant other was breathing down their necks, begging them to go straight, or because life outside was preferable to the grinding boredom of prison. The big boys, the real hard men, rarely found the road to Damascus.

'When was Kennedy banged up?'

Oxslade shrugged. 'Four years ago.'

Probably arrested before the birth of the Assets Recovery Agency, Tallis thought, an organisation set up to claw back funds from organised crime. It had been a disaster, its powers dissolved and responsibility handed to the Serious and Organised Crime Agency. No wonder SOCA was groaning under the strain. Kennedy was, Tallis wagered, most likely still in the money. Oxslade seemed to read Tallis's thoughts.

'We put a restraining order in place as soon as we kicked off with a criminal investigation so that Kennedy couldn't shift any assets abroad,' Oxslade said. 'Problem was he already had stuff in Spain.'

'Not known for being entirely co-operative.' In fact, as far as extradition proceedings between the two countries went, there was a good level of co-operation. Lots of villains who'd thought they could flee to Costa whatever had come in for a nasty surprise. Money and assets, however, were a different matter.

'Can say that again.'

The Dutch, by contrast, Tallis remembered, were brilliant. But interesting though this was, they weren't really cutting to the chase. 'Working backwards, I'm assuming that Kennedy's sentence was around the eight-year mark.' Usual deal: out in half the time.

'Longer, actually.'

Tallis raised an eyebrow. Kennedy must have been a very good boy in prison, or perhaps he simply had an effective brief. 'How big was his criminal empire before he got caught?'

'Hard to put an exact figure on it. As I said, like a lot of these guys, he was involved in the construction industry.'

'As a front?'

'For real. He was highly successful and well respected in business circles. There's a lot of major buildings in Birmingham that have the Kennedy stamp on them.'

'So his criminal enterprise was a hobby?' Tallis smiled.

'Hardly. Any illicit racket and Kennedy's name would pop into the mix.'

'But nothing strong enough to finger him with?'

'You got it.'

'All the usual culprits? Drugs, prostitution, guns?'

'I don't think the bloke could help himself, to be honest,' Oxslade said. 'He didn't need the money. He was into it for kicks, for the adrenalin rush.'

Yes, Tallis thought, and as any fool knows addictions are hard to kick. He decided to adopt a different tack.

'What's your bust rate like?'

Oxslade broke into a satisfied smile. 'We're hot.

Recently, we pulled in a white gang for twenty million. There are two other smaller gangs subject to ongoing investigations, one Asian, one West Indian. Added to that, we've just crossed the i's and dotted the t's on paperwork to take down a bloke in Holland.'

'Sounds impressive. To what do you owe your success, do you reckon?'

'Teamwork and first-rate intelligence.'

'Any of these guys involved in terrorist activities?'

Oxslade looked shocked. 'Not on our patch.'

Would he know? Tallis wondered. He was beginning to feel like he needed to talk to someone higher up the food chain. Then an outlandish thought crossed his mind. Had Garry stumbled across Johnny Kennedy? Oxslade was still speaking.

'Although I've heard rumours that certain gangs in London have connections. But that's all it is—rumour. No hard evidence.'

'See, I've got a bit of a theory,' Tallis said. 'What with all this terrorist stuff, I reckon too many of us are focused in one direction.'

'There's certainly an enormous amount of resources going into counter-terrorism,' Oxslade said, his expression earnest. 'It's considered to be *the* main threat to national security. The public are far more worried about being caught up in a random terrorist attack than of becoming the victim of organised crime. Yet chances are that, during their lifetime, they will be. Comes down to perception, see. The public feel removed from it.'

'You mean,' Tallis said, 'they read about criminality in the newspapers but it has nothing to do with them. Gangsters inhabit a different world. Joe Public doesn't understand that every time he accepts a pirate tape, receives knock-off goods or visits a prostitute who might have been trafficked from Eastern Europe, he's part of the problem.'

'Absolutely,' Oxslade agreed.

And on that final note of accord, Tallis thanked Oxslade for his time and walked out of the pub.

On his return, Stu, his old firearms mate, was waiting for him. By the way he was half-sprawled on the doorstep, Tallis could tell he was hammered. He looked around for Stu's car, a horrible piss-coloured Peugeot. Stu hotly insisted he'd had it spray-painted champagne. Thankfully, champagne or piss, it wasn't there. Stu must have got a cab, or bus. He wasn't sober enough to have walked.

'Paul, you old bastard.' Stu beamed, staggering un-steadily to his feet and clapping him on the back.

Christ, Tallis thought, a naked flame within fifty metres of him and he'd ignite like an Apollo spaceship. 'Thought you were on the wagon.'

'I fell off,' Stu said proudly. He was jutting his chin out the way he always did when he'd had a few. Tallis reckoned it was Stu's way of checking his teeth hadn't melted.

'You'd best come in,' Tallis said, steering Stu out of the way so he could get his key in the lock.

Bundling Stu into the sitting room and onto a sofa, he went

through to the kitchen and put the kettle on. 'Where's the pisser?' Stu called out, his Glaswegian accent thick as tar.

'Bathroom's through there,' Tallis said, grabbing Stu's elbow, hoiking him up and pointing him in the right direction. Tallis had dismal visions of urine splashed all over the tiles and shower unit. While Stu was carrying out his ablutions, Tallis made coffee, adding an extra heaped spoonful to Stu's mug. He wondered what the hell had sparked Stu's decision to reach for the bottle. By the time the kettle boiled, Stu was back on the sofa.

'Your flies are undone,' Tallis said, placing a mug in front of his friend.

'Fuck me, so they are,' Stu said, zipping up his trousers.

Tallis gave him a long hard look.

'What?' Stu said. 'Not seen a cock before?'

'Do me a favour,' Tallis said, edge to his voice. 'How the fuck do you think you'll ever go back into firearms the state you're in?'

Stu jutted his jaw out. 'Doesn't make any difference, dry or tight as a tick. They don't want me back.'

'Who said? Surely—'

'It's official, Paul. Had it from the top.' A look of intense pain entered his red-rimmed eyes. His shoulders sagged. He looked utterly defeated. His voice when he spoke was low and reproachful. 'Anyway, what's the point? Seen the new guidelines? We're all supposed to be clobbered up with Tasers. Great if you want to frighten the pants off a minor offender, useless against an armed psycho.' Tallis flashed back to his recent skirmish in Turkey. He'd found the prospect of being stunned into paralysis by thousands of volts not a particularly attractive one. Oddly enough, several pilot schemes to arm ordinary coppers with the damn things were already under way. He didn't think that was a very good idea either.

Stu continued to complain. 'Bullets are being replaced by peace pamphlets. Only people we're gonna piss off are Greenpeace.'

'And what about you? What about self-respect and discipline, all those values you hold so dear?'

Stu blinked, opened his mouth to speak then rubbed his face with both hands. They were trembling. Jesus! As Tallis looked at Stu he saw a vision of what might have been. Christ, he'd been lucky. 'Look,' he said more gently. 'You want to stay in the service, don't you?'

'What for?' Stu said, belligerent.

'There must be other avenues, for God's sake.' For the life of him, none immediately sprang to mind. He pressed on. 'Don't throw everything away over this. You've done brilliantly up to now. This is just a blip. Stay here tonight and sober up. You can kip on the sofa. But for Chrissakes, Stu, you're going to have to get your life sorted.'

He expected a barrage of foul-mouthed abuse. It didn't happen. Stu hung his head, took a snatch of coffee. Neither of them said anything for a while. 'Spoken to Oxslade?' Stu said finally.

'Yes.'

'Get what you want?'

'Sort of.'

Stu nodded. 'He mention Napier?'

'In passing.' Oxslade's very words, Tallis remembered.

'Did he tell you he was at Headquarters this afternoon?'

'Napier?'

'Four o'clock, according to my source.' Oxslade wouldn't have seen him. He had been at the FSS, Tallis remembered. 'Any idea who he was meeting?'

Stu shook his head. 'Looks like SOCA are on the swoop again,' he said, leaning back into the sofa and closing his eyes.

11

STU was gone by the time Tallis got up the next morning. He found a scrawled note left on the coffee table conveying thanks and expressing apologies. Tallis picked it up, briefly thought about his friend, walked through to the kitchen and looked out of the window. Two blackbirds were hopping around the garden on the lookout for worms. He reckoned they were husband and wife. The bigger of the two was yanking up poor unsuspecting invertebrates and shoving them into the mouth of his mate, presumably for her to take home to the kids.

The phone rang, jettisoning Tallis out of his feathered reverie. It was Crow. The irony wasn't lost on him.

'You owe me.' Crow sounded incredibly pleased with herself.

'I seem to remember you concluding our last telephone conversation in a similar vein.'

'That was before I knew what I know now,' she said, resplendent.

'Which is?'

Crow let out a raspy laugh. 'How about we meet for a drink?'

'I live one hundred and twenty miles away, in case you've forgotten.'

'Only take you two and a half hours by car.'

'You haven't seen the car.'

'Last time you were poncing about in a Z8.'

'Borrowed.'

'Well, borrow it again. The place I had in mind is full of filthy rich.'

'You're not making this proposition sound any more attractive.'

'Come on, where's your sense of adventure? I knock off at noon.'

Tallis looked at his watch. It was doable. Just. 'This better be good.'

'When have I ever disappointed you?' she said, a grotesquely flirty note in her voice. 'Meet me at the Swag and Tails, Fairholt Street, Knightsbridge, one o'clock.' Then she clicked off.

Tallis took the train then tubed it. It took him two attempts to find the street due to the pub's tucked-away location. Surrounded by charming terraces, festooned with hanging baskets and planters, it was as pretty as any high-class country pub you'd find in the Cotswolds. The clientele had much in common—extreme wealth, talk of big deals and country-house pursuits.

Crow was already seated, her ample frame caught in a

blast of afternoon sunshine pouring in through the windows. She'd obviously gone to some trouble. Her hair was washed, her clothes ironed. Nothing, however, could relieve the crumpled appearance of Crow's skin, or the thread veins in full cry across her cheekbones. As Tallis approached, she looked up and grinned. Same bloody awful smile, he thought, finding it curiously endearing. Perhaps it was the simple familiarity that struck a chord. He looked at her glass. It was three-quarters empty. Some things never changed. 'V&T?'

She winked. 'Make it a double.'

Tallis went to the bar, all bleached blonde wood, and pushed his way through a scrum of blokes downing champagne. No sign of a downturn in the economy here. He ordered a pint of Adnams Bitter for himself and took a sip while the barman was sorting out Crow's drinks. Tallis ordered two large V&T's to save himself the bother of having to break away at an inopportune moment.

'Very thoughtful of you,' Crow said, looking like a chemistry teacher as she mixed a lethal quantity of vodka with tonic. She took a taste, shivered slightly and surveyed him admiringly. 'Nice tan.'

'I brown easily.'

'So I see.'

'This is all very nice, Micky, and delighted as I am to be in your company, I'm keen to know what you've managed to turn up.'

Crow grinned, enjoying her brief moment of power over him. 'Our two piss-taking poets,' she began, 'were found dead three days ago in a disused warehouse in Southall. They'd been beaten to death with iron bars. Word is they were in debt to the Turkish Mafia. The killing bears all the hallmarks. They go in for that kind of thing, apparently,' she said, as though exchanging gossip about someone's sexual proclivities.

So much in debt they'd risk going to Istanbul to kill one of their own countrymen? 'You sure they're the same guys?'

'According to the set of forged passports found at the bedsit they shared in Acton. DNA confirmed their real identities: Mitchell Reid and Nathan Brass.'

And, educated guess, that same DNA would tie them to the hit in Turkey. He studied Crow with something approaching admiration. No looker, but she was bloody good at her job. And sharp. 'Previous form?' Tallis said, quietly filing the information away.

'Reid, twenty-seven years of age, originally from Manchester, lived in London for the past year. Before that, resided in Birmingham. Started out with petty thieving, nicking cars, escalating to drug running then taxing.'

Ripping off drug dealers, Tallis remembered. There'd been quite a vogue for it in the naughty '90s. The best plans were the simplest and it didn't get much simpler. There'd usually be at least two thieves who, by paying attention to the local grapevine, would discover a stash of drugs and often large quantities of money in the flat or premises of another more serious player. Either by stealth or brute force, they'd enter the building, put a gun to the head of the said dealer then steal his stash. The whole incident was usually accompanied by a fair amount of violence. Clearly, the 'victim' was in no position to go to the police. It could, however, have serious consequences for the thieves if they were caught. 'Dangerous occupation,' he chipped in.

'Not kidding. Brass, also known as Spider on account of a tattoo on his hand, was a real hard case, thirty years of age, early history of assault, threats to kill, supplying arms. Born in Tipton, West Midlands, Brass and his mate Reid hooked up there and finally bunked off to the smoke together. Talking of which, I'm desperate for a fag.' To compensate, she took a deep slug of her drink, her eyes narrowed.

'What are we talking, big league or small time?' Tallis said.

'Depends on your point of view. Small in London, big in Birmingham. They'd originally worked for a bloke called Kennedy.'

'Oh, yeah,' Tallis said, sounding as disinterested as possible.

'Not heard the name before?' Crow said, razor-sharp.

'Can't say I have.'

'Got sent down for a stretch so Reid and Brass decided to try their luck in the capital.'

'Looks like their luck ran out. What exactly did they do for Kennedy?'

'Bottom-rung stuff. Extortion. Dirty work when it needed doing.' Crow eyed him, making him feel like a piece of meat on a rack. 'What's your interest?'

'Personal. The journalist I told you about was a friend.'

'Morello?'

'You knew him?'

Crow shook her head. 'Heard about the killing on the grapevine. After your call I followed it up.' She took another healthy slug of vodka. 'Strange, this Turkish-Birmingham connection. Reckon the motive was revenge?'

'How do you work that out?'

'Pissing on someone else's patch?'

Crow was shamelessly fishing, Tallis thought. Even she couldn't make that one stack up. Tallis remained noncommittal.

'Don't have any better ideas?' Crow grinned.

'None.' He smiled, pushing his empty glass towards her. 'Your round.'

Tallis reluctantly disentangled himself from Crow an hour later. In spite of her somewhat blokey image, something he suspected she'd cultivated to maintain her own position in what was still a male-dominated environment, she was a decent woman and he secretly enjoyed winding her up and sparring with her. His parting shot was to ask her to keep him posted with regard to hard evidence establishing Reid and Brass as the same two men who'd pulled the trigger on Garry Morello, although he guessed Gayle would also let him know.

'It will cost you more than a few drinks,' she said with a louche smile.

'Dinner, then.'

He spent the train journey back considering the implications of his most recently acquired information. Who'd paid for the contract to kill Garry? Who'd paid for the murder of Reid and Brass? Crow seemed to think the Turkish Mafia were involved in the death of the two young killers, or was that a red herring? And what about Kennedy? Simply a loose connection, or something heavier? Either way, he reckoned he needed to go with his original thinking: Kennedy had not gone straight. No matter what Oxslade believed, no matter that Tallis had never met Kennedy, experience told him that Kennedy was back in the game, smarter, more devious, but definitely back.

As soon as he got home, he showered, changed, found a pad and pen and, powering up his Apple Mac, negotiated his way to Google and punched in 'Johnny Kennedy'. He had fifteen useful hits. Three items focused on the trial resulting in Kennedy's ten-year sentence, two on his links to several sites of redevelopment, with an additional four references to what had once been Kennedy Holdings and its connection to a well-known business consortium, two on his alleged involvement in dodgy dealing in the Balkans, three on a road accident in which Kennedy's only son had been seriously injured and—Tallis's eyes widened—one minor piece on Kennedy's early release from prison. Why? he wanted to know. Not keen on staring into a screen, Tallis printed off everything he could find and read it as it shunted out of his printer.

Kennedy was variously described as charming and charismatic. Certainly, if the picture was anything to go by, he seemed to fit the depiction. Square-shouldered, firm-jawed, he looked capable rather than cunning. His grey hair was close cut. He had good bone structure. Tanned and muscular, dressed in a sober well-cut suit, he looked like a man at the pinnacle of his career. He had been forty-eight when he'd gone inside, which made him fifty-two now, Tallis estimated. It was reported that he was worth upwards of thirty million, something Oxslade had failed to put a figure on, Kennedy's occupation allegedly entrepreneur, a catch-all phrase much beloved by those who have champagne lifestyles and only a passing acquaintance with Inland Revenue.

Kennedy's business acumen seemed truly astounding for a poor lad who'd left school at fourteen and fallen through the system. As Oxslade had already confirmed, Kennedy had, at one time, owned his own construction company and made heavy inroads into a number of flagship building projects. You didn't normally reach those kinds of dizzy heights without either great connections or some nefarious dealing along the way, something strongly suggested by the prosecution, Tallis noticed. If the QC was to be believed, Kennedy's currency was terror. He was feared and worshipped in equal measure. Tallis felt a flash, cold as ice, ripple along his spine. His father had had the same effect on those around him, he remembered, particularly Dan. Thoughts of his father's forthcoming funeral chased through his head. He caught hold of them, pinned them in the outer reaches of his consciousness and read on.

True to criminal form, Kennedy owned various properties abroad, including a villa in southern Spain. Interestingly, Tallis thought, he also owned a place in Hvar, a fashionable town on the Dalmatian coast, famous for its commercially grown lavender. While all this was interesting and gave Tallis a context, one piece of information fired out of the page and shot him between the eyes. Immediately, he was transported to Turkey, to the street where Garry Morello's blood was running into the gutter, his dying words echoing in Tallis's ears. 'Report,' Garry had gasped. *Report.* Was it simple coincidence that Kennedy's soubriquet as an up-and-coming thug had been *The Reporter*?

12

TALLIS reread his notes—Johnny Kennedy, abandoned as a baby outside West Bromwich hospital, West Midlands, mother never found. He owed his name, apparently, to two West Bromwich Albion football players popular in the 1950s: Joe Kennedy, who played centre half; and Johnny Nicholls, inside forward. Brought up in a combination of care and foster homes in the Midlands, a fertile breeding ground for a future life of crime, Kennedy quickly got involved in all the lower echelons of criminality—minor theft, car nicking, drug running. He'd also spent time inside for firearms offences and gained a suspended sentence for receiving and handling stolen goods. His nickname, however, had been earned from a particularly despicable form of aberrant behaviour: robbing the recently bereaved. Tallis glanced away, teeth grating at the man's callousness. In a stroke, his connection with Kennedy felt entirely personal.

Tallis returned to his notes. Kennedy was no illiterate. Wherever Kennedy was, a stack of newspapers followed. Had become a bit of a standing joke, although his reasons for such interest were far from amusing. While later on in his career he could honestly say that he was checking out the business sections, keeping his eye on the markets, in the early days the obituary columns had been the focus of his concentration. Not the pages of the great and good, but the tiny personal sections, those that announced no flowers and the date of the forthcoming funeral. While the grieving family had been out paying their last respects, Kennedy had been in helping himself to anything on offer.

Climbing the ladder through the well-tried and trodden route of enforcing, Kennedy had developed a fearsome reputation. It was alleged that he'd once buried a recalcitrant debtor's pet dog alive. Horrible enough, but he'd carried out the deed in front of the man's wife and children. By the time Kennedy had been in his middle twenties, he'd already graduated to serious dealing, wiping out any opposition along the way. His idea of debt consolidation was loan sharking with all its concomitant violent sidelines.

Ten years later, he had been living well. He'd had his fingers in all sorts of pies, mainly the construction industry. And this was what struck Tallis as Kennedy's greatest achievement for, during those later years, he'd managed to rid himself of his crazy-guy image and cultivate an aura of kindness and respectability. He was no longer a foulmouthed thug but a softly spoken man who looked after people, those outside the law admittedly, but people none the less. He was like a current-day Godfather. This was the secret of Kennedy's success and explained his ability to engender a devout and loyal following. Either they didn't know…Tallis shuddered with distaste…or didn't care about Kennedy making a mint shifting heroin by exploiting UN convoys in former Yugoslavia. Something else Kennedy was brilliant at cultivating: contacts. In spite of Kennedy apparently going straight, Tallis had a real feel in his gut that Kennedy could be useful in his current quest. Thing was, would Kennedy talk to him?

The next morning Tallis did some more phoning around, starting with Finn Cronin, a journalist and mate he often turned to when needing information. He started off with the usual preamble, enquiring about Finn's eldest child and Tallis's godson.

'Just made it into the under-sixteen cricket team.'

'Send Tom my congratulations.'

'Will do. Now, what do you really want?' Finn said, shrewd as ever.

Am I that easy to read? Tallis thought, worried. Maybe only to his closest friends, he hoped. 'Heard of a bloke called Johnny Kennedy?'

'Part of the American Kennedy clan?'

'Closer to home.'

'Singer?' Finn said hopefully.

'Former Midlands crime baron.'

'Can't say I have, but that doesn't mean much.'

Not Finn's patch, Tallis thought. 'I want to do some digging into his background.'

'Last time you said that I ended up moving me and my family to a safe house,' Finn groaned. Tallis pulled a face. How could he forget? Caught up in a deadly conspiracy where everyone with whom he'd come into contact had wound up dead, Tallis had done the only thing he could to protect his friend: told him to go to ground.

'This is different. The man's gone straight.'

'What did he do—find God?'

Actually, Finn could be right, Tallis thought. Kennedy's son's accident might have had a profound effect. He wouldn't be the first man to turn to religion after suffering personal trauma. Shit, he thought, sensing a hole in his theory. Perhaps Kennedy really had become an upright, law-abiding citizen. He pressed on regardless. 'I need basic background information about his family. His son was injured a couple of years ago in a hit-and-run. I want to find out more about it. Also want to know if Kennedy's married, any other kids, that kind of thing.'

'Human interest,' Finn said.

'You got it.'

Finn promised to see what he could turn up. Cutting the call, Tallis phoned Max, another friend and City financier. Most unusually, Max's mobile was switched off. Tallis resorted to calling him at work. Mistake. His secretary was in stonewalling mode.

'Mr Elliott isn't taking calls this afternoon from anyone.'

'I'm not anyone,' Tallis said, humour in his voice.

'I'm sure you're not,' the secretary said crisply, 'but the answer's still the same.'

'Can I talk to you, then?' Tallis said.

'Me?' Outrage mixed with shock.

'I didn't catch your name.'

'My name is irrelevant.'

Oh great, one of these *I don't have to give my name therefore I'm not accountable* merchants. 'Surely not… Monica, isn't it?' he said, plucking it from a deeply recessed part of his memory bank.

'Miss Morton.'

'With an o or an e?'

'I'm sorry?'

'Max has told me so much about you,' he rushed on. 'All good, of course. Perhaps you'd be kind enough to pass on my very best wishes and tell him I'll try to catch him at home this evening.'

Three minutes later, Max returned his call. 'Paul, good to hear from you.'

Tallis smiled a *Thanks, Monica* and stuck to the same theme he'd followed in his conversation with Finn, the emphasis this time on Kennedy's financial acumen.

'He was quite a respected figure before his spectacular fall from grace,' Max said. 'Most of us didn't have a clue about his extraneous activities.' That was a good one, Tallis thought. He'd never heard the word 'extraneous' used to describe some of the more vile things Kennedy had sanctioned. As with countless bosses before him, Kennedy had learnt to distance himself from the dirty end of business, employing others to carry out his bidding. 'He's actually done Birmingham a power of good,' Max enthused. 'Helped various youth initiatives, put money into charities and foundations…'

'You make him sound saintly.'

'Far from it.' Max laughed, low and long. 'But you had to admire his business sense. His philosophy was founded on simplicity.'

Bashing people's heads in, Tallis thought. Didn't get much simpler than that.

'He basically acquired property when values were low and got shot of them when they rose,' Max said. 'Moved eventually into the commercial sector, including retail and shopping developments.'

Tallis asked Max if he could find out more about the source of Kennedy's money now, how he operated his current business.

'Give me twenty minutes,' Max said.

And Tallis knew that he would. It was one of the many things he loved about the man. Max always delivered. Tallis put on the kettle, took a leak, made himself a cup of tea and ate two digestive biscuits.

'Right,' Max began when he called back. 'Current property on the outskirts of Solihull.'

An image of golf courses, leafy suburbs and affluent householders floated in front of Tallis's eyes. It was reputed that life expectancy in Solihull was several years more than in central Birmingham.

Max was still speaking. 'The property is in his wife's name.'

'Which is?' Tallis said, picking up his pen.

'Samantha Sheldon, a former model, I understand.'

Weren't they all, Tallis thought, cynical as hell. 'Go on.'

'Kennedy apparently salted a lot of cash away in

offshore accounts, usual culprits: Caymans, Brazil, Cuba, Switzerland, Jersey.'

'Jersey?' Tallis expressed surprise. 'Thought that was tightly controlled.'

'Officially it is.' Max lowered his voice. 'Depends who you know. I could tell you a tale of a certain bank where one of their employees died in extremely mysterious circumstances. Rumour has it the bloke was laundering money for al-Qaeda.'

Christ, Tallis thought, them again. What or where were the connections? *Were* there connections? 'Getting back to Kennedy,' Tallis said, 'when he was involved in the construction industry, would he have had much contact with suppliers abroad?'

'Turkey, maybe. The cheap price of their steel has seen many British suppliers go under.'

'What about now?'

'I was wondering when you'd come to that. You said he was running an online company distributing building supplies to trade.'

'Uh-huh.'

'That's not all he's running.'

'Tell me more,' Tallis said, wits sharpening.

'Incinerators are the name of the game, apparently designed for animal waste.'

Oh, yeah? 'Where's he supplying to?'

'In the UK?'

'Further afield.'

'Countries like Iraq, Iran and Saudi.'

* * *

'He's worth cultivating.'

'You make him sound like a plant,' Asim said.

'He fits the profile,' Tallis insisted hotly. 'He ticks the right boxes.'

'Not any more. He's out of the game. Simply because Reid and Brass worked with him all those years ago means nothing.'

'But the Turkish connection…'

'Because the bloke bought some steel?'

'Aren't you forgetting something? He's supplying incinerators to the Middle East.'

'So are a lot of companies.'

'All right,' Tallis said, breathing deeply, 'then what about Morello's last words?'

'Too much of a stretch.'

Tallis closed his eyes. He really didn't know what was expected of him. Using his brain was obviously not part of the job description.

Asim seemed to sense his frustration. 'Look, all I'm saying is that you're too fixed on Kennedy. You need to get out and about and find out who's doing what now.'

Tallis threw his head back and laughed. 'That's rich. Wasn't so long ago you were telling me how well the law enforcement agencies were working together, security service, police, SOCA, Counter-Terrorism, all chums in the fight against terror? One phone call should do it. You don't need me,' he said, deliberately cutting the call.

Silence. The air seemed to sweat and throb. He felt suddenly heavy and lifeless, as though someone had taken out his batteries. Now what? Was he behaving like a prima donna? Had he pushed Asim too far? Would Asim relent? Would he play ball? His phone rang. He eyed it warily, picked up.

'It's complicated,' Asim said, smoothly continuing the call as if their minor spat had never taken place.

Always is, Tallis thought. 'The truth is you don't want anyone to know what you're up to, me included.'

Asim didn't deny it. Instead he said that he'd see Tallis on Friday. 'We can talk then.'

'But it's my father's funeral.'

'I know.'

'You've sprung Dan?' Tallis said, wary.

'Yes,' Asim said coolly.

Tallis wondered how much it would cost.

13

TALLIS felt as if there was a tsunami in waiting. It was very quiet, very still, an undertow of evil in the air. Eyes drifting towards borders of blue sky, he saw a speck on the horizon, moving closer, disturbing and redistributing the atmosphere. Then he heard the sound, muffled at first, growing more distinct until he could make out the unmistakable whop-whop of a helicopter circling overhead. Clearly, the police were taking no chances with Dan. Tallis looked across at him, met his brother's stony stare, felt a crackle of hostility, wondered what he was thinking, mainly in a bid to avoid all the uncomfortable thoughts piling through his own mind. When he saw Dan, he was reminded of Belle. Reminded of Belle, he remembered all that he'd lost. He should have felt murderous. Now in a position of power over his older brother, he should have been triumphant—all his enemies vanquished.

He felt hollow.

They were standing outside the crematorium, his family and a couple of dozen or so mourners, local farmers, men who'd served in the police force with his father from way back. Tallis's mother was talking to the vicar, a young man who looked out of his depth and who'd never known the deceased. Hannah and her husband, Geoff, were trying to keep their three kids under control. The two boys, dressed in long trousers, whined with impatience, the little girl, his niece, Orla, skipped about, chatting animatedly to her doll. Tallis, trying to distract himself from the proceedings, picked her up and swung her onto his shoulders, making her squeal. Several disapproving looks were thrust in his direction.

At last, they were ushered in. Two police officers, each cuffed to Dan, one on either side, made a motion for their prisoner to move. Tallis automatically glanced over, wondering how Dan felt as a former detective chief inspector to be on the receiving end of British justice, and caught Dan's eye. If Dan could have spat in his face, he would have done, but Tallis wasn't close enough. Instead, Dan mouthed, 'Loser.'

Tallis stared back expressionless, knowing any reaction would translate as weakness and give his brother the advantage. Controlled as he was, he couldn't ignore the physical responses of his body: dryness in the mouth; sweat gathering in his armpits; skin itching with suppressed adrenalin. Inside his head, he thought, *Murdering bastard*.

Tallis pushed on ahead with his mother, Hannah and her family falling into step behind, all of them, apart from Dan and his minders, who sat at the back, finally shuffling about and taking their places in a long row at the front. His father had chosen a piece of music from Elgar, with which

Tallis was unfamiliar, for the walk-in part of the ceremony. Although there were to be hymns, he felt glad there would be no Te Deums, no Creeds, no Communion, nothing demonstrably religious.

When everyone was seated, ushers wheeled in the coffin. A casket destined for the fires of hell, Tallis thought, shocked by his bitterness of spirit, ashamed, too. He glanced to his right, saw the obvious distress ingrained on his mother's features and took her hand. She squeezed his tight, craving his support. It was strange, but he almost envied her because he knew that his mum's reaction was normal, her emotions pure and uncomplicated. Whatever he believed, his mum had loved his dad. So was he the odd one? His sister, meanwhile, on his left, was dabbing at her eyes with a tissue, clearly upset. For God's sake, he thought, what was wrong with him? The words in his head echoed eerily. How often had his father stood over him and demanded to know *What's wrong with you, boy?* For the rest of the service, Tallis tuned out, pretended he was watching a play. Might as well have done. The man described in actorly terms by the vicar was not the one he recognised to be his father.

When the curtains drew across for the final act, Tallis felt a strong sense of release and relief. He hoped it would last, hoped he wouldn't remain haunted by his father's jeering spirit. His mother, stoic as always, made no sound. Only Dan wept.

Gently taking his mother's arm, Tallis guided her out of the chapel. He noticed Asim outside, skulking near a monument of an angel. Beautifully dressed in a light-weight charcoal-grey suit, dark black tie, white shirt, Asim looked every inch a mourner. He turned his dark head, looked across, an expectant expression in his deep brown eyes.

'I want to try and have a few words with Dan,' Tallis's mother whispered in her son's ear. Tallis nodded, taking the opportunity to steal away from the small crowd, mildly amused by the presence of a dark-skinned man at his father's funeral. Dad's racist soul must be spinning, he thought.

'Walk and talk,' Tallis said as he approached.

Asim nodded though neither of them spoke at first. When Asim finally broke it was with one word. 'Kennedy.'

'The man who's gone straight,' Tallis said, watching a wagtail swoop out of the sky, perch on top of a tombstone and relieve itself.

'Your cynicism is duly noted.'

'And well founded.'

Asim flashed a smile.

'He was released early from prison,' Tallis stated, as if this explained everything.

'Our Home Office makes rather a habit of releasing prisoners early,' Asim said dryly.

Tallis wasn't buying it. He turned, faced Asim, eyeball to eyeball. 'Kennedy's turned informer, hasn't he?' That's why you want me to leave him alone.

'I'm not at liberty to say.' That meant yes. Tallis wondered when he'd ever get used to the coded dialogue beloved by spooks. Problem was different levels of secrecy.

'Wasn't hard to work out,' Tallis said, picking up the pace again. They were heading down a path far away from the others. A smell of ashes was in the air. Tallis didn't like to conjecture on its provenance. 'As soon as my contact in Organised Crime mentioned the team's high success rate, something gelled. Comes down to the mechanics of the Organised Crime Division.' Oxslade hadn't lied to him, Tallis thought. He simply hadn't known the truth. Asim still didn't say anything.

'When intelligence finds its way into the department and is pooled, it can come through any number of routes. None of the officers know the source of information. In fact, it's policy. And why? *To protect informers.*'

Still Asim remained silent.

Tallis stopped walking and whipped round. He felt suddenly and unaccountably angry. Maybe it was the whole stupid sodding spy thing, or maybe it was the fact that his father, dead or alive, engendered that sort of emotion. 'In this game you can only trust a small number of people.'

'Not even that many,' Asim chipped in with a mild smile.

Which was true. There was a superb irony about what he was engaged in. Deception was key, that and being at ease with it. Basically, Asim was hiring people like him who engendered trust yet broke it on a daily basis. In fact, Tallis hadn't trusted a single human being in a very long time, but that was neither here nor there. 'But *you* are supposed to be the exception to the rule. As much as you value me being straight with you, you have to be straight with me. I'm not in your bloody club or on your official payroll so you owe me that, at least. You knew, didn't you?'

Asim met his eye, slowly nodded. He had the bearing of a man who was totally in control, as if he knew exactly what was going to happen next. 'All right, but, like I said, it's not that simple.' He indicated that they walk off the path and through the graveyard. 'Johnny Kennedy, code name Michael Shaman, is proving to be the best informant West Midlands Police ever had on their books. Through him, they've managed to locate and bag a number of players and bust several high-rolling deals. Naturally, they want to run this guy for as long as they can.'

Until it either gets too dangerous for Kennedy, Tallis thought, or he reaches the end of his shelf life. Often they amounted to the same thing. 'And they don't want anyone else getting their hooks into him.' Tallis also knew how long it took to persuade a man of Kennedy's standing to become a grass. Fundamentally, he was being asked to sign his own death warrant. Tallis wondered what particular lever they'd used to coerce him into taking such a momentous decision.

'However, Kennedy is one sharp operator,' Asim said. 'We know that he visited the Byzantine café the same week Morello was in Turkey.'

Tallis felt his gut sharpen. So that's why Asim had changed his mind, he realised. 'What was he doing there?'

'According to his handler, building up his cover.'

'For what?'

'Drug dealing.'

'You mean they let him go unchaperoned?' He thought gangsters were subject to tight control orders. In the same way that terror suspects had their movements restricted, high courts could impose similar constraints on those involved in organised crime. Not that it had done a fat lot of good. To his certain knowledge, seven suspected terrorists had already skipped and dropped beneath the radar, a couple suspected of having links to two failed bombings in London and Glasgow.

'Remember, he was a big player,' Asim said. 'If Kennedy alters his behaviour, people are going to get suspicious.'

'Fair enough, but still seems risky. He could have been up to anything.' Tallis's mind flashed back. Maybe Garry had seen Kennedy talking to someone he shouldn't have. Maybe that's what Garry had meant. Maybe Kennedy was responsible for Garry's murder. That same stabbing feeling he'd experienced before in connection to Kennedy suddenly assailed him once more. If he found out that that bastard was responsible for Garry's death, he'd nail him personally. 'How do you read the situation?' Tallis said. He listened very hard to the answer.

'Kennedy may or may not be playing a straight bat. Everything you've found out about his Middle East connections is true.'

'The incinerators.'

'That doesn't mean to say he's actively involved in stoking terrorism,' Asim added.

Right, now they were getting to the nub of it. 'But you want me to find out?'

'Yes.'

It appeared that Asim was asking him to work along-side Organised Crime. They'd never wear it. He expressed his doubts.

'This is going to be run as a dual operation,' Asim said enigmatically.

'What? You mean not even the Organised Crime Officers running Kennedy are to be told what's going on?' He was aghast.

'No.'

Tallis kept on walking. This time it was his turn to remain silent. There were too many variables. Not only would he have to find an in to Kennedy and gain his trust, but also evade his protectors in the police. It couldn't be done.

'Effectively, you'll be going in cold. We could, perhaps, assist in creating a credible introduction.'

Tallis reeled his memory back to one of Asim's earlier approaches. His pitch had been that there wasn't enough information filtering through from the Muslim commu-nities. Added to that, a change in strategy was strongly sus-pected that the threat, rather than being home-grown, was going to come from abroad in the form of overseas-born suicide bombers. 'An attack from outside. That's where the money is,' Asim had said. And a nightmare to trace, expose and dismantle, Tallis had thought at the time.

But what most spooked Tallis, a fragment of intelligence based on informer information suggested that certain elements of organised crime wanted an in on the action. While their role was to fund terrorism, their reward was confusion and chaos, providing a perfect smokescreen for criminal activities. Tallis knew only too well that informers could be wrong, or have their own agendas. And since the information had filtered through, things had gone eerily quiet.

'Why not simply work with Kennedy's handler?' Tallis said. 'Cut me out of the loop?'

'Like I said, we don't want to alert anyone to what we're up to.'

'Why not?'

'Muddies the waters.' Asim blinked enigmatically.

And if it went wrong, it would be someone else's fault. He understood the logic. SIS, the new remodelled former MI6, had got so trashed by politicians for failing to find the intelligence for weapons of mass destruction, half of them had ended up being disbanded and sent to some far-flung outpost. It didn't do to nail one's colours to the mast. Too easy to be hoist by them. So much for working together, Tallis thought grimly. 'What exactly do you want me to do?'

'Get close to Kennedy.'

'How close?'

'Close as you can. We want to see what he's really made of.'

Oh, great, Tallis thought. If Kennedy's really gone straight, the cops will pick me up. If he's bent, and dabbling in terrorism, I could find myself at the business end of a gun again. Still, he'd survived earthquakes and the dark side of Turkish hospitality. Then inspiration struck. He shared it with Asim. 'The spider-mite analogy,' Tallis announced cryptically.

Asim looked intrigued.

'The spider mite eats all the plants in your planter. Two solutions to the problem—either you treat the plants with a soapy solution, which doesn't do them a lot of good, or you put in another mite who will chomp them all up.'

'You think Kennedy could be our big bug?' Asim said, dark eyes shining.

'Why not? If his connections are as good as we believe, we can use them to our advantage. Maybe Kennedy could be the bait.' Something he knew from experience would appeal to Asim. Quite where he stood on the issue, he wasn't certain. Had Belle's death made him a harder individual? he wondered.

'We're slightly running ahead of ourselves,' Asim cautioned. 'First, we need to find out what, if anything, Kennedy's up to. After that, we can make a proper assessment. Only problem is time.'

Dead right, Tallis thought. In novels, the infiltrator penetrated a network with indecent speed. It could take months, years to infiltrate a network. Likewise, radicalisation, as it was termed, was never a sudden life-changing event. 'You sure I should go in cold?'

'Less people who know, less chance Kennedy has of rumbling you.'

Tallis wasn't happy. 'One word about me from Kennedy to his handler and I'm sunk.'

'Not necessarily. They may decide to let you run and see where you lead. By rights, they should alert Counter-Terrorism and then we step in. Your main difficulty is getting Kennedy to trust you over and above anyone else. You'll have to make it look attractive for him to defect. Either that, or appeal to the base side of his nature.'

Become like him, Tallis thought. He still didn't like it. It had taken Joe Pistone, aka Donnie Brasco, six years to infiltrate the Bonnano family. He'd got the equivalent of five minutes.

'Need a go-between?' Asim said.

'A go-between?'

'Someone you can use for communication.'

'I've got you.'

'Might prove tricky to get information out once you're in the field, as it were.'

'I'm sure I'll find a way.' Tallis shrugged.

Asim flashed an insistent smile. 'Someone to cover your back, then.'

'Thought you said the less people who know, the better.'

'Kennedy's handlers, yes. This woman…'

'Fuck, no.'

Asim threw Tallis a penetrating look. 'You have a problem with women?'

'Of course I bloody don't, but—'

'Think about it.'

'I have thought about it.' Asim probably wanted to

draft her in as a girlfriend. Tallis couldn't think of a worse idea.

'She's good, plenty of experience as a police officer, Organised Crime, actually. Different force, of course.'

'I'm sure she's exquisite, but my answer remains the same: no.'

'Pity,' Asim said, eyes flickering across the graveyard to where a woman was standing. He motioned for her to come forward.

'Screw you, Asim,' Tallis muttered under his breath, before taking a good hard look. The hair was dark and luxuriant, skin olive-coloured and lightly tanned, eyes the colour of green chartreuse. She was wearing a long navy coat, knee-high black boots, heels not too high. Had to be about five six, slender build without being skinny. He estimated her age as being early thirties. If this was what was on offer, he should have had serious second thoughts about back-up. He should have been an unrepentant convert. He was a red-blooded male, after all, but the only thing he could envisage was heavy-duty complication.

'Charlie Lavender,' she said with the warmest, most engaging smile imaginable.

'Tallis,' he spoke softly.

'I've heard all about you.' She continued to smile.

He thought he'd quickly pass over that one. 'Very nice to meet you.'

'Asim's filled me in on the job.'

Tallis cast Asim a thin smile. 'Presumptuous of him.'

Lavender continued undaunted. 'I understand your reservations, especially as it's critical to the operation that your cover isn't blown, but I'm really going to act as no more than a shadow.'

Tallis met her eyes, held her gaze. He liked the fact that she wasn't like some kid pleading to go on the mission, that she was simply trying to reassure him that she could do the job. She probably could. She exuded professionalism.

'I like to operate alone.'

She met his eye. 'To all intents and purposes you will.'

Tallis dropped his gaze. 'I don't think it will work.' He glanced at Asim.

To her credit, Lavender didn't seem fazed. Her expression remained calm and serene. Asim said nothing. Like a fool, Tallis fell into the classic trap of feeling the need to fill in the silence. 'Where's your local beat?' he asked her.

'Devon and Cornwall.'

'Bit different, then.' He was thinking boat theft, mucky DVDs.

'Yeah,' she said, green eyes glinting. She wasn't remotely defensive, but Tallis instantly got the picture. *Don't dare patronise me.*

'You're sure you won't change your mind?' Asim said to Tallis. 'I'd feel a lot happier if you had some sort of cover.'

Tallis looked from Asim to Charlie. Wow, those eyes were magnificent, and she had a really nice, open and attractive face. 'Nothing personal, Charlie, but I'd rather do things my way.'

'Fair enough.' She smiled. 'Your call.' She turned to Asim. 'I'll go and wait in the car.'

'Thanks,' Asim said.

Tallis watched her retreating form, noted the confident lilt in her stride, the way her hips swung ever so slightly.

'You'll let me know if you change your mind?' Asim inclined his head. There was mischief in his eyes.

Was Asim playing matchmaker? Tallis wondered. 'Sure.'

'One distinct advantage that will definitely work in your favour,' Asim said, returning to business again.

'What's that?'

'You bear a strong resemblance to Billy Kennedy.'

'Johnny Kennedy's son?'

Asim nodded.

So they wanted him to play the emotional card. Dangerous. He looked into Asim's eyes. Why did he get the impression that Asim was ten steps ahead of the game? He guessed it explained why Asim was a spook, and he was a humble mercenary, the word derogatory and immediately unappealing. And it wasn't even true. He wasn't in it for the money, but neither could he say that he harboured clear political ideals, something that would have made him deeply unattractive to his masters. People with ideals were difficult to control. No, he simply had a strong inbuilt sense of right and wrong. The trouble with this game, as he was rapidly discovering, it was often hard to tell the difference.

Tallis looked up into a sea of blue sky then glanced back towards the remnants of his family. A security van had arrived. Dan was being escorted towards it ready to be bundled into the back. If it hadn't been for his brother, he thought, his and Asim's paths would never have crossed.

Asim was speaking. 'Once you're in, usual routine. You have free rein. No trace to us. Money put in your bank account. If you need to contact me…'

'It's all right, I'm familiar with the drill.'

14

IT WAS agreed that Tallis should conduct his own surveillance. It wasn't ideal. Teams were far better suited to the job. One bloke assigned as the trigger man—who reported when the subject was on the move—another to follow, the third to oversee the stopping place. By the simple law of averages, a single tail could easily have his cover blown, or lose sight of the target, especially one who was, to use the jargon, target-aware, and had a personal entourage to protect his back care of the cops. Yup, single-handed surveillance was utterly foolhardy and Tallis knew it, which was why he felt guilty for blowing out Charlie Lavender, especially for confusing reasons he hadn't begun to process. He was also forced to bear in mind that Kennedy was under extreme pressure and could, at any time, behave unpredictably. Solid back-up would have been preferable for such an eventuality. Against this, Tallis relished the freedom and solitude of working alone. Always had.

Before he got started, he shopped for basic equipment. This included a camera, binoculars, a Dictaphone, penlight torch, notebook and pen, maps, two large sheets of green

netting and a waterproof rucksack. For his own personal
comfort, he invested in a flask, the type of high-energy
foods that wouldn't leave a trail of wrappers and debris and
a quantity of Ziploc-type polythene bags in case he needed
to relieve himself in an inconvenient place. He also bought
two jackets, one reversible, a brilliant aid to disguise, and
the other fluorescent, the type worn by building-site
managers and highways personnel.

Next came the planning stage. He already knew
Kennedy's main address. A drive-by established that his
house was well hidden from trees and at the end of a drive
with CCTV cameras sitting astride the electronic gates.
Checking with an ordinance survey map, Tallis discovered
that Shakenbrook House could be accessed via swimming
across a deep pool situated outside the property's extensive grounds. As yet, he didn't know whether that
boundary had any form of protection, either by an alarmed
fence or guard dogs. He was banking that the pool alone
was deep and deadly enough to deter intruders. A rummage
through some boxes he'd never unpacked since he'd
moved to the bungalow yielded a snorkel and a diver's dry
suit. Several years old, the suit still fitted, if tight across
his more muscular shoulders.

A quick shoot through the Internet turned up the whereabouts of Kennedy's online business, which was based in
Lye, deep in the manufacturing heartland of the West
Midlands. Relieved to discover that it wasn't on an industrial estate equipped with nosy parkers and CCTV, or in
some office block with numerous exits, Tallis planned to

carry out his surveillance from the belfry of a derelict church. He had basic knowledge of Kennedy at his finger-tips, yet he badly needed to study him in his own habitat, his comings and goings, habits and routines, his known as-sociates, before he made an attempt at blustering in.

First things first. He might be a one-man operator, Tallis thought, but mode of transport could be variable and indeed desirable. With this in mind, and as it was Saturday and brilliantly fine weather, Tallis headed out of town in his old Rover and, skirting Kidderminster, drove towards the leafier environs of Bridgnorth, a small market town that had recently undergone serious redevelopment. His desti-nation was a bikers' café.

The place, up an incline and having a commanding view of the main road, was unmissable. Tallis scanned at least a hundred bikes, of all descriptions, as he pulled into the car park. Riders, some of them Hell's Angels dressed in full regalia, gathered inside and outside the café, strutting their stuff like peacocks trying to attract a mate. Tallis found it deeply heart-warming even though he got as pissed off as the next man when buzzed by a biker. This lot were probably heading down to Wales, a popular weekend destination.

As predicted, Oz, a guy who way back when Tallis had once had the honour of arresting for stealing motorbikes to order, was deep within the crowd, swigging coffee from a glass beaker that looked as though it had been designed in the 1950s. He was an extraordinary-looking man. Big with a shock of white-blond hair and blue eyes, he had the sallow kind of skin that tanned easily. Tallis often pulled his leg about it, putting his looks down to his convict roots. Weirdly, in spite of their history, they'd become friends, mainly because Oz regarded Tallis as his personal saviour. After a short time in prison, Oz had gone straight, met the right girl and set up his own business. This, apparently, was all down to Tallis. On seeing him, Oz's eyes lit up and he strode towards him.

'Well, I'll be fucked.' Oz's accent was a curious mix of Midlands and Melbourne. 'Bit far out of your comfort zone, in't you?'

Could say that again. Tallis didn't mess about by enquiring how Oz's toolmaking business was going. Instead, he ran his request straight past him. That's the sort of bloke he was dealing with. Oz didn't appreciate pleasantries.

'Got a Triumph Daytona in my garage,' Oz told him.

'Bloody hell. How did you manage to snaffle one of those?'

'Rare as hen's teeth,' Oz agreed with a cheeky grin. Contacts again, Tallis thought, not money, not what you knew, not violence. 'Goes like a dingo with its arse on fire,' Oz enthused. 'I managed to clock 140 up the Bewdley bypass last week, and it's forgiving, much more robust than a Ducati.'

'Road legal?' Tallis grinned.

'Cheeky fucker.'

'How much to have a lend of it?'

'Nah, mate. You're all right.'

'Come on, I might dent it, or something.' He'd done a lot worse. On his last job, he'd borrowed Max's Z8. Before handing it back, he'd paid to have a crater panel-beaten out of it and a full re-spray after a contretemps with a Rottweiller. Curiously, the dog had been unscathed by the experience.

'You'd best be sure to bring it back in mint condition, then.' Oz laughed. 'How long do you want it for?'

'A week, maybe less.'

'How soon?'

'Soon as.'

'I'll give my old lady a ring,' Oz said, pulling out his mobile. Four minutes later, he'd got it sorted. 'Cheryl's in all afternoon. She's got the keys. Might have to put some petrol in the tank.'

'All right if I leave my motor at your place?'

Oz looked out and surveyed the car park. 'You still driving that shit Rover?'

'I'm sentimental.' Tallis grinned.

'Mental, for sure.'

Yeah, Tallis thought, hit the nail on the head.

Christ, Tallis thought, standing in Oz's garage. *Daytona.* He should have known. Bright yellow. Even a bloody pensioner walking his dog would sit up and take notice. He was tempted to hand the keys back to Cheryl and start all over again but he had another idea. Maybe the fact the bike was so noticeable would work in his favour. It was so blatantly obvious, he couldn't possibly be suspected of doing anything underhand. And he was only going to use the machine for a short spell. After that, he could revert back to his battered old motor. Which brought him back to habitats again. In a classy area the bike would fit in beautifully, the Rover better suited to a rougher environment. Decision made, he allowed himself a full minute lost in love and praise, marvelling at the hawk-like lights, the sassy instrument panel, then wheeled the mean machine out onto the drive, put the keys in the ignition, turned and gunned the engine. Amazing.

The next morning was muggy and pouring with rain. By the look of the depth of the front, it was set in for the day. Great weather for rural surveillance, Tallis thought. No shadows to give his position away, fewer people out and about, noises muffled. He'd already packed up his gear the night before. He wore his dry suit underneath his jeans, sweatshirt and leather jacket.

South-west of Birmingham, it took him twelve and a half minutes to drive the eight kilometres at warp speed to Solihull. Oz was right. The Daytona shot down the road like the gas was mixed with rocket fuel.

Following the route he'd plotted from the OS map, he found himself in a semi-rural location with a scattering of old and newly refurbished houses on both sides, fields leading off. Still early, a Sunday, curtains were closed; most people either in bed, in church or, more likely, heading for the nearest retail park. From somewhere off, he heard a dog bark. Kids, if there were any, were probably shackled to computers.

After a casual glance around, he wheeled the bike down a track off to his left, past a field on his right, lots of trees giving him cover. At the end of the track, there was a five-bar gate, no padlock. A battered-looking sign announced that there was a bridle path, which looked overgrown to Tallis's eyes. Walkers were exhorted to close the gate after them, keep to the path and away from the lake. Another sign, more recent by the look of it, warned that trespassers would be prosecuted. A life-belt attached to a metal pole sticking out of the ground signalled a warning. Not exactly what you'd call inviting, Tallis thought.

The gate swung open after a bit of pushing and shoving. Tallis wheeled the bike through into a field covered in cowpats, flanked by hedges on three sides. To his right, there was dense woodland and barbed wire. To his left more field and green. Ahead lay the pool and Shaken-brook, an elevation of the house clearly visible through the rain and trees.

Tallis leant the bike against the fence. First, he peeled off his outer clothes, including his boots, dropping them to the ground. Next, he opened the rucksack and took out one of the pieces of green netting. It measured six feet square. He moved quickly, partly because it was chucking it down, partly because he wanted less opportunity for someone to spot him, his greatest fear children or someone walking a dog.

Stuffing his clothes under the bike, he draped the netting over the lot to break up the shape and deflect the light from the bike's reflective surfaces. A few bits of branch and twig completed the effect. Nobody, unless they were specifi-cally looking, would notice the extra bit of bush and foliage ostensibly growing along the fence.

Winching the rucksack onto his back, he tied his boots together, draping them round his neck. They'd get wet but would give protection for his feet if he needed to cover open ground, something he wasn't planning on doing.

He made his way down to the water's edge quickly. Surrounded by grasses, the water pea green and lethal-looking, it wasn't an attractive prospect. He slid in rather than making an entrance with a splash. The extreme cold penetrated his suit, taking him by surprise.

He kept to the side of the lake, a longer route round, but less dangerous. Tallis knew the centre could prove a death trap, the water suddenly dipping in depth and temperature. Hypothermia was his greatest enemy. Rain was coming down heavily now and bouncing off the lake's surface, making it roil and bubble. It suited him, anything to break up his body shape. He swam slowly, deliberately, no sudden movements to attract the eye. Close-up the water was really black, thick and brackish-looking, its green appearance simply a reflection of the unbroken blanket of trees growing overhead. He felt as though he was swimming through swamp.

His next major obstacle would be getting out without being seen. With nothing to cling onto, he would have to try and float his way to cover and hope there was an overhanging branch or piece of hedgerow he could grab hold of to yank himself out. He glanced at his watch: 07.05 hours. The closer he swam the more the house came into view. And what a view! Georgian, with at least six bedrooms, pale green shutters at the windows, both upstairs and down, creamy-coloured rendering that would take an army to paint, ornate fanlight over the front door, Shakenbrook rose out of the landscaped gardens like an ocean liner in the middle of the Pacific. He hadn't a clue whether the Kennedy family were early risers or not. He could only be guided by the position of the drapes. Downstairs' were closed. Upstairs they were open. In fact, with his 20-20 vision, he could see movement in one of the bedrooms. Narrowing his eyes, he made out a male, short grey hair, tanned, white towel tied loosely round the waist, exposing a well-built and toned torso.

Shit, Tallis thought. From an elevated position like that, Kennedy had a much better chance of looking down and spotting him. To avoid detection, he was going to have to call on all his former military experience to avoid being shown out. The basics were second nature—patience, confidence, discipline. The only thing he could do was wait, tread water, try and keep out of Kennedy's ten o'clock and two o'clock line of vision.

For almost an hour, Tallis kept his eyes levelled at the open bedroom window. Wasn't just Kennedy now. A naked woman was walking back and forth, oblivious to the stranger watching below. A smile crept across Tallis's face. If he had to be stuck in this God-awful bog, at least the view was outstanding. Slim-shouldered and with a nipped-in waist, legs long and lean, the blonde had the kind of breasts he'd only seen on page-three girls. Couldn't be much more than middle thirties, he reckoned, judging by the muscle tone and tautness of her skin. Kennedy was a lucky man.

It also said something about him. You had to be powerful and influential to pull a bird almost twenty years younger than yourself.

Another fifteen minutes and the shine started to wear off. Tallis was struggling hard not to shiver. Every time the blonde passed the window, she had another bunch of clothes in her hand. Wish to hell she'd get on with it, he thought. Having never lived with a woman properly, he'd no idea it took them that long to choose what to wear. He was almost crying out, pleading with her to stick on the nearest pair of trousers and shirt. Christ, she'd look terrific in a bin-liner, he thought, bleeding with frustration.

More minutes passed. More discussion. By the time Kennedy and the woman Tallis took to be Samantha Sheldon exited, his feet and legs were almost numb. The thought of lying in a hollow for any length of time was not immediately appealing, but he knew he had to get up and out of the water fast before either of them could reach the downstairs area. Luck was on his side. Near to the edge of the lake was a handsome weeping willow tree. It had also stopped raining.

Tallis pushed his way slowly through a thick bed of reeds, finding purchase. Every single action, each breath, was carried out with a minimum of movement and maximum of control. Eventually, he found himself near enough to be able to clasp hold of a dangling branch and ease his frozen body onto solid ground. The tree would provide great cover for an observation post, he thought. About to crawl forward again, his luck ran out.

Tallis held his breath, lying silent, the distinctive smell of cigarette smoke alerting him to the simple fact he had company. Then he saw the man—wasn't too tall, medium build, brown-haired, no outstanding features other than the fact he was dragging on a fag, crossing the lawn and heading in his direction. Tallis knew that if he stayed put, he'd be discovered. Any sudden movement would yield the same result. With a heart that was leaping against his ribcage, he did the only thing he could—slid back into the murk and prayed to God he wasn't spotted.

Immobile, eyes wide open, focused on the man who, finger and thumb grasping the filter of his cigarette, continued to move slowly and deliberately towards his position. Gaze scanning, checking for intruders, everything about him shrieked enemy on the lookout. Then Tallis spotted the jacket he was wearing, open down the front. Double fuck, Tallis cursed. It revealed a holstered gun.

In spite of the cold, a sheen of sweat coated his brow.

The man came closer, moving cat-like, the smell of tobacco stronger. He was almost near the spot where Tallis had hauled himself out. Was the ground flattened? Tallis wondered. Had he left behind some remnant of his presence? He held his breath, wondered if a clever game was being played. He half expected the bloke to drop his cigarette, pull out his gun, fire and ask questions later. To his horror, Tallis watched as the fag end was tossed from the fingers, butt ground into the dirt with the heel of a boot, hand reaching…

Tallis lowered his chin further into the water, closed his eyes, felt intense heat on the top of his head. Dear God, he thought, I've been shot. His hair was suddenly warm and wet, blood running down his face, he imagined. No, wasn't running, gushing. A memory of Garry Morello's final moments flashed through his mind. Except there was no pain and, apart from feeling frozen, Tallis felt very much alive. He prised open his eyes and let his gaze travel upwards. Fuck's sake, he thought, seeing the bloke zipping his fly, I've just been pissed all over.

Thirty minutes later, Tallis had recovered his equilibrium. After watching the man's retreating form, he'd pulled himself back out onto more solid ground and burrowed deep into the bowels of the willow tree, a fine specimen of ancient vintage if its foliage was anything to go by. Not that it helped with heat loss. Although it wasn't cold for September, the length of time he'd already been in the water meant his body temperature had taken a tumble. He seriously risked losing control and precision in his movements, something that could get him blown out.

Dropping his rucksack onto the ground, he opened it, took out a pair of thick woollen socks and put them on his feet and, having decanted a couple of pints of lake from his boots, strapped them on. Next he fished out his Thermos flask, pouring the contents into a plastic beaker, the taste of hot sweetened coffee as it slipped down his throat joyous. After that, he unwrapped and took a bite from a chocolate bar, taking care to clear away the wrapper.

Feeling a hundred times better, he took out binoculars and camera, notebook and pen, and the other sheet of netting, which he draped over himself to reduce the risk of compromise. From his concealed position, he had an excellent view of the front of the property and the approaches, including the carriage lamps studding the snake-shaped, block-paved drive. To watch the back of the house would mean crossing the grounds, something that could only be carried out effectively in darkness. Maybe tomorrow, he thought.

By using the zoom facility on his camera, he had a perfect view of the downstairs drawing room—iris-blue-coloured furnishings, baby grand piano in one corner, marble fireplace with bookshelves on either side. There he observed Kennedy freely moving around talking to his wife, who'd arranged herself on one of the two sofas. Nice outfit. Tallis smiled appreciatively. The wait had been worth it.

The sound of a vehicle rumbling up the drive grabbed his attention. He glanced at his watch: 09.09 hours. The engine note signalled a four-by-four. Sure enough, an ugly-looking Jeep powered across the gravel, a woman driving, two children strapped into the back. She pulled up, got out of the vehicle, let out a little girl with long blonde hair trailing across her shoulders. The child definitely looked to be older than his niece, he thought, zooming in, probably six or seven years of age. The way she skedaddled across the drive towards the house suggested that she knew the place well. Tallis narrowed his vision, snapped off some shots, his eyes moving to the front door. It was open,

Kennedy standing in the entrance. He was wearing a brilliant white shirt, open-necked, navy chinos. His eyes, which were heavy-lidded, had lost their vulpine quality. The smile was broad and warm as he swooped down and picked up the child, tickling her as only a father would. In that brief moment of time Tallis found it difficult to believe that Kennedy was the bastard he'd heard so much about.

After a brief, amiable exchange, Kennedy moved back inside with his child, the woman heading off down the drive in the Jeep. After that, nothing much seemed to happen. Hours ticked by. Tallis used the time to scan the area, dividing the ground in front of him into sections and examining each. During one of the sweeps, his gaze locked onto another building to the right of the main house, some distance away. With the aid of his binoculars, he could make out what looked like a summerhouse. Further inspection revealed an octagonal structure with a roof of beaten copper. There were drapes at the windows, cushioned seating in bold navy and gold stripes. It would make a good doghouse after a row with one's other half, Tallis thought, not that he ever imagined someone like Kennedy feeling the need for one.

Next, Tallis measured the distance between his hide in the willow tree and the main house. Although the light was bad, often making objects and people seem further away, he estimated the length between the two points to be roughly the same size as a football pitch. This was further corroborated by the fact that when Kennedy popped out of his house, Tallis could identify him clearly. At one hundred metres, definition was clear. One hundred and twenty metres and more, distinguishing details start to blur and become indistinct.

For the next two hours, Tallis scanned, watched, and waited. He noted Kennedy cracking open a bottle of bubbly at noon, speaking to a soberly dressed middle-aged woman with a clipboard several minutes later, and the bloke who'd pissed on him at 12.37. Their discussion lasted no more than seven minutes during which Kennedy's body language was relaxed, his face showing no sign of strain. An hour later, another bloke entered the frame. Coal-skinned, black hair in dreadlocks, and with the kind of build you saw in a local gym, he looked every inch a henchman. More discussion took place and then he disappeared. As there was no sign of a vehicle, Tallis could only surmise that he was staying somewhere in the house.

By two in the afternoon, and estimating that the family would soon be eating Sunday lunch, Tallis decided to head off. Kit packed away, and on the point of sliding back into the pool, he heard the sound of another vehicle travelling up the drive. He dropped back down, edged forwards, using his elbows, stomach flattened into the soggy ground. Stealthily drawing back a curtain of leaves, he was in time to see a black BMW draw up and a single white male step out. Tallis blinked. The man was thinner. Skin drawn back tightly across the skull, green eyes glinting, head shaved. The front door opened, Kennedy's main man standing there in greeting. Tallis's eyes clicked back to the man who'd just stepped out of the Beamer. Even in the lesser light, he felt he'd recognise that venal smile from two kilometres away. Was this an official visit from the master, or something else? Either way, he wondered what business exactly had brought Kevin Napier to Shakenbrook.

15

NAPIER stayed for two hours. Three of them, Kennedy, Napier and Pisshead, as Tallis had christened him, spent much of that time in the summerhouse. Was this where Kennedy felt most at home, or where he couldn't be overheard, or both? Tallis thought. Like most former police officers, he knew of tales of handlers getting too close to their informants, but so many rules and regulations were now in place, procedures to follow, it was no longer that easy to circumvent the system. *Know a guy called Kevin Napier?* It had been Garry's opening gambit, Tallis remembered.

Back at home, after a hot bath and meal, Tallis continued to mull over the day's observations. Perhaps, as Asim had intimated, Napier had been posted to Turkey; SOCA had a large network overseas. It would explain how his and Garry's paths had crossed. And as Asim had said, Kennedy had been seen at the Byzantine café only a few weeks before Morello's death. *We know that he visited the Byzantine café the same week Morello was in Turkey.* What was he doing there? Was Napier babysitting Kennedy, or was something more sinister going on? Had Kennedy contacted his old mates and ordered the hit? No, Tallis thought, he'd turned informer. He was one of the good guys now. However things were viewed, Tallis decided to take a leaf out of Asim's book. Never accept the first version of events.

That evening he called Gayle Morello, but got no reply. Leaving a brief message of support, he rang off with the promise of calling again soon. Bored with the thought of television, he wandered outside. The rain had stopped. Sunshine flooded a lawn pocked with molehills. The blackbirds were going mental. Tallis immediately spotted next-door's cat sitting on one of the brick pillars supporting the wall. The cat eyed him venomously. Something in its arrogant expression reminded him of Napier. Unreeling the hose from the wall, and switching on the outside tap, he swung round and blasted it with water, watching as it dived for cover. Then the home phone rang. Tallis went back inside, picked up the call in the living room. It was Finn.

'Got the information you wanted.'

'Fantastic,' Tallis said, reaching for a pen and notebook.

'Sure you know what you're getting into?' Finn's voice was sober.

Tallis tried not to sound like he noticed. 'Why do you say that?'

'My source told me that Johnny Kennedy once had some poor sod thrown off a motorway bridge.'

'Gangster folklore,' Tallis said, dismissive. 'So what have you got?'

Finn let out a sigh, seemed to be on the point of saying

something then changed his mind. 'Johnny Kennedy married Rena Lennox in 1976, had a son, Billy.'

'Same year?'

'Fashionably ahead of their time, year before.'

Making Billy the same age as me, Tallis thought.

'The marriage foundered two years later. Kennedy got custody of Billy as Rena was deemed unstable.'

'Unstable?'

'She had a drink problem. Died ten years ago. Kennedy married former glamour model Samantha Sheldon. They had a daughter, Melissa, born shortly after Kennedy was sent down for fraud.

'During the time Kennedy was in the clink, Billy was involved in a hit-and-run, the driver a bloke coming back from a party held by Birmingham City Council.'

'Drink drive?'

'No.'

Tallis rested the pen on the table. 'Then why did he flee?'

'Panic, fear, confusion. He turned up an hour later at his local nick and gave himself up.'

'Very public-spirited of him.'

'Want a name?'

Tallis flipped over to another page, picked up his pen again. 'Yup, go ahead.'

'Simon Carroll.'

'What was the outcome?'

'According to witnesses, including three other men travelling in the car at the time, it was Billy's fault. He stepped out in front of them.'

'Deliberately?' Tallis frowned.

'Never established.'

Tallis scrawled some more. 'Know where this bloke Carroll lives?'

'He rather sensibly moved out of the area. Reported he fled to the West Country.'

'Know his former address?'

Finn told him.

'And what was Carroll's occupation? You said he was coming back from a party held by the Council.'

'He was a planning officer, part of a planning management team specialising in retail.'

Tallis made a note. 'Do we know much about him?'

'My source on the *Post* reckoned he was a bit of an earnest type, eager to please, to better himself.'

Interesting take, Tallis thought. Journalists, Finn possibly the exception, were more often concerned with the personality and character traits of victims rather than offenders.

'Something you may find of interest,' Finn said, 'I've downloaded a photograph of Billy Kennedy, taken before his unfortunate accident, and emailed it to you.'

Tallis thanked him and, after a bit more disconnected conversation, hung up. It was only when he was face to face with Billy Kennedy that Tallis understood what Asim meant. He himself really did bear an eerie resemblance to Kennedy's son.

* * *

Early next morning, Tallis was back on the beat, destination Lye. He'd already exchanged the Daytona for the Rover for the day

Kennedy's online outfit, Sheldon Building Supplies, could be found in a short row of shops with a Tesco Express on the corner, a dozen or so parking slots at the front with a time limit of two hours. Nearby lay a derelict chapel, the place Tallis had already selected from the ordnance survey map as a possible vantage point for covert surveillance.

Tallis pulled up, got out and, taking the fluorescent jacket from his boot, put it on. Next, he bought a sandwich and sauntered past the double-fronted unit. At 7:02 a.m., it wasn't yet open so he took the chance to take a good look through the windows. Inside, it appeared to be pretty much like any other office—rows of desks, banks of computers, telephones, white board at the back with target figures. A second storey suggested the premises extended further, something that could be confirmed once he was in situ in the chapel.

Making a mental note of the approach, Tallis carried out a 360-degree recce of the target area. With a few notable exceptions, the general environment was fairly rough—broken-down-looking boozers with cracked windows, one having a dirty brown door near the entrance marked 'Off-Sales,' 1930s-style semis where you walked in the front door and swiftly found yourself out the back, small industrial workshops. Shift-workers and cleaners with tired eyes trudged the dirty streets before making way for the next wave of manual labourers.

Like all the shops in that row, the unit had a staff entrance

at the rear. Unlike the others, it had two private parking
spaces and warning signs to that effect. By 7:20 a.m., Tallis
had moved the Rover and parked it in a dossy-looking back
street where it suited the natural habitat, and had installed
himself in the belfry of the old chapel. Stinking of urine,
littered with bent lager cans, cigarette butts and used
syringes, it was clear others had been there before him.

At 7:30 a.m. a small, sandy-haired man, mid-forties,
emerged from around the corner, walked along the row
and, taking out a fistful of keys, entered the premises.
After removing his jacket, he spent the next half an hour
crawling under tables and desks then checking light fittings
and telephones. Looking for listening devices, Tallis
thought, making a note. By 8:00 a.m. four others had
joined him, two men, two women, and the place was
rocking. Tallis took photographs, made more notes, observing that upstairs was a lot more palatial in décor than
down. Prints on the walls, big expensive-looking desk,
lush blue-grey carpet, leather sofa and chairs, this had to
be Kennedy's office, he concluded.

At 8:30 a.m. a black Land Rover with tinted windows
cruised towards the rear of the block. Further inspection
confirmed that Pisshead was driving, Kennedy seated on
the passenger side. The Land Rover pulled into one of the
private parking slots, Pisshead alighting from it first, furtively checking that the coast was clear before allowing
Kennedy out and into the building. After brief discussion
with those downstairs, Kennedy disappeared to his lair in
the top storey where he remained for several hours.

For the rest of the week, Tallis watched faces and routines. Although Kennedy frequently changed cars and venues, there were definite patterns of activity. Alternating between the Rover and Daytona, Tallis tracked Kennedy's haunts. A picture was starting to emerge of a man with certain enthusiasms. He liked racehorses and casinos, fast cars, not fast women. In contrast, two days before, Tallis followed the Land Rover to a dilapidated club in Oldbury. Kennedy spent an hour inside with his minder. After they left, Tallis decided to check out the place for himself. Ten youths stopped what they were doing and turned their surly eyes on him. Some were playing pool, others cards. Adopting his very best Black Country accent, Tallis fell into the role of a motorbike courier who was lost. Ignoring him, the lads relaxed, returned to their pool cues, those at the card table playing a game called Shithead. Couldn't be anything exotic like Canasta or Chemin de Fer, Tallis thought, edging his way out.

Twice, Kennedy attended a private medical clinic in Edgbaston, near Birmingham city centre. It was one of those places where there are ornately laid out paths and benches in the grounds, the service gold-plated, and the staff look fresh instead of knackered. Having no idea why Kennedy was there, Tallis could only presume he was suffering from high blood pressure or some other stress-related illness, a common condition for informers.

The Land Rover came in for special consideration. With reinforced glass, armour plating and tyres, the type of add-ons more often reserved for the likes of the security

services, the vehicle indicated either a man worth protecting at all costs, or someone still very much in the game.
But the strangest discovery of all was that someone else
was also watching. And that someone was a woman.

And it wasn't Charlie Lavender.

Tallis took a circuitous route to his bungalow. He'd spent
what, on the surface, seemed a wasted day staking out
Shakenbrook. Nothing of note had happened. Nobody,
other than the usual suspects, made an appearance. No
Napier. No clandestine meets in the summerhouse. In spite
of everything that hadn't happened, Tallis felt quiet satisfaction. He'd discovered a weak spot in security.

Each morning Samantha and Melissa were driven to
school in a top-of-the-range Lexus by the dark-skinned
heavy. No armour-plating, no bulletproof tyres, always
the same time, always the same route. Likewise, the afternoon run, with the exception of Tuesday when the kid
had a music lesson, was carried out with a similar
monotonous if dangerous regularity. With a plot already
hatching in his mind, Tallis aimed to contact Asim that
evening. Freshly out of the shower and about to make a
start on dinner, he received an unexpected visitor.

'How did you get my address?' Tallis demanded
sharply.

'Stu,' Oxslade replied, cool. 'You going to let me in?'

'Sure,' Tallis said, opening the door, leading the way,
hastily clearing the sofa of newspapers. Fortunately,

anything connected with Kennedy was out of sight in his bedroom.

'Don't bother,' Oxslade said. 'This won't take long. I'm off to Holland in an hour.'

'Cheese and clogs?' Tallis said conversationally.

Oxslade was deadpan. 'Cannabis and cocaine.'

By his stony expression, Tallis had already worked out that this was no social call.

'Understand you've been snooping round Johnny Kennedy.'

Fuck, Tallis thought. Who'd rumbled him? Then he remembered the bloody woman watching Kennedy, *watching him*. Denials were pointless. Not that Oxslade seemed that interested. 'You could get hurt,' he said in a cocky, challenging tone.

'By your own admission, Kennedy's no longer in the game. How could I possibly get hurt?' Tallis smiled.

'Look, mate, I'm just warning you.' Oxslade's eyes flashed pale.

Tallis dropped the friendly stance. 'Who sent you?'

A heavy flush spread from Oxslade's neck to his cheekbones. His reply was imperious. 'Nobody sent me.'

Tallis didn't believe him. SOCA, he thought. He bet Napier was involved, nothing to do with the bloody woman at all. Only one way to resolve it—pull rank, mutter security services. He didn't. Instead he thanked Oxslade for the tip-off and wished him well in Amsterdam. 'I hear the Red Light district is impressive,' he said, firmly shutting the front door.

* * *

In spite of wanting further clarification of his role, he didn't call Asim immediately. He cooked himself sausage and mash, ate it while reading the *Birmingham Mail*, and slept like a dead man. The next morning, he got up and went for a three-mile run. Nagging at the back of his brain, he harboured the maddening thought that Asim was not being entirely straight with him. No surprises there. Asim, if previous dealings were anything to go by, specialised in dissembling. Tallis still found it frustrating. What the hell did Asim know that he didn't?

He kicked hard off his left foot, feet pounding the pavement, really starting to motor. From his time in the police, he knew that a team of specially trained officers handled informers. Although they could be of any rank, they consisted of a contact, a surveillance officer and undercover officer. Tallis marked the woman he'd spotted as the surveillance officer. She was OK at her job, but not that accomplished. He felt certain deep in his gut that she hadn't rumbled him.

After a shower and breakfast, Tallis drove in the direction of Bearwood. Rows of nine-storey blocks of flats jutted into a jagged skyline. Although there was a sign for an arts centre, Tallis couldn't think of a place less likely to host one. Cops were out in force. A black man who wandered out in front of him as he pulled up at some lights looked as though he'd been smacked on the nose and was still suffering the after-effects of concussion. Driving through different layers of deprivation and shattered-looking streets, Tallis eventually came to a respectable road of Victorian houses that reminded him of parts of North London. Simon Carroll had lived in number thirty-one.

A bloke with acne answered the door. Tallis arranged his expression into a warm smile.

'Wondered if you could help me, mate. Trying to track down Simon Carroll. Understand he used to live here.'

'Can't help you.' The homeowner was already closing the door. Tallis put his foot inside, jamming it. The man's expression turned to one of pale fear.

'Take it easy,' Tallis said calmly.

'B-been gone two years,' the bloke stammered. 'West Country.'

'I know that,' Tallis said evenly. 'Any idea where?'

'Didn't leave a forwarding address.' His eyes were clicking from Tallis to the road and back again.

'Is there some problem?' Tallis said, easing his foot back from the doorframe. 'Course there was. Why else was acne chops behaving like he had the Grim Reaper up his rear?

'He'd received death threats,' the man said, slamming it shut.

So that's how the police got their hooks into Kennedy, Tallis thought. He didn't like to think about what had become of Simon Carroll.

16

ASIM agreed to meet. Tallis got the impression that the next stage of the plan was about to be implemented. Why else would he be invited to London for a debrief? Any grand hopes of going to Thames House, MI5's headquarters, however, were quickly dashed. Asim suggested a row of shops round the corner from Richmond tube station, the venue a back room above a shop selling slug pellets and gardening paraphernalia.

To Tallis's surprise, there were two others in the room, a bloke roughly the same age as himself, tall and lean with dark blue eyes that appeared almost brown, and a petite-framed woman with short bleached-blonde hair and full lips painted the colour of damsons. Neither looked as if they wanted to be there. In fact, the atmosphere in the room was several degrees north-west of genial. What a contrast to the welcome he'd received from Charlie Lavender. Tallis groaned inside, an image of her smile flashing through his mind.

Asim introduced the team, as he referred to them, as Sean and Roz. Tallis was introduced as David. He sus-

pected nobody was operating under real names. Made him
ponder on what Asim was really called.

It was straight down to business. Tallis gave an account
of his surveillance, most specifically a recce report on
Kennedy, details of the vehicles he owned, the area in
which he lived, where he worked, entry and escape routes
to both known establishments. He also mentioned
Kennedy's personal history, associates and contacts, including Napier. Asim said nothing, simply listened,
Sphinx-like.

'Something else you should know,' Tallis said. 'I had a
visit from West Midlands organised crime section. They
know of my interest in Kennedy.'

Sean raised his eyes heavenwards. Roz clicked her tongue.
'You've shown out,' she said, voice ladled with contempt.

'No, I haven't. *They* showed out. *I* stayed undercover.'
Tallis turned his gaze on Asim. 'That's right, isn't it?'

Asim didn't answer. 'The plan goes ahead.'

'But I'm compromised.'

'Not necessarily.'

'Asim, this isn't going to work,' Sean broke in. 'He's
way out of his depth,' he added, inclining his head in
Tallis's direction. Tallis felt himself flush, not with indignation but with embarrassment. Now that the tables were
turned, he suddenly realised the position he'd put Charlie
Lavender in. Wasn't very nice.

Asim flicked a smile. 'Think I'll be the judge of that.'

'Sean's right,' Roz said, eyes darting, red lips pulled back
to reveal the two front teeth in her upper jaw overlapped.

'What's your plan?' Asim said, ignoring both operatives, addressing Tallis the way an indulgent uncle spoke to a favourite nephew even though Tallis believed he and Asim were roughly the same age.

Tallis cleared his throat, addressed Asim only, told him about the weak spot, how he'd mapped out the school run, how they could strike.

Roz was off again. 'For Chrissakes, this isn't downtown Chicago.'

'Think you'll find your intel's out of date,' Tallis said with a provocative smile. 'Come to think of it, when was the last time you two set foot in the Midlands?'

'What, leafy bloody Solihull? Fuck you.' Sean's blue eyes smouldered to brown.

Tosser, Tallis thought, saying nothing.

'Fine,' Asim said, his voice cold and commanding. 'Roz, Sean, you can leave.'

Sean's mouth went slack. 'What?'

Roz half smiled, clearly unsure whether she'd heard correctly. 'You're not serious.'

'I think you've made your positions clear,' Asim said, a dangerous timbre in his voice. 'Prejudice in one form or another has been responsible for many of the world's evils. I'm not prepared to sacrifice another life on its altar.'

'Hey, Asim,' Sean said, breaking into a shaky laugh. 'No need for this. We just don't want David here to get hurt, that's all.' He offered a smile to Tallis, who viewed him with the same disdain as if Sean had shaken him down for money. Sean looked at Roz, who dropped her gaze and shrugged.

'Good.' Asim nodded, a calculating smile on his lips. 'Then you'd better listen to what the man says.'

And they did.

They were poring over an ordnance survey map of the area for a third time. The plan was simple: Sean and Roz were to stage an abduction of Mrs Kennedy and her child, and Tallis was going to play the hero and come to their rescue. Everyone knew that what was intended carried a high risk of injury, or worse. Although concern for Kennedy's wife and child was paramount, they also had to take into account other road-users. For this reason, the interception had to take place early in the morning, early in the journey, before the rural landscape became urban.

They'd already established the route, possible escape paths, timing, vehicle and ID of the driver, a twenty-eight-year-old West Indian known as Desmond 'Dread' Williams.

'He'll be armed,' Tallis told them.

'Naughty, naughty,' Sean said. Now that he'd been told exactly how it was all going down, he'd started to put forward sensible suggestions. He also had a nice sense of humour. About Roz, Tallis felt less certain, probably because she said little, let alone found Sean's asides amusing.

Tallis pointed out that Dread favoured the Ingram Mac 10, a popular weapon with Yardies and black gangs. From the shade of the willow tree, he'd watched Dread swagger and show his latest toy to Pisshead. 'What about us?' Tallis said, regarding Asim.

'Sean and Roz will be armed. For authenticity's sake, you won't.'

'Fabulous,' Tallis said, unsmiling.

'Sorry, but that's the way it has to be. You start waving a firearm about and you'll look like part of the plot.'

'Can't I have a piece in my glove compartment?'

'Only piece you'll be needing is a hands-free phone.'

Tallis wasn't persuaded but he knew better than to argue with Asim, especially in front of the others.

Sean turned to Roz. 'Better take a look and familiarise ourselves with the terrain soon as.'

'When are we going in exactly?' Tallis asked. 'I don't recommend Mondays unless you fancy getting stuck behind a refuse collection lorry.'

A date was arranged for five days' time.

It was decided that Roz would act as trigger. A lay-by close to Shakenbrook gave a clear and unobstructed view of the entrance. From there, Roz, riding a motorbike, could confirm the Lexus was being driven with the target occupants inside, and give Dread's direction of travel. Less than a kilometre down the road, Tallis would already be in position at a junction from which he'd pull in behind the Lexus.

'Think he'll notice?' Sean said.

Depends how stoned he is, Tallis thought. That was the other thing about Dread. He liked his ganja. Had also been known to smoke the odd rock of crack. 'No special reason for him to be suspicious. Even if he is, there are no lights to jump, no roundabouts to drive round twice, no places for a U turn.' Tallis was actually a bit more concerned

about his battered old car. Wouldn't look cool for it to
break down in the middle of the operation. He made a
mental note to run a maintenance check.

As if Roz had read his mind, she asked what he'd be
driving. He told her.

'How far are you going to get in one of *those*?'

'The plan is for you to allow me to escape. What would
you prefer, a bright red Ferrari? Might as well paint *I'm
coming to get you* on the bonnet.'

Roz bit her lip and glared.

'He's right,' Sean said, glancing grudgingly at Tallis.

'Comes down to authenticity.' Tallis grinned before
turning back to Roz. 'I'm sure you could play dead, or
something. Give me a head start.'

She flicked a cold, disdainful smile. 'I'll be too busy
sorting out Mr Dread.' Carrying out the hard part was what
she meant, Tallis thought, considering what kind of a
woman she was, a ball-breaker, or vulnerable as hell.
Again, he remembered Lavender, her charm, her quiet
confidence. Oh, fuck, he thought, shaking the image of her
out of his head. He asked what they intended to do with
Dread. Everyone looked at Asim.

'We're going to put him on a plane back to Jamaica,'
Asim said. 'Police want to question him about a murder
in Kingston.'

They returned to the map. Sean tracked Tallis's intended
route. 'You'll be the eyeball,' he said.

And the cavalry, unless it went tits up, in which case
he'd be the fall guy, Tallis thought.

'I'll be waiting here at the choke point,' Sean said, indicating a spot on the map. 'Roz, you cut through using the bridle path. I'll pull out in front—'

'What are you going to be driving, a Sherman tank?' Tallis interrupted.

'A specially reinforced Land Rover,' Asim chipped in, 'not unlike our Mr Kennedy's preferred mode of transport.'

'Roz pulls her piece,' Sean continued. 'I move in. Between us we disable Mr Dread…'

'And in the meantime, I rescue the woman and child, reverse like fuck up the road and become the hero of the hour.'

Simple.

17

THE rendezvous, three kilometres from Shakenbrook, was a boarded-up petrol station-cum-store that had recently gone out of business.

It was cold for the time of year and there was a weird cloud formation in the sky as if the blue were crusted in fungus. Tallis was wearing dark clothing so as not to draw attention to himself. Sean followed the same dress code. Roz, an earpiece dangling from her ear, was dressed in leathers. She looked strangely sexless, Tallis thought, suddenly reminded of the hit in Turkey. It made him reconsider the identity and sex of the individual who'd fired three bullets into Garry Morello's chest. He remembered that Crow still hadn't got back to him.

They decided to keep to a simple system of communication—target vehicle Car 1, the Rover Car 2, Land Rover Car 3, bike Romeo. At 7:35 a.m. each drove to their positions. Tallis parked, taking care to align all four wheels so that he didn't appear to be on the lookout for someone, turned off the engine, checked his watch, estimating that in ten minutes the Lexus would be emerging from the drive. He didn't suffer from nerves. He was too busy watching and waiting, eyes clicking from front to mirror to rear. Which was how he spotted the police car coming up behind him. Great, he thought, sticking on his hazards, wondering what the hell he was going to do if, in a few minutes' time, Roz gave the standby signal. Sure enough, the police car pulled up. A lone officer got out. 'Problem?'

'Flat battery,' Tallis said. 'Fortunately, help's on its way.'

'Better move it,' the officer said. 'It's obstructing the highway. There's a short piece of verge back there. I'll give you a hand.'

Tallis gave a weak smile of thanks. With no choice but to comply, he climbed back inside, letting the handbrake off, and steered the vehicle away from the junction and away from his prime view of the road. Christ, Roz would have his rear in a sling for this. So would Sean. So would Asim.

Two minutes later, he was back in position, praying the copper wouldn't return and frantically checking his mobile phone for missed calls. Nothing. Worse, it was well past the hour. Eventually, the call came through at 08.30. It wasn't standby but stand down.

Undeterred by the false start—maybe the child was ill, Tallis pointed out—they reconvened the following day. This time things started more smoothly, but Tallis fizzed with nerves. Bang on 08.05 Roz called. 'Standby, standby, Car 1 has left target residence, turned left onto the road, heading north. All targets are in vehicle.'

Tallis responded by turning his engine on. 'Car 2 in

position,' he said. Three minutes later, the Lexus came into view and shot past at speed. Tallis called, 'Contact, contact,' pulled out, flooring it, hoping to God Dread was so busy looking ahead he wouldn't be checking his mirror. As added protection, Tallis used every single hill and bend in the road as cover.

'Romeo to Car 3,' Roz said, 'heading for choke point.'

'Car 3 in position,' Sean said.

'Car 1 ahead, no deviation, driving in excess of sixty miles an hour,' Tallis said. Christ, he must get through brake pads, he thought, watching as the Lexus's rear lights flashed on and off as it slowed abruptly for the bends. So far, he'd only seen two other cars on the road, both travelling in the opposite direction. Tallis kept his eyes glued to the Lexus, foot glued to the accelerator. The Rover was starting to judder a bit now, unused to being thrashed. 'Car 1 passing church on nearside,' Tallis reported to the team. And, shit, tractor. With breathtaking daring, the Lexus speeded up and sailed past, narrowly missing a lone car coming from the opposite direction. Tallis tried to do the same, but another car popped into view, the driver blasting his horn, forcing him to drop back behind the tractor, which was rumbling down the road at snail's pace. Swearing like a junkie in need of a fix, it was another five hundred metres before he was able to pull out. Road ahead clear, the Lexus was nowhere to be seen.

Tallis sped off again, eyes skimming the empty horizon, bend after vacant bend, before admitting defeat. 'Total loss,' Tallis reported, his gut twisting with failure.

Nobody spoke then Roz came on the air. 'Contact, contact. Car 1 heading towards position.'

Where was she exactly? Tallis thought, frowning.

'Car 3 on standby.' Sean sounded clinical and calm.

They've changed the plan, Tallis thought, smacking his foot down, hammering the engine, eyes scanning the open road for sight of the Lexus. As he rounded the second of two bends, he slammed on his brakes, skidding to a halt, the scene before him a vision of chaos. He saw the bike first, or rather bits of it splayed across the road, the Lexus sideways on, caved in where it had been rammed, the Land Rover the other side, sandwiching it. Dread was out of the vehicle, staggering, blood pouring from a wound to his head. Sean was also out, armed, shouting abuse and orders to the terrified females, their screams rending the air. His cue to move, Tallis leapt out of the car and ran. Sean opened fire, deliberately allowing the bullets to go high and wide, Tallis dodging in case. Yanking open the offside rear door, he saw the woman's face, eyes shot wide, pupils dilated with terror. He grabbed her hand. 'Come with me.'

'What?' She pulled back, teeth chattering, resistant.

'Look, I don't know who the hell you are, or what's going on, but we're all going to get shot if you stay here. It's a fucking killing zone.'

Something seemed to click in her head. She nodded, struggled out. 'And you, little one,' he said, scooping up the child, running flat out with them both towards his car. Out of the corner of his eye, he saw Roz lying motionless, blood spreading onto the tarmac, not playing dead, but dead.

All around them was noise: feet pounding, men shouting, shots ringing out. Something skimmed Tallis's ear. Glancing back, he saw Dread, raising his weapon, lining him up for another go.

'Get in,' Tallis shouted, pushing the child on top of her mother. Throwing himself into the driver's side, he turned the ignition, revved the engine, saw Dread stagger and start to fall, blood bloom and blossom on Sean's T-shirt. Jaw clenched, Tallis twisted round and, thrusting the gear into reverse, put his foot flat down on the accelerator, laying rubber, speeding back up the way he'd come. When he looked back in his mirror, both men were on the ground.

It had been a disaster.

'Either of you hurt?' They were pointing in the right direction, away and on open road, the little girl sobbing uncontrollably, her mother doing her best to calm her.

'A little bruised. It's nothing.' Now that she was out of immediate danger the woman recovered and seemed very controlled. They had that much in common, at least, Tallis thought. Or, perhaps, it was more a case of both of them being very good at masking their emotions.

'What the hell was that all about?'

She was slow to answer. 'Business. My husband is a powerful man. He has many enemies.'

'We should call the police.'

'No.'

Tallis glanced in the rear-view mirror, saw the look of

absolute certainty, recognised that this was indeed Kennedy's woman, blonde, blue-eyed and beautiful. An image of her naked flesh flashed before his eyes. 'But those people tried to kill you.'

'Not kill me, take me.'

'Same difference,' he said. 'I really think it best if—'

'My husband will know what to do.'

'But—'

'He'll want to thank you,' she said, looking out of the window. She'd put a hand to her face and was brushing a stray hair back over her ear.

'We'll call the police once we've spoken to him,' Tallis said, insistent, playing the good citizen. He wondered what Asim was doing—probably issuing orders for a clean-up squad to move in. He didn't like to think of Sean, much less of Roz.

'Yes,' she said without conviction, then, leaning forward, she introduced herself. 'I'm Samantha Kennedy. This is my daughter, Melissa. You are?'

He paused. Tallis had realised that in revealing his true identity, Kennedy could easily find out that he had once been a firearms officer. On the other hand, he was an officer who'd left the service crushed and disillusioned. As every professional crook knew, disillusioned ex-coppers could be bought. Disillusioned ex-coppers could prove invaluable. He was going with the truth.

'Tallis.'

'Unusual name.'

'Paul Tallis,' he explained. 'Where should I take you?'

'My office,' she said, giving him an address on the other side of Birmingham.

It turned out to be a storage unit in Walsall. Tallis triangulated the position in his head. With Solihull and Lye, it completed Kennedy's geographical power base, he thought, pulling into a car-parking space. Perhaps this was the real seat of power, but, then, why would Mrs Kennedy risk taking him there?

Samantha Kennedy took her daughter's hand and led the way up two stone steps and into a narrow entrance with a closed door, punching in a code on the wall to allow access. Unlike most offices, it didn't appear customer friendly. Tallis wondered what type of business was carried out there. Perhaps this was where the incinerators were made or supplied. When he asked, he was told import and export. Tallis nodded and looked down and smiled. The little girl looked up, staring at him with big solemn eyes.

The entrance opened out into a large reception area with no receptionist. Tallis scoped the room. Two CCTV cameras positioned from different angles. Alarm winking high up in the right-hand corner. Large desk. One chair. Glass screen that he guessed was one-way. Cheap carpet the texture of Brillo. Samantha smiled sweetly and asked him to wait while she fetched her husband. Tallis watched as she punched in another code, clicked the door open and, taking the child, walked through into what looked like a hall. Five minutes later, Tallis began to sense things slipping through his fingers, a feeling confirmed by the appearance of Pisshead. The expression in his eyes was not one of welcome.

He should have seen it coming, Tallis thought, feeling a devastating left hook connect with his jaw. Teeth rattling, he made several deductions—his assailant was no novice, it took skill to throw a punch like that off the front leg, and he was a left-hander. Tallis absorbed the blow, staggered a bit—he was supposed to be some innocent do-gooder, after all.

'Hey, what are you doing?' he pleaded, putting both his hands up defensively.

Pisshead didn't seem in the mood for listening. In fact, he was putting on quite a show. 'We know so don't play games, you fucker. Who sent you?'

What did they know? Tallis thought. Was this bluff or intelligence? He fell into the role of simp. 'Look, let's talk. Ouch, can you stop doing that, please? *Please.*'

Adrenalin was coursing through his body, screaming at him to fight or take flight. By doing nothing, the receptors in his brain, instead of flicking off the pain facility, switched it on. This was really hurting. When the next two blows landed, nasty left jabs, he changed his mind. Everything that had happened in the past twenty-four hours erupted and boiled over, exacerbating Tallis's already dystopian view of the world.

He went in hard and fast. Pushing his right hip forward and, bending slightly at the knees, bringing him level with Pisshead's jaw, he threw his left fist upwards, twisting and powering through with a devastating uppercut. Pisshead rocked, just about managed to stay on his feet, but Tallis, in no mood for taking prisoners, followed up with a right cross, employing all of his considerable body weight, hammering his assailant on the jaw. Swiftly realising the change of game plan, Pisshead tried to come back with some defensive moves, but he was no match for Tallis's rage and recklessness.

'Want some?' Tallis yelled, lurching his body forward, whiplashing the front of his head into Pisshead's nose. Blood sprayed across the room. As Pisshead put his hand to his face, Tallis launched himself at his opponent, cannoning into him, and pinned him across the desk. In a split second he was sitting astride him, his hands around the man's throat. Eyeball to eyeball, the man's breath and spittle and blood on his face and hands, close quarters, close combat. He pressed hard. The man was trying to jab him away, twisting and wriggling, but Tallis's grip was strong and unforgiving. A dreadful rattling sound rasped from the guy's throat, eyes beginning to strain and bulge, heels kicking and drumming on the floor. Then the rear door flew open.

Tallis glanced up, saw Kennedy standing there but was too enveloped in his own personal mist of madness to stop. Still Pisshead writhed and squirmed, each movement weaker than the one before. He was like a fish breathing its last. Still Tallis pressed down, expecting the crack and break, then felt something solid on his arm. He looked down. It was Kennedy's hand, wasn't clamped in restraint, but rested there, light as a feather, as if Kennedy were holding him in reverence. Tallis's gaze travelled up, locked onto Kennedy's dark eyes, seeing something in them that made him want to give up the fight and stop. Kennedy as peacemaker, he thought wildly as he let the man go and, breathing heavily, staggered back.

Kennedy approached Pisshead, extended a hand and helped him to stand. 'Get cleaned up then get this man a drink,' he said, indicating Tallis. Pisshead nodded, swaying slightly, his hand still locked round his throat from where Tallis had tried to squeeze the life out of him. When he'd gone, Kennedy turned to Tallis, regarding him with something approaching awe.

'I always think that violence is the last resort of an ill-educated man.' He spoke softly, his accent less broad than Tallis had imagined it would be. Perhaps he'd tried to lose that, too. 'John Kennedy,' he said, extending a hand.

Tallis didn't take it. 'Disgusting way to treat a good Samaritan,' he said, taking out a handkerchief and wiping his mouth.

'For which I apologise.'

'That goon work for you?'

'Gabriel is one of my more enthusiastic employees.' Kennedy smiled.

Certainly no archangel, Tallis thought.

'Are you hurt?' Kennedy enquired. 'I can arrange for a doctor.'

'Not necessary.'

'You sure?'

'Nothing that won't heal.'

Kennedy perched his rear on the desk, crossed his arms,

placing one foot in front of the other in a relaxed gesture. 'You put up quite a fight.'

So you were watching, Tallis thought. Close up, he noticed Kennedy's eyes, which were the colour of wet slate, were even more arresting. It wasn't easy to tell what was going on behind them. 'Used to be in the army.'

'Special Forces?'

'Royal Staffordshires.'

'Just merged to become the Mercian regiment, I believe.'

'That's right,' Tallis said.

'Joined with Worcestershire, Sherwood Forest and Cheshire to form a multi-battalion unit. Part of the Defence Secretary's shake-up of the army,' Kennedy added, sounding none too impressed.

Well informed, Tallis thought. 'With a predictable cut in jobs.' He smiled thinly.

'And what do you do now?' Kennedy said.

'Unemployed and looking for work.'

The door swung open. Gabriel appeared with a brandy balloon two fingers full. Face swollen and red, a wodge of tape and cotton wool over the bridge of his nose, he handed the glass to Tallis.

'I think you owe our knight in armour an apology,' Kennedy said in a voice guaranteed to brook no dissent.

'Yeah, 'course,' Gabriel said, obedient. 'Sorry about that. Misunderstanding.' He stuck out his hand. Tallis took it, noting the belligerent light in the man's eyes. Didn't blame him. Not only had a stranger tried to kill him but his boss was rubbing his face in the dirt.

Kennedy dismissed Gabriel and turned back to Tallis. 'My wife said you were called Paul.'

'Tallis, that's what I prefer to be called.' By people like you, he thought.

Kennedy gave a small smile of acknowledgement. 'Tell me what happened out there.'

'Your wife didn't say?' Tallis took a gulp of brandy. It tasted as smooth as toffee until it hit the back of his throat and turned into a fireball, a metaphor for Kennedy maybe.

'She's upset and when women are upset…' Kennedy flicked a knowing smile '…they're good on detail but not the big picture.'

Tallis didn't agree. His motto was never to underestimate a woman. Not that he told Kennedy this. Instead, he talked of how he'd been driving along, minding his own business, until he noticed the Lexus. 'Moving like the wind.' Tallis smiled appreciatively.

Kennedy shook his head, let out a sigh. 'If I told Desmond once, I told him a thousand times to cut his speed.'

'Certainly brought out the boy racer in me,' Tallis said. 'Not that it did much good. An old Rover's no match for a machine like that.'

'This other bloke, the one with the gun.' Kennedy leant forward slightly. 'Describe him.'

Tallis did, although his description was a far cry from the man he knew. He was especially careful to leave out the unique colour of Sean's eyes. Not only would it indicate they'd already met, it seemed too private, too personal.

'And what was this man driving?'

'A Land Rover, black. That's all I noticed. It was only a fleeting impression. I didn't spot the registration or anything.'

Kennedy nodded thoughtfully, flicked a smile that suggested Tallis was doing well. 'Any sign of police?'

'No. Naturally, I suggested to your wife we call them, but she seemed reluctant. Perhaps we could call them from here,' he said, looking around as if searching for a landline.

'We'll discuss that later,' Kennedy said briskly. 'I'd like to get a clearer view of what we're dealing with first.' He asked Tallis to continue.

'Like I said, me and the Rover were hammering along. Next I knew there were a couple of double bends. I began to come out of the second bend and the pile-up was right in front of me. Lucky I didn't drive into the back of it. There were bits of bike all over the road. At first I thought it was a straightforward accident, bike hits car, car goes into oncoming vehicle, but then I heard the shouts, saw the guns, heard your wife and child being threatened. That's when I acted.'

'You didn't think first?'

'What was there to think about?'

'You were taking one hell of a risk.'

'Two blokes want to have a shoot-out, it's up to them, but there was a woman and kid involved. I couldn't run away from that.'

Kennedy blinked his eyes. 'Did you see what happened to Desmond?'

'Last I saw, he was on the ground with the other bloke. Didn't look good. I think he'd been shot.'

Kennedy studied him some more, then broke into a smile. 'Courage like that deserves a reward.'

Tallis raised his glass. 'This will do me.'

'A shot of second-rate brandy in return for saving my family?' Kennedy scoffed. 'I have a much better idea. Come,' he said, moving forward, clapping his arm round Tallis's shoulder.

Tallis followed as Kennedy punched in a code and walked him through to a hallway in which there was a lift and control box. Taking out a key, Kennedy inserted it into the box and twisted it once clockwise, twice anti, presumably deactivating some kind of alarm. Satisfied, he indicated they move towards the lift. As the doors drew apart, a man was standing inside. He was about five feet ten, muscular, head and upper body top heavy for the rest of him. His eyes looked like someone had put two slits in his face. Kennedy invited Tallis to step in, which he did. Kennedy followed. Glancing at the panel, Tallis established there were four floors. The heavy pushed the button marked 'B' for the basement. Nobody said a word.

Tallis felt the sudden weight of double-cross heavy on his shoulders. A cold image of torture, of vomit and pissing blood, of execution swam before his eyes. When the doors slid open, he had a hard time persuading his legs to move. Kennedy stepped out first, Tallis next, the heavy bringing up the rear.

It looked as if they were in a small underground car

park, apart from the fact the lighting was exceptionally bright and the cars were all new. Tallis looked around him, waiting for some other thug to appear, wondering how many he could lay out before the final curtain. So convinced that Kennedy was going to slot him, Tallis didn't hear what he was saying. 'Of course, if you'd like to come to some other arrangement, I'm open to offers.'

'What?' They were standing stock-still.

'The car.' Kennedy smiled.

'Yes?'

'The Aston Martin Vanquish is mine, but I guarantee any one of these will bring out the boy racer in you.'

Tallis followed Kennedy's wolfish gaze, eyes travelling to the bonnet of a black Italian stud motor, a Maserati, then skimming to the bright yellow TVR next to it and, next to that, the latest Audi TT in gunmetal grey. The earlier model, the *I've got balls, shaved head and an earring through my ear lobe* version had never appealed. This was poetry.

'Go on, what do you think?'

Tallis stared at him. The man was offering him a car. He couldn't believe it. Nobody had offered to buy him a car in his life. He looked back at the TT, wondering what Kennedy would expect him to say, for he was in no doubt that this was some kind of test.

'You like it?' Kennedy beamed.

'Yes, but…'

'It's yours.' Kennedy pulled the keys out of his pocket and pushed them into Tallis's hand.

'No, I can't. Wouldn't be right.'

Kennedy reached up, put his arm around Tallis's shoulder and squeezed it. 'Nothing more than you deserve.'

Weighed up against the indescribable thrill of having a car actually given to him, he had to balance the realisation that he, too, was being bought, or at least his silence was.

'It's all taxed and insured, if that's what you're bothered about.'

'No, it's—'

'I can dispose of the Rover for you.' Get rid of the evidence, Tallis realised. He clearly wanted the whole matter hushed up. Kennedy was speaking again. 'The less said about what happened today, the better. In fact, I'd rather you kept the whole incident to yourself. Seems to me that whoever tried to kidnap my family failed royally.'

Kennedy's eyes lasered into Tallis's. They really were extraordinary, Tallis thought, in this light like the colour of mercury. What was it Samantha Kennedy has said? *My husband is a powerful man.* 'I understand,' he murmured.

'I'm sure you do. Now,' Kennedy said, businesslike. 'You'll be wanting to get on your way. I'll arrange for one of my employees to drive the car round the front for you. You can pick it up outside.'

And with those final words, Tallis was escorted back to the reception area and out of the building.

The car was a dream to drive. Bigger than the original, lower slung, and with a lightweight aluminium frame, not only did it move with the speed of a cheetah but looked terrific inside and out. He felt as if he'd gone from the ridiculous to the sublime. In a less tangible sense, he knew he'd crossed the line, been bought and paid for.

Back in the familiar confines of his bungalow, Tallis wondered how things would pan out. Would Kennedy contact him sooner or later? If later, would Asim close the entire operation down? The initial plan had been clumsily executed, the human cost too great. Although he'd barely known Sean and Roz, he felt bad for them, and guilty. It had been his idea, his plan. He bore a certain amount of responsibility for it having turned out the way it had. As for himself, he'd come within a whisker of losing it in Kennedy's office. If it hadn't been for Kennedy stepping in, he'd have killed Gabriel. Rage was an emotion with which, up until now, he had been unfamiliar. As a former firearms officer, maintaining control at all times had been a given. But that had been then. Since Belle's violent death, he was a changed man. Yet to come that close to recklessness was so alien, it made him wonder if he was the right man for the job. Or, perhaps, it made him exactly the right man for the job. In a dark moment, he wondered whether he'd fallen into a role preordained for him by his violent father.

He followed every news report on the radio, scoured the TV channels for coverage, checked the headlines on broadband. One minor mention on BRMB at noon, and ranked fourth in the great scheme of things, there was an isolated report of a shooting in Solihull, believed to be a product of gangland overspill. That was it.

For the rest of the day, Tallis spent a considerable amount of time trying not to think too deeply about Sean and Roz, instead sitting in the TT, studying the manual, plinking every button, playing in it like a small boy with a new MP3 player.

Asim called at nine that evening. Tallis braced himself. As feared, Roz was dead, Sean in Intensive Care but stable. Thank God, Tallis thought. 'What happened to Dread?' Tallis he asked.

'Gone to the great crack house in the sky.'

Asim asked how he'd progressed. Tallis told him.

'So no plans to take you on, or further ensure your loyalty?'

Tallis preferred not to think of the various and painful ways his allegiance might be further secured. The car was a carrot, the stick he could do without. 'He didn't ask for a date, if that's what you mean.'

Asim let out a low chuckle, but Tallis could tell he was disappointed. He wondered whether Asim was having second thoughts. There wasn't a shred of evidence, as far as he was aware, tying Kennedy to terrorism, either by being actively involved or having dealings with others who were. Would Asim waste any more money or Tallis's time on what was essentially a shot in the dark? And what was to prevent Kennedy from going to his handler and re-porting everything? Except instinctively Tallis didn't think he would. And that's what kept him interested. 'This place you went to,' Asim said, 'anything in particular jar?'

'If Kennedy's seen the light, he's doing a bloody good impression of retaining his old image.'

'He has to be careful,' Asim said. 'With gang culture,

E.V. SEYMOUR 207

image is all. To be any other way is to expose himself to the accusation of weakness, or colluding with the enemy.'

'If, as you say, he's got the police onside, does he still need a retinue of thugs? That bloke Gabriel tried to beat the shit out of me.'

'Ah, thereby hangs a tale.'

'Like to explain?' He felt too tired for cryptic clues. The events of the day, the week, the month were starting to catch up with him.

'Not at this precise moment.' And on that mysterious note, Asim hung up.

18

SEVERAL days passed. It was after the weekend and Tallis was over at his mother's, helping tidy up the garden. It was still and warm, with only a hint of chill as the afternoon descended into evening. Copper-coloured leaves peppered the ground. A sickly smell of overripe fruit and decay scented the autumn air. The heavy roar of tractors from adjoining roads and fields clamoured in his ears.

He'd mowed the lawn, weeded some of the beds and got a nice bonfire going with the garden remains. It was an old man's job, he thought, layering more twigs and leaves onto the mound, yet strangely satisfying. He understood the allure of the fire and the heat and the burning, and the way the pile was slowly reduced to ashes. His mother came out to him with a mug of tea and a plate of digestives. He took them from her with thanks. She looked at him and smiled. It was a rare moment of love and companionship, son and mother together.

All too brief.

Tallis noticed it first, growling down the narrow lane outside the house, as out of place as a Georgian mansion in the middle of the Sahara. His mother followed his gaze, mouth slack with wonder as it pulled up outside the cottage. 'What's that?' she said.

'A Maserati.'

'What's it doing here?'

Tallis didn't answer. He was watching, mind racing, trying to work out how they knew where his mother lived, what message was being sent.

Gabriel climbed out of the car. He wore a charcoal-grey suit, well cut, white shirt, black tie, sunglasses to hide his ruined face. He walked slowly round to the passenger door, opened it and reached inside, taking out a vast bouquet of flowers packaged in cellophane with a big yellow satin bow tied round the base. With a sober stride he walked to the wooden gate, unhitched and pushed it open, walking through. He looked neither to his right nor left. His focus was Tallis's mother.

'Who is he?' she said, a tremble in her voice.

'It's OK. I'll take care of it,' Tallis said, stepping in front of her, putting the solid weight of his body between Gabriel and his mother. A cold, awful anticipation of something quite horrible spread through his entire body. Pressure built inside his head. He felt as though someone was scraping a metal file against the inside of his skull. Had Gabriel come for payback? Did he carry a weapon beneath the bouquet? Tallis couldn't tell anything from the man's body language and without seeing his eyes it was impossible to work out the motivation. His only fear was for his mum. His mouth went dry.

Gabriel stopped, held out the flowers. 'These are for Mrs Tallis.'

'For me?' Tallis heard his mother exclaim.

'From Mr Kennedy.'

'But I don't know a Mr Kennedy,' she said, popping out from behind Tallis. 'Do you know him, Paul?'

'Yes,' he said, shooting an arm out to protect his mother, eyes trying to bore through Gabriel's lenses.

'He wishes to express his condolences for your recent loss,' Gabriel said respectfully.

Tallis's mother reached over and took them. 'Well, that's very kind of him. Who is he, Paul, someone you work with?'

'That's right.' Gabriel's smile was glacial.

'Paul, for heaven's sake, why didn't you say?'

'Well, erm…'

'Is this the man you were telling me about?' she said, more animated now. 'The client who gave you the company car?'

Tallis remembered the lie, opened his mouth to speak.

'Mr Kennedy is a very generous employer,' Gabriel butted in, clearly enjoying Tallis's distress.

'He certainly is,' Tallis's mother agreed, beaming happily. 'Do thank him for me, won't you?'

Gabriel said he would, indeed, then turned on his heel, walked back the way he'd come, climbed back into the car and, engine growling, drove away.

Tallis stared after him. He was reminded of an old Chinese proverb: be careful what you wish for.

He'd certainly got what he wanted, but not the way he wanted it.

* * *

In the early hours of Wednesday morning, Tallis's mobile phone rang. It was a summons. He was ordered to look out of the window. Grabbing a pair of boxers and stumbling into them, he went into the front room and hitched back the curtains. A black taxi was waiting outside in the road, light on, a figure in the back.

'Get dressed,' the voice said. 'We're going for a ride.' Click.

Washing his face with cold water, he tried to think out the moves, another game, or confession time? In five minutes he was dressed with no answers.

'Mr Kennedy, do you know what time it is?' Tallis said, waving his hands around, standing outside the cab on the pavement, indignant.

''Course I do. Now, get in.'

'Look, I'm not really up for this. I don't want to cause offence or anything and you can have the car back if you want to, but I don't want any bother.'

'Don't be stupid.'

'Oh, and my mum says thanks for the flowers and you shouldn't have,' Tallis said, plunging his hands deep into his jacket pockets, hopping from one foot to the other in a pantomime of anxiety.

'You going to keep standing there, or what?' No threats, no anger. 'Come on.' Kennedy suddenly grinned, making it sound as if he were offering the chance of an irresistible adventure. 'We've both done our homework so where's the problem?'

What homework? Tallis shrugged his shoulders as if he

didn't have a clue, and clambered in beside Kennedy. The driver was told to move it.

'I love a city at night,' Kennedy said with passion. 'Especially Birmingham. Can't beat it. Powerhouse of Europe, I say.'

'Thought London was the centre of the universe,' Tallis said, pulling up the collar of his leather jacket. Christ, it was cold.

'No way.'

'The centre of commerce, then,' Tallis persisted.

Kennedy snorted with derision. 'You can do business anywhere these days.'

Drugs, guns, trafficking, Tallis thought. He disagreed with Kennedy. London was the hub, always would be. Birmingham, Liverpool, places like Bristol were young pretenders by comparison.

'No congestion charges,' Kennedy continued, 'overheads are lower, expenses cheaper, not so likely to be blown up by terrorists and no sodding Met to contend with.'

All hugely interesting. 'Why am I here?'

'Because I invited you.'

Tallis gave him a slow sideways look. 'And why does everything you say sound so reasonable?'

Kennedy burst out laughing. Whether it was tension, or the infectiousness of Kennedy's laughter, Tallis joined in. 'I like you, Tallis,' Kennedy said, putting an arm around him, squeezing his shoulder. 'Shame you were a copper. Not my favourite people'

Tallis felt himself freeze. Did he imagine the extra dig into his shoulder blade? 'Mine neither, not any more.'

The pressure on his shoulder didn't ease. 'I guess that was why you were able to handle yourself so well.'

Tallis said nothing.

'Gather you had a spot of bother,' Kennedy said elliptically, his face pale, almost green, in the moonlight.

How wonderfully understated, Tallis thought, remembering the young woman he had been ordered to kill in the mistaken belief that she had been a suicide bomber. 'Still bitter?' Kennedy said.

'As battery acid.'

'Not sure I know what that tastes like.' Kennedy laughed lightly. He removed his arm. Tallis realised how physically powerful Kennedy still was. 'So, what have you done since?'

'Bit of this and that. Worked in a warehouse as a security man for a while.'

'Bloody waste.'

'Bloody stupid,' Tallis cursed. 'We're on high alert for terrorism, and the police get rid of their best people.'

Kennedy looked out of the window. He wasn't biting, Tallis thought. They were driving in the direction of Aston University past the student bedsits.

'Ever go to university?' Kennedy asked him.

'No, after school I went straight into the army.' Then joined the police and trained as a firearms officer before a spectacular fall from grace, eventually fetching up with the security services, Tallis thought, mentally ticking off the list.

'My son went to university.'

'Your son?'

Kennedy didn't seem to hear, just carried on looking out of the window. 'Are you a religious man, Tallis?'

'No.'

'So you don't believe in punishment for wrongs?'

'Not by a divine force, no.'

Kennedy nodded as though seriously considering Tallis's answer. A thoughtful man, Kennedy had a way of making everyone he talked to feel special, Tallis suspected.

Various landmarks came and went. Kennedy raved about the planned redevelopment of the Rotunda and the area around the Mailbox. 'It's going to be a real asset to the city, bring a bit of class, good for the economy, too.'

'Seat of capitalism,' Tallis said, testing Kennedy's reaction.

'Nothing wrong with that.'

More streets, more turnings. 'See this,' Kennedy said, at last, pointing out of the window at a building site. 'This is my baby.'

'Yours?'

'I put the money up for it. Know anything about construction?'

'Not much, other than I'd like to live in something other than a bungalow.'

Kennedy let out a laugh. 'Construction's the business to be in,' he said with enthusiasm. 'Ever heard of the Concrete Club?'

Something dinged in Tallis's personal database of criminal activity. Mafia hoods, he thought, States, way back.

'It's where a contractor adds a percentage to bids and

passes the inflated costs to a developer or overall contractor. Ever considered why the cost of the Olympics has spiralled?' Political incompetence, Tallis thought, shaking his head. 'Because you can bet your life some crook has got his fingers in the pie. Won't be obvious,' Kennedy said, in answer to Tallis's astounded expression. 'It will be deep down at sewer level. Urban Dark Arts, I call it. Been going on for decades.'

'What are you suggesting exactly?'

'I'm suggesting even the brightest stars of the law-enforcement agencies haven't got a fucking clue whether it's Wednesday or Thursday. They're good at convicting the minnows—makes the crime statistics look nice and tidy—but the sharks...' Kennedy shook his head with vigour. 'They get away with it time and time again. Believe me.'

Tallis took a deep inner breath. 'Are you a shark, Mr Kennedy?'

Kennedy turned towards him with a smile that bore a striking resemblance to a hammerhead. 'Think of me as a great white.'

'Then how come your wife and child almost fell into the jaws of a barracuda?'

He was taking a risk. For half a second Tallis swore the earth stopped turning. He could feel the older man's breath on his face, his own breath caught in the back of his throat. Kennedy had acted *agent provocateur* in the conversation, throwing him lines, challenging him. What was he playing at? 'Fair point,' Kennedy said at last.

'Have you any idea who was behind it?' Tallis asked softly.

'Ideas, yes. Evidence, no.'

The cab ground to a halt. Tallis looked out and saw that he'd been driven round in a circle. 'Your patch again,' Kennedy said, reaching across and opening the door. Tallis climbed out, crossing round the back of the cab to the pavement, wondering if he'd blown it. Illuminated by dingy street lighting, the bungalow looked even more depressing. A rear window slid down. Kennedy poked his head out, looking at the street. 'See what you mean. What you need is a proper job with a proper salary.'

'Not that easy to find.'

Kennedy agreed, stuck his head back inside.

'Well, thanks,' Tallis said uncertainly, turning on his heel. Was that it? Interview over? Yup, he'd definitely blown it. He started to walk up the path. He was almost at the front door when he heard Kennedy call out his name. Tallis turned.

'Do you like boxing?'

'Performing or watching?'

'I know how you perform.' Kennedy grinned. 'Watching, of course. There's a fight on tonight at the gym I use. You up for it?'

'Sure.'

'Be ready for nine. I'll send Gabriel round to collect you.'

Can't wait, Tallis thought.

19

HE'D never seen anything like it. This wasn't boxing. It was carnage. Two men locked in sweaty no-holds combat, six fights in all.

Booze flowed. Money changed hands. Strict anti-smoking legislation was ignored with flamboyance, a thick fug of cigar smoke sucking out any oxygen in the heat-infested gym. As for the crowd, he thought he'd been transported back to ancient Rome. They wanted ears torn off, noses bitten, hair ripped out. They wanted blood, of which there was plenty. Like modern-day Shylocks, they demanded their pound of flesh. And the women were considerably more vociferous and foul-mouthed than the men. Tallis looked across the table to where Samantha Kennedy was sitting, caught her eye, saw the twinge of embarrassment, or was it something else? She looked quite beautiful, regal almost, a honey-coloured glow to her skin.

They were nine others at the table, the Kennedys, a racing trainer and his wife, and another older couple who Tallis hadn't caught the names of, Gabriel, the thug in the lift who Tallis had found out was called Justin, and a

strange wiry character, Donald Brooker, Kennedy's so-
licitor. It was clear from the way they were talking they'd
been many times before. Kennedy introduced Tallis to the
others as a personal friend. The elevated association
worked like a protective charm. Nobody asked him questions. Nobody put him on the spot. Even Gabriel treated
him with respect. Tallis was one of them for the night.

While Kennedy ordered more champagne, a drink Tallis
wasn't fond of, Tallis tried to get a feel for the dynamics.
Gabriel and Justin were definitely on duty. Neither drank.
Neither smiled. Eyes clicking from Kennedy to the other
punters, both watched for something out of place, for a
spark of trouble. Gabriel's place as second-in-command in
Kennedy's empire was self-evident. Justin, Tallis
reckoned, was next in seniority.

The couples were all over the Kennedys, the men, dressed
similarly in dogtooth check jackets particularly nauseating
in their admiration. Clearly delighted to be part of the circle,
and wanting to impress, each was trying to outdo the other
with gags and horseplay. Kennedy smiled politely but Tallis,
catching his eye, saw no warmth in his expression. Signalling for Tallis to join him at the makeshift bar, Tallis pushed
his chair back, made his excuses as another heavy bounced
off the ropes and onto the deck, his opponent descending on
him like a hyena on a wounded antelope.

'God save me,' Kennedy growled. 'If I have to listen to
another one of those so-called jokers, I swear I'll throw the
pair of them into the ring.' Something about the venom in
his voice persuaded Tallis he wasn't joking. 'Now, let's

have a proper drink. I can't abide all that gassy stuff. Recipe for indigestion.'

'Why order it, then?'

'Got an image to maintain.' Kennedy winked. 'And,' he said more seriously, 'Sam loves it.'

Tallis pulled out his wallet. 'My round.'

'Wouldn't dream of it,' Kennedy said, staying his hand. 'Whisky all right?'

Tallis said it was. Hell, was he going to suffer the next morning.

In spite of the bar being three deep, it was like watching the Red Sea part as Kennedy moved through the throng. Nothing was said. Nobody really looked. Kennedy's presence alone appeared to cause a chemical reaction. Blokes simply glided out of the way. Bartenders vied to serve him. Tallis was beginning to think he could get used to this kind of celebrity treatment.

Then he saw her.

Christ, she was walking straight towards him. Instinctively, he turned away but he'd witnessed enough to know that she was dressed in an indigo-coloured silk trouser suit, the cut of the jacket revealing that she wore nothing beneath it. Bracing himself as she passed within a hair's breadth of him, he noticed she wore no definable perfume. He thought her skin smelt of warm sand, of heat.

Once they'd got their drinks, Kennedy walked him over to a quiet spot away from the noise and action. Tallis gave a surreptitious glance around the hall. No sign of her. Lavender, the great illusionist, he thought. Not a great believer in coincidences, he wondered whose idea it was to have her follow him.

'Never got the chance to talk much about you last night.' Kennedy's heavy-lidded eyes studied him over the rim of his glass.

'Nothing much to tell.' Tallis shrugged.

Kennedy looked surprised. 'Served in the armed forces, worked as a copper, became part of an elite undercover firearms team—nothing much to tell?'

Tallis resisted the strong temptation to ask from whom he'd got his information. 'Ancient history.'

'And losing your dad?'

Tallis flinched. He was the one supposed to be exploiting the emotional angle, not the other way round. 'No big deal.'

Kennedy arched his eyebrows.

'We didn't get on.' An understatement.

Kennedy leant towards him, his voice almost a whisper in Tallis's ear. 'You hated him.'

'I didn't care enough to hate him.' Tallis found himself flushing with the lie. To hate, you had to care. Tallis felt wrong-footed by Kennedy's intuitiveness. It wasn't what he'd expected. He snatched at his drink. An uncomfortable silence descended between the two men. Finally, Kennedy broke it.

'You said you were looking for work.'

'That's right.'

'Someone like you might be valuable to my organisation. You have, after all…' Kennedy paused, his eyes more dark grey than ever '…particular skills.'

Tallis nodded slowly, holding the man's gaze.

'Because you're a smart guy, I expect you're already aware of my criminal history.' Breathtakingly honest, Tallis thought, immediately suspicious. 'You also know of my many business interests,' Kennedy continued, 'and, as you probably realise, it's not possible to reach my elevated position without a certain amount of ruthlessness. I'm sure you understand a man in my powerful position has certain enemies.'

'I understand.'

'What you must also understand is that I prize loyalty more highly than love. If you betray me or go against me, in any way, I will destroy you.'

What the hell was his game? Tallis thought. Kennedy was an informer, working with Organised Crime Officers. Like Asim had pointed out, he had a role to maintain, but this was stepping well outside his zone. Was Kennedy playing both sides against the middle? Was the lure of criminality stronger than the desire to reform? Was he playing them all for fools? And what had he really been up to in Turkey?

'I won't betray you,' Tallis said. Strangely, he found the prospect of doing so unsettling.

'Good boy.' Kennedy took his left hand in both of his, squeezing it warmly. Tallis imagined it was the way a loving father might congratulate an obedient son.

'He's taken the bait too easily.' Tallis was speaking to Asim. He'd been back ten minutes. It was three in the morning and his head was aching with alcohol and nerves.

'You underestimate the impact you've made. Kennedy never really got over the tragedy of his son's accident.'

I prize loyalty more highly than love. 'No,' Tallis insisted. 'He's up to something. How's he going to explain me to his handlers, for a start?'

'He'll come up with a reason.'

Tallis wasn't convinced. The police weren't stupid. 'He wants me for his dirty work.'

'Think he's kicking with both feet?'

Playing informer while continuing his own nefarious activities.

'It's the only explanation that makes sense.'

'Has he given you a job description yet?'

'No.'

'Then don't worry.'

'Something else,' Tallis said.

'Yes?'

'Lavender.'

'What of her?' Asim's tone was neutral.

'She was at the fight.'

'Did you engage with her?'

'What do you take me for?' Tallis snorted.

'Did she engage with you?'

'Of course not.'

'So she was entirely professional?'

'I thought we'd agreed I go in alone. I don't understand what she was doing.'

'Still got your jacket on?'

'Yes, what—?'

'Check your right-hand pocket.'

Confounded, Tallis slipped his hand into his jacket. To his amazement, there was a mobile phone inside. He switched it on. There was one message.

'Play it,' Asim said.

Tallis did. 'Hi, Tallis, sorry to sneak up on you like that. Just letting you know I'm here if you need me. Over and out, Charlie.'

'Told you she was good.' Asim laughed. In spite of being duped, Tallis couldn't help but smile in agreement. 'Now, get stuck in there with Kennedy and see what you can turn up.'

Tallis didn't have long to wait. He'd been asleep for barely four hours when his doorbell rang. It was Gabriel, looking remarkably chipper.

'Boss wants to see you.'

'What, now?'

Gabriel glanced at his watch. 'You've got twenty minutes.'

Tallis let out a grim sigh. He felt like shit. 'All right,' he said, making to close the door.

'Boss said I'm to wait inside.'

Tallis let out another sigh.

'I'll make myself useful.' Gabriel's mouth fell into a rare transforming smile.

Relenting, Tallis let him in. 'Mine's black with two sugars,' he called over his shoulder, heading straight for the bathroom.

As Tallis shaved and showered, he could hear Gabriel

busying in the kitchen. True to his word, four minutes later, a mug of instant appeared. Tallis consumed coffee as he dressed. Amazed at his capacity to bounce back after a heavy night, he gave himself a quick scan in the mirror, checked the shine on his shoes and told Gabriel he was ready.

They went to Lye. Seemed strange to be entering the unit in an official capacity, Tallis thought, glancing briefly up at the church tower, his nerves jagging. Bending down, he made out he was retying a loose shoelace and glanced back up. Spotted the camera lens. Was this Charlie behaving carelessly, or someone else?

'You coming?' Gabriel said tersely.

'Sorry.' Tallis straightened up, followed him into the office where the same three men and two women he'd spotted during his earlier surveillance were seated at computer terminals. He heard one of the men assure a customer that the sand ordered was of the same type delivered. Obviously some hitch, he was doing his best to explain and smooth things over in best customer-relations fashion. The older chap, the one who had the keys to the building, was sitting staring into his terminal as if he'd lost everything on the horses.

Kennedy appeared from a doorway. 'Tallis,' he said, voice booming across the room, 'come and meet the team.' Swift introductions with job titles followed. The morose-looking man was Jim Repton, office manager. Even though he didn't know the bloke, something definitely seemed up, Tallis thought as he was shown upstairs to the second storey and Kennedy's private suite. There he was given a brief rundown of the history of the business, number of customers, the extent and range of building materials supplied. During this, Kennedy's many phones never seemed to stop ringing. Sometimes he offered to call the person back. Other times, he picked up, the conversation brief, to the point and definitely criminal. Didn't he realise that his calls could be traced? Tallis listened, mesmerised. Then, cool as you like, he quizzed Kennedy about distribution, quantities, marketing and advertising. It took him some time to work out that they were not talking in code, that the business was legitimate, that it wasn't fronting for something else.

'So basically you're middle men for the building trade,' Tallis said.

'Yes.'

'Is that how business is traditionally done? I thought builders preferred to visit merchants in person, see the material, touch it, and negotiate the best deal. Are they really going to be persuaded to use an agent via the Internet?'

'It demands a change of attitude, granted, but think of the time saving. All the customer has to do is press a few buttons, his order is dispatched immediately and, within twenty-four hours, he has the supplies. It's reliable, simple and cost-effective.'

Tallis wasn't convinced. He had mates in the building trade. They liked nothing better than to bomb down to the latest trading estate and jaw. 'Does the business necessitate travel abroad?'

'You mean do we sell internationally?'

'Yes.'

'Not yet.'

'But you envisage a time when you will?'

'Who knows?' Kennedy smiled. 'Now, my other business over in Walsall, that's a different kettle of fish altogether.'

'Yeah?'

'We make and supply incinerators for animal waste.'

'Big market?'

'Growing by the day thanks to new EU regulations. Had a trade fair recently at the National Exhibition Centre and took a lot of orders from abroad.'

'Any countries in particular?'

'Very popular in Saudi for some reason. Other than that, Iraq, Iran, Romania, Turkey.'

'Turkey? Nice place for a holiday.'

'Too bloody hot. Visited not long ago. A few days later and I'd have been caught up in that earthquake.'

'Lucky.' Tallis smiled, examining Kennedy's face for signs of guilt and seeing none. A knock on the door concluded the conversation.

'Come in,' Kennedy said.

It was Jim Repton. 'Wondered if I could have a word in private.'

Kennedy glanced at Tallis. 'We're all friends here.'

Repton looked decidedly uncomfortable. 'It's OK,' Tallis said, making a move to get up. 'I can make myself scarce.'

'Stay.' Wasn't an invitation. From Kennedy, it was an

order. Tallis obediently remained where he was. 'Well, Jim, what's up?' Kennedy began in a convivial manner.

Repton glanced down at the floor. 'It's my son.'

'Darren?'

Repton nodded. 'He was jumped last night, got beaten up bad, really bad.'

'Know his attacker?'

'Two boys he goes to school with. They've been bullying him for months.'

'Speak to the school?'

'Got nowhere.'

'Police?'

'No.'

'Why not?'

'It's not that simple.'

Kennedy flexed his fingers, making the knuckles crack. Tallis was reminded of a scene from *The Godfather*.

Repton swallowed, acutely uncomfortable. Next came a rambling account of everyday urban anti-social behaviour. 'One of the boy's fathers, he's a nasty piece of work, lives round the corner from us. Got this dog, see, a Doberman. Walks round the neighbourhood with the thing as though he owns the estate. It's always scaring the life out of people. My wife, she doesn't like dogs, frightened of them. Got bitten by an Alsatian when she was a nipper. So she's out walking to the shops and this thing, the Doberman, comes at her, no lead, no muzzle. Fortunately, a neighbour pulled her into his garden and closed the gate on it, but she was really shaken.

'Mad as hell, I went round to see the bloke, told him…'
He broke off, cleared his throat, Adam's apple squeezing
up and down like it had a life of its own. 'Anyway, he
smacked me one, threatened he'd set the dog on me and
my wife and kids. If I went to the police, he said he'd kill
me.'

'And you believe him?' Kennedy said, voice low.

'I do. My son…' He faltered, tears filling his eyes.
'Doctors say he may lose the sight in one eye.'

It's a police matter, Tallis thought, and any medic worth
his salt would report something as serious as that to the authorities in any case. The problem probably lay with the
lad. Tallis would bet he was suffering from a bad case of
victim amnesia.

'What do you want from me?' Kennedy said.

Repton swallowed hard. 'I want you to make it stop.'

Kennedy nodded, took out a pen. He asked Repton for
names, addresses, descriptions of the man and the boys.
He asked what the thug in question did for a living.

'Mechanic.' This seemed to delight Kennedy. He then
asked for the name of the garage.

'Go and grab yourself a cup of coffee and go home to
your wife and son. Tell them not to worry. Tell them everything will be fine. And here,' Kennedy said, scribbling
down a note and handing it to Repton. 'This is the name
of my private doctor. Give him a ring and tell him I sent
you. He's the best man to look after your son. Ask him to
send the bill to me.'

Tallis looked on. He'd witnessed the most extraordinary

demonstration of power, seen Kennedy as he really was: a fixer, an avenger, nemesis. When Repton left in a flurry of thanks and gratitude, Kennedy picked up his phone, spoke to Justin, gave him the low-down and asked him to wait twenty-four hours so that the intended victim was lulled into a false sense of security, then sort it. Tallis had visions of the dog being buried alive with its master.

'Right, where were we?' Kennedy said, as if he'd just asked his secretary to pop out and buy an anniversary card for his wife.

'Turkey,' Tallis said.

'Home of heroin barons.'

'Thought the Turkish government had cleaned up.'

'They have, which is why the kingpins have relocated here. Heroin is still being shipped direct.'

'That the real reason for your last visit?'

Kennedy broke into a big, beaming smile. So that's what Garry had been trying to tell him. Drugs, pure and simple. Nothing to do with terrorism at all. He wondered if Napier knew about Kennedy's extra-curricular activity. It was one thing to play along, another to actively solicit for business. Perhaps that's why he'd paid a visit to Shakenbrook, Johnny's palatial home, to put Kennedy back into his box. But sitting there, in front of the man, it didn't take him long to alter his view. Napier was no match for Kennedy. Not many people were.

20

TALLIS spent the next four days being talked through the workings of both the legitimate and illegal side of Kennedy's businesses. On the surface, Kennedy employed around forty personnel. Tallis reckoned at least half had extra-curricular duties. As yet he'd not been offered a professional role, his only remit to be present during certain hours of the day and night, whenever Kennedy dictated. The incinerators, Tallis discovered, were manufactured in a workshop at the Walsall site.

'On-site burial of animal carcasses is illegal,' Kennedy explained.

The farmers in Herefordshire, where Tallis had grown up as a boy, sent their fallen stock to the hunt kennels. He told Kennedy this.

'Still can but it poses a number of bio-security risks. Nobody wants to take chances after foot and mouth, swine fever, blue tongue, let alone the prospect of bird flu. Incineration really is a much more efficient method. For something as large as a cow, we make this brand,' he said, pointing out a machine. 'Comes with a trolley and winch to help load the carcass into the incinerator.'

'Front loading?'

'Yes. All the operator has to do is select the appropriate burn programme and walk away.'

'That it?'

'Simple.' Kennedy smiled.

Ashes to ashes, Tallis thought, feeling mildly uncomfortable.

Most of the employees were from Eastern Europe. Asians, he noticed, were conspicuous by their absence. Bearing in mind they made up a large percentage of the population, Tallis felt surprise, something he expressed to Kennedy.

'Where you've got Asians, you have police raids.' Kennedy gave a shrug. 'And police raids are bad for business.'

By business, Kennedy meant the brothel that masqueraded as a massage parlour. The quantities of drugs that got shipped through the haulage company that was nothing more than a front, but Kennedy's real skill was in his list of contacts. He knew what was going on, what was being planned, who was next for the chop. No wonder the police wanted him as an informer, Tallis thought. The constant barrage of visitors to Kennedy's establishments, some of them known faces, also proved a revelation.

Twice, Tallis overheard Kennedy recommending a particular individual for a certain type of job, the jobs in question armed robbery and extortion. He also listened in as Kennedy gave a masterclass on the most effective method for getting hold of knock-off booze, a fake passport and firearms. A dissertation on drugs went along familiar lines. Kennedy no longer considered the profit margins in cannabis to be rewarding, Ecstasy not cost-effective, cigarettes and bootleg liquor too competitive. Cocaine and heroin, however, were the name of the game.

The real problem, he stated, was taking money from A to B to pay for drug shipments. No longer could you rely on a courier to deliver a suitcase full of notes. More and more, Western drug barons were adopting the centuries-old system of *hawala*, a means of transferring money without actually moving it, the main advantage being that it's untraceable. The more time Tallis spent in his company, the more open Kennedy became. Although he had the protection of the police, for a sharp operator he was behaving like an ingénue. Which meant only one thing. Kennedy was on to him.

And still no whiff of terrorism.

That night, Tallis caved in.

The day had been less than satisfactory. He felt as if he was on a trail leading nowhere. Feeling too lazy to cook, he'd succumbed to the instant charm of fish and chips from the chippie and got caught out by a bad bout of indigestion. Downing some antacids, he'd started to read a book written by a couple of Americans on the first Gulf War but, after winding up going over the same paragraph twice and still not taking in the information, switched to the TV. With nothing of consequence to view, he flicked on the radio, catching the ten o'clock news announcing the usual mix of job cuts, death and destruction. He turned it off.

He'd locked the phone Lavender had given him in an old cash box that he kept behind the back panel of his bath. A determined individual could easily find it. Tallis's precautions against theft, however, were aimed at the opportunist criminal, the less intelligent type who regularly burgled the homes in his area. Taking a screwdriver from a drawer in the kitchen, he walked into the bathroom, undid the screws from the panel and hoiked out the box, taking it through to his bedroom where he held a set of keys.

The phone, a tiny, functional, no-frills brand, sat like a grenade in the palm of his hand. Switching it on, it immediately sprang into life, ready and primed for action. Why am I doing this? Tallis thought. *I'm here if you need me.* That's what Charlie had said. But what sort of need did she have in mind? To the point, what sort of need did he have in mind? He wasn't about to call to enlist her professional help. His motivation didn't stem from a feeling of guilt for snubbing her. He wasn't even interested in discussing her sleight-of-hand technique for dropping the phone into his jacket pocket. No, he was calling her for the worst of reasons: because he felt incredibly alone. Checking the call history, he punched in the number. Lavender answered after three rings.

'Hello, Tallis.'

He could hear the smile in her voice, made him feel glad. 'Neat trick, the phone. I'm impressed.'

'That was the idea.'

'Liked the outfit, too.' Christ, why on earth had he said that?

'Didn't think you noticed.'

'It's my job to notice things,' he said, recovering with cool.

'Naturally,' she said, gracious. 'Everything OK?'

'Fine.'

'Just checking in, then?'

'No.'

'Oh?'

She sounded slightly wrong-footed, he thought. Made him smile. 'The day after you went to the fight club, was that you in the belfry, watching Kennedy's place in Lye?'

'You have to be kidding. I was catching up on my beauty sleep. Is there a problem?'

'No.' Possibly one of Napier's oppos, he thought, or someone from the original organised crime team running Kennedy.

'Simply eliminating me from your enquiry,' she joked.

'Something like that.' He laughed.

'Then I'm glad I could be of help.'

He could have asked whether she was under Asim's control, whether he'd gone ahead and put her on the job anyway. He could have asked what her orders were. He asked none of these things.

'That it?' she said, breaking the silence.

'I guess it is.'

'Goodnight, then.'

''Night, Charlie.'

* * *

The following evening, Tuesday, Tallis was invited to Shakenbrook for dinner. Samantha answered the door. She was wearing a dress of royal blue that matched her eyes, cinched in at the waist, the neckline demure. With her hair pinned up, she looked elegant without being studied.

'Come in.' She beamed. 'Johnny sends his apologies. Been held up, but promises to be here as soon as he can. What can I get you to drink? A glass of wine, soft drink?'

'Tonic water?'

'Ice and slice?'

'Terrific.' He felt torn between surveying the sway of her hips and the incredible grandeur of his surroundings. The hall was the same length as his bungalow. Triple-height, it was dominated by a pair of ornate, wrought-iron staircases that led up to a galleried landing. The floor was tiled in cream upon which sat two enormous thick Chinese-style rugs. The walls were painted crimson and were decorated with works of art. There were several studies of Samantha, clothes on, clothes off. He wondered whose idea that was.

Samantha guided him into the drawing room, a place with which he was already familiar. As he sank into the nearest sofa, Melissa, Kennedy's daughter, popped her head around the door.

'Hello, again.' Tallis smiled.

'You should be in bed, Liss,' her mother said reprovingly.

'But Daddy's not home.' Melissa scooted into the room. In a pair of pale lilac pyjamas, she looked utterly cute,

Tallis thought, feeling a dark pang of guilt for deliberately exposing the little girl to danger.

'And won't be for some time,' her mother said.

'Look, Tallis,' Melissa said, proudly showing him a mobile phone.

'This yours?' Tallis said, taking it. Brand-new, a Samsung. What on earth did a little girl need a mobile phone for? he thought. He made all the right noises and handed it back to her.

'Come on, school night,' Samantha said, taking her daughter's hand. 'Say goodbye to Tallis.'

'Can I give him a kiss?'

Tallis wasn't sure whether it was a ploy to evade bedtime, or whether Melissa was giving her tiny female feathers the chance to flutter. The modern world continued to confuse him. Little girls played hard to get, lads hard to ignore. Perhaps it was the horrible onslaught of evolution. In fifty years' time, he imagined there'd be four-year-old boys with five o'clock shadow.

'Think you ought to ask Mr Tallis,' Samantha said, a smile playing on her fabulous face.

Tallis inclined his cheek, felt the soft brush of the child's lips against his skin. 'Goodnight, Melissa,' he said with a smile.

And then they were both gone.

Tallis scoped the room. Nothing busy, muted colours, traditional furniture, many, many photographs. To his surprise, only one subject was portrayed, from baby to toddler, from boyhood to man. Tallis picked up the nearest frame. The lad was smiling to camera. He was wearing football kit, arms crossed, knees spattered with mud, one foot resting idly on a football, looking the business. Tallis replaced the photograph and picked another. This was different, the subject older. The dark-eyed, troubled expression on the young man's face bothered Tallis. He wondered if the eyes conveyed some horrible premonition of what would be.

'Billy,' Samantha said, handing him a glass.

Tallis put the photograph back. 'Is this him on graduation day?'

'That's right.'

'What degree?'

'Architecture.'

'Clever guy.'

'And not afraid of hard graft. Have to have a minimum of seven years' training, five as part of a full-time degree then another two years spent working in an architect's office. Johnny wanted him to join the family business.'

Tallis wasn't sure how to respond. Which bit? he thought. Billy didn't look much like an enforcer. Samantha saw his dilemma and laughed. 'The construction side. This was all before Johnny went down.' *Went down*. Tallis smiled inside. So much more elegant than *went to jail*.

'Hungry?' she said.

'Yes, but shouldn't we wait for Johnny?'

'He told me we should go ahead.'

'Fair enough,' Tallis said.

They ate in a dining room with arched windows, giving

it an ecclesiastical atmosphere. The table was long and dark, as were the furnishings. Place settings for two were laid at one end. As Tallis sat down, he noticed a slot machine, big and brash, tucked into a recess. Baffling.

The woman Tallis had seen with the clipboard when he'd been carrying out surveillance on the house waited on them. It transpired her name was Stephanie. He wondered what conversations she'd been party to, what secrets she could tell. The food was simple but good. Asparagus soup to start, *Johnny's favourite*, followed by chicken roasted with garlic.

'How did you two meet?' Tallis said, this time accepting a glass of wine. He glanced at the bottle. *Côtes de Nuit Villages*.

'Through Billy. I was his date for the night.'

'Blimey!'

She threw back her head and laughed. 'Wasn't as weird as it sounds. It was a formal arrangement. He wanted an escort to go to a posh dinner in London and I obliged. After that, it became a bit of a regular thing. He wanted eye-candy and I wanted to be wined and dined. One night, he brought me here and I met Johnny.'

'Love at first sight?'

She smiled, said nothing.

He studied her. She didn't look like a gangster's moll. He wondered how long it had taken for her to discover what Johnny really did, whether it had been too late to pull out by then, or perhaps she'd fallen for him and it didn't matter. 'What did Billy think?'

She broke into a fond smile. 'He was pleased. His dad had been on his own for a long time. Johnny and Billy's mum got divorced when he was little,' she explained. 'She was a drunk, so Johnny had custody of Billy.'

If you believe that, you'll believe anything, Tallis thought. 'Father and son must have been close.'

Samantha raised her hand, crossed her fingers. 'Like that.' The smile faded. She didn't come across as being dominated by Kennedy, but there was definitely caution in her eyes. The photographs said it all: Kennedy was consumed by what had happened to his son.

The door suddenly swished open, revealing Kennedy on the threshold. Tallis had the impression he'd been standing there for some time. Kennedy's wife stood up, walked towards her husband, kissed him lightly. 'I'll ask Stephanie to organise some food.'

'A sandwich is fine,' Kennedy said, picking up a glass from a side-table and helping himself to wine. 'Is she looking after you?' he said, pulling up a chair.

'Royally. It's been very nice, thank you.'

'My pleasure.' Kennedy's smile was so genuine and affecting, it made Tallis feel uneasy. Again, Tallis felt an unfamiliar emotion tugging at him. He guessed Kennedy was just old enough to be his father. Time to wrong-foot him.

'Can I ask you something?'

Kennedy nodded, took a slow sip of his drink, clearly giving himself time to prepare.

'What's with the slot machine?'

'A reminder of my roots.' Kennedy beamed effusively.

'Used to spend hours in amusement arcades. Loved the noise, the rattle and hum, the thought of getting rich quick. You want a go?' He pulled out some change from his pocket.

By the time Samantha returned with Kennedy's favourite bacon and sausage sandwich, Tallis was quite enjoying himself. He was revisiting that old boyhood thrill of seeing a row of cherries line up and yield a clatter of coins. He handed his winnings to Kennedy, who politely told him to keep them.

'Got any plans for Saturday?' Kennedy said, walking back to the dining table.

'Not especially.'

'What do you normally do?'

Tallis didn't do normal any more. He shrugged. 'Get up late, pick up a paper, have a pint down the local, chat with the lads, either watch the sport on the telly or go to a football match.' He hadn't actually had a Saturday like that ever, but he knew plenty of blokes who had.

'Which team do you support?'

Tallis hesitated, sipped his wine. What would Kennedy expect? Birmingham City, Aston Villa, Wolves? 'West Bromwich Albion.'

'Top man.' Kennedy smiled broadly. 'Anyway, I've got a little job for you.'

What sort of job? Tallis silently wondered.

'Up for it?'

'Sure.'

'Good,' Kennedy said with a slow, satisfied smile. 'Keep Saturday free.'

* * *

By Thursday evening of that week, Tallis was glad to be released from duty. Reports had filtered through in the morning about the fate of the unfortunate bully and his dog. Both had been found dead with multiple injuries, brains splattered out, below a large multi-storey car park not far from the garage at which the dead man had worked. Apparently, the victim's distressed wife had informed police that her husband suffered a history of depression. Tallis didn't like to speculate on the nature of the type of threats used against the poor woman for her to come up with a tale like that. He felt genuine shock at what was, on every level, a spectacular and unrestrained demonstration of force. He didn't like to think about a son who'd lost a father. Maybe it was a bad sign. Maybe he was becoming desensitised.

He'd arranged to meet an old schoolmate in Wetherspoons. Barry worked in the demolition industry. Mad, obsessive and continually looking for the bigger bang, demo guys, like scaffolders, were a breed apart. For them, demolition was the ultimate buzz. Big boys' toys. In common with firearms officers, they remained 'dry' when working. Barry, by the look of him, was making up for lost time.

'Paul,' he said, staggering a bit. 'Wha' can I get you?'

Tallis asked for a soft drink.

'Fuck me,' Barry said, shaking his head in disapproval. He was as thin as a stick, pale-cheeked with a scrub of short, dark hair. 'You haven't got God, or nothing?'

'Antibiotics,' Tallis explained, falling back on a tried and tested ruse.

Didn't work. After disappearing through a scrum of people, Barry reappeared. 'Ditch the pills, and drink this,' he said, pushing a pint at Tallis, some of the beer sloshing over his hand. Tallis hadn't the energy to argue and took a gulp. It tasted terrific.

'There,' Barry said, delighted he'd got a convert. 'You're looking muscled up. Been working out?'

'Not really,' Tallis said, taking another pull of his pint.

'Seen Griggsy?'

'He's here?' Tallis said, glancing around for Barry's mate from work, the noise in the bar pounding his ears and apparently affecting his eyesight. The place seemed inhabited by fifteen-year-olds pretending to be twenty-five-year-olds.

'Fuck knows why. He's become a fuckin' vegan, given up booze completely.'

No wonder his desire for a soft drink had caused alarm. 'No kidding.'

'Got into all that Eastern mysticism lark. Meditates and all.'

Tallis made a sympathetic grunt. Nothing surprised him any more. 'So how's business, Barry?'

'Good. Just taken down a tower block, a shit thing thrown up in the '70s.'

'How do you go about something like that?' Tallis said, drinking his beer, feeling his body limber up and slip into relaxed mode.

'Preparation,' Barry said, suddenly quite lucid. That

was the other thing about demolition men. Get them on their favourite subject and there was no stopping them. 'Can't afford to have any margin for error. You're putting people's lives at risk if you cock it up. And gone are the days when you got out your ball and chain and *accidentally on purpose* knocked down a wall.'

'Why would you do that?' Tallis said, perplexed.

'Usually to give someone a bit more land. Anyway,' Barry said, taking a slurp of his beer, 'with this particular job, we set off a small explosion to scale first to find out what we need explosives-wise for the bigger job. No point going in half-hearted,' Barry said, wiping his mouth with the back of his hand. 'Then we cut out holes in the structure to weaken it so that when it comes down, it comes in one piece. Beautiful it was,' he said, eyes glinting with excitement.

'Done this factory in Leicestershire couple a weeks ago. That was good. Proper smash and mash.'

'Smash and mash?' Tallis frowned.

'Smash anything of importance before you blast it. Windows, chimneys, knock out stud walls. Not rocket science. I mean, if you're tearing down a bridge, stands to reason you remove the supporting girders first.'

'You must have to work with police and council officials.'

'Oh, yeah. They help with evacuating people. Don't want anyone killed, or property and cars damaged. Health and safety.'

'Going back to the tower block, how much explosives you use?' From the corner of his eye, Tallis registered

Griggsy moving their way. He was short, no more than five-six, big smile on his face like always. Fortunately, some things never changed.

'One-twenty pounds in all.'

'And two miles of detonation cable,' Griggsy chipped in.

'Talk of the devil,' Barry said amiably.

'Wotcha!' Griggsy said.

'What's all this?' Tallis joshed, looking pointedly at Griggsy's glass of tomato juice.

Griggsy's grin grew wider. 'Barry told you, then.'

'He has. When did you take the pledge?'

'A year ago, since I found Vishnu.'

'Vindaloo?' Barry said, frowning.

'Vishnu,' Tallis repeated louder, voice competing with the ear-bleeding sound of techno-pop.

'The Hindu god, you daft tart,' Griggsy bellowed.

'Happy for you, mate,' Tallis said, 'but don't you find it a bit of a strain? I mean, no more pies, no fish and chips—'

'No beer,' Barry broke in, his face a picture of misery.

Griggsy let out a laugh. 'It's a way of life.'

'Must be hard,' Tallis said.

'If something's difficult to do, it's more difficult to let go of,' Griggsy said, draining his glass.

'Another?' Tallis said.

'Nah, catch you lads later.'

'Probably going home to bed,' Barry muttered reproachfully, watching Griggsy push his way through the crush.

Tallis wasn't listening. He was thinking about what Griggsy had said. *Some things were difficult to let go of.*

After another couple of hours, Tallis meandered back home. He'd been in bed three hours when his mobile rang. Immediately awake, he picked up. It was Kennedy. Another drive around the cityscape, Tallis thought, unimpressed.

'Gabriel is missing.'

Good, Tallis thought.

'Police turned up outside his home and took him away.'

Tallis scratched his head. Kennedy wasn't making sense. 'He probably jumped a red light.' Or pushed somebody off a high building.

'You don't understand. They weren't real police officers.'

'How do you know?'

'I know.' The hard edge in Kennedy's voice could have pierced sheet metal.

Tallis reached for his jeans and started putting them on. 'Any ransom been demanded?'

'No.'

'Any ideas on the players behind it?'

'Fuck's sake, that's what I want you to find out.'

Tallis had never heard him so tense. 'Johnny,' he said, 'how much does Gabriel know?'

Long pause. 'Fucking everything.'

'All right,' Tallis said, doing his best to calm Kennedy down.

'Get over to the storage depot. Justin will be there.'

Terrific, Tallis thought. He wanted brains, not brawn.

But he'd been right about Justin's place in the great pecking order. Gabriel's disappearance meant the equivalent of a promotion.

'And when you do find Gabriel,' Kennedy said, his voice suddenly quite cold, 'I want you to kill him.'

21

'WHY?'

Tallis was in the reception at the Walsall operation, the place Gabriel had tried to beat the crap out of him. Justin stood like a statue in the corner, arms folded, face hard and immobile.

'Gabriel fucked up,' Kennedy snarled.

'Because some louse decided to kidnap him?'

'Because he'll sing like a songbird.'

'You don't know that.'

'Yes, I do.' Kennedy broke into a cold and calculating smile. 'Torture always guarantees the truth.'

Suddenly the thin veneer of civilisation seemed to crack and shatter.

'And what truth would that be?' Tallis stared at Kennedy with a stony expression. What was Kennedy afraid of, that word of the various workings of his criminal activities would get out, or that he was working as an informer? Except none of his men knew, apart from him. Or had Gabriel found out? If so, he could understand Kennedy's anxiety.

'I'll explain when the job's done,' Kennedy said, voice tight.

'Explain now.'

Kennedy paled with fury. At once Tallis glimpsed the essence of the man—balled with anger, ruthless. He thought Kennedy was going to smack him. Then he seemed to get a grip. 'I've got men out there searching, shaking down, door to door.'

'I don't care.'

'*Don't* disappoint me.'

'I'm not a fucking animal.' Or *your* fucking animal.

'You've killed before.' Kennedy met his eye.

Tallis allowed a slow smile. This was a test. He should have known. But was Kennedy really prepared to push it all the way, to cross that irrevocable line? 'That was different,' he said, milder now. 'I was following orders.'

'And now you're following mine. Justin will take you to the armoury.'

The armoury? What armoury? Without a word, Kennedy deactivated the alarms, allowing Tallis and Justin access to the lift. Kennedy got out at the first floor, Tallis, under Justin's instructions, the second. Justin was clearly taking his elevation in authority seriously.

Tallis followed him down the corridor to a counter area, behind which was a steel door. Justin punched in a code, releasing the door to an Aladdin's cave of weaponry. There were rocket launchers, Uzis, Kalashnikovs—deadly spray and contain weapons beloved by rebel soldiers—machine-guns, bolt-action rifles, pistols and revolvers. Without a word, Justin picked up a Heckler & Koch self-loading pistol, Tallis a Glock 17. His last thought as he left the building was that he was up to his neck in trouble. With so many bad guys surrounding him, intent on pushing him off course, it was going to be difficult, if not impossible, to find his own moral sat nav.

Tallis drove. If he thought Gabriel was a royal pain, Justin was in a league of his own. In his experience, people like Justin fell into one of three categories: enthusiastic amateur often with a low IQ; smart and cunning; and those with psychopathic tendencies. Justin fell into the last classification. Besides having the bearing of a man dying to freshen up the gene pool by culling it, he was brash and, Tallis suspected, harboured a burning desire to see him fail so that he could establish himself more firmly in the power vacuum left behind. Not Tallis's first choice of partner.

It was agreed they'd head for Gabriel's place, a two-bedroomed semi-detached house in a particularly rough bit of Brierley Hill, the sort of wasted area where pubs served industrial-strength cider, and car parks were badly lit.

There wasn't much light, the sky the colour of graphite. In spite of the hour, spindly-looking youths drinking from cans hung out on street corners, arses hanging out of their jeans.

As soon as they arrived at number eighty-three, Tallis clocked an empty light blue Citroën parked on the drive, the driver door half open. 'Does that belong to Gabriel?'

Justin confirmed it did. Tallis pulled over. Evidence of trouble was clear from the moment he stepped onto the blood-spattered pavement. Approaching the crime scene, he felt sure Gabriel had put up a fight. The bushes adjoining the property were beaten down. There were drag marks all over the gravel, dents in the car. And there was more blood. Tallis scanned both sides of the building. Even in an area where people saw plenty and said nothing, it was inconceivable the fight had taken place without remark.

Somebody had heard something.

A quick flash of light from the window next door confirmed his suspicions. Against Justin's advice, Tallis walked round and, seeing the doorbell hanging by a thread, rapped at the door. There followed a steely silence.

'They won't talk,' Justin growled.

'Could pretend we're coppers.'

'Even less chance of them talking,' Justin sneered.

'All right, smart-arse. You try.'

A big, calculating grin spread over Justin's muscular face. He turned to the door, pulled out his gun and with one shot blasted the lock and walked in. Face to face with a terrified householder, Justin, expression set like old granite, snarled, 'Johnny Kennedy sends his regards.'

The man, a big West Indian with rolling eyes and a Tipton accent, needed no further prompts. In the space of one minute and thirty seconds, they learnt that three men had 'arrested' Gabriel, two uniformed officers, one in plain clothes, all Middle Eastern in appearance. Tallis found it far-fetched, to say the least.

'You're absolutely certain?' he said.

'They weren't black.'

Turkish perhaps? Tallis asked him. The man said he didn't know, too busy watching Justin stalk around the narrow confines of the living room, muttering to himself, picking things up, briefly examining them, putting them down, his pumping frame threatening to erupt into violence. 'Did they say anything?' Tallis persisted.

'Yeah, they asked for his name.'

'And he gave it?'

The West Indian's eyes clicked from Tallis to Justin. Didn't look happy. 'He asked them why.'

'And what did they say?' Tallis said, attempting to refocus the man's attention.

'Said they wanted to talk about drugs, something to do with a delivery.'

'They what?' Justin spat, cracks in the granite.

'Shut up,' Tallis told him, turning back to the house-holder, ignoring Justin's vile expression and the curse underneath his breath. 'Anything else?'

'They said that they knew he worked for Johnny Kennedy, that they wanted to take him down the police station. Man, everything kicked off. I didn't see nothing else,' he said, spreading his hands.

'Which way did they go?' Justin's voice, from the corner of the living room, was like the low growl of a wounded tomcat.

'Don't know, man.'

'What car were they driving?' Tallis said, throwing Justin a back-off look. More muttering ensued.

'Didn't see. Too dark.'

Absolutely right there, Tallis thought. Outside was an expanse of unbroken black. So how come he'd seen so much? And could he really hear that clearly? 'And they were definitely police?'

The man nodded furiously. 'Yeah, like I said.'

Kennedy must have got his information from his handler in the organised crime department, or through Napier, Tallis thought. That's how he knew that the police officers were bogus. Did that mean that the real cops were also looking for Gabriel? This was a scenario that was getting more complicated by the second. It was just what he'd been afraid of. It had been an idiot idea for Asim to run it as a joint operation. There were too many people, too many competing agendas. There was nothing else for it, Asim would have to step in and assume total command. West Midlands' finest Organised Crime Officers and SOCA would have to be kicked off the case.

Tallis and Justin returned to the car. 'Don't you ever fuckin' disrespect me again.' Justin glared.

Tallis glared back, felt a pulse tic in his neck, opened the door and got in.

Justin climbed in the passenger side. 'Just 'cos Kennedy thinks you're the blue-eyed boy doesn't mean the rest of us—'

'Yeah, yeah. And for the record, my eyes are brown. Now, do you want to ride or walk?'

To Tallis's surprise, Justin shut up.

Exploiting every piece of local knowledge, Tallis checked out lock-ups, garages, disused buildings, stretches of wasteland, railway bridges, anywhere Gabriel might have been taken. They started in Brierley Hill, worked out towards Oldbury, Dudley, Gornal and Tipton, tracking towards West Bromwich. Throughout, Justin kept up a running commentary of his boss's reputed exploits, throwing a chilling spotlight onto Kennedy's past.

'Ever heard of a bloke called Gamble?'

'Shane Gamble?' Tallis said, mentally attuning. Gamble: well-hard Midland gangster, served time for armed robbery and died after an attack in the prison showers.

'That's him. Kennedy took over his patch after he got sent down. They say that he decimated Gamble's men.'

'Oh, yeah?' Tallis watched the shifting shadows of dawn breaking over the city. How different from Turkey. There the light seemed to flick on in one go.

'Decimating,' Justin said, taking pleasure in each syllable. 'Old Roman practice—'

'For every ten men, one put to death.'

'Yeah,' Justin said, giving him a sly sideways glance, 'but how?'

Tallis glanced across. 'Knowing the Romans, crucifixion, I guess.' The thought made him shudder.

'Worse.' Justin was positively slavering.

'Yeah?' Tallis said, apprehensive.

'Strung 'em up and beat their bodies with hammers.'

Tallis tried not to react. He kept his voice low. 'Are you saying Kennedy did that?'

'Straight up.'

How the hell had he got away with it? 'What did he do with the bodies?'

Justin turned and grinned. 'What do you think the incinerators are for?'

The anonymous tip-off came shortly before nine in the morning. Kennedy relayed the message in person, his parting words to Tallis: 'Don't forget I gave you the order to kill Gabriel.'

They were directed to a lock-up near a canal bridge in Perry Barr. First they drove past, checking for any outwards signs of activity, then, chucking the car up onto a piece of wasteland, headed back on foot. It was slinging it down with rain.

'You can go in first and I'll cover you.' Justin winked. 'Boss's orders.'

And if I don't shoot, you will, Tallis thought, with me in the firing line. Talk about Hobson's choice.

The brown-painted door was closed and padlocked, suggesting that whoever had taken Gabriel had left. Not that Tallis was taking chances. He pulled out the Glock, crooking it between thumb and forefinger, his left thumb locked over his right, automatically taking care not to get in the way of the slide. Heart rate accelerating, mouth dry, everything around him seemed to shrink into the background.

Instinctively, he knew to go for body mass, one in the abdomen, one in the chest, setting up a tsunami effect, the ensuing shock so massive it would kill anyway. Except Tallis didn't want to kill, and certainly not on Kennedy's orders.

He glanced at Justin and nodded. Putting his ear to the door, he listened hard. Nothing. One shot broke the lock, the next he was in, weapon raised.

It was as silent as a vault. Death beat the air. It felt as tangible as having disinfectant rubbed against raw skin. Justin came up close behind. 'Fucking smell,' he muttered, Christ, if they dished out degrees for grumbling, Tallis reckoned Justin could have an honorary.

He looked around for a light-switch, couldn't find one. Justin pulled out a pocket torch, shone it around, the small beam finally highlighting the source of the smell and diabolical tableau.

'Looks like you're off the hook,' Justin said, disappointment registering in his voice.

Which was more than could be said for poor Gabriel, Tallis thought, feeling cold and empty.

22

GABRIEL had not died easily. Some psycho had worked on the premise of fingers and toes, followed by kneecaps and elbows, working up to the more essential bits. Strung up, Gabriel had also had his tongue cut out.

Kennedy came to ID the body for himself. He'd recovered his composure and seemed almost relieved. Tallis couldn't work him out. Kennedy might be glad that Gabriel was no longer in a position to talk, but how was he hoping to conceal Gabriel's disappearance and keep this somewhat inconvenient hiccough from the police? With a chill, he remembered Justin's remark about incinerators.

Kennedy made several phone calls. Tallis waited and watched and noticed the phone. Brand-new Samsung: Melissa's.

'Christ, I'm hungry,' Kennedy said. 'You?' he asked Tallis.

Not really. He found blood and viscera had an appetite-suppressing effect on his digestive system. 'Hungry as a lion.' He smiled cheerily.

'Me, too,' Justin chimed in.

.

'You'll need to stay here, oversee things,' Kennedy said, curtly clicking shut the phone and putting it into an overcoat pocket. 'Tallis, you're with me. I know a great little greasy spoon. You can drive.'

Tallis could almost feel Justin's eyeballs lasering into his back as he walked out of the killing zone.

In the car again, Tallis demanded answers to questions. 'Are you going to tell me why you wanted Gabriel dead?' The thought that Kennedy might have set up the whole episode suddenly entered his mind.

'Patience. You need to take a right here.'

Tallis indicated, glanced at his rear-view mirror, took the turning. 'You said Gabriel knew everything.'

'That's right.'

'You mean the nature of the business.'

'Yes.'

'Like me.'

Kennedy smiled. 'You're still a pup. Haven't been with me long enough to know all the ins and outs.'

Tallis wondered what exactly, apart from the obvious, Kennedy was trying to protect. 'You thought Gabriel was going to inform on you, right? He might have done.'

'Have to wait and see,' Kennedy said, cool.

'Never had time for grasses.' If Tallis hoped to provoke a strong denial, it wasn't forthcoming. Kennedy's reply was philosophical.

'We live in an informer society. Our wonderful nanny-state government has seen to that. Every year hundreds of so-called "friends" tip off Inland Revenue, Customs, you name it, about a neighbour or member of their family who they suspect of fiddling the taxman. Councils have even recruited little kids to spy on litter louts and report on them. In this industry, however, grassing up has always been an occupational hazard.'

'Fucking people over, I call it,' Tallis said.

'Left here.'

Tallis glanced at the mirror again. Yup, they were being followed. He was sure of it in spite of the originality of the disguise. A lilac-coloured VW Beetle, artificial flower poking out of the dash, was not everyone's immediate choice for undercover surveillance. The Golf engine under the bonnet, however, ensured that it could put in a swift and robust performance when necessary. He looked again, saw the indicator suddenly flashing left. Female driving. He felt strange relief that it definitely wasn't Charlie Lavender. Last thing he wanted was of his image of her to be spoilt. He took another look. Probably the same woman he'd seen watching the offices. Possibly the person behind the camera lens in the tower. Clear of the turning, he pulled over, blew her a kiss as she drove past, and saw the flush of red on her neck and cheek when she glanced in her rear-view mirror. Yes, he thought, same woman.

'What the hell are you doing?' Kennedy burst out.

'We were being followed.' Tallis reeled off a description, including the registration. 'Familiar?' Kennedy shook his head, no sign of recognition in his seal-grey eyes. 'Is there another route we can take?' Tallis asked.

'Go back the way we came, down to the roundabout and take the third exit.'

Tallis threw the TT into reverse. 'A witness said the guys who came for Gabriel were Turks.' A lie, but he wanted to study Kennedy's reaction. Tallis glanced across as he looked left and right to check it was clear to pull away.

'Them again,' Kennedy said with disdain.

'Didn't run into anyone in particular last time you were there?' Tallis said, sliding up the gears.

'Saw lots of people.' Kennedy shrugged. 'Did you know Turks have taken control of half the European heroin market? They used to be what we call the facilitators—'

'Contact men,' Tallis pushed in. Like you, he thought. Then another more compelling thought crossed his mind. 'Facilitator' was a word used in terrorist circles to describe a mastermind.

'Not any more,' Kennedy spoke. 'They've joined the game. Got a number of bases in Birmingham, but I expect you already knew that.'

'They also have quasi-terrorist links with organisations like the Grey Wolves,' Tallis said pointedly.

'So I'd heard,' Kennedy said, dismissive.

Tallis ground his jaw. Kennedy was behaving re-markably like a man who was not only back in the game, but also on top of it.

Tallis decided to push his luck, see what Kennedy was really made of. 'You don't have a view?'

'On what?'

'Terrorism.'

''Course I do. Fuckin' ragheads, sick of the lot of them. And this government,' Kennedy said, banging on again, voice thronged with contempt, 'just love 'em to bits.'

'How do you work that out?' Tallis was genuinely bewildered.

'Gives them the opportunity to turn this country into a fuckin' police state. One more politician droning on about frigging ID cards to prevent us from being blown to bits on our streets and I'll scream. It's here,' he said, indicating a row of shops with a café on the corner. 'Park in the private slot.'

The service was outstanding, the food less so. Tea, poured out of huge metal tea urns, was thick enough to stand a spade in. While Kennedy tucked into bacon, sausages and eggs, Tallis tried another approach.

'Think Gabriel's death is connected to the attempted kidnap?'

'Of my wife and daughter?'

Tallis nodded. Kennedy surveyed him slowly. 'Maybe.'

'What's the motivation?'

Kennedy popped a piece of bread into his mouth, chewed it well and swallowed. 'If I knew that, I'd be a very smart bloke indeed. Now, eat your breakfast before it gets cold.'

When they'd finished Kennedy announced a change of plan. After a visit to the offices in Lye, he asked Tallis to take him to the clinic.

'Not feeling well?' Tallis asked.

'Never felt better,' Kennedy said, unsmiling.

The medical centre was situated halfway between Harborne and Bournville, posh areas of Birmingham, the latter home to the Cadbury chocolate empire. Tallis recognised the clinic from his time on surveillance. The cars in the car park were a steal-to-order thief's wet dream. Tallis counted a Bentley Arnage in among the Jaguar convertibles and Porsche Cayennes.

The entrance was cool and inviting. No smell of bodily fluids, disinfectant or old age. Nursing staff were good-looking and friendly and, without exception, white Caucasian. As soon as Kennedy's shoe hit the plush carpet, he had everyone's attention. 'Afternoon, Mr Kennedy,' rang out in unison.

'How's Billy today?' he asked a tall brunette with flashing eyes.

'Enjoying the sunshine,' she replied, smiling warmly. 'He's in the garden room.'

'I'll see myself there. Come on, Tallis,' he said, turning towards him. 'Time I got you up to speed.'

They walked down a wide corridor, doors off, modern art prints hanging on the walls, classical music piped out of a sound system overlaid with the sound of trickling water. Reminded Tallis of the Basilica in Turkey.

Two men, one seated, one walking towards them, greeted Kennedy.

'All right, Rex?' Kennedy said, shaking the man's hand.

Rex nodded. He was an academic-looking individual, clean-shaven, with fashionable oblong-rimmed glasses.

After a brief exchange and introductions, Tallis was asked to remove his jacket, socks and shoes. The man who'd been seated, a short, colourless individual with steel-grey hair, patted him down, obviously checking for wires and weapons.

'It's all right,' Kennedy said as Rex studied the Glock Tallis was carrying. 'He can have it back later.'

To Tallis's surprise, Kennedy then took off his socks and shoes. Ritual complete, Rex punched in a code to the door behind them. As it sprang open, Kennedy entered, followed by Tallis.

The reason for bare feet became immediately obvious. They were walking into a bubble. The walls were padded, the floor was padded, no sharp corners, no furniture, everything smooth and round. Even the light in the room was moderated by gauze drapes at the windows. The air seemed unusually pure, as if they were standing on top of a mountain in Switzerland. Tallis glanced up and saw two filters, one at each end, embedded in the ceiling.

'Hello, Mr Kennedy.'

Tallis looked across the room. A middle-aged nurse dressed in a dark blue top and loose white trousers was sitting on the floor, legs apart. Between them, half lying, half propped, upper torso supported, rested the ruined body of a man.

Kennedy fell to his knees and crawled towards him. 'Hello, Billy,' he said. 'How are you doing, mate?'

At the sound of his father's voice, Billy's head, which seemed too big for his emaciated frame, lolled to one

side, mouth flopping open, saliva spuming forth
followed by a grunting sound that seemed to come deep
from his diaphragm.

'Yeah,' Kennedy said tenderly, stroking his son's pale
cheek, 'it's your old dad, isn't it?'

Without any fuss, as if the routine had been carried out
hundreds of times before, Kennedy gently swapped places
with the nurse. Tallis crouched down, acutely uncomfortable
at intruding on private grief. The man in front of him was
hardly recognisable as the same young man in the photographs. Sure, he had neatly cut dark hair, his clothes casual,
T-shirt and jeans carefully chosen to resemble any other
thirty-something. But physically he was a wreck. Features
slack and distorted, his eyes looked as if something in them
had died long ago. One arm hung down from his shoulder
inert, the hand a claw, fixed as if in rigor mortis, the other
arm curled in, spastic. His legs were thin and wasted. The
only area of bulk was around the lower half of his trunk.
Tallis guessed Billy was wearing incontinence padding.

As for Kennedy, he bore no resemblance to the thug
who only hours before had given orders to kill, who had,
in his time, cheerfully taken the lives of others. He was
simply a father taking care of his son. And he was doing
it brilliantly. Humbled, Tallis felt something dark stir inside
him. If his own father had shown him even a modicum of
the same regard, how different his life would have been.

When Billy was settled, Kennedy asked Tallis to come
over. 'He doesn't like sudden movements so approach
him slowly.'

Tallis dropped on all fours, quietly creeping along, a fleeting memory of playing with his sister's children flashing through his mind. When he was close enough to feel Billy's spittle-laden breath on his face, see the vacancy in his injured eyes, Tallis gently took Billy's hand in his, felt the slab of cold flesh, and wondered how long a human being could survive such disability.

'He was hit by some louse driving a car,' Kennedy explained, his voice dull and without inflection. 'Dragged for 400 metres. Bits of his skull fractured and penetrated his brain. Broke both legs, his arms, shattered his pelvis, ruptured his spleen. Didn't think he'd pull through.' Kennedy suddenly erupted, his voice rising in a howl of pain then falling, eyes blinded with tears and rage. Tallis didn't speak. What could he say? He felt as if he knew nothing about suffering. Nothing at all. Kennedy was speaking again, softly, coldly. 'Did you know that when a moving head comes to a sudden stop, the brain continues to travel? Does a fucking lot of damage.' Kennedy bowed his head, kissed the top of his son's damp hair, and whispered in his ear something that Tallis failed to catch.

'Who was driving?' Tallis asked softly.

'A prat,' Kennedy said. 'Stupid prat.'

Not cunt, not bastard. Seemed a very inconsequential word for someone who'd mown down your son, Tallis thought, for he didn't doubt that in Kennedy's mind, Carroll was guilty of a grave offence. Why else had Simon Carroll been sent death threats?

'Hit-and-run,' Kennedy spat out, 'and he got nothing

more than a fine and points on his licence. You call that justice? I call it corruption. Fucking police. And they have the cheek to come after people like me. That's right, isn't it, Billy?' Kennedy leant forward, hugging his son to his chest. Billy grunted and howled. 'He likes you.' Kennedy beamed, looking up at Tallis, a strange light in his eyes.

Tallis smiled uncertainly. Take your word for it, he thought.

'You haven't forgotten about tomorrow, have you?'

'Saturday, no. Kept a space in my diary especially.' Maybe he'd find out about those repeated connections to Turkey, and why Gabriel, and even Garry, had been killed.

'Big learning curve.' Kennedy was still smiling. Only the eyes said something else.

23

TALLIS didn't go straight home. He found a back-street pub where his face wasn't known and ordered a pint. 'I Will Survive' was belting out of a sound system. Before he sat down, his mobile rang. It was Crow.

'Forensics have definitively linked our two poets to Morello's murder in Turkey,' she said without preamble.

'Thanks for letting me know.'

'One good turn deserves another.'

Tallis took a pull of his pint. He knew there had to be a catch.

'Is Johnny Kennedy gold-plated, or what?' Crow said.

'Don't know what you mean.'

'Every avenue to him has a sod-off sign on it.'

'In case you've forgotten, I'm out of the game.'

'And I'm Jordan.'

Word association conjured up a bizarre image of Crow leaning towards him, exposing a fair expanse of what he imagined would be stretch-marked cleavage. Tallis took a big breath. 'As far as I know, Kennedy's turned over a new leaf. He's got legitimate businesses.'

'That take him to Turkey.'

'It's a nice place for a holiday, Micky.'

Big pause. 'All right,' she said, 'I'm going to tell you something in confidence.' She paused again, as if she were suddenly having second thoughts. 'I really shouldn't be telling you this.'

'Go on,' Tallis encouraged softly, automatically turning away from the bar.

'In less than seven hours a big operation is getting under way to smash a fairly major Turkish drugs ring.'

'There are hundreds of established Turkish crime syndicates in London.' Tallis shrugged.

'It's not in London, it's in Birmingham.'

As soon as Tallis got out of the TT he knew someone was waiting in the shadows. Couldn't see, couldn't touch, was unable to smell the presence of another, but some other highly developed sense confirmed the threat was real. He still had the Glock, and took it out, feeling the compact shape mould instantly to his hand.

From out of nowhere, a voice sounded. 'Long day at the office?' Then a man Tallis didn't recognise stepped out onto the path, illuminated by the security light, and introduced himself as Gavin Shaw.

'I work for West Mids,' he added, cool and calm, fearless.

'The building society?' Tallis said, droll, keeping his gun aimed and steady. He noticed the stocky build, the scar on his forehead similar to one he carried on his own, light brown hair, grey eyes.

'He's one of ours,' another voice said. Although he hadn't heard it in a long time, and there seemed to be more grain in the tone, Tallis recognised it immediately. He didn't move a muscle.

'Shall we go inside?' Napier said, emerging from the rear of the bungalow into the chill light of the moon. Thin, face lined and older than his years, Napier still cut an imposing figure.

'Why not?' Tallis's curiosity was starting to burn a hole in his head. He threw a set of front-door keys to Shaw, which he caught. Tallis motioned with the gun for Napier to follow his colleague inside.

Nobody sat down. All three men stood in the galley kitchen. Tallis placed the gun carefully on the work surface nearest to him, within hand's reach. He said nothing, watched them with wary eyes. In spite of an impressive show of confidence, it became clear to him that neither man was happy with either being there or with what he was about to divulge. Shaw, hands folded in front of him, short torso leaning against a cupboard, started the ball rolling.

'I'm an Organised Crime Officer and Johnny Kennedy's handler,' he announced, eyes fixed on Tallis. 'Your every move has been monitored by Kennedy.'

'My every move?' Did he tell you he ordered me to kill a man? Tallis wondered.

'We've had you watched,' Napier said, smug.

'I know,' Tallis said, seeing some of the shine fade from Napier's expression. 'Lilac VW Beetle. The driver showed out on my first day's surveillance. Before you consider using her again, for mobile work I suggest she undergoes a period of retraining.'

'You arrogant shit,' Napier spat.

Tallis ignored him. 'Just remember where you are. This is my home, my territory,' he said, looking pointedly at the weapon sitting on his work surface. 'What I don't understand is why you're telling me all this. An informer's identity, especially one of Kennedy's calibre, is supposed to be top secret.'

'Which is why even our own Organised Crime officers are kept in the dark,' Shaw concurred.

Including Nick Oxslade, Tallis thought, realising that Oxslade had genuinely been trying to warn him off. Maybe he wasn't such a bad bloke after all. 'Let alone someone who's just returned to civvy street,' Tallis said with a smile.

'That might be what you told Kennedy,' Napier said, mouth twisting. 'But our intelligence is somewhat better.'

Tallis arched an eyebrow, decided to let it drop. Asim, he thought. That's what Napier meant. 'I'm interested to know what pressure you used on Kennedy,' Tallis said.

Shaw answered. 'The disappearing man.'

'Simon Carroll?' Driver of the car that almost killed Billy. Shaw nodded.

'Are we talking disappeared as in disappeared, or dead?'

'A badly decomposed human head and severed leg were washed up on the beach near Start Point in Devon eighteen months ago. Scientists identified the body parts as Carroll's.'

'You're saying Kennedy issued orders from prison?'

'Wouldn't be the first.'

'But how did you know it was him?'

Shaw glanced at Napier who answered. 'We were tipped off.'

By whom? Tallis wondered. 'And what of the person who carried out the killing?'

'Never found.'

Probably bumped off, Tallis thought.

'So you gave Kennedy a choice?'

Shaw gave a slow nod.

'But I thought the judiciary had clamped down on all that.'

'Depends,' Napier chipped in.

'On what?'

'The level of information.'

Tallis met Napier's eye and reeled back to 1991, recalling a conceited man with an image to uphold, who hated competition, who, even when he'd made the most appalling mistake, blamed others for it. Had Kennedy led Napier to believe that he could give him something so momentous that his reputation would be secure for ever? Somehow Tallis didn't think it was the whereabouts of the unrecovered gold from of the Brink's-Mat bullion robbery. 'Is that supposed to explain why you've given the man such a free hand? How do you know Kennedy's not running rings around the lot of you? Business as usual.'

'Desperate times require desperate measures,' Shaw said.

'Sprat to catch a mackerel.' Napier broke into an

unlovely smile. Tallis noticed he had several molars missing. His breathing was noticeably fast and shallow. Excitement, not nerves, he deduced. One thing was clear: they were letting Kennedy run.

'Kennedy's no sprat,' Tallis said, remembering Kennedy describing himself as a great white. 'Expect you want to know my involvement.'

'We know.' Napier's voice was a snarl. Sweat broke out across his brow, even though it wasn't particularly cold in the room. Shaw flashed him an anxious look.

'Thing is,' Shaw said, clearly trying to run the conversation in a different direction, 'Kennedy isn't your average informer. He is the best of the best. He's put his life on the line over and over again.'

Yes, Tallis thought, Kennedy had. Why would he give so much for so little? All he had to do was serve the time. This way he'd always be running, always looking over his shoulder, waiting for that knock at the door, the bullet in the head.

Shaw was still speaking. 'You only have to look at the fount of high-grade information involving drugs and huge amounts of money…'

'Like the drug bust going down in the city in a little under five hours' time.'

'How the hell—?' Shaw began.

'Which we're hopeful might lead to other criminal activities,' Napier butted in, ignoring another warning look from Shaw. Tallis realised just how rare and valuable Kennedy was to Napier, indeed to the Serious and Organised Crime Agency. The track record for nailing anyone higher than a tea-boy was not a particularly good one. When they'd stumbled across Kennedy, a veritable Mr Big, they'd believed they'd struck gold. 'Including possible terrorist plots,' Napier added. Bingo! Tallis thought. Kennedy would prove even more valuable to the security services.

From the cold light in Napier's eye, Tallis knew that Asim had been stamping all over them, that whatever they had accomplished, whatever they were about to achieve, was about to be snatched away and they both resented it like hell. Then another thought struck him. 'Does Kennedy know about me?'

Once more Shaw and Napier exchanged glances. 'Gabriel does,' Shaw offered.

'Gabriel?' Tallis said, astounded.

'He's our man on the inside.'

'To shadow Kennedy?' Jesus, was that why Kennedy wanted him dead? Tallis thought.

'To protect him.'

'But Gabriel's dead.'

'What?' Shaw said, eyes narrowing.

Tallis told them both what happened. Shock, then anger registered in both men. And fear—of losing an officer, of screwing up an operation, of receiving a bollocking and possible demotion. Oh, he understood only too well and was glad to be outside that kind of gladiatorial arena.

Tallis rewound Kennedy's more recent history with the police, imagined and went through the operational moves in his head. First, Kennedy comes under the spotlight of West Midlands Organised Crime Officers on the ground. Pressure applied, he turns informer and moves into a slightly different circle, coming under another chain of command headed by Shaw. Second, and because of Kennedy's high-profile status, SOCA start sniffing around in the form of Napier who in turn takes over operational command, although Shaw remains in place as Napier's handler. Third, and because of a whiff of terrorism, Asim, under the auspices of MI5, assumes overall responsibility, cutting out any number of other agencies on the way. In effect, Napier and Shaw were receiving a kiss-off. *Thanks, chaps. Go back to what you're used to and let the experts take over.* That added up to an awful lot of egos being bruised, an awful lot of individuals pissed off. And he was bang slap in the middle of it.

'Something you should be aware of,' Tallis finished up, 'Kennedy ordered me to kill Gabriel.'

Shaw shook his head. 'No. Doesn't add up.'

'It's not the sort of thing I'd get wrong.' He also told them about Kennedy's extensive armoury.

Napier, who'd been listening intently, suddenly spoke. 'He's testing your loyalty.'

'Testing it?' Tallis said, his voice a howl of frustration. 'He wanted me to kill the man.'

Nobody spoke. Eventually Shaw broke the deadlock. 'Aren't we forgetting something? Someone got to Gabriel first.'

Napier shrugged, in a *shit happens* fashion.

'You still haven't told me what you're doing here,' Tallis said, beginning to feel the discussion sliding off course.

'We want you, Paul, to take Gabriel's place,' Asim said.

Three pairs of eyes swivelled to the doorway where Asim, sleek and composed, was standing.

Tallis raised his gaze to the poorly painted ceiling. *Ten steps ahead, Asim*, he thought. 'They've known all along?' he said, casting Asim a reproving look.

'Not exactly.' The dissembling expression on Asim's face was one Tallis instantly recognised.

'Would have been simpler if we had,' Napier said, curt and pale.

Too bad, Tallis thought. Napier was pissed off to be missing out on his moment of glory; he, however, remained more concerned about his personal safety. Without realising it, he and Gabriel had been working on the same side. His back had been protected. But now Gabriel was dead and the Organised Crime team had been shown the door, he was, in effect, completely on his own. 'How can I possibly take Gabriel's place?'

'Because you're already in so now we can change the rules,' Asim explained smoothly.

Tallis stared at Asim with incomprehension.

'Let's just say as of…' Asim broke off to glance at his watch '…an hour ago, Kennedy's agreed to work with us.' The *us* meaning the security service. No more Shaw, no more Napier. Goodbye, SOCA.

'Not much of a stretch,' Napier muttered. 'He'd already crossed over months before.'

Yeah, to your side, Tallis thought, so that you could take the credit. 'More importantly,' Tallis said, looking at Asim, 'has he agreed to work with me?'

'Absolutely.' Tallis wondered who had delivered the news and how Kennedy had taken it. He imagined the conversation had gone something like this. *You know that guy you've taken a shine to, Johnny? Well, really he's one of ours. You're going to let him look after you, make sure you and your family are protected. In return, every scrap of information, any link, however tenuous, between organised crime and terrorism, we want to know about it, and you're going to use Paul Tallis as your conduit. Got that?*

'You're both on the same side now,' Asim confirmed.

To do what exactly, bar the obvious? Tallis thought. It seemed to him that some nugget of information was being withheld. Deciding to bide his time, he thought he'd let the conversation roll, see where it led. He glanced at Shaw, who appeared to be taking an avid interest in a scuffmark on the kitchen floor. Napier, by contrast, couldn't prise his dead-eyed gaze from Asim. Christ, the sound of conflict in his ears was deafening.

'Our threat level is about to be raised from severe to critical,' Asim explained. 'We've notified airports so they can step up security.'

Bet they'll be thrilled, Tallis thought. For some time now airports had borne the financial brunt of extra protection, the government, apparently, not keen on footing the bill. Tallis wondered what specific intelligence had been received to warrant such a move, or, after the wilder accusations of turning a blind eye levelled after 7/7, was it simply a case of nobody wanting to slip up, nobody wishing to be the person to ignore a potential warning?

'We've received a tape,' Asim continued, ' allegedly from al-Qaeda, which is currently being looked at.'

Meant nothing, Tallis thought. Threats of violence were a-Q's stock in trade. The publicity it generated kept them in business even when they were too strapped for cash to operate. Conversely, Tallis was aware that while some thought al-Qaeda was a spent force financially, plenty believed the organisation to be well funded. Whatever the truth, there was no such thing as bad PR.

'We have other concerns, partially based on intelligence gathered abroad,' Asim continued, glancing in Napier's direction as if to give him the credit, although Tallis suspected the information was more likely to have been sourced by the Secret Intelligence Service. 'Some of the details cross-match with information supplied by Kennedy.'

'What information?'

'As we thought, there's to be a change of tactics.'

'Bombers coming in from abroad?' Tallis said, stony.

Asim nodded. 'Plenty of young malcontents willing to blow themselves and innocent members of the public into eternity.'

Yes, but, my God, it takes planning, Tallis thought. Simply smuggling a bomber into the UK via circuitous routes across European capitals, the forged papers, the securing of safe houses, procurement and transportation of explosives, the cultivation and nurturing of a faceless, anonymous network of movers and shakers and all the little people in between, the whole thing was a logistical and, from the enemy's point of view, security nightmare. At any point the threat could be leaked and busted wide open. Unless, he contemplated, you have Organised Crime on your side to provide a direct, helping hand?

'The bombers, from which countries exactly?' Tallis said.

'The usual suspects,' Napier answered.

Tallis imagined Asim liaising with the SIS who'd then tip off those co-operative foreign security services whose countries might provide a route through which a bomber might travel.

Napier was still talking. 'The point is, Kennedy thinks he's found a link via someone in Turkey.'

Tallis could hardly believe it. If it was true, the man was suddenly a hero. This was the missing piece of info he'd been waiting for. Then again… 'Thinks or knows?'

'Knows is too strong a word,' Napier said, surly.

Now he understood Napier's frustration and rage. Napier had hoped to keep this under SOCA's remit. He'd wanted to be the one to follow the investigation, to establish the evidence, to be the first to crack the news and foil the plot. Think of the accolades. 'Not that it matters,' Tallis said. 'The operation is already compromised.'

'Are you saying Gabriel talked?' Napier glared accusingly.

'I'd have talked,' Tallis said, spreading his hands. By

now, everyone probably knew that Johnny Kennedy was a grass. 'You didn't see what was done to him.'

'I'll need to come up with a cover story for the family,' Shaw said, morose.

What an interesting conversation that should prove to be, Tallis thought grimly.

Nobody said anything for a moment or two. Tallis looked at Asim for guidance. Would he pull the plug or go ahead? 'Napier's right,' Asim said. 'We don't know Gabriel talked.'

Tallis shrugged. High-risk gamble. 'So Kennedy's real reason for being in Turkey was an attempt to establish the evidence?' Nothing to do with drugs at all.

'He was trying to check out a contact,' Napier said, deadpan.

Tallis exchanged glances with Asim. *Faraj Tardarti*, the Moroccan with a-Q connections Tallis had killed in Turkey. Christ, was it possible Napier had tried to shut Garry up? Then, remembering Asim's obvious disinterest in Garry's death, was it possible that MI5 were behind the hit? Or what about Kennedy? Men who he'd had associations with had carried out the killing. He was getting a very bad vibe about all this.

'Right, then,' Asim said, indicating that it was time for Shaw and Napier to make tracks. 'Thanks for all your hard work, guys. Really appreciate it. Like I've said before, your role in this is now officially over, but we're still all in this together.' He smiled with the supreme confidence of a man who knew they weren't.

'Not happy,' Tallis said as the front door slammed shut.

'They'll get over it.' Asim grinned.

'So I'm supposed to waltz into Kennedy's pad tomorrow as if nothing has happened.'

'As if nothing has changed,' Asim corrected him. 'You won't be entirely alone.'

Tallis resisted the temptation to raise an eyebrow. Please, let it be Lavender, not some faceless bod from the security service, counter-terrorism, Special Branch, or any one of the other myriad wings of law enforcement. 'And what am I to do exactly?'

'Kennedy, as you've already discovered, has many important British contacts.'

'Local villains.'

'Don't underestimate him,' Asim warned.

Tallis didn't. He never had. Something in Asim's hard expression brought him up short. 'What is it?' Tallis asked.

'Valuable though Kennedy is, you are probably wondering why we are focusing all our attention on him.'

Tallis said nothing. He didn't need to. He only wondered why he hadn't been kept in the loop before now.

'We've received uncorroborated intelligence suggesting that Kennedy has direct involvement in terrorism.'

'When? Today, or weeks ago?' Tallis flushed with irritation. 'While I've been boxing in the dark, busting a gut, you've been in receipt of this rather important fact.' He wondered who the source was.

Asim shook his head. 'Not fact. That's my point. It may be an entirely false allegation.'

Tallis wondered if this was American-led intelligence.

Either way, he felt unappeased. 'What about Napier's claim that Kennedy's found a link in Turkey? You said yourself that information Kennedy supplied cross-references with info from the SIS.' Jesus, was Kennedy that daring, that cunning? And why was it that a part of him was shrieking *yes*?

'Look, Paul, Kennedy may well be useful to us in the way you originally suggested.'

By leading us to the criminal organisation involved in terrorism, Tallis recalled. He felt flat, inert. He wanted to believe it, but...

'And, as such, your role, ostensibly, is to protect him,' Asim said evenly.

'While trying to uncover any direct evidence that he's playing a dirty game.'

'That's right. Ever heard of the old Mafia-style Commission?' Asim said.

Tallis shook his head.

'Set up by Lucky Luciano in the 1930s as a means to create links between all the major Mafia families and ensure co-operation for criminal ventures,' Asim said. 'With incredible skill, Kennedy has created his own version.'

'And the first meeting is tomorrow afternoon,' said Tallis, rallying. For the first time in a while he had the drop on Asim. The pleasure of seeing an expression of complete surprise on Asim's face was marvellous. 'It's all right. I've already received my invite to the party,' Tallis said, smiling.

24

AT SEVEN-THIRTY the following morning, Tallis drove to a link-detached house on an estate in Coventry. Letting himself in, he was delighted to find that he already had company. Lavender was wearing black motorbike leathers.

'Right, then, first things first.' He grinned. 'I'll make the coffee.' By this very simple act he was trying to say he was sorry for doubting her.

'Sounds good to me.'

'You cool with all this?' he said, filling the kettle with water and putting it on.

'All what?'

He flicked her a direct look. 'This is going to be one hell of a change from Devon and Cornwall.'

She laughed softly. 'What are you saying, that I'm a numty?'

'A what?'

'Devon slang for stupid person.'

'Christ, no. But this could get rough.'

'For you, yes.'

'For both of us.'

Their eyes met. The air seemed to tingle. 'I'll take my chances,' she said.

Tallis nodded, first to drop his gaze. 'So what have you been told?' he said, rummaging through a cupboard and locating a jar of instant.

'It's all in there,' she said enthusiastically, pointing to a thick folder on the coffee-table. 'Target information. Addresses. List of known associates. Business interests. Kennedy's history, criminal and personal. Details of time spent in prison. Kennedy's deal with DCI Napier. Contact sheets with his handler, DI Gavin Shaw. Shall I go on?'

'Mind if I take a look?'

'Help yourself.'

Tallis picked it up. The file was marked 'Top Secret, Johnny Kennedy, code name Michael Shaman.' Eyes scanning the early text, it all seemed pretty much in order. No unexpected or unpleasant surprises. Then it got interesting. A whole paragraph had been blacked out. Tallis remarked on it to Lavender. She gave a shrug. 'I guess it's connected to the evidence linking Kennedy to Carroll's murder.'

Tallis sat back and thought about it. Often in such cases it was the individual paid and hired to kill and dispose of a victim who talked, not that it always played well with the courts. He'd known of instances where evidence like that had been ruled inadmissible. How else had Shaw and Napier put the squeeze on Kennedy? he wondered. He went back to the file. Kennedy's medical notes in prison told the story of a man devastated by his son's accident.

In the immediate aftermath he was moved to the hospital wing of Winson Green Prison, where he was heavily sedated. There followed a regime of anti-depressants, and for a time Kennedy was put on suicide watch. Tallis knew how much Kennedy loved his son, but even he found it hard to believe the depth to which the man had fallen. Perhaps even more amazing was his slow but steady rise from the pit of despair.

'Here,' Lavender said, putting a mug down in front of him. 'No milk, sugar's there,' she added, pushing a spoon and a bag of granulated towards him.

'Thanks. Sorry, I was supposed to get that.' He looked up, studied her face. A perfect oval, her features were symmetrical, pupils large. Unlike at the fight club, she'd reverted to no make-up again. Still looked great. She really had the most enchanting smile.

He returned to the file, turned the pages. Next up, Simon Carroll, the driver responsible for the devastating injuries to Kennedy's son, Billy. In spite of escaping a custodial sentence, he'd swiftly gone into hiding in the West Country, last known address in the small market town of Kingsbridge supplied. Reported missing by his wife after he failed to return from work at a nearby business park, he was found seven weeks later. Body parts washed up on the beach, just as Shaw said, Kennedy suspected of ordering the killing and police gathering enough evidence to nail him on a conspiracy to murder charge. Tallis read over the interview notes. Kennedy didn't even deny it.

Why not? Tallis thought, sitting back, trying to work it out and failing. He returned to the file. Shaw's contact sheets revealed an amazing tale of revelation and betrayal. In the six months following Kennedy's decision to turn informer, he offered hard information on the identity of a contract killer, the names of two violent armed robbers who'd carried out a series of thefts in London, the whereabouts of a man suspected of killing a schoolgirl in West Lothian. The text was liberally sprinkled with names and addresses of dealers, times and locations of drugs deliveries by boat, lorry and courier. It was only when he'd flicked through to the end that Tallis realised a chapter was missing. No mention of Tardarti or Garry, or even Kennedy's trip to Turkey. Had Kennedy taken off of his own accord? Surely that was impossible. Somewhere along the line, he suspected Napier's involvement.

'Interesting, huh?' Lavender smiled.

'This is fine,' he said, tapping the file and putting it back down on the table then, leaning forward, meeting her luscious green-eyed gaze, he said, 'But this is what you really need to know. Kennedy is suspected of being directly involved in terrorism.'

Two hours later, after Tallis had described his own personal observations of Kennedy, they'd made a full risk assessment, discussed logistics, codes, radio communications, target addresses, vehicles used by the main players, and covered every eventuality. Between them there were no

secrets. Trust nobody, Asim had told him. Sometimes, especially if your life depended on it, you had to.

'How do you think Kennedy will react?' Charlie said.

He almost found her more engaging when she was
serious. Part of his brain wondered exactly how old she
was, whether she was married, had a boyfriend, husband
and kids maybe. 'To my change of allegiance? He'll be
nice as pie to my face, scheming behind my back.'

'As long as it stays at scheming, we'll be all right.'

'Yeah,' he said, standing up, indicating the meeting was
over. 'You clear, then?'

'As crystal.'

'See you later.'

'I'll be ready.'

'Where are you staying?' he blurted out as she
reached the door.

She grinned. 'I'm heading back to my digs in Halesowen where I'm going to phone my mum and dad and tell
them I'm all right.'

'Sure, of course,' he said, trying to sound a bit more
businesslike. After wishing her good luck, he waited and
watched her leave. Cute rear, he thought admiringly as she
hammered up the road riding a top-of-the-range Yamaha.
The sight of the motorbike spiked a chain reaction. Picking
up his phone, he decided to give Gayle Morello a call. It
rang three times. A bloke answered. He had a northern
accent, wasn't in-your-face northern, softer like the Dales,
Yorkshire. Tallis asked to speak to Gayle.

'She's not up yet. Who's calling?'

Tallis told him.

'Paul,' the man said, seeming to make the connection. 'Friend of Garry's.'

'Yeah,' Tallis said.

'I'm her brother.'

'Glad she's taken my advice.'

'Yeah?' The man sounded baffled.

'I told her she shouldn't be alone.'

'Oh, right. Look, can I give her a message or something?'

'Just wondered how she was. Gather the police have identified Garry's killers.'

'Yeah. Looks like Garry poked about where it wasn't appreciated.'

'Poked about?' An unfortunate choice of words, Tallis thought, bridling. Suddenly, he heard a woman's voice in the background. 'Is that Gayle?' he said, straining to make it out.

'No, I told you she's—'

'Hello, Paul.' It was Gayle Morello.

'Sorry to disturb you. Your brother made a valiant effort to put me off.'

'Unfortunately, he's rather undiscriminating.' There was freshness in her voice, amusement even. Good, she was starting to move to a different plane, where the days weren't all entirely bad and filled with despair. From experience, Tallis knew it might be only a temporary respite.

'I was saying to your brother—'

'Stephen,' Gayle helpfully interposed.

'Yeah, Stephen, that I heard the police identified the

blokes responsible. Did anyone ever mention the name Johnny Kennedy to you?'

'No.'

'Garry didn't mention him either?'

There was a brief pause. 'No. Is it important?'

'Maybe. I'm not honestly sure.'

'He mentioned some Moroccan. Damned if I can remember his name.'

Tallis felt his stomach lurch. 'Tardarti.'

'Goodness, that's right.'

If Garry had been so careful, why the hell would he have let Tardarti's name slip? 'You told the police this?'

'I couldn't quite zero in on the name. Think it's significant?'

Yes, but he didn't understand how. He felt as if he were drowning in tons of disparate pieces of information, none of which seemed to be apparently linked. 'Don't worry about it.'

He heard a burble of voices. Gayle told him to hang on. She must have clamped a hand over the receiver because the line went very quiet.

'Sorry about that,' she said. 'Someone at the door.'

'No worries. Gayle, about the funeral…'

'We haven't got a date yet. There've been some complications with bringing Garry's body back.'

'Oh?'

'Bureaucratic stuff,' she said, sounding philosophical. 'And there's still people to contact. A lot of Garry's mates work abroad.'

'Yes. Sorry. But you'll let me know?'

'Of course, Paul.'

'Right.' He was about to wrap up the call when Gayle asked when he'd be next in town. 'Not sure. Bit busy with work at the moment.'

'Pity. It would be nice to get together. You know, to talk about Garry.'

'I'll call you.'

'Don't leave it too long, Paul.'

After making a phone call to Crow and running the usual gamut of flirtatious and not so flirtatious suggestions, he asked her to check a couple of things out.

'I'm on the case,' she said. 'Seen the news this morning?'

'Not yet.'

'You should.' Click.

He walked into the plainly furnished sitting room and switched on the television to *News 24*. Sure enough, there were reports of joint police raids with Customs and Excise on a number of premises throughout the city with an estimated haul of 200 kilos of Turkish heroin worth over £25 million. After that, he left the safe house in Coventry and, to confound even the most persistent tail, deliberately took a tortuous route, watching out for anyone pulling in behind him, speeding up, slowing down and indulging in the odd U-turn. He drew the line at jumping a red light to see if anyone was daring enough to follow. He didn't want West Midlands's finest breathing down his neck.

Kennedy had asked Tallis to pick him up from Shakenbrook. As Tallis headed up the S-shaped drive, he kept a watchful eye out for Lavender, but saw no sign of her. Good, he thought.

Flanked by a stone-faced Justin, Kennedy greeted Tallis with typical warmth. It seemed strangely paradoxical to Tallis that he was now playing protector to the man he'd tried to expose. From now on, Johnny Kennedy was effectively his principal.

'I've got some coffee on the go in the summerhouse,' Kennedy said affably. 'Want some?'

'Thank you,' Tallis said. He felt uncertain. This really felt quite odd.

Kennedy dismissed Justin, giving him orders to go straight to the clinic. Once they were alone, Kennedy began to laugh. 'It's all right, Paul,' he said, clapping him on the back. 'You didn't have me fooled for one moment. Always reckoned you were a bit special.'

Tallis turned, looked into Kennedy's laughing eyes. Either he was bluffing or he was cleverer than even he'd given him credit for.

'To business,' Kennedy said, purposefully leading the way over lawns soaked with autumn rain.

The summerhouse was smaller inside than Tallis had imagined. Just about room to swing a cat. He sat down close to Kennedy, who poured coffee from a cafetière into a plain white china mug, which he handed to him.

'Sugar?' Kennedy said, offering him a spoon and a packet of sugar lumps.

Tallis took two cubes, chucked them into his mug and

stirred. 'I've got some cartons of cream somewhere,' Kennedy said, opening up one of the seats to reveal a cold compartment inside. It struck Tallis that Kennedy seemed to have the answer to everything.

'No need. I'm good.'

'Well,' Kennedy said, sitting down, looking long and hard at Tallis. 'At least we no longer have to play stupid games with each other.'

'That's the idea,' Tallis said, unsmiling. He didn't want Kennedy to run away with the thought that they were best chums. 'About Gabriel. Think he talked?'

'I'm working on the premise he didn't.'

Why? Is that what you've been told to say? Didn't exactly square with Kennedy's behaviour at the time, Tallis remembered. 'Nothing rattling your alarm bells? No threats, no strange occurrences?'

'Everything's fine. Business as usual.'

What a relief, Tallis thought, sharp enough to realise, however, that true revenge was never usually dispensed with speed. If Kennedy's treachery had been revealed, those in the know might take their time. 'You did well this morning.'

'The Turkish haul.' Kennedy smiled. 'Actually, it's not where it's really happening.'

'What isn't?' Sometimes Kennedy had an obtuse way of speaking that Tallis found confusing. He wondered if it was a deliberate ploy.

'Three-quarters of heroin comes from Afghanistan, smuggled in direct via India and Pakistan.'

Now he was getting the drift. 'And Asian dealers in Birmingham have major links with Pakistan and India.'

Kennedy nodded. 'Why bother importing through Turkey?'

'When you can cut out the middle man and improve your profit margins?' So all that blarney about visiting Turkey for a drugs deal really was a smokescreen. At least Napier seemed to have got that bit of intelligence right. And then it dawned on him. The reason there was no mention of the visit to Turkey in the file was because SOCA had stepped in at that point of the operation, leaving Shaw out of the loop.

'Asian gangs also have major links with terrorist organisations.'

Tallis felt his stomach crease. 'You know that for a fact?'

'It's a good supposition. Think about it.'

'Christ, is this the so-called intelligence you gave MI5?'

Kennedy's response was to stare with burning eyes. 'I believe I know the identity of what you blokes call a fixer.'

Tallis understood the phrase, the kind of man who facilitated travel to places like Pakistan for terrorist training. 'You're certain?'

The burn in Kennedy's eyes grew brighter. 'Do you trust me?'

'I trust you to tell me the truth,' Tallis said, cool. 'I can't protect you unless you do.'

Kennedy flashed a smile. 'Good answer.'

'And do you trust me, Johnny?' It was the first time Tallis had ever used his first name.

'I trust you as if you were my only son.'

Tallis stared at him, silent. Was this emotional black-mail or genuine affection? Careful, Tallis thought, don't be seduced.

Even though they couldn't be overheard, Kennedy leant towards him. 'You know about the Commission?'

Tallis nodded. 'A modern-day gathering of current crime lords. I'm presuming it was set up as a sensible measure to ensure co-operation and prevent turf wars.' It suddenly occurred to him that, with Kennedy spilling the beans at regular intervals, the need for a Commission where everyone could close rank and protect each other's backs would seem even more vital. 'I'm also guessing that it provides the means for you to work together in criminal endeavours.' Including terrorism, perhaps.

'Doing well.' Kennedy smiled.

'As far as the law's concerned, would I be right in thinking your aim is to provide a united front against it?'

'Partially,' Kennedy said. 'Put it this way, the Commission's aim is to keep the law at arm's length. We don't, therefore, want to draw the law's attention by, for instance, killing a police officer, an act, under the Commission's rules, which is punishable by death, I might add.'

'Good to know,' Tallis said dryly. 'What about buying people off?'

'The thorny topic of bent coppers.' Kennedy smiled. 'Yeah, it happens.'

Tallis knew. His brother Dan had been one of them. 'How long has the Commission been in action?'

Kennedy shrugged. 'Twenty years.'

'Twenty?' Tallis couldn't believe his ears. How come police hadn't tumbled to it? He felt as if all his years in law enforcement had counted for nothing.

'Naturally, some of the faces have changed due to natural wastage,' Kennedy said matter-of-factly. 'But some of the blokes I deal with I've known for a very long time.'

'So there's a good level of trust between you?'

Kennedy didn't flinch. 'There is. You get to know these men, how they tick, how their policies, plans evolve and change. Nothing stays the same in this business, Tallis. You probably know that better than anyone. It's a case of keeping up to date, reading the market and adapting to it. Cocaine is the drug of the moment. It's halved in price so it's as accessible to punters living in Sutton Coldfield as in Surrey. You only have to walk into the toilets of any club and pub in the city centre to see the evidence—devil's dandruff, they call it,' he said with a wry smile, 'but crack is the drug of the future. We're already seeing an increased demand. When it comes down to it, it's all about the money.'

'And what are you all about?' Tallis's change of direction was deliberate, as was the hardness in his expression.

'Family,' Kennedy said. 'If I hadn't turned, I would have missed seeing my daughter grow up. I wouldn't be able to spend time with Billy and care for him.'

Sounded plausible. And yet… 'Going back to my original question,' Tallis said. 'About the Asian connection.'

Kennedy nodded. 'There's an Asian gang headed by a

bloke called Ahmed. Runs a cab company and a couple of garages, legit on the surface. Known him for a while. He's highly educated, comes from a good family, and took over chairing the Commission while I was inside. He's the man you need to watch.'

Tallis studied the older man's face, looked closely into his eyes. It all sounded so outlandish and yet Kennedy had, to date, delivered. Time and again, as Shaw had already pointed out, he'd put his life on the line. If word leaked out about his treachery, he was a dead man. Thing was, in spite of Asim's more recent disclosure, there was no evidence to support the allegation of terrorist activity. Even Asim was keeping his cards stubbornly close. As far as Tallis could see, and notwithstanding the change in the threat level, which as far as he was concerned went up and down like a tart's knickers, it was all rumour and speculation. Without something harder, MI5 would do nothing more than watch Ahmed, add him to a long list of others. Depending on resources, he would either be watched closely or hardly at all.

'When you went to Turkey you were seen with a Moroccan.'

'Faraj Tardarti. I believed him to be Ahmed's contact. I went in under the pretext of arranging a drug deal.'

'Tardarti was involved in supplying drugs?'

'If the price is right,' Kennedy said, dismissive, 'most people are.'

Only in the circles you keep, Tallis thought. 'Wasn't that risky?'

'Life's a risk.'

Tallis didn't buy it. He flashed a smile. 'Talking of risk, you need to pay serious attention to overhauling your security. Justin's a loose cannon.'

'He's loyal,' Kennedy countered.

I prize loyalty more highly than love, Tallis remembered. 'Your choice, but I'd prefer you make more use of Rex. He's older, less likely to overreact, more likely to think first.'

Kennedy rubbed his chin. 'Yeah, I'll go with that.'

'Good. As for here,' Tallis said, looking out of the window. 'The lake is a gift to anyone who wants to infiltrate your property.'

'It's a swamp. You'd have to be mad to try and cross it.'

Tallis smiled. 'You know better than anyone that sanity has nothing to do with matters of security. Get it properly fenced off, for Melissa's sake, at least. You also need to seriously watch your back when you go into a building and when you leave. At present, you're far too sloppy. You should also make a point of altering your routines. It's no use simply relying on basic anti-surveillance techniques.'

'Served us well enough in the past.'

'The past is a foreign country.'

'Very smart.' Kennedy cracked a smile. 'But before you give me any more lectures, I'd like to show you something.' He stood up, indicating for Tallis to follow. They went back outside into the rain. Tallis glanced up and saw a fleet of clouds skidding past. Kennedy took him to the west wing of the house towards the indoor squash court and wine cellar. They passed through a barn, empty save for a stinking vat of what looked like silage. Tallis commented on it.

'It's a digester,' Kennedy explained. 'Waste products are fed into it to provide energy for the house.'

'Didn't know you were a green fan,' Tallis commented.

'There's a lot you don't know about me,' Kennedy flicked back with a smile.

Once inside the main building, they came to a door with an entry code. Kennedy punched in a number and the door slid open to reveal a control room. From the threshold, Tallis saw a boiler, a generator, an air-conditioning unit and various pieces of hi-tech equipment. Walking in further, he was faced with a wall of video cameras for monitoring and tracking intruders.

'Here, check this out,' Kennedy said, opening a door to a panic room fully equipped with bunk beds, sanitation and enough supplies to feed an army. Tallis stared in wonderment. 'Escape tunnel's that way.' Kennedy pointed to a door beyond. 'You were saying?'

Tallis shook his head and smiled. Back out into the main body of the house again, he told Kennedy that he would stay with him at all times.

'I can promote you to lieutenant,' Kennedy said.

'Might be tricky. How are you going to explain me to your chums? They're not going to like the fact I was a serving police officer.'

Kennedy smiled. 'They won't know. We'll give you a different name. We'll call you Milton.'

Tallis shook his head again. 'These guys are smart. A false name isn't going to cut it.'

'No,' Kennedy said, grave. 'But if I give my word, it will.'

'So I'm to take Gabriel's place?'

Kennedy nodded darkly.

'Why did you ask me to kill him?' Tallis's expression was direct and unforgiving.

'I wanted to see how you'd react.'

'You were taking a risk.'

'Not really. Like I said, I had you sussed. I knew you wouldn't shoot,' Kennedy said, slate-eyed. Before Tallis had the chance to respond, Kennedy fired another question. 'Do you realise what you're getting into? If you're unmasked by any one of these people I've told you about, to a man they will happily come after you and pay to watch you suffer agonies.'

'Which brings me to one final point,' Tallis said, his voice rock hard. 'You ever try to pull a stunt like you did with me and Gabriel, pitting me against another man, and I'll kill you and feed you bit by bit to one of your own incinerators.'

Kennedy broke into a wide smile. 'Time we got going. Wouldn't look good to be late for my own meeting.'

25

TALLIS'S orders were to drive Kennedy in the Land Rover to the clinic, the place scheduled for the meeting with the Commission. First, Kennedy put on a bulletproof vest. He offered one to Tallis, who accepted. Probably the most sensible precaution he'd taken lately. That, and having Charlie Lavender on side, he thought. Although he took a less than obvious route, Tallis was pleased to see her astride her motorbike, powering down the road behind him. She wore traditional black leathers. He absently wondered what she'd look like beneath them. Steady, he thought.

The journey was without incident. Taking a piece of his own advice, Tallis asked Kennedy to direct him to the rear entrance.

'Why?'

'Like I already told you, when you leave this car to go inside, you're most vulnerable.'

Reluctantly, Kennedy complied. Justin was waiting. 'All clear,' he told Kennedy. 'Rex and Darren are in place.'

'Make sure everyone is checked before they get into the building. Don't want any cock-ups.'

'Yes, Mr Kennedy,' Justin said, studiously ignoring Tallis.

Tallis followed Kennedy inside. 'I understand you're a dab hand at languages.'

'Some,' Tallis admitted. Fluent in five, could make himself understood in three Arabic dialects, had only a shaky command of Russian. He'd always fancied having a crack at Mandarin but hadn't had the time.

'We're a pretty multinational group,' Kennedy explained, as if he were talking about a UN peacekeeping force. 'It would be useful to know about any unguarded, off-the-cuff remarks.'

The reception area was much as it had been last time, except for the staff. Tallis recognised two men from the Walsall premises ostensibly manning the phones, the bulges in their jackets telling a different narrative. As he followed Kennedy down an unfamiliar corridor, Tallis spotted two other armed men flanking doorways, one definitely a face from another slice of his history. He'd recognise that bad skin anywhere.

'Afternoon, Pat,' Tallis said, walking past.

'Afternoon, Mr Tallis.' The bloke smirked.

Tallis did the maths: Patrick Simms arrested in 1997 for possession of a shotgun without a licence, later convicted in 2000 for attempting to smuggle an automatic and pistol into the country after a 'holiday' in Eastern Europe.

The interior landscape changed. The garden room lay off another wing of the building. This section looked more corporate, less like a clinic. They came to a door with a time lock on it. Kennedy punched in a code, releasing the lock. The door, made of reinforced steel, swung open to reveal a conference room in which a long table, to rival those used for Cabinet meetings, was laid for twenty guests, each place with its own notepad, pen, glass and bottled water.

Kennedy took a seat in the middle. He asked Tallis to pull up a chair beside him. 'Like I said, we're a broad church,' Kennedy began, giving Tallis a jaw-dropping précis of those likely to be in attendance. 'The Colombians have pulled out. No offence taken, they're notoriously suspicious of who they deal with. Could have got some of their bottom-rung players, but didn't see much point. I heard along the grapevine that one of the major cartels has a woman fronting it.'

Tallis stared at him. Surrounded by white noise, he felt something click more firmly into place in his mind, forcing him to briefly wonder how Crow was getting on.

'You listening?' Kennedy said tersely, as a father might discipline a child.

'Sure, you were saying about one of the Colombian cartels fronted by a woman.'

'What you have to remember at all times is respect,' Kennedy said. 'Everyone believes that the Yardies are the big face-savers. They're not. The Albanians and triads corner that particular market.'

From what Tallis knew of the Albanians, he could believe it. He was part Croatian himself so he had some experience of their peculiarities. 'You've only mentioned international crime families—what about British?'

'Coming to that,' Kennedy said. 'Asians have taken the high ground here in Birmingham. Yardies mainly run the show in Bristol, Hell's Angels in Plymouth, but they won't come because they never publicly admit they're anything other than a group of fun-loving motorcycle enthusiasts.' Tallis smiled, remembering Oz. Perhaps he ought to view Oz's mates in a different light. 'Then you've got various outfits representing Liverpool, Manchester, Doncaster…'

'Doncaster?' Tallis expressed surprise.

'Important connection to the north-east,' Kennedy said matter-of-factly. 'Nottingham's on the slide with a nasty power vacuum developing since a main man got banged up.'

'Gunn by name, gun by nature,' Tallis said, referring to Colin Gunn, who had been responsible for a notorious reign of terror until his arrest for conspiracy to murder.

'And let's not forget London,' Kennedy said. 'Turks heavily embedded in the north, but there are about five other major crime families, including the Adams family.'

'Whose boss is serving time for money-laundering,' Tallis chipped in.

'See, you're not so wet behind the ears.' Kennedy grinned. 'You actually work for MI5?'

'No.'

'Thought not. You're too grounded. More of a mercenary.'

'I prefer to think of myself as a freelance.' Tallis smiled. He had often thought of himself as a mercenary, but coming from Kennedy's lips he found himself resisting the man's cold-blooded assessment.

The first of the crime lords and their seconds-in-command began to trickle through twenty minutes later. It had to rate as one of Tallis's more surreal experiences. It was a bit like being at a high-class cocktail party, everyone greeting everyone, asking after family and, in Kennedy's case, villains making solicitous enquiries about Billy, his son. One constant thread of conversation was the recent drugs bust in the city that morning.

Tallis was introduced to a smiling Sicilian whose boss, by all accounts, headed an outfit specialising in stolen fine art and black-market anti-obesity drugs. From the other side of the room, Kennedy was deep in conversation with a large, dough-faced man from Manchester who'd recently diversified into cannabis importation, as he put it.

'Yeah, but the profit margins are crap, Steve,' Kennedy was saying.

Steve let out a loud, throaty laugh. 'Be surprised. Customs are busting a gut on Class-A stuff. All I'm doing is using a bit of common,' he said, knuckling his forehead. 'Nothing like cashing in when everyone's looking the wrong way.'

While Steve moved off to greet a wiry-looking Russian with feral features, Tallis watched Kennedy fall into thick conversation with a huge black man who spoke in an incomprehensible Bristolian dialect coupled with Jamaican patois. If Kennedy's information was correct, the guy was the king of crack cocaine. He'd somehow managed to survive turf wars and numerous attempts on his life. Tallis reckoned the West Indian was no more than twenty-five. He looked edgy and unpredictable, like he'd sampled too much of his own product. The rate he was going, Tallis thought, he probably wouldn't see his next birthday.

Every time the door opened another face arrived. Tallis observed two mean and Mediterranean-looking men slide into the room unnoticed. Both took a stand away from the others. Tallis slowly positioned himself so that he could listen to them. It didn't take him long to work out they were Turks. Ergul and Alpi, as he soon discovered, were bemoaning the fact they'd lost twenty-five million pounds' worth of heroin.

The door swished open again. On the threshold stood a tall, handsome-looking Asian. Dressed in an expensive suit, his sophistication and presence went well beyond the clothes he wore. Tallis had the impression that this guy had learnt to control the expression on his face and the give-aways of body language a long time ago. Kennedy rushed over to greet him, calling him by name, Ahmed's light Midlands accent confirming his geographical status. So this is the would-be terrorist sympathiser, Tallis thought, never taking his eyes off him. Like most criminals, he didn't look mean or evil, or give the slightest hint that he was capable of taking someone's life, let alone aiding and abetting the bombing of hundreds of people he didn't even know.

By now the room was filling up more quickly. There was a definite protocol. Seconds-in-command talked only to seconds-in-command. Among the bosses, there emerged some curious alliances. The Italians and the triads seemed to have a number going with high-tech crime, involving counterfeiting. The Russians appeared to be hooking up with the Albanians in their pursuit of sex trafficking. As with all gatherings, there were those Tallis suspected he might like if they didn't go round murdering and torturing people, and those he'd never want to share the same air space with in a million years.

Kennedy, however, made no such distinctions. He was polite and effusive to everyone. Although there were no class differences, it soon became clear from the seating arrangement who held most power. While the seconds-in-command stood silently behind their bosses, the heads of state, as Tallis regarded them, elaborately and with a great deal of shunting around, took their places. He was reminded of an all-star pop concert at Wembley some years ago. It had taken bloody ages for the class acts to step onto the stage.

Kennedy took his place opposite a fearsome-looking Albanian called Vasel. Next to him sat a thin-faced Chinese man who represented the oldest and one of the largest criminal organisations. Mr Wo was at pains to point out that he was not speaking only for himself but for the other three major triad gangs. Observing the softly spoken Chinaman, Tallis found it hard to believe such a harmonious-sounding individual was part of the same group that had meted out extreme violence in a Birmingham restaurant a few years before over a loss of 'face'. Ahmed, Tallis noticed, was seated closely to Kennedy's right. He would not have been surprised to see either Kennedy pulling out a written agenda or a secretary taking the minutes.

After a brief welcome by Kennedy, debate swiftly

followed. It included a thorough précis of joint operations, the smuggling of arms top of the agenda, a résumé of the state of the drug market in the UK and where certain products like crack cocaine could be more successfully introduced, marketed and increased, followed by the promotion or otherwise (meaning elimination) of certain individuals within the various organisations. The names of a number of high-profile people within the judiciary and political circles were also bandied about, some of whom Tallis recognised as being eminently bribable. Then things took an unconventional path.

'Where's Gabriel?' It was the meaner of the two Turks, Ergul.

All eyes were on Tallis.

'My fault,' Kennedy said smoothly. 'Let me introduce you to Milton, my new second-in-command.' He glanced behind him, looking up at Tallis. They'd already arranged to give him a suitable pseudonym. He was simply known as Milton.

'That because your old one's dead?' Vasel let out a laugh, displaying an appalling set of broken and discoloured teeth.

Tallis couldn't see Kennedy's face but, from the way everyone was looking, he could picture his embarrassment and irritation.

'That's true,' Kennedy said slowly, with great precision. 'How did you find out?' The suspicion in his voice was obvious.

The Russian answered. 'We have all lost good men, one way or another,' he said, looking around the table. The

Italian nodded. 'After our last meeting one of my men was abducted. It was not good, not a clean kill,' he said, shaking his head ruefully.

'We is suffering, man,' the West Indian said. 'Nothing is cris. Yannerstan? Got a bird dog in the house, man.'

Shit, Tallis thought. The guy means an informer.

'Yeah, how else did we get busted?' Alpi burst out. He was tall, rake-thin, with twisted features.

'Tell your man to shut up, Ergul,' Vasel said, picking his teeth with a dirty finger.

Ergul, flat-faced and pudgy, did as he was told, speaking aggressively to Alpi in rapid Turkish. Only Tallis understood what was really being said. His gut felt as if it had been lanced with a laser.

Kennedy spoke, trying to restore some order. 'Gentlemen, in the circumstances, I'd like to call a sidebar.'

To Tallis's dismay, this was met with a unanimous murmur of agreement. He tried to catch Kennedy's eye as he and the other seconds-in-command were forced to file out of the room. Either Kennedy was lost in concentration or deliberately ignoring him. Perhaps he'd planned it from the beginning, Tallis thought suspiciously, outwardly playing ball, inwardly continuing his own terrorist agenda, whatever that was. Always at the back of his mind, he knew that Kennedy's success lay in his ability to deceive. If he was a master at deception, he could also be a master of disinformation.

Out in the corridor, the 'lieutenants' were shepherded into another oblong-shaped space. Formica tables, four chairs at each, the room resembled the type of enclosed and dingy place where jurors waited before selection. Nobody sat down. Everyone stood, backs to the wall, at arm's length from the man next to him. The bonhomie that had kicked off the proceedings suddenly vanished, to be replaced by stone-faced looks and hard *don't mess with me* expressions. The heat was on. Everyone felt under threat. As the newcomer, Tallis knew that he fell under most suspicion. Wasn't logical. Simply human.

Like the rest, he was wondering about what was being discussed. The Sicilian looked at his watch. The Albanian's henchman did the same. Others followed suit. Tallis didn't need to look. He had an internal and accurate sense of time, and reckoned they'd been inside alone for forty minutes. Fifteen minutes later the door opened, Rex and Darren giving the all-clear. Tallis watched the faces as they filed out. He'd expected them to be grave and stern. Only Ahmed seemed vaguely troubled, although it was difficult to detect from the calm expression on his features. The others seemed buoyant, jubilant, as though stirred to action by a great leader. Kennedy came out last of all. He too was smiling. Tallis wasn't fooled. He'd seen that strange light in his eyes before.

Suddenly he got the unholy feeling that he was stepping into a dead man's shoes.

26

AS SOON as the others left, Kennedy's demeanour changed. Gone the smile, the warm expression. Face set like weathered concrete, he told Tallis he was going to see Billy.

'What happened in there?' Tallis asked, falling into step beside him.

'Not now.' Curt, angry.

Tallis caught Kennedy's arm. 'You might have talked to Gabriel like shit, but you're not doing it with me.'

'Take your hand off me.' Kennedy's eyes flickered dangerously.

Tallis had the unpleasant sensation of feeling like he was caught in the crosshairs of an automatic weapon. In that moment he understood what Kennedy was capable of. No stretch at all to link him to Garry Morello's murder. 'Not until you tell me what went on, or am I going to contact my superiors and say you no longer wish to co-operate, that you've changed your mind?'

'Tell them what you like,' Kennedy said, bullish.

Tallis dropped his voice. 'Perhaps some of your colleagues might like to know what you're really about.'

'Fuck you,' Kennedy snarled. 'I've been saving your arse.'

'The only arse you're intent on saving is your own.'

'Get out of my way.'

'Everything all right, boss?' It was Justin. Christ, Tallis thought, how long had he been standing there, how much had he overheard?

'Fine,' Tallis answered, never taking his eyes off Kennedy.

'Everything's good.' Kennedy twitched a smile. 'Make sure we're all secure, would you?'

Justin nodded, threw a vicious glance at Tallis and lumbered back down the corridor. Tallis caught up with Kennedy, grabbed his arm again.

'I've pulled off something quite remarkable,' Kennedy spat, still visibly furious. 'It wasn't easy in there. Those blokes' default setting is suspicion. Some of them didn't care for the look of you. They wouldn't hesitate in ordering a hit. Now, with your permission, I'd like to see my son.'

Tallis released him. For reasons he didn't understand he felt quietly ashamed. 'Sure, I'll pick you up in twenty minutes.'

'Back entrance,' Kennedy stated, voice drenched with sarcasm.

'We've put Ahmed under surveillance,' Asim said.

'Good.' Tallis was standing in his kitchen, watching a spider demolishing a fly. 'What have you got on him?'

'Nothing that would stand up in court.'

It didn't sound to Tallis that they had very much at all. Not on Ahmed. Not on Kennedy.

'Two things you need to understand,' Asim said. 'In this business, terrorists have a very different timeframe to the rest of us. They play a long game.'

'They're not averse to opportunism,' Tallis pointed out. 'Change of government, appointment of a new Home Secretary, announcement of Olympics all triggered a spate of attacks.'

'Agreed, but their overall policy is one of attrition. They're marathon runners, not sprinters.'

'What's the other thing?'

'Most contact takes place with mirrors,' Asim said.

'Somebody who knows somebody who knows somebody else.' He was thinking of the Moroccan, Tardarti, again. Had he really been a contact man, a cog in the machine, or had he been more important, the facilitator who organised a campaign?

'Often making it extremely difficult to establish a concrete chain of evidence,' Asim said.

'And leaving the door wide open to Chinese whispers. How the hell do you know that the information relayed back is accurate, that it hasn't morphed into something entirely different?'

'We don't. That's why we have to check and double-check our sources. The Turkish authorities originally flagged Ahmed up to us a while ago, although, in their assessment, he didn't pose a terrorist threat at the time. We formed the same conclusion.'

'So what's changed?'

'The company Ahmed keeps. For some time he's been

regarded as a low-grade follower. He hasn't been caught with his hands in the cookie jar, but he has links to those who we suspect, at some stage, might. He's also suspected of funding certain individuals to return to both Iraq and Afghanistan to support insurgents.'

Exactly as Kennedy had stated, Tallis thought, and if Ahmed was fuelling insurgency, it explained why the Americans were sniffing around. Also explained their interest in Tardarti, with whom Kennedy suspected Ahmed had had links beyond the business of drug dealing. What it boiled down to was connections and the means to those connections, something Asim and his ilk strived for every single day. Kennedy was also in the connections game and, Tallis recognised, so was he.

'And Kennedy, is he under surveillance, too?'

'He is so you can relax for the next twenty-four hours.'

Make the most of it was what Asim meant, Tallis thought. He had no doubt that the next few days would prove to be testing ones. 'Terrific.'

'You don't sound happy.'

'Not every day you have a run-in with a crime lord.'

Asim let out a laugh. For someone with responsibility for the safety of the nation, he sounded remarkably relaxed, Tallis thought. 'Any news on the videotape sent care of a-Q?'

'Ninety-nine per cent certain it's the real deal. Usual narrative, threats of retaliation for Britain's role in Iraq and Afghanistan, decadent Western values, plus there's the additional seasonal aspect.'

'Seasonal?'

'Nothing like putting the fear of God into the general public on the run-up to Christmas.'

'Christmas? That's over two months away.'

'I can tell you're a last-minute shopper.'

Tallis let out a laugh. His Christmas-present list extended to his mother and his sister's kids. 'Surely, if al-Qaeda is in bed with a bunch of Asian gangsters, they're hardly going to warn of an attack. The tape's nothing more than a cheap publicity stunt.'

'You're having a real credibility problem with all this.' Asim's voice was ringed with concern.

'Comes back to Kennedy.'

'Still don't trust him?'

'I don't know.' At least he was being honest. In this game, trust was a rare commodity. Come to think of it, so was honesty.

'GCHQ, the government's main listening base, at Cheltenham have been monitoring Kennedy's mobile and home telephone calls for some time. Nothing untoward's been thrown up.'

'How many phones are they monitoring?' Tallis gave a snort. 'The guy could open his own Carphone Warehouse, and he uses his daughter's mobile.'

'We know,' Asim said, cool. 'Look, intelligence supplied to date has been superb. Single-handedly, he's given Organised Crime Officers details of villains responsible for money-laundering, people traffickers. I could go on, and, remember, this is all aside from the drugs busts.'

Sounded to Tallis as if Asim was backtracking. Closer to the truth, Asim couldn't afford to ignore the unverified intelligence that had landed on his desk, but Kennedy's actions seemed to speak louder than words. At this point in time, Kennedy looked clean.

'I don't doubt he's cracked the *Guinness Book of Records* for making British informer history,' Tallis said with heavy cynicism, 'but he's embarking on different territory this time.'

'We're all embarking on different territory, Paul. Frankly, with the current state of affairs, we need all the help we can get. Problem we've got is we can't watch everyone all of the time. There simply aren't the resources.'

And sometimes you have to dance with the devil, Tallis thought.

That evening he cooked steak and treated himself to a bottle of decent wine the colour of dirty crimson. He enjoyed neither and cleared it away, wishing he had a dog to feed his meal to. He would have enjoyed the companionship, too. Loneliness was not a natural state for him, although it had plenty of advantages. Life was less complicated. He could please himself.

Opening the back door, he went outside, sat on the step and looked out across the garden. For a fleeting moment he sensed he had company. He called out, thinking it was Charlie—if he was honest, hoping it was. No reply.

He got up, stalked the small perimeter, peering into bushes, expecting next-door's cat to scoot across the grass. Nothing. Must have been the wind whistling through the trees.

He retreated to the back step, the concrete cold against his rear. He felt as if he was losing his touch. He regarded himself as being good at reading situations and people, but lately he'd begun to doubt his own abilities. Even Asim had him worried. He was too much the puppet-master, which was probably why he'd chosen not to be as open with him on the phone as he should have been. On impulse, he pulled out his mobile and punched in a number. The recipient answered almost immediately.

'Hiya!'

'Hello.'

'All well?'

'Fine.'

'Good.'

Tallis cleared his throat. 'I wanted to hear your voice.'

'Is that the only reason you called?' Charlie Lavender laughed.

She had a good laugh. It was low and earthy, no staccato notes. Tallis decided to change the mood music, put it onto a more businesslike footing. 'You're aware of the latest intelligence on Kennedy?'

'That, rather than being a suspect, he's on the trail of a terrorist plot involving organised crime, yes. Not sure I exactly understand the motivation. Terrorists need nobody's help. There are enough of them, either home-grown or threatening, to pour in through our porous borders from Afghanistan, Iraq and Jordan, without having to do dodgy deals with those they consider to be infidels.'

'See your point. On the other hand, no self-respecting

organisation, al-Qaeda or otherwise, ever turned down the chance of funds or safe houses.'

'But what's in it for organised crime?'

Tallis thought about what Kennedy had said about keeping the law at arm's length. Suddenly, it began to make sense. 'Easy. As long as terrorism continues to dominate headlines, it takes a lot of heat off the Mr Bigs. While the police are searching for terrorists, they can carry on business as usual. Basically, it's in their interests for the law to be looking in the wrong direction.' No different from the Mafia. History proved that they were masters at taking advantage of political strife and instability.

'Christ, you really think so?'

'I do.'

'Let's hope Kennedy busts the plot wide open, then.'

'Yeah.' And that was the problem. Kennedy might have contacts, but could he discover and identify the players, transport routes, safe houses, cells and targets? A major problem with a terrorist outfit like al-Qaeda was its compartmentalism: one cell gets shown out and sealed off but without compromising the other cells in the structure.

'You don't sound too hopeful. Are you a pessimist, Tallis?'

'Realist,' he said. 'You?'

'Optimist, through and through.'

'Good. And on that optimistic note I'd better let you go.'

''Night, then, Tallis. Talk again soon.'

'Yeah.' Look forward to it, he thought, closing his phone.

He sat a while longer. The conversation with Lavender

had helped sharpen his focus in a surprising area. Kennedy had crept underneath his skin in a way he couldn't quite explain. Some of the time he hated the man, other times he admired him, no, felt warm towards him, moved by him. Tallis didn't believe himself to be a fool. Psychologically aware, he understood the emotional dimension, the hidden dangers, yet the image of Kennedy with his boy was impossible to erase from his mind.

Neither could he forget the power of Ergul's words to Alpi at the meeting.

You're right. He's the man who killed Tardarti.

27

TALLIS checked in with Rex first thing. He was told that Kennedy was spending the day quietly at Shakenbrook with his family but had left orders that, should Tallis call, he wished to speak to him.

'Put him on,' Tallis said, studying his nails, wondering what was going to be dropped on him this time. All thoughts of a peaceful Sunday went out into the long grass.

Kennedy's tone was immediately repentant. 'I'm sorry about yesterday. Shouldn't have spoken to you like that. I apologise unreservedly.'

'Doesn't matter. Stressful situation for both of us.'

'No, I was wrong.'

'Well, never mind. It's forgotten.'

Brief silence. Was that it, Tallis wondered, or was there more?

'There will be another meeting of the Commission in five days' time. It will take place in London, easier for some of the blokes to get there.'

Tallis felt his nerves sharpen. Why so soon? What was

going on? Was this as a result of the sidebar? 'Where exactly?'

'Won't know until the last minute. Even then the venue is likely to be changed.'

'Pity.' We could get the place bugged, he thought.

'Security,' Kennedy said, as if reading his mind. 'Naturally, I'd like you to be there.'

'That's good.' You don't have a choice, Tallis thought. He supposed it came hard for a man used to calling the shots to being on the butt end.

'Thing is, I like you, Tallis…'

'Mr Kennedy, we have a professional arrangement and—'

'Yeah, yeah, not cool, but allow an old guy a little indulgence. You're the same age as Billy, did you know that?'

'Erm…'

'He'd have been strong, like you. *Was* strong. Smart talker, too, knew his stuff. Takes after his old man in the good looks department, of course.' Kennedy let out a laugh riven with sadness. 'So proud of him, you know. Didn't tell him when I should have done.'

Tallis dug a fingernail into the soft part of his hand. He's playing you, he thought. He knows your weakness and he's going for it.

'Listen to me go on,' Kennedy said, more cheerful. 'Have a good day, Tallis. Look forward to seeing you tomorrow.'

''Bye, Johnny, and thanks.' Tallis cut the call, cursing his momentary loss of judgement. *Johnny*, indeed.

Deciding to go for a run, he changed into sweats and

trainers and went out onto the street. A British Telecom van was parked a hundred yards down the road, one bloke sitting inside reading a newspaper, the other outside studying a telegraph pole.

'Morning,' one of them said as he sped past. Seven punishing miles later they were still there as he jogged back up the road.

'Don't you blokes ever get a day off?' He grinned, pausing briefly.

'Twenty-four-seven, mate.'

Tallis met the guy's eye. Maybe, he thought, maybe not…

Tallis returned to find a blackbird flapping around in his sitting room. From the sooty marks on the furnishings, it had obviously taken a tumble down the chimney. Opening all the windows, he managed to shoo it out. The next hour was spent clearing up dirt and bird crap. In the back of his mind he remembered his late grandmother, a Croatian national, telling him that a bird in the house meant a run of bad luck. Something he definitely didn't need right now, he thought grimly.

He took a long hot shower and dressed. Starving, he cooked himself bacon and eggs for a late breakfast, eating it in silence. No radio, and definitely no television. That leaves the rest of the day to kill, he thought, washing up. Truth was, he didn't know what to do next so that, when his mobile rang shortly after noon, he picked it up with a sense of relief.

'Lunch at my place.'

'Shall I bring flowers?' Tallis said, tense.

'Lavender would be nice.' Click.

Picking up his keys, he went outside, scanning the drive. The B.T. blokes, or whoever they were, had gone. There were no familiar or unfamiliar faces. Satisfied, he climbed into the TT, reversed out onto the street and drove down to the main road, heading through Birmingham and back out towards the general direction of Coventry. Deliberately overshooting to Rugby, he doubled back, eventually pulling into the tired-looking estate and parking the car in the street some distance from the safe house. There was no sign of Lavender's Yamaha but, then, he didn't really expect to see it on show. Letting himself in, he found her standing in the kitchen. She was wearing jeans and a tight black sweater that hugged the curves of her body. Her face, again without make-up, shone with radiance. He wondered if some of it might rub off on him.

'At least the code worked even if it was a bit 007.' She beamed.

He let out a laugh. 'Thank God you came to my rescue. I was seriously thinking I'd have to do something boring like mow the lawn.'

'Glad to be of assistance,' she said, still smiling.

'What I meant—'

'Is that you're in danger of becoming an adrenalin junkie.'

Tallis flashed a grin. Had she got him here under false pretences? Did she expect him to take her in his arms? Should he? 'You dragged me all the way here to discuss my mental state?'

'I wanted to show you my holiday snaps.' She handed him a stack of photographs. The smile faded.

He shot her a puzzled look, took them. The subject in all the shots was the same: a man, medium height and build, neatly cut short fair hair, eyes blue, no particular distinguishing features, mid-thirties at a guess. Tallis ran through the photographs for a second time, paying more attention to the locations, which were familiar to him—the road opposite the clinic, streets running adjacent to the premises in Lye and Walsall, outside the greasy spoon where he'd eaten breakfast with Kennedy after Gabriel had been killed.

Charlie was studying his response intently. 'Recognise him?'

'Never seen him before in my life.'

'You should have done. It's you he's tailing.'

Tallis looked up. 'Not Kennedy?'

She shook her head. 'You're his target. He's taken photographs of you and tried to follow you back home yesterday, but your counter-surveillance routine paid off.'

Thank God it had become second nature, Tallis thought. 'Could be MI5.'

'Wouldn't waste their time.'

'Thanks.'

'What I meant…' She flashed a cheeky smile. 'They're already overstretched.'

'And unable to spare any more resources,' Tallis said soberly, remembering his conversation with Asim.

'Anyway,' she said, 'why, in heaven's name, would they be watching you? You're practically one of them.'

THE MEPHISTO THREAT

Nice of you to say so, he thought. It wasn't exactly how Sean and Roz had made him feel, he remembered. 'One of yours then?' He meant Organised Crime. He wondered if Napier or Shaw were trying to muscle their way back into the inquiry, a supremely foolish move. He put the possibility to Lavender.

'No,' she said, adamant.

Tallis raised an eyebrow.

'I've already run a check.'

He drew up a chair.

'Coffee?' she said brightly. 'I brought milk with me this time.'

He would have preferred a shot of whisky. 'Thanks,' he said.

'Any ideas?' Charlie said, flicking the kettle on.

'Some, but none fit.'

'Problem shared and all that?'

He looked up into eyes so green they dazzled him. She was always smiling, he noticed. He couldn't make out if this was part of her naturally cheerful disposition or whether it was a cover for nerves. 'Remember last time we talked?'

'And you told me about the Turkish connection.'

'Right,' he said. 'Two of those guys at the Commission, part of the so-called Turkish Mafia, recognised me as the man who killed Tardarti.'

'How the hell do you know that?'

'I speak fluent Turkish.'

'And they actually spoke in front of you?'

'In front of everyone, actually.'

The kettle flicked off. Charlie turned, hurriedly made coffee, spooning sugar into his mug.

'You remembered.' He smiled.

'It's my job to remember things.' She smiled back, the hint of a blush on her cheeks. She pulled up a chair next to him. He could feel her knee close to his, her breath on his face. She tapped the photos with a finger. 'This bloke isn't Turkish.'

'No.'

'So he's not connected to them. Next idea?'

'Could be any one of the gang members' goons or associates.'

'Think that's likely?' she said.

'Every single one of those dons, for want of a better description, believe there's a bird dog in their midst.'

'A what?' she frowned.

'In twentieth-century parlance, a receiver of stolen goods, but there's an older meaning—a watcher, an observer, somebody who lies in wait.'

'Like the old CIA expression, *We have a stranger in the house*, meaning a mole.'

CIA? Tallis thought. He immediately remembered Koroglu, the hard bastard American working alongside Ertas in Turkey. When a man grabbed your balls, you didn't forget him in a hurry. Revealing nothing, he agreed. 'Back in the 1940s it also referred to a pimp, or someone who attempts to steal a girlfriend from another man.'

'Basically, someone's onto things,' she stated. 'Makes it dangerous for Kennedy.'

Perhaps that accounted for Kennedy's bad temper the

day before. Tallis scratched his forehead. If the Americans
had tipped Asim off about Kennedy, and MI5 weren't seen
to be taking any action, had the Yanks decided to take the
law into their own hands? Or had he got it all wrong? A
part of him dearly hoped so. And that wasn't good. He told
Charlie about Kennedy speaking to the members of the
Commission alone. 'He reckons he's persuaded them that
his credibility, and mine, is unimpeachable.'

'The fact he lost one of his own men would seem to
bear that out.'

'That's what bothers me.'

She took a sip of coffee, gave him a shrewd look from
underneath a set of long dark lashes. 'You suspect
Kennedy's kicking with both feet.'

Outwardly playing the informer, supplying high-grade
information while secretly supporting terrorism, was what
Charlie meant. 'Maybe.'

'Why?'

'Search me.'

Charlie didn't say anything for a moment. 'This little
private conference he called. You have absolutely no idea
what was discussed?'

'None.'

'And they all emerged looking a damn sight happier
than when they went in?'

'Apart from Ahmed.'

Charlie gave a sigh. 'Which adds up if Kennedy's right
about his connections.' When she spoke next, there was
strain in her eyes.

'But if he isn't. If he's playing his own game, you pose a threat, and Kennedy has access to a lot of people.'

'And I won't necessarily know who to watch out for.'

Charlie picked up one of the photos. 'Maybe he's one of them.'

28

HE SHOULD have thought of it before.

After leaving Charlie, he drove to an off-duty chemist and bought a pair of disposable gloves, the type that hairdressers wore for mixing peroxide and bombers used for making bombs. Next, it was straight to Lye. Parking outside, in Kennedy's private slot, he got out of the TT and casually glanced up through a mist of falling rain to the church tower. No glint of a long-range lens. No sign of a watcher. Whoever was tailing him seemed to have taken the day of rest seriously.

As newly appointed head of security for Kennedy, he held the master keys to both sets of premises. Taking out the appropriate bunch, he let himself in. Once inside, he dropped the deadlock to prevent unwelcome guests then, pulling on the gloves, set about booting up all six computers downstairs. It took him an hour and a half to sift through the various files. Satisfied that he'd seen nothing of startling import, he went upstairs to Kennedy's office suite. Punching in the code, the door sprang open. First he turned the place over, checking drawers, dossiers, a diary.

He found a black-bound notebook with lists of names that read like a rogues' gallery. Careless, Tallis thought, or another masterstroke from the lord of misinformation? On the point of putting it away, he spotted one entry at the top of a page at the back. Underlined twice, one word, it read: *Mephisto*. What the hell did that mean? he wondered.

Careful as a bank manager, he returned everything to its rightful place. Next, he switched on Kennedy's computer. As he waited for it to boot up, he went to the window, took a look outside. Four kids were playing football in the road. An old man carrying a plastic bag was shuffling along the pavement. Other than that, it was quiet, the rain a natural deterrent.

Tallis took a seat in Kennedy's leather chair, half expecting him to walk through the door and give him a bollocking. For a moment Tallis sat there flexing his shoulders, trying to loosen his thinking and get inside the man's head, work out his motivation and if he was playing it straight. Family was all, Kennedy had said. Probably the only true words he'd ever spoken. Then why jeopardise it, Tallis thought, or did Kennedy fondly believe that when his work was done he'd be given a new identity for himself and those he loved? Aside from the inherent difficulties of the witness protection programme, there were two problems with that. No such deal had been offered, and how did you hide a man who needed twenty-four-hour specialist nursing care?

Not much of a techno-person, Tallis clicked through each application, methodically opening and checking folders, the most startling revelation the virtual absence of business data, legitimate or otherwise. Instead, the computer told its own grim story. File after file revealed downloaded reports and articles on pioneering treatment for brain-damaged victims. He felt like he was reading an obituary for someone who had not yet died. Billy's accident had nearly killed him, but it had killed a chunk of his father, too. Tallis sat back, felt sudden tension in his neck. He understood only too well Kennedy's despair. When Belle had died, something inside him had also expired.

Tallis closed down the machine, left the office, thinking he'd make the next stop the Walsall site, when, suddenly, the alarm went off. He raced downstairs. Quickly taking in the scene, he could see no signs of forced entry. The deadlock was in place, exactly as he'd left it. Through the windows everything was as before, except the old man had gone. Alarm must be on the blink, he thought, or perhaps there'd been a power surge. Not so unusual in wet and windy weather. Walking through to the tiny kitchen, he checked the box to the alarm. The time—18.34—was flashing. Tallis punched in the code to disable it and pushed it to reset. Satisfied, he made a quick tour of the offices, double-checking everything was as it should be then opened the door, locked it behind him and walked out into the rain. He was on the point of getting into the TT when he experienced a sudden rush of fear.

Next was pain. Then darkness.

He came round care of a bucket of cold water thrown into his face. The back of his skull hurt badly. He was stripped down to his boxers, his wrists and ankles roped tightly together. His feet inches from the floor, his arms were above his head and he was suspended from a large metal hook that jutted out of the ceiling. A chain ran in a Heath Robinson kind of affair from the hook to a winder and lever attached to the wall—except there was nothing eccentric or quaint about the effect on his body. The cramp in his shoulders was agonising. He felt entombed in pain.

There was no window. Four walls, brick and sweating with condensation, enclosed him in a cell measuring no more than nine by nine. A smell of mould and rot hung in the dead air.

Gasping, blinking under the brutal glare of a strip light, he thought for a terrifying moment that someone had kidnapped him and flown him back to the detention centre in Turkey, his fears unassuaged by the sight of his captors.

Ergul, the head of the Turkish Mafia and a member of the Commission, spoke first. 'You will tell us the truth,' he said darkly. 'First, we want to know how long your boss has been passing information.'

'What information?'

'Don't play games.'

'Johnny knows a lot of things.'

'So you don't deny it?'

'I do. He's no grass.'

Ergul looked at Alpi, his second-in-command, by far the more benign-looking of the two men. Alpi turned to Tallis, smiled and then from nowhere produced a length of electric cable. One sharp lash across Tallis's bare shoulders convinced him he was wrong. Six more followed.

'Guys,' he said through gritted teeth. 'You've got this all wrong. Johnny's suffered too, you know, losing one of his best men.'

Alpi exchanged dead-eyed looks with Ergul. Oh, God, Tallis thought, were they responsible for Gabriel's terrible suffering? A vision of the man's mutilated body flashed through his mind. Had Gabriel told them that Kennedy was an informer? Another vicious crack across his already bruised skin brought him rushing back to the present.

'We know,' Ergul said, putting his face close to Tallis's. Already, Tallis could feel sweat pouring from his brow, underneath his arms, in his groin. All he could do was keep talking, playing the innocent. Whatever he did, he mustn't break.

'All you know,' he said, alarmed by the pain rushing through the upper half of his body, 'is that someone's striped up your mates.'

'Johnny Kennedy,' Ergul spat.

'No.'

Alpi's fist shot out, connecting perfectly with Tallis's left eye. 'It's not true,' Tallis moaned. Another blow hit Tallis across the mouth, splitting his lip. 'You keep doing that and I won't be able to talk,' he muttered.

All at once, his world turned sideways. Alpi had worked a lever dashing him down, the side of Tallis's head taking the full force as it connected to the roughened floor, wrists and ankles burning as they strained against the rope. Roughly righting him, cranking him back up, Ergul started in again.

'You're lying.'

'If Kennedy grassed you up,' Tallis said, trying to get his breath, 'why didn't he name you? Why didn't *you* get a knock at the door?'

Another flash of pain, this time the blow aimed at his kidneys. Christ, Tallis thought, his mouth filling with bile, they weren't interested in answers. They simply wanted to use him as a punchbag for their aggression. Apart from the agonising pain, he felt his face grey and ooze with sweat.

'What's your name?' Alpi said, his voice soft and beguiling.

'Milton,' Tallis said, adopting the pseudonym he and Kennedy had devised for the meeting with the Commission.

'Your real name.'

'Milton.'

'You lie.' Alpi looked at Ergul and nodded. Fear, bright and glistening, broke out over Tallis's body. He could smell it. This time the whiplash broke his skin, the pain searing. Blood, warm and viscous, trickled down his back.

'Your name is David Miller.'

Fuck, Tallis thought. They knew about his Turkish adventure. He could just about believe word had leaked out, but how in hell's name did these two-bit psychos have that much detail about his identity? Did they have mates in the Turkish police? Then he remembered the American connection. He'd said himself that the CIA had a long history of using organised crime to further their ends. Hell, he'd even pointed out to Asim that the CIA had recruited Mafiosi to kill Castro.

'You were working for Mr Kennedy, yes?'

'No.'

'He sent you.'

'No.'

This time Tallis was dropped onto his knees. Without a word Alpi placed his bony hands either side of Tallis's shoulders and dug his fingers in deep, hitting the pressure points. Tallis twisted and gritted his teeth, almost blacking out with pain.

'He wanted you to do business with the Moroccan, Tardarti.'

'No, you have it all wrong.'

'What was it, a drug deal?'

'Yes,' Tallis moaned.

Ergul signalled to Alpi. Tallis was roughly hoisted back up. He thought his shoulders might dislocate.

'No,' Ergul spat, 'you wanted to talk about bombs.'

'Not true.'

'But something went wrong. Perhaps you were not offering enough money.'

'You're talking crap.'

'Tardarti did not trust you.'

'I never talked to Tardarti.'

'You feared he would expose your plans to fund terror-ism so you killed him.' Where the fuck did they get their information—educated guess, or wild supposition? Without warning, Tallis flashed back to the detention centre and Koroglu. *Tell him that we know he intended to meet the Moroccan. Tell him that he had already contacted him in Britain.* Even then, the Americans had already had a line going on Kennedy, but Kennedy, under his new status as an informer, was untouchable so they were using the Turkish Mafia to root out his associates. These guys weren't pissed off about a cut in their takings, he thought, looking blindly at his interrogators, because the CIA was paying them handsomely for extra-curricular services. It wasn't that outlandish. He bet a lot of shady stuff went on without the knowledge of international governments so that, in the final outcome, they could be protected from grave political consequences.

Alpi suddenly dropped the lever. This time Tallis was ready, feet hitting the floor first. Next, he was seized by both men and manhandled onto a chair. To his surprise, Alpi undid the rope binding his arms then, taking his left wrist and with one deft perfectly choreographed movement, broke the bone. So unexpected, so coldly premeditated and carried out, this time Tallis let out a scream of agony.

'If it wasn't bombs, what was it?' Alpi's words were wheedling.

'Nothing.' He felt sick. Dots were dancing before his eyes. The floor was moving, so were the walls.

'When did you plan to plant these bombs?' Ergul said, drawing up another chair, planting himself inches away from Tallis.

'I didn't.'

'Where?'

'Nowhere,' he groaned. Jesus, change the fucking record.

'London, Frankfurt, New York?'

'No…'

When Ergul gripped his injured wrist, Tallis fainted.

Tallis came to with the smell of Ergul's breath on his face, the sting of Ergul's hand across his cheek. The pain from the injuries to his body and shattered wrist was something he'd never experienced before. Had someone handed him a knife he would have cheerfully cut his own throat to escape it.

'I know nothing,' Tallis groaned, trying to set his stall out again, anything to delay the next round of torture.

'But that's not true,' Alpi said with a glittering smile. 'Johnny sent you to talk to Tardarti about bombs, yes?'

'How many more times? No.'

Ergul shook his head, pulled up a chair, his flat features level with Tallis's chin. Worryingly, he rested a podgy hand on Tallis's knee. The line of the cartilage bore a four-inch scar, the remnants of an old injury picked up during training in the army. It never gave him any trouble. Until now, he thought, bracing himself. These guys seemed to know every weakness, not just of the human body but his body.

'In our meeting with the Commission,' Ergul said, 'your boss was extremely eloquent.'

'He's an eloquent man,' Tallis said, sweating with the dread of random violence, the consequent suffering.

Ergul smiled and nodded, glad, it seemed, he'd reached consensus with his victim. 'He talked much about the threat of terrorism, the way the British government is finding more and more ways to meet the challenge…'

'More legislation, more surveillance, more sharing of

data, more crime-fighting organisations,' Tallis slipped in helpfully. He knew, at least, how Kennedy thought.

'Exactly, my friend,' Ergul said. 'More and more devious methods to restrict the powers of the ordinary citizen and damage good businessmen like ourselves,' he said, glancing up at the ever-grinning Alpi. Tallis followed his gaze and saw, with horror, that Alpi had pulled out a flick-knife. 'Which is why he asked all of us to join together, to fight fire with fire,' Ergul continued. 'I believe it is based on the old judo adage of drawing your enemy close enough so that you can throw them.'

'Makes sense,' Tallis said, hating the tremor in his voice.

Ergul grinned. 'So that he can actively aid and abet terrorism…'

'No. That's not true. You can't infer he supports terrorism simply because he wants you to unite against the law.'

'We have intelligence,' Ergul hissed.

From your paymasters, the Yanks, Tallis bet. 'Bullshit.'

'Do not pretend,' Alpi said, pointing the knife at Tallis. 'We need solid information. We need dates, times. If you continue to lie, we will cut you slowly bit by bit and mail the body parts back to your family. We could start with your cock.'

'I'm not lying,' Tallis burst out.

Slap. Tallis resisted the temptation to spit in his tormentor's eye.

'It is clever, no?' Ergul said slowly. 'To cause confusion, to distract attention, we crime lords are encouraged to take ever more risks. Your boss even suggested *we* get involved in terrorism.'

What? 'Crap. I don't believe you.' They were just shooting a line to get him to talk.

'So that while the police are hunting down terrorists,' Alpi said in a wheedling voice, 'we can continue to do business as usual.'

Tallis let out a bitter laugh. Christ, he'd said the same, almost word for bloody word, to Lavender. He thought of her lovely smile, her laughter, and the unlikelihood of ever hearing it again. 'Business as usual?' Tallis spat. 'You won't be able to shit without a licence. Those freedoms you say are being restricted will simply disappear for good. You'd be handing the government a gift, and Kennedy's much smarter than that. He'd never encourage it. He loves his family too much, his city, this country.'

Ergul grabbed Tallis's knee, dug his fingers deep into the line of the scar, twisting. In spite of the shooting fire in his joint, he slammed his head forward, smashing into Ergul's face. While Ergul shot backwards, overturning his chair, Alpi grabbed Tallis round the throat in a claw hold. Tallis tried to struggle but the more he did, the stronger Alpi's grip on his larynx. Christ, Tallis thought, with every second that passed not only was he nearer to unconsciousness but death. One extra squeeze and his larynx would break. Too long, and his brain would start to starve of oxygen. At best, he'd end up like Billy.

A terrible rattling noise issued from his throat. He made every attempt to struggle, arm flapping, bulging eyes searching frantically for the knife. One last effort, he thought, one last attempt to nail this bastard and escape the bloody jaws of death. Then he saw it: bright, glittering and seductive. One-handed, Alpi had flicked open the blade. He was swinging his knife-hand back and Tallis realised with terrible clarity that he was about to die. And what a way to go, he thought crazily, picturing the thrust and plunge and twist of the blade into the side of his neck, the rush of his blood cascading onto a floor covered with filth.

Then the door burst open.

Alpi's head exploded in a blast of bone and blood and tissue. A deathly scream ricocheted round the cell as Ergul's body received a burst of machine-gun fire. Slipping in and out of consciousness, Tallis was aware of shouted orders, of being untied, of someone taking off their shirt and covering him. Next, he was lifted carefully, gently, and taken to where the air smelt fresher. Before darkness consumed him, he imagined he was in the loving arms of a father, that he was his son.

29

'YOU'RE making good progress.'

'Who are you?' Tallis stared at the man.

'Your doctor.'

Tallis was in bed. His left hand and arm were partially encased in plaster. There was a large dressing on his back, a light bandage on one knee. He felt muzzy.

'Mr Kennedy asked me to look after you, the doctor explained with a smile that denoted he felt honoured by the request.

Tallis glanced around at the pale green walls, the French windows, orange autumn light sifting through the glass. From his bed he had a fine view of the gardens. Two wagtails shot along the lawn at speed. The clinic, Tallis thought. How useful to have a friendly quack on site who didn't ask questions. He wondered whether the man was a specialist in the treatment of bullet wounds as well as torture.

'How long have I been here?'

'Two days. We had to sedate you. Fortunately, the wrist was a clean break.'

Tallis threw back the covers, awkwardly swung his legs

round, attempting to plant both feet on the floor. He felt hollow-eyed, swathed in exhaustion. 'Where are my things?'

The doctor's expression shot through with alarm. 'Mr Tallis, I really don't think—'

'And my phone. I need my phone.'

'You really are in no state to—'

'Keys to my car.'

'I strongly advise—'

'Hell, man, at least find me a pair of shorts.'

The door swung open. 'What's all this?' Kennedy said, advancing on Tallis.

The doctor instantly paled. 'I did warn him in the strongest of terms, but he wouldn't listen.'

'It's all right, James,' Kennedy said. 'Leave this to me.'

The sight of Kennedy alone triggered a host of thoughts Tallis hadn't begun to elucidate. Ergul and Alpi were stooges for the CIA, but was there truth in their assertion?

Kennedy broke into a wide smile.

'What?' Tallis said. He felt extraordinarily agitated. Maybe they'd pumped him full of amphetamines or something. After all, Kennedy was in the right business.

'You're standing stark bollock naked looking as if you want to take the whole world on.'

'I'd like some clothes.' Tallis knew he sounded pissy.

'I'll arrange it, but first you eat and then we talk.'

'But—'

'Tallis, everyone who matters is being kept in the loop.'

'There've been no terrorist attacks?' Please, God, Tallis thought.

'We're safe for the time being.'

And you would know, Tallis thought, immediately quashing the thought. 'I still need to get up,' he insisted, feeling very unwell indeed.

'Another twenty-four hours of bed rest isn't going to make any difference to anyone other than you.'

Tallis looked into Kennedy's eyes, eyes that in some lights appeared to be without guile. He didn't know what he believed any more. Perhaps that was good. In the great scheme of things, opinions counted for little. 'How did you know where to find me?'

'My patch. My job to know.'

Wasn't a very plausible argument, Tallis thought, feeling far too muddled to debate the whys and wherefores. 'Why did you save me?'

'Because I could. Is that good enough?' Kennedy twitched a smile.

'Yeah.' Tallis smiled uncertainly. 'Thank you.'

He must have fallen asleep. When he awoke it was pitch-black. He switched on the overhead light, eyes blinking and adjusting to the shifting shadows. A set of clean clothes had been placed on the only chair in the room. Both his watch and phone had thoughtfully been left on the side-table next to the glass and jug of water. He picked up the watch: 03.43. Wincing with pain from the lacerations on his back, wrist throbbing, he gingerly slid out of bed and took the phone to the window, switching it on, wondering if he had enough battery. Sure enough, the phone bleeped into

action, notifying him that he had two missed calls, one
from Lavender, one from Asim. He played both.
Lavender's was along the lines of *Has something happened
and get in touch*. Asim's was more coded: *Trouble on the
horizon from our friends in America*. Damn right, Tallis
thought.

Four bars appeared in the right-hand side of the screen.
He had power. He had a signal. Protocol dictated he call
Asim. Instinct led him to Lavender.

'Great to hear your voice,' she said, sounding not the
least bit sleepy.

'Thought that was my line.' He smiled.

'I was told to stand down until further notice. What the
hell happened?'

Tallis told her.

'I should have followed you.' She sounded glum.

'Tail-end Charlie.' He laughed.

'Very funny.' She didn't sound amused. It was the first
time, he realised, that she'd suffered a sense of humour
failure.

'You can't track me twenty-four hours a day.' Pity, he
thought. The idea of having her near held real appeal.

'Those Turkish bastards got dangerously close to
nailing Kennedy as an informer,' she said. 'I wonder why
they didn't tell the rest of the Commission.' Because they
had bigger fish to fry, Tallis thought. 'Think they were
behind Gabriel's killing?' Lavender said.

'Beginning to look that way.' Or their American em-
ployers bore the responsibility. He hadn't told her about

Ergul and Alpi's claims of Kennedy's incitement to terrorism. Asim could pick the bones out of that one.

'So what happens next?'

'I'm going to speak to Asim, see if there's been any developments. There's another meeting of the Commission
on Friday.'

'Why?'

'Interesting, huh?'

'Yeah, but so soon.'

'Is that a problem?'

'Will you be well enough?'

'If I'm well enough to speak, I'm well enough.' He
smiled again. He really liked hearing her voice. She felt
like the only bit of sanity in a very crazy world.

'Same place, same time, then?' She laughed.

'Actually, no. We're heading down to London.'

'Great, gives me a chance to dress up.'

'Don't think they're planning a meet at a fashion house.'

'Heard the phrase when in Rome,' she joked. 'I'll stand
out like a sore thumb tricked out in leathers.'

That he very much doubted, but he saw her point. 'What
had you in mind?'

'Wait and see,' she said playfully. 'Something else.'

'Yeah?'

'The fair-haired guy.'

The bloke who'd been tailing him, he remembered.
'What about him?'

'Think he's in the mix?'

Tallis paused, trying the notion out for size. 'Either he's

with the American contingent or he's working a number all of his own.' Or maybe there are too many drugs flowing through my bloodstream, Tallis thought.

Next he called Asim, gave him the equivalent of a debrief.

'And they definitely mentioned the name David Miller?'

'That's what spooked me. I reckon Koroglu and his paymasters at the CIA recruited Alpi and Ergul to spy on Kennedy and his associates. The Americans are convinced that Kennedy is involved in terrorism.' Something, Tallis suspected, they'd long ago leaked to Asim. 'They already had a line going on him in Turkey, then I pop onto the scene, first in Turkey then here in Britain as Kennedy's right-hand man. As far as they're concerned, I'm part of the alleged plot. You mentioned we had trouble with our American friends.'

'Lots of sabre rattling. With the foreign adventure costing the American presidency dearly, the hardliners are looking for scalps.'

Everyone knew the love affair was over, Tallis thought. The Transatlantic alliance was in shreds over Iraq. The climate had changed from one of admiration to one of mutual suspicion and blame. Not even a change at the top was going to shift that kind of mindset overnight.

'We're largely applauded for our intelligence and skill at averting terrorist attacks. However, in some quarters it's believed that we're not doing a good enough job at weeding out extremists. They're particularly sensitive because, according to a declassified document, the US is under threat from a-Q sleepers.'

Tallis thought again about the fair-haired stranger who'd been tailing him. Was he back on the trail? He mentioned the prospect to Asim. 'Lavender spotted the guy and took photos. Locations include the clinic and premises at Lye and Walsall.'

'And this individual appeared on the scene before your abduction? Hell of a coincidence.'

Yeah, Tallis had to admit. Either that, or there were an awful lot of different people after him.

'Get her to email the photographs to me,' Asim said. 'As for the guy they call Koroglu…'

'So he does have a name?' Probably a Brad or a Grady, Tallis thought spitefully.

'I've got no specific intelligence of his involvement,' Asim said, neatly sidestepping the question, 'but I think it might be a sensible precaution for you to avoid home ground. Either stick with Kennedy, or use the safe house. You've spoken to Lavender?'

'Yes.'

'So she's up to speed on Friday's meeting?'

Tallis confirmed that she was.

'I'm going to put measures in place to have the main players monitored.'

'Is that a good idea? We only need someone to slip up and the whole meet's off.' And the cell, if there was one, would be shut down for ever.

Asim paused, clearly considering the merit of Tallis's argument. 'It's critical you don't let Kennedy out of sight.'

'What if we have another sidebar situation?'

'Let's hope you don't. Whatever happens, yours and Kennedy's cover must not be blown. Sure you're up to it?'

He wasn't. He needed rest and time to heal. Fortunately, only his left wrist was broken. Had it been his right, he'd have been in serious trouble—that was his gun hand. Tallis assured Asim he was good to go. 'Something else,' he began. 'When I was going through Kennedy's stuff, I found a notebook of names of contacts. Right at the back there was one name that didn't seem to fit in with the rest.'

'Yeah?'

'Mephisto.'

'That it? Mephisto, not Mephistopheles?'

'Does it make a difference?' Tallis said, scratching his head.

'Didn't you study Goethe at school?'

'Goethe?'

'Late eighteenth-, early-nineteenth-century German dramatist.'

'Grease was the closest I got to drama.' He'd heard of Goethe, of course, but to say he'd studied him at school would be a lie. Kennedy didn't strike him as being the highly educated type so what was such a reference doing in his notebook?

Asim was in full flight. 'Goethe wrote *Faust* in 1808. It was considered to be his masterpiece. Faust was a legendary magician who was said to have sold his soul to the devil. Mephisto is another name for the devil.'

Christ, Tallis thought, although, for the life of him, he couldn't see the connection. Unless…

'What about the Turks' claims about Kennedy?' Tallis said.

'About him inciting the crime lords to commit terrorist acts? Has to be bluff,' Asim said firmly. 'Every piece of intelligence has to be looked at and taken seriously,' Asim said, calm in his voice, 'but do you really think he'd be that stupid?'

'Or that devious.'

Asim said nothing for a long moment. *'If* he's about to do what they say, he's achieved something quite remarkable.'

I've pulled off something quite remarkable.

That's what Tallis was afraid of, he thought, Kennedy's words after the Commission meeting, hurtling back to haunt him.

30

THREE days to get back to physical fitness, Tallis thought, gingerly taking an electric razor to his chin, the energy required making him feel more like a return to bed.

After a careful shower and full English breakfast brought to his room by a smiling nurse, he picked up his bedside phone and asked the receptionist on the switchboard to find a number. When she called back, he asked for a line out. There followed several minutes of tedium during which he listened to numerous recorded messages until, eventually, he was connected to a human voice. Tallis stated his name and address and, explaining his query, asked for clarification. Less than forty seconds later the operator told him what he'd already suspected.

'No, sir, no British Telecom vans in your area on Sunday or, indeed, that week.'

He bet they were American intelligence officers. For all Tallis knew, with the high level of technology available, the CIA was transmitting images of him straight back to Langley for some spook to pore over and draw the wrong conclusions. To think more clearly, he decided to go out into the garden. The sky was an odd colour, pale blue with streaks of dragon-fruit red, signalling more rain. It felt good to be outside, in the fresh air, air he'd thought he'd never breathe again. Tallis walked the circuit as quickly as he could. His knee was better than it should be and, although his wrist continued to ache, the wounds on his back gave him the most trouble. He felt as if someone had taken a blowtorch or sandblaster to his skin.

Yet, in many ways, these were the least of his problems. Too much anxiety, or in his case rank fear, was not good for the human psyche. Lately, he'd had spades of it. And, on Friday, he was about to receive another helping. However professional and experienced he was, the days leading up to the all-important meeting of the Commission would be the most nerve-racking he'd ever encountered. He could take every precaution, examine every angle, bring every iota of judgement to bear, but situations like that were always volatile. Anything could happen.

Finding a bench, he sat down, tried to think logically. Kennedy had yielded diamond-quality information, had risked his life, and saved the skin of a man he barely knew. Kennedy had also arranged to have a man and his pet killed, had, on the face of it, given orders for another, an undercover police officer no less, to be dispatched. He had also continued to carry out his less than legitimate activities, admittedly with a staggering level of leeway from on high. Good guy or bad guy? Except, of course, there was no such thing. Whether villain or upstanding citizen, everyone was flawed. Simply depended on the shade and degree.

So, Tallis asked himself, was Kennedy bad enough to incite terrorism? Didn't exactly fit with his image of shopping Ahmed, the head of the Asian Mafia in Birmingham, to the authorities. Neither did it fit with Kennedy, family man, who loved his city, loved his country. That left him with his original scenario: Ergul and Alpi had been working for the Americans via the Turkish police, that's how they got their information, wrongly as it turned out, and now they were responsible for trying to forge a link between Kennedy and terrorism that didn't exist. Conclusion: Kennedy was a force for good. Trust, Tallis reckoned, was in short supply in his line of work, but sometimes you had to break the rules. On that basis, he decided to take an enormous leap of faith. It was high time he put his belief in the man who'd saved his life.

'Penny for them.'

Tallis looked up, smiled. It was the man himself. 'Thinking.'

'A very dangerous occupation.'

'How so?'

'Easy to talk yourself into a corner, or a position that isn't tenable.'

Tallis gave a tired smile, continued to look out across the grass. 'We didn't talk last night.'

'You fell asleep. Didn't see the point in disturbing you,' Kennedy said softly.

A tender image of someone watching over him flashed through Tallis's mind. He banished it immediately.

'What are we doing in London?' Tallis said.

'Speculating on who will fill Ergul's dirty boots.'

'The meeting was called before Ergul and Alpi decided to abduct me.'

'Everyone's jittery at the moment. It's right we stay in touch.'

'So there was no specific reason?'

'Like I said, we're being supportive of one another. It takes the spotlight off me,' Kennedy said, dropping his voice several semi-tones.

No, Tallis thought. It would be safer to go to ground. 'Known Kevin Napier long?'

'You ask some bloody odd questions.'

Tallis laughed. 'There's more where those came from.' Kennedy joined in.

'In answer to your question, no. Why?' Kennedy said.

'Wondered, that's all. Knew him from when I was in the army. We fought alongside each other in the first Gulf War. He was in a tank regiment.'

'Gotcha. Yeah, he mentioned something about the war. I thought maybe he'd been injured or something.'

Tallis expressed surprise. 'Why would you think that?'

'Not a chap I'd say was in the best of health. Got a sodding awful cough, for starters. Frankly, he makes the Grim Reaper look bloody gorgeous.'

Tallis let out a laugh but now that Kennedy had articulated it, he saw his observation contained the ring of truth. Napier really was very bony. The last time they'd spoken, Tallis had noticed that he'd been sweating profusely. He'd put it down to Napier's anger and passion for argument, but perhaps he was wrong. Perhaps Napier really was a sick man. Then another thought struck him: Gulf War syndrome. Tallis had been one of the lucky ones. It was believed that the illness was connected to the toxic cocktail of drugs administered to protect against biological and chemical weapons. Reports alleged that the army had used unlicensed drugs with which to vaccinate their soldiers. Except, if Napier was so ill, he felt puzzled that it hadn't come to SOCA's attention. Every operative had to undergo biannual tests with the unit psychologist. Anything untoward would have been flagged up in Napier's assessment—unless he was exceptionally skilled in the art of deception.

Time to lob another stone in the pond. 'If terrorists were to hit the city, where do you think they'd strike?'

'Bloody hell,' Kennedy said. 'I don't know. Not my field.'

'I know that,' Tallis said evenly. 'But educated guess.'

Kennedy took some time to respond. 'A landmark. Somewhere symbolic. I don't know, maybe the Mailbox. Centre of capitalism and all that. A lot of construction going on there, and it includes the BBC. Or maybe somewhere people feel safe? Who knows?' Kennedy shrugged then looked at his watch. 'I've got a problem with one of the sites. I need to make a couple of phone calls.'

'What sort of problem?'

'A leak round one of the glazing units. It's soaked into the plasterboard we supplied. Not suave in a ritzy penthouse apartment costing £500K, especially as the developers have got half of Birmingham's glitterati and local bigwigs assembling there for a beano in a few days' time.'

'Whereabouts?'

'The Rotunda,' Kennedy replied.

Tallis twisted round, skin smarting, amazed. 'You didn't tell me you did that kind of business.' A former office block in the centre of the city, the Rotunda, at eighty-one metres high, had loomed like a sleeping giant. Tallis had always thought the cylinder-shaped listed building rather ugly, probably because it had been derelict for so long. Recently, it had been transformed into a giant glass construction.

Kennedy winked and smiled. 'They don't know it's me, Johnny Kennedy, they're dealing with. If they did, they wouldn't touch me with a barge pole.'

'How did you get round that one?' Tallis imagined Kennedy dispensing very large bungs.

'The development company, I'm delighted to say, have a very ethical and principled approach to redevelopment.' He grinned.

This was even more confusing, Tallis thought, mystified. 'You're going to have to help me out.'

'If the materials required aren't too specialised, the developers like to use local suppliers, local workforce, too. Good for public relations, bringing employment to the city and feeding money back into the economy. Everyone's happy.'

'And these developers are based where?'

'Head office is in Manchester. 'Course, they've got managing directors and associates who are Birmingham based, but they don't do the essential ordering and hiring and firing. They have underlings for that.'

'So when they source suppliers, as long as the company has a respectable front, decent track record…'

'People like me can get a slice of the action.' Kennedy winked. 'By the way, I'm known as Mr Sheldon—sleight of mouth.'

Samantha's maiden name, Tallis recalled.

31

KENNEDY asked Justin to drive them to the clinic. Tallis wondered if it was for another of his shady meetings. It wasn't. Kennedy wanted to spend time with Billy. He asked Tallis to join him. 'He's not been too well,' Kennedy said. 'Chest infection.'

Tallis felt most reluctant, but didn't wish to risk either Kennedy's wrath or disapproval. Besides, he had his orders. Kennedy was under his protection.

'Fine,' Tallis said, 'Justin, you stay here until we're finished. When we leave, we'll go in my car. You take the Land Rover, act as decoy.'

'But—'

'Do as the man says,' Kennedy stepped in.

Justin, his face a mask, nodded and turned on his heel.

This time Billy was in bed, his face pale and white against the pillows, a bubbling sound emanating from his chest. An intravenous drip was attached to a vein in his arm. A facemask hung above the bed, presumably to supply oxygen, Tallis thought, looking at the cylinder nearby. Saliva dribbled out of Billy's twisted mouth. On seeing his father, recognition seemed to blossom in his all-but-dead eyes.

'Hello, my son,' Kennedy crooned, pulling up a chair and taking Billy's stiffened hand. 'It's your old dad.'

Billy groaned unintelligibly, eyes flickering, irises rolling upwards, nearly disappearing.

'That's right. Look, I've brought Tallis to see you. Remember, he came before. I told you all about him. He's come to look after us.' Kennedy turned to Tallis and nodded a smile. Tallis, acutely uncomfortable, smiled back. Kennedy leant over his son, running a hand over his boy's sweating brow. His mouth was close to Billy's face. 'Sam sends her love as always and Liss sends her big brother a kiss.'

Billy began to rock. His groans grew louder.

'See.' Kennedy turned to Tallis. 'He's smart, my boy. He knows what's going on.'

Tallis flashed another nervous smile. He didn't like hospitals at the best of times, but this whole encounter was deeply upsetting. He couldn't understand why Kennedy wanted him there. What was he trying to prove?

Kennedy turned back to Billy. 'Got a joke for you, son. He likes jokes,' Kennedy told Tallis with a grin. 'There were these three mice down the pub, having a few drinks, larging it up, showing off to each other, they were. Anyway, one mouse says to the other, "Guess what, went home last night, found this nice hunk of cheese in a mousetrap right outside my front door. Know what, I snaffled that piece of Cheddar right out of the trap, sweet as you like. How's that for skill and daring?" So this other mouse, he says, "That's nothing. I went out on the town last night, did two lines of rat poison and I'm still squeaking." Then there's this other mouse, a little mouse, and he doesn't know what to say. See, he's modest, in a different league to his mates. Know what he says, Billy?'

Billy let out a groan that sent a metallic shiver down Tallis's spine.

'The little mouse says it's time he got off home because it's his night to shag the cat.' Kennedy burst into a roar of laughter so infectious Tallis found himself laughing, too.

At last, Kennedy pulled out a handkerchief and wiped his eyes. Next he told Billy about the problem he'd had with the Rotunda. 'Made a first-class job of it,' Kennedy said. 'Same people who developed Fort Dunlop. Always said it was ripe for improvement, didn't you, son?

'Remember me telling you about all that glass,' Kennedy prattled on. 'They've got seventy-two panes on each floor, seventeen floors encircled by glass bands.'

Suddenly Billy let out an ear-shrieking howl, filling the room with what Tallis could only describe as fear. Billy's wasted body thrashed alarmingly beneath the bedclothes. Kennedy got up, caught hold of his son, yelling at Tallis to press the alarm. At once nurses and doctors were running from all directions. Tallis shrank back, heading for the corridor. Out of the corner of his eye he saw a doctor administer an injection. Thirty minutes later Kennedy emerged, the emotional drain on his features evident.

'Billy's asleep. Come on,' he said. 'I want to go home.'

* * *

The weather had taken a terrible turn. Rain pelted down like straight-edged needles, lancing the ground. Sky, dark and brooding, echoed with the sound of distant thunder. It had all the ingredients for flash floods.

Tallis and Kennedy made a dash for the TT and threw themselves inside.

'Does he often have turns like that?' Tallis said, starting the car and pulling out onto the road, almost skidding on a lake of surface water.

'Only when he's upset.'

Tallis wondered what had triggered the outburst. He was going to ask but Kennedy's posture signalled the matter closed.

Tallis decided to vary the route by driving through the urban industrial maze of Cradley and Halesowen then picking up the M5 heading south before turning off and connecting to the M42, a road sometimes beset with heavy traffic and roadworks. Within five minutes of taking off he noticed Charlie Lavender's bike aquaplaning several cars' distance away. He switched on radio communication.

'Papa, Romeo, radio check.'

'Romeo, okay over,' Charlie's voice sounded.

'Papa, okay out.'

He drove in silence for the next couple of miles. The noisy combination of wipers scooting back and forth across the windscreen, rain hammering on the roof, concentration stretched to the limit meant he could hardly hear his own thoughts. The conditions were quite atrocious. Virtually impossible to see further than the car in front,

Tallis kept his hands steady, foot off the brake, light touch on the accelerator, eye flicking to the rear-view mirror. That's when he saw it.

'Don't look round,' he told Kennedy. 'We've got company.'

Volvos didn't normally excite him, but the dark blue car behind was an S60, second generation, sporty in looks and performance with plenty of grip and terrific for long-distance journeys. The driver was white, his companion riding shotgun black. Both wore baseball caps, the brims pulled down hard over their faces. In spite of the drab light, they wore sunglasses. Tallis knew Volvos were often used as unmarked police cars. If this was one of them, they were in trouble.

Kennedy glanced into his side-mirror. 'You sure? Look like a couple of dealers to me.'

'One way to find out,' Tallis said. 'Papa to Romeo receiving,' he said, taking care not to dip his head and alert his pursuers.

'Romeo, go ahead,' Charlie's voice came back.

'We have company, over. Dark blue Volvo.'

'Roger that. Touch red.'

Tallis tapped his brake pedal lightly, the bright glow indicating not only where he was but where the Volvo was.

'Romeo received. Moving up. Registration, wait,' she said, pausing before reeling off the Volvo's number using the phonetic alphabet. 'Two males in car. Over.'

'Am going to lose them. Do not pursue.'

'Say again.'

'Do not pursue. Over.'

Pulling out abruptly into the outside lane, Tallis floored it, plumes of water spraying from the sudden increase in traction. Sure enough, the Volvo skated out, lights blazing through a shield of grey. Fuck, Tallis thought, watching as the Yamaha exploded into the outside lane, briefly fishtailing as it skidded on the wet tarmac. Lavender either hadn't heard or was disobeying orders. Memories of Roz and Sean bolted through his brain.

Rain slashed the ground, surface water everywhere. Visibility was down to no more than three hundred metres, the lights of oncoming vehicles gauzy and indistinct. Tallis urged the TT forward, ninety miles an hour, ninety-five, -six, -seven…

Still the car was in pursuit. Without indicating, Tallis changed lanes, zipping into the middle then right over to the slow lane, dropping down the gears then speeding back up, pulling out in front of a lorry on the underside, the result an angry blast of horn and air brakes.

'Sorry, mate,' Tallis muttered, pleased that his actions had mixed things up nicely, but it wasn't long before the Volvo was back in business.

'We don't want those bastards following us to Shaken-brook,' Kennedy spat, twisting round.

'Don't worry. There's only one of them,' Tallis said, glancing anxiously in his rear-view mirror for sight of Lavender. Must have fallen back, he thought, ignoring the crease of alarm in his stomach at the sight of an ambulance and two police patrol cars heading off in the opposite direction, sirens screaming. Whatever had happened, they'd lost radio contact.

He was really flying now, the speedo pushing one hundred and twenty, one hundred and twenty-three, -four, -five…

He tried every manoeuvre he knew, but nothing shook off the tail. These guys were good, professional. If anything, the weather seemed to be working in their favour. Most of the time he was driving blind. He was setting the pace. All they had to do was keep up. At junction five, Tallis veered off for Solihull, no indicator, expertly dropping down a gear, tightly controlling the car. Still the Volvo kept pace even as he headed for the town centre.

'What the fuck you doing?' Kennedy said, hands gripping his thighs.

'Trust me. This is where the fun begins.'

They were in leafy suburbia, the outer reaches of town. Without warning, Tallis stuck his foot down, cut up a Saab, whose driver promptly gave chase, the Volvo having no choice but to drop in one car behind. For two streets, the Saab drove bumper to bumper, the driver mouthing and throwing hand gestures like he had a bad case of Tourette's.

'Now we're fucked,' Kennedy said as they approached traffic lights changing to red.

'Don't think so,' Tallis said, flooring it, leaving the Saab standing then watching in horrified amazement as the Volvo pulled out, weaving in and out of oncoming traffic until it, too, was safely over the other side.

Only one ace left to play, Tallis thought, spotting a

multi-storey car park. He turned in, grabbed a ticket, went through the barrier then, feeling the muscles of his sphincter pinch, stuck his foot down, tearing up the levels, travelling helter-skelter, up three, down two, up one, the TT's tyres screaming, until finally he reversed into a space and waited. Sure enough, the Volvo showed, flying up to the next level. Out of sight, Tallis slipped out of the space and down the other side, shooting out of a cordoned-off staff exit with the same tight trajectory of a bullet from a gun.

The Volvo was nowhere to be seen.

'That's screwed them,' Kennedy growled.

Tallis hoped so, but for how long he couldn't say.

'You worried me back there,' Kennedy murmured as they were pulling into Shakenbrook.

'What, a big tough guy like you?' Tallis laughed.

'Thought you were going to lead those bastards here.'

'If they're as serious as I think, they already know where you live.'

'No way. House is in Sam's mother's maiden name.'

A bit circuitous, still traceable, Tallis thought, especially if you're the CIA. 'Whatever, I think it best we keep a low profile until the meet in London. You cool with that?'

'Suits me. The businesses can largely take care of themselves.'

'It's not just you. This includes Samantha and Melissa.'

Kennedy's nostrils pinched together. His mouth formed a frown. 'Sam won't be happy, especially with

Melissa missing school. Neither will the school, come to think of it.'

Made Tallis smile. The man who entertained no qualms about killing was reluctant to offend a head teacher. 'It would only be for a week or so, until things have died down.'

'What makes you say that?' Kennedy sounded edgy.

'What?'

'You said a week or so. You expecting something to happen?'

'I wasn't being literal,' Tallis said. 'I meant for as long as it takes.'

Once they were back home, Kennedy went upstairs to shower and change. Tallis elected to go to the control room. From there, he phoned Lavender, relief flooding through him as she picked up the call.

'You're all right?'

'Soaked through but safe.'

'Christ, you had me worried.'

'Didn't know you cared.'

Tallis swallowed. 'I—'

'Who were those guys?' Lavender scooted in, much to Tallis's relief.

'No idea.' The Yanks again, he thought.

'I've run a vehicle check and come up empty.'

That could mean one of two things. Either they were using false plates or fake vehicle licensing papers. 'Managed to shake them off for now, at least.'

'Are you going to tell Asim?'

'When I get around to it.' He didn't want to go running to the boss every time something out of the ordinary took place. He informed Lavender that he intended for them to lie low until the trip to London, that he would call soon.

'Think something big is about to go down?'

'According to Kennedy, no.'

'You don't believe him?'

'It's not that. I'm simply not sure how much he can control events, how much power he actually has.'

'Thank God, at least, Ahmed's under surveillance.'

Tallis murmured agreement and cut the call. Afterwards, he stood for an hour checking and rechecking the screens, half expecting to pick up their pursuers on one of the monitors. Giving orders to one of Kennedy's men to watch for intruders, he returned upstairs to the drawing room, where he found Samantha looking out of the window. She turned as he entered, and smiled. Beneath the perma-tan he thought she looked pale. He knew better than to say so. Good-looking women were most easily offended.

'You won't see much out there,' he commented. 'Weather's terrible.'

'I like rain. Makes me feel protected.'

He inclined his head. 'You don't feel safe?'

'Only when you're around.'

Her eyes met his. In other circumstances, he might have viewed it as the beginning of a chat-up line. In other circumstances, he might have been tempted to take advantage. For a brief moment he felt entirely thrown by her blue-eyed gaze. It was then that he wondered how much she knew of Kennedy's defection, how much or, more likely, how little she'd been consulted, or her feelings been considered, how much she recognised the dangers not simply for herself but for her daughter. Kennedy, alone, had been the main man, Sam and Melissa relegated to the role of bit-players, subordinates in a deadly and dangerous game.

'Well, you're stuck with me, then.' He laughed lightly, breaking the tension.

'Drink?' She smiled.

'Tonic water would be good.'

'Ice and slice?'

'Why not?' Thank God for small, familiar rituals, he thought, watching her open the drinks cabinet. The moment had obviously passed.

'You realise,' she said, handing him the glass, 'the difference you've made to our lives.' Oh, dear, Tallis thought, he'd been hopelessly over-optimistic. 'Johnny's in particular,' she continued, sitting down, indicating for Tallis to join her. 'Before you came along, he was much more closed down about Billy. It was as if his son was a taboo subject. He didn't welcome discussion. He's much more relaxed now, thanks to you.'

Tallis was about to protest, but Samantha was in full flow. 'You see, Johnny and Billy hadn't always got on.'

'No?' This was interesting, Tallis thought, settling back into the sofa.

'Billy had experienced problems trying to find work. He reckoned he was dismissed from at least two architects' offices when they discovered who his father was and got wind of his criminal connections. For a while nobody would touch him. It led to a lot of argument. Of course, I was stuck in the middle.'

'Never an easy place to be,' Tallis said, mind tumbling. Were Kennedy's strong feelings for his son based on guilt?

'Things eventually began to work themselves out when Johnny was inside and then there was the accident.'

'I heard Johnny took it very badly.'

'What father wouldn't?' Samantha said. 'It was a difficult and worrying period for all of us. I'd never seen my husband like it before. He was absolutely inconsolable. God help me, but at the time I wondered whether it would have been almost better had Billy died.'

Tallis sipped his drink. He knew exactly what she meant. 'Who arranged for Billy's care? Must have been tricky with Johnny inside.'

'I did. Don't think I slept for the first week, but I knew it was vital to act quickly and get the best treatment money could buy. It's what Johnny would have wanted, what he would have done. He always wanted the best for Billy.' To the exclusion of everyone else, even his own wife and daughter? Tallis wondered. 'Strange really, I feel guilty for all those bad feelings I had at the time, for feeling so hopeless. I'm glad Billy's still with us. It's somehow given Johnny the chance to catch up for the years he was inside, to make amends, I suppose,' she said uncertainly, glancing away. 'He really is a terrific father,' she said, turning back towards him, bringing her little finger to her mouth and biting the corner.

'You don't need to persuade me. I've seen how he is with Billy. And Melissa,' he added hastily.

She flashed a grateful smile. 'With you here, like I said, he's much more comfortable, more at ease.'

'It's very kind of you, but you credit me with too much. I can think of a far more credible reason.'

Samantha's mouth fell slightly open. Her eyebrows formed little arrowheads. It was as if she'd failed to persuade him of something she needed convincing of herself.

'Time,' Tallis said.

'Talking of which,' Kennedy said, his footfall soft on the thick carpet, 'isn't it about time we ate? I'm starving.'

Tallis glanced at Samantha, saw the colour drain from her face. For a taboo that was supposed to have been broken, she was immensely cagey.

Dinner was convivial enough. There was no business talk. Tallis felt grateful. While it was important to stay focused, to be utterly prepared for the critically important meeting on Friday, it was equally important to keep Kennedy calm. The conversation revolved around Melissa, Kennedy's love of football, countries he'd like to visit, including Croatia. This was Tallis's cue for talking about his grandmother's homeland. When Samantha briefly left the room, Tallis took the opportunity to ask Kennedy if he was all right with the current arrangements.

'Sure,' Kennedy said. 'Everything's just cool.'

Good, Tallis thought.

It was after midnight. Tallis was sitting in the summer-house, the only place as far as he could deduce that was consistently and reliably bug-proof. He was talking on the phone to Lavender. He'd told her about Billy's dramatic turn in the hospital and how the doctors had been forced to sedate him. He also told her about his hunch. Lavender seemed unimpressed.

'You don't think Billy's key?' he said, at last.

'No, I don't.'

Tallis let out a sigh. Maybe he'd got it wrong. His gut feeling was strong yet entirely inexplicable. He couldn't rule out the simple fact that his feelings were misplaced. That's what happened when you entered the sphere of a man like Kennedy. 'All right, I bow to your superior judgement.'

'Thank God for that. I was beginning to wonder what tale I was going to have to spin to explain your latest line of thinking.'

'So your feelings weren't entirely altruistic?'

'Let's leave my feelings out of this,' she said, a playful note in her voice.

'Lavender, are you flirting with me?'

'Would you like me to?'

He looked around him, peered out into the darkness. What kind of a question was that? Funnily enough, when Belle had been alive, he'd always been up for a bit of flir-tation because it had meant nothing to him. He'd already

THE MEPHISTO THREAT

got the woman of his dreams. And now? He couldn't deny he'd entertained the odd fantasy about Lavender, clothes on, clothes off. 'I guess I wouldn't say no.'

'Good. I'll remember that next time we talk.' And then she was gone.

32

TALLIS spent the following day running maintenance checks on the vehicles and supervising the security arrangements for Samantha and Melissa. He was glad of the distraction—it helped control the mounting tension. Rex was given strict orders to have the control room manned at all times. Anything worrying and he was to report directly back to Tallis. Justin, meanwhile, was tasked with running the unit in Walsall. To Tallis's surprise, he seemed quite happy with the arrangement. He wondered what Kennedy had promised him by way of a sweetener.

It was agreed that Tallis, suitably loaded up with painkillers, would drive Kennedy in the Vanquish, both the Land Rover and TT used as decoys in case they had company. Tallis made arrangements for the TT to be dropped back at his place afterwards to further confuse an enemy. According to Kennedy, the meeting was to take place in London at noon, the final destination to be agreed at the last moment.

'Where do you think it will take place?' Tallis asked Kennedy.

'A sparsely populated location.'

'Bit difficult seeing as we're heading for the capital. Who makes the final decision?'

'Take it in turns. We're a democratic lot, you know.' Kennedy smiled obliquely.

'I'd love to say I believe you. Whose turn this time?'

'Ahmed's.'

Oh, Tallis thought, relieved that Ahmed was being watched by MI5.

That evening Tallis retired to bed early, not that he expected to sleep. There were too many variables, too much at stake. The grave possibility that word of Kennedy's betrayal had been leaked continued to plague him.

He was housed in one of the guest rooms in the west wing, the east reserved for what Kennedy called his staff. The en suite bathroom alone was the size of Tallis's bedroom in the bungalow. It was agreed that they'd leave around 8:15 a.m., after the decoys had gone their separate ways. After checking his room for any listening devices, Tallis phoned Lavender.

'Hope you've got your finest haute couture at the ready.'

'And stilettos suitably sharpened.'

He wondered what her legs were like. So far he'd only ever seen her in jeans and leathers. 'Nervous?'

'Should I be?'

'Probably.' No point in lying.

'Let's say I've a healthy respect for our enemies.' Good answer, he thought. 'Are you going to be fit enough to drive?' she asked.

'I've got enough medication to fell a rhino.'

'Will you be clear-headed enough?' Lavender's voice was shot through with alarm.

'Don't worry. The doc's come up with a suitable cocktail. Might turn me into a junkie but that's another story.'

'What are you driving?'

Tallis told her.

'If it's good enough for 007, I guess it's good enough for you.' She laughed. 'Does it come complete with rocket launchers and ejector seats?'

'If only. Think you'll be able to keep up?'

'Piece of cake.'

'What the hell are you driving? Didn't think the budget extended to Lamborghini.'

'Depends whose budget we're talking about.'

'Oh, yeah, meaning?'

'Wait and see.'

'God, you're infuriating.' He laughed.

'Infuriating and conscientious. After your call, I spent some time checking old information.'

'Uh-huh?'

'At the time of the accident, Billy Kennedy was taking heavy-duty anti-depressants.'

'How did you find that out?'

'I have my ways,' Charlie said, mysteriously.

Tallis considered Charlie's news. 'You think he really stepped in front of the car deliberately?'

'Wouldn't like to say. It could be that he was so doped up he wasn't concentrating.'

'Yeah, that might explain it.'

'It doesn't really change things, does it?'

'I guess not.' Except it made him wonder quite how much Billy looked forward to those visits from his father.

The Vanquish was a joy to drive once they hit the motorway. Tallis found the six-speed Formula 1 style paddle-shift gearbox confounding to start with until Kennedy talked him into switching the gearbox to automatic mode.

'Only until we hit major tarmac,' he explained.

Ever watchful, Tallis saw no sign of a tail. Neither did he spot Lavender, which was more disappointing than worrying. The ride and handling was so superb he fancied showing off a bit. They were moving from the M42 onto the 6 when Tallis caught sight of a sparkling red Ferrari Spider moving from the middle lane into the outside lane. In four and a half seconds it was hot on his rear, the noise it made loud enough to blow his pants off.

'Fuck me.' He grinned.

'Problem?' Kennedy said.

Tallis shook his head. 'Back-up.'

For the next ten miles they played cat and mouse, Lavender proving to be as tenacious as his next-door neighbour's moggy. When a police car homed into view on the opposite carriageway Tallis immediately killed his speed, Lavender, pulling over into the middle lane, following suit.

'Thank Christ for that,' Kennedy said. 'What's she like, your girl?'

'She's not my girl.'

'You fancy the pants off her.'

'Don't be soft.' Tallis felt the skin on his neck flush.

'It's all right. You're allowed.'

'What the hell does that mean?'

'All I'm saying,' Kennedy said with a big sigh, 'is that in your line of work you have to take your fun where you can find it.'

'That right?' Tallis felt a sudden cold and unaccountable rush of anger. How dare this bloody man give him life lessons?

They didn't speak again until they joined the M1. Kennedy broke the silence. 'Those guys yesterday. I've done some asking around. So far come up empty. Leads me to think it was you they were after.'

'Yeah?'

'I guess a bloke like you has his fair share of enemies.'

'None that I'm aware of.' Who was he kidding?

Kennedy looked out of the window. 'I envy you.'

Tallis glanced across. There was strain in his voice. For the first time Tallis noticed grey-blue shadows underneath Kennedy's eyes. He seemed to be fighting an urge to say something momentous. 'You all right, Johnny?'

Kennedy didn't answer.

'Johnny?'

'Do you find it difficult?' Kennedy blurted out.

'What?'

'Doing this.'

'Driving the Aston, looking after you, track—?'

'The deception, pretending you're someone you're not, becoming a bad guy to defeat people like me.'

'Believe me, I'm having difficulty understanding who the bad guys are exactly.' Tallis laughed lightly, his attempt at humour falling on stony ground judging by the hunched set of Kennedy's shoulders. Tallis continued in a more serious vein. 'Deception is no more than playing a part, falling into a role, something we all do. You, of all people, understand that.'

'Oh, I do. But I never said it was easy.'

Tallis had to think about that. He was at ease with what he was doing, yes, and lying came naturally to him. Was that the same thing? 'As for wanting to defeat people like you— your words, not mine,' he added, 'it's not what I'm about.'

'No?'

'You're part of a much bigger picture.'

'Defence of the realm and all that,' Kennedy said.

'Yeah, if you like. We're in this together.'

'And when it's all over?'

I go back to my life and you go to God knows where. 'Step at a time, Johnny.'

Kennedy's mobile rang as they passed the turning for Milton Keynes. From the sound of it, Tallis thought the caller was Ahmed, or at least one of Ahmed's men, that there was a change of plan. Kennedy was clipped and precise. 'Yes, got that,' he said, glancing at his watch. 'I'll see you there.'

Kennedy closed his phone. 'We're to drive to Bedford. There's a farm not far from Sandy.'

Where the Headquarters of the Royal Society for the Protection of Birds was located, Tallis thought, remember-

ing a school trip there a long time ago. The RSPB, a grand
lodge in a Tudor style of yellow brick, was set in rolling
countryside. Glancing in the mirror, he saw the Spider two
cars behind. Kennedy followed his gaze. 'She won't be
able to follow. We're to meet at a drop-point, a lay-by concealed by trees. From there we'll travel in a number of 4x4s
to the farm.'

Tallis didn't like it. 'You OK with that?'

'Sure.'

Whatever he thought of Kennedy, he had to admit the
man had balls. Tallis alerted Lavender. 'Papa to Romeo receiving?'

'Romeo, go ahead.'

He told her of the change of plan and the fact that she'd
have to drop back and drop out.

'Say again.'

Tallis repeated the message. 'And no breaking orders
this time,' he added sternly.

'Roger that.'

Didn't sound happy, Tallis thought. He turned to
Kennedy. 'Looks as if your tip about the type of possible
location was spot on.'

After being frisked by Ahmed's men, they shared a bumpy
ride up a narrow farm track with Steve, the cannabis
importer from Manchester, and his heavy.

'You heard about Ergul?' Steve said, his pale complex-
ion the colour of congealed lamb fat.

'Bad business,' Kennedy said, shaking his head. Tallis

looked straight ahead, pleased that sunglasses were de rigueur for a second in command. 'Think it's an inside job?' Kennedy continued.

'Hard to say. I know we've had some problems but this feels different.'

'I agree. Nobody's had the balls yet to knock off a capo.'

'You and your Mafia slang.' Steve grinned.

'Born in the wrong country.' Kennedy let out a laugh.

'Wrong century, more like.'

Tallis looked out of the window at the changing land-scape. Having skirted the river Ouse, they were climbing steadily upwards, heading north, pleasant countryside replaced by more desolate-looking scenery. At last the farmhouse, or what was left of it, came into view. It was surrounded by broken-down caravans, old cars, sheds and rubbish piled high. As they pulled into a yard, Tallis saw three other 4x4s already parked. Ahmed came out of the front door and greeted Kennedy with a smile that was both warm and deferential.

'Mr Wo sends his apologies. He has suffered a close bereavement.'

'Sorry to hear that,' Kennedy said. 'The others were able to make it?'

'All apart from our Turkish friends.' Ahmed's dark eyes glittered.

'You know who's taking Ergul's place?'

'Rumoured to be Erol.'

Kennedy nodded sagely.

Then Ahmed's gaze turned to Tallis. 'You've been injured, I see.'

'Yes.'

'My fault.' Kennedy laughed. 'Bit of sparring that got out of hand.'

Ahmed nodded, eyes unsmiling. 'For reasons that will be made clear, Johnny, we thought it best to confine all talk to ourselves. Your man may wait with the others.'

Shit, were they being deliberately split up? Tallis thought. All his worst fears came into the sharpest of focus. This was exactly the type of variable that had worried the life out of him. Somebody somewhere had got wind of Ergul and Alpi's suspicions, and confirmation of Kennedy's betrayal. No doubt about it, they were both doomed, caught in a trap, the end of the road. From the expression on Kennedy's face he thought the same.

'Is this really necessary?' Kennedy said, glancing at Tallis, flashing a nervous smile.

Ahmed's gaze was unswerving. 'It is.'

Tallis looked around him. He was unarmed. He had one wrist in a cast. There were two other men apart from Ahmed. He could probably take them down, but that left whoever else was in the house. Perhaps Asim's operatives were nearby, not that he could see them. Seconds passed then he caught the burble of low voices coming from a nearby barn, a brief laugh, the comforting sound of human voices.

'You'll find refreshments in there,' Ahmed said, signalling to one of his men to escort Tallis out of earshot. With a brief backward glance at Kennedy, he made his way slowly in the direction of the noise. As soon as he entered he smiled to himself. Here we go again, he thought. With luck, the only danger facing him was boredom.

As he'd thought, same old faces, same damn routine. Only change was the environment. The barn smelt of straw and dried-on cow shit. Wind whistled through the thinly plastered walls. A wooden refectory table laden with food and drink butted up against the far wall.

Most 'lieutenants' milled about in a desultory fashion, some helping themselves to food and drink. Tallis exchanged greetings with the Sicilian he recognised from last time, studiously avoided eye contact with the Albanian and Russian contingent and nodded politely to a Bristolian Yardie. Pouring himself orange juice, he decided to try and talk to Ahmed's right-hand man, a short, stocky bloke with bent features. Didn't get far. As soon as Tallis opened his mouth, he was thrown a glare as devastating as a flame-thrower. He'd be about as much use as an a-Q operative with amnesia, Tallis thought, neatly sidestepping him and helping himself to a plate of samosas. He ended up hovering on the periphery of a conversation between the Sicilian and the dreadlocked Yardie about the cost-effectiveness of crack as opposed to straight cocaine.

'Ting is, you get fifty lines from an ounce of coke, almost eight times that in rocks of crack,' the Yardie said. 'At home we supplies the smackheads with free crack to get 'em hooked.'

Not forgetting the prostitutes, Tallis thought. Acting as a stimulant, it meant they could work for longer hours and, unlike in the case of heroin, there were no obvious off-putting physical symptoms, like atrocious skin. With its highly addictive qualities, it really was becoming a scourge, and the Yardies in Bristol and the rest of the United Kingdom were raking it in.

The meeting lasted a little short of five long hours, the bosses emerging into the open with much backslapping and fond farewells. Ahmed remained inscrutable as ever. Kennedy, Tallis noticed, was also giving nothing away. Just going through all the genial motions, making the right noises, pressing the buttons. Twenty-three minutes later, they were back in the Aston. Lavender, parked up near the junction to the motorway, picked up the tail as they headed for home.

'Well?' Tallis said as soon as they were back in the car. He noticed that Kennedy's breath smelt of alcohol, his clothes of cigars.

Kennedy shook his head as if he had a fly buzzing in his ear. He asked Tallis to pull over and told him to check the car for listening devices. Tallis did. There were none. Back in the car again, he asked Kennedy what had trans-pired. Kennedy glanced at his watch.

'I need to talk to your man and soon. We've got roughly forty-eight hours to avert the biggest bomb attack Bir-mingham has ever seen.'

33

AFTER a brisk change of plan and direction, Tallis drove Kennedy to a pretty guesthouse, with leaded panes of glass and hanging baskets, in the original part of the old coaching town of Hatfield. Tallis got the impression that the 'No Vacancies' sign in the window was down to there being no guests rather than a surfeit of them. A homely looking middle-aged woman with greying blonde hair showed them to their room, a welcome speech on her lips, ruthless intelligence in her eyes.

Asim was waiting for them, as planned. He was sitting in the corner of a room decked out in chintz and old furnishings. Spread out on a huge double bed, with three pillows leaning in a straight line across the headboard, were several maps of Birmingham. Asim looked tired, Tallis thought, spotting the dark shadows underneath eyes that usually sparkled with vitality. The shirt he wore looked a day old and lacked its customary crisp creases. This was a man under pressure.

With no smiles, no handshakes, they got straight to the matter in hand.

'The bombings are scheduled to take place on Monday,' Kennedy announced.

'Plural?' Asim said.

Kennedy nodded gravely. 'The first is scheduled to go off at eleven in the morning in the centre of the Mailbox—' pointing to the map '—the second five minutes later at New Street Station, the third,' he said, pointing to the Bull Ring Shopping Centre, 'here. Five minutes after that, care of a paramedic attending the scene, the next bomb blast.'

'What?' Tallis said, aghast.

'Inventive, isn't it?' Kennedy issued a cold smile.

Cowardly was nearer the mark, Tallis thought with a chill. Christ, how many people would be slaughtered? How many maimed and crippled for life? 'A massive bombing campaign like that requires sophisticated planning. Where did the explosives come from?'

Kennedy shrugged. 'I don't know.'

Why not? Tallis thought.

'We are talking explosives, aren't we?' Asim said, a hawkish expression in his eyes. 'This isn't some form of dirty bomb?'

'No,' Kennedy answered firmly, 'Ammonium nitrate.'

A *good for cities* bomb favoured by the IRA, Tallis recalled, its main advantage that it could be driven hundreds of miles without the risk of detonation.

'Method of delivery?' Asim said.

'Suicide bombers, except, in addition, at the Bull Ring they plan to use one of those street-cleaning machines as camouflage.'

Tallis immediately thought of the several bombers waiting for the signal. He was thinking in terms of cells, of sleepers, each individual assigned a specific role. He thought also of those past their usefulness ready to blend anonymously back into society again once the job was done.

Asim nodded, didn't flinch a muscle. 'The bombers, are they already in the country?'

'Yes.'

How? Tallis thought. Which routes?

'Recognise any of these faces?' Asim said, producing a set of surveillance photographs.

Kennedy stared, scratched his jaw. 'No,' he said slowly.

'Sure?'

'Yes.'

'For fuck's sake,' Tallis railed, 'we need concrete, verifiable evid—'

'Addresses?' Asim said, shooting Tallis a back-off look.

Kennedy gave Tallis a long, slow stare.

'Johnny,' Asim said, his voice an order, forcing Kennedy to drop his gaze and oblige.

'Thing is,' Kennedy said, 'it's not only Birmingham they plan to hit.'

Asim's eyes narrowed to two thin straight incisions. 'What? You never said that.'

'The Turks are also involved. That bloke, Tardarti...'

'What about him?' Tallis said.

'It turns out he was the mediator. He had links to both Ahmed *and* Ergul.'

That turns everything upside down, Tallis thought. So Ergul was trying to frame Kennedy to cover his own duplicitous tracks. Rather than the other way round, Ergul and Alpi had been playing a clever game with the Americans.

'It's quite simple,' Kennedy said in answer to Tallis's stunned look. 'Britain is perceived to be drifting by a significant section of the Muslim community. There's a fear of further national, political and moral decline. A small, marginalised minority welcome the destruction of Western values.'

'Yeah, yeah,' Tallis said, having heard it all before. 'They want to bounce us back to the seventh century.'

Asim let out an irritated laugh. 'Please, we don't have time for this.'

'Well, you should,' Kennedy barked. 'You might learn something.'

Tallis glanced at Asim. He'd never seen the guy put in his place before, still less by a former top villain. Asim wearily signalled for Kennedy to continue.

'You've also got a general population who feel oppressed by an increasingly prescriptive and dictatorial and isolated government…'

'That's only your take,' Asim said, a surly note in his voice. 'You're not telling me that disaffected voters would like the implementation of Sharia law?'

'Agreed, but what you have to admit is that while you guys are running around like demented football hooligans, a power vacuum is opening up.'

'Step into the gap, organised crime,' Tallis said.

'Providing an opportunity for both terrorism and criminals to prosper in a joint, mutually acceptable venture,' Kennedy finished with a dry smile.

'Most illuminating,' Asim said, visibly rattled. 'But where's the second hit?'

'Manchester. I don't know the location. It's scheduled for Tuesday.'

'How many?'

'One, as far as I know. Presumably, it will prove more tricky as the whole nation will be on high alert.'

'The new Turkish kid on the block, rumoured to take Ergul's place, is a guy called Erol,' Tallis told Asim. 'Worth tracking him down.' Folding his arms, Tallis turned back to Kennedy. 'And Ahmed gave you this juicy information in front of all the other blokes?'

'No.'

'So it was one mate to another, man to man, on the quiet?' He tried very hard to keep any hint of suspicion or sarcasm out of his voice. It was really, really important he got the facts straight in his mind.

'We have a close working relationship,' Kennedy said, icy.

'Close? He's taking one hell of a risk by shooting his mouth off to you.'

'He trusts me.' Kennedy's eyes flickered. 'He didn't want me or my family getting hurt.'

'He warned you?'

'Yes.'

'And there's me thinking there was little or no honour among thieves.'

'What the fuck do you mean?' Kennedy said, testy.

'I mean that when I was being interrogated by those two Turkish goons, they had a different tale to tell.'

Tallis felt Asim's eyes bore into the side of his face. Screw that, he thought. He'd made a decision to trust Johnny, to put his faith in him. Something about Johnny's story was off, and even though he had no evidence to support it, he was seriously beginning to think that his trust was misplaced. 'They said you were inciting the rest of the bosses to violence, to terrorism to be precise...'

'Bollocks.'

'Or were you intending to provoke hostility between them,' Tallis needled, ' to trigger a turf war and provide a nice big cloak for terrorist attacks?'

'You going to let him talk to me like that?' Kennedy snarled, looking at Asim.

'And judging by that hashed-up piece of Western philosophy you just treated us to thirty seconds ago,' Tallis continued, unappeased, 'I'm inclin—'

'Right,' Asim said. 'Paul, we'll be taking over from now. Your part in the operation's finished.'

'But—'

'We need to close the net on Ahmed and bring him and his co-conspirators in.' Don't call us—we'll call you, Tallis thought bitterly. He found himself identifying with Shaw and Napier. Now he knew how they must have felt after being so unceremoniously axed from the operation. He had images of people being picked up at airport terminals and on motorways, arrested at their places of work, offices and garages searched, computers seized. It would probably all be carried out with a minimum of fuss, the public unaware that yet another attempt at terrorism had been foiled. Asim continued speaking. 'As for you, Mr Kennedy, we'll make suitable arrangements for you and your family to go into hiding.'

'What about my son?'

'We can take care of him.'

'But—'

'We don't have much time,' Asim said, brusque.

'What if I don't want to go?' There was a glint in Kennedy's eyes, belligerence in his voice.

'Johnny,' Tallis said. 'You'd be a fool.'

'What's it to you? You don't believe me, anyway.' Kennedy was white with anger. His eyes burnt with reproach and hurt.

As Tallis looked into the older man's eyes he felt unaccountably small for doubting him, and immediately regretted his outburst. 'It's not that,' Tallis said gently. 'I'm paid to look at alternatives, that's all.'

'Not any more, son.' Kennedy flicked a cynical smile. 'This bloke…' he gestured towards Asim '…has just given you the chop.'

34

BEFORE he left, Kennedy offered him a job. 'I need protection. You can give it.' Tallis refused. Kennedy begged.

'Sorry,' Tallis said, handing him back the keys to the Aston and patting him once on the shoulder. 'Good luck, Johnny. It's been good knowing you.'

He turned on his heel and walked down the stairs and out of the guesthouse, the middle-aged woman nodding at him briefly in the hall before he made his final exit. For a moment he stood alone on the pavement, rootless. The sky was the colour of chalk dust, the day losing light. The mission was over, he told himself. The informer had finally delivered and was about to fly. Unprofessional of him, but even now, and in spite of all, Tallis knew that he would miss Kennedy. A flash of car headlights caught his attention. It was Lavender, parked opposite, a little way down the road.

'Want a lift?'

He smiled warmly and crossed over, slid into the seat beside her. 'Nice,' he said, admiring her suit, which was white and hand-stitched at the collar. Legs, long and lean in her heels, were fabulous. His eyes travelled to her face. Her hair was tied back. She was wearing earrings—gold oblong-shaped with a single diamond. Her perfume filled the car. It smelt expensive. For the second time since he'd met her, she was wearing make-up and looked terrific, more womanly than before. 'You look like a suave city executive.'

'I nearly died when I heard we were diverted to that farm. Luckily, I had a change of clothes in the back.'

'You what?' Tallis said, in amazement.

'Parked a mile down the road, changed and hiked the rest of the way in my jeans and wellies.'

'Bloody hell, Lavender, do you never do as you're told?' She threw her head back, the laugh issuing from her mouth drowned out by the engine's roar. He couldn't help but laugh, too.

'That's better. You looked absolutely shattered standing there on the street.'

'Probably because I haven't had more than a few hours' sleep in the past two weeks.'

'I didn't mean like that,' she said, a serious note creeping into her voice. 'You looked lost, somehow, bereft.'

'Stop, you'll have me crying in a minute.' He flicked a smile.

She flashed him a grin that managed to be both cheeky and admonishing. 'You always so flippant?'

'Only when I'm in the company of beautiful women.'

'Smoothie,' she said laughingly, a pink glow cresting the top of her cheekbones. In profile, she had great bone structure, Tallis thought. For no joined-up reason he wished he hadn't eaten the samosas on offer. He reckoned his breath reeked of garlic. 'So where were you exactly?' he said.

'At the foot of a hedge about four hundred metres away.'

'You saw the players?'

'Uh-huh.'

'Including Ahmed and Kennedy?'

'Sitting at opposite ends of the table.'

Not so close, then. 'Did you see them confer in private?' he said, his eyes never leaving her face.

'They wandered off to another room for a couple of minutes.'

'That all?' Was it enough? he thought.

'I'd say so. Why?'

Tallis told her, watched as her eyes widened. 'Christ, tell me these maniacs are going to be picked up.'

Tallis confirmed that they were.

'And Kennedy?'

'He's supposed to go into hiding with his family but he's resisting tooth and nail.' He wondered what would happen to Kennedy's boys—Justin, and Rex and Pat, and the others.

'Why?' she said, incredulous.

It was a good question. 'Search me. He's a dead man if he doesn't.'

'Talking of dead men, you still think Kennedy played no part in your friend Morello's murder?'

'I don't see how. Kennedy had enough going on without ordering hits on investigative journalists.' He briefly wondered whether Crow had managed to find out the answers to some of his more off-the-wall questions. He imagined her leaving message after message on his answering-machine at home. Then another thought crossed his mind. Was it safe to return? What about the men who'd followed him, the tall, fair-haired guy?

'You hungry?' she said, puncturing his thoughts.

'Ravenous.'

'Good. There's a place I know en route.'

It turned out to be a restaurant with rooms off the beaten track near the town of Northampton. He liked the place on sight. The bar was modern, the seating area rustic with lots of wood, low lighting and squashy leather sofas and chairs. In one corner was a baby grand piano with a young musician, a good-looking, blond-haired bloke, accompanying a dark-haired girl perched on a bar stool, singing a medley of old jazz numbers. The adjoining dining room flickered with candlelight and tables buzzed with chatter and conversation. Front of house was run by a shiny-eyed Polish girl. She asked if they were dining.

'Haven't booked, I'm afraid,' Lavender said. 'Could you squeeze us in?'

'Sure. Would you like a drink at the bar first?'

Lavender looked at Tallis. 'Great idea,' he said. The cocktail of painkillers was starting to wear off. Given a choice, he preferred a pint of beer to its chemical counterpart. They ordered drinks and took them to a corner table.

'How's the wrist?' Lavender said, taking a sip of wine, Argentinean, dry and white. She had taken her jacket off.

The sleeveless top revealed impressively toned arms, slim and brown, the muscles smooth, unknotted. She had tiny wrists, unlike her breasts. A hint of bra strap, thin, lacy and white, winked at him.

'Throbbing.' He smiled winsomely.

She looked at him over the rim of her glass. She really was quite a looker, less heart-stoppingly beautiful than Belle but still a head-turner. He immediately hated himself for making such comparisons.

The waitress came along to take their orders. Tallis plumped for chorizo and pork meatballs with linguine in a tomato sauce, easy to eat one-handed. Lavender chose sea bream on a bed of roasted Mediterranean vegetables. He ordered a bottle of wine because he liked the accompanying blurb on the wine list. It was, apparently, mostly Merlot with a little bit of Cabernet Sauvignon, no Cabernet Franc. The conversation was light. He discovered that she had two brothers and had always been a bit of a tomboy.

'Hence the fascination for fast cars.'

'Motorbikes are more my thing, actually.'

He also discovered that she'd joined the police because her dad was a police officer.

'Like me,' Tallis said. Except unlike him in so many respects. When Lavender talked of her father there was softness in her eyes, pride in her voice. She clearly adored the man. 'And you enjoy the job?'

'I love *this* job,' she said, eyes shining. 'You don't think you're the only maverick in town, do you?'

Tallis let out a laugh. 'Now I understand how you got to drive a Ferrari. You're working for Asim.'

'Pushing the envelope. Seconded to him is nearer the mark.'

'Wonder why he didn't mention it.'

'Didn't consider it important.' She shrugged.

Different levels of secrecy, more like. 'Is Lavender your real name?'

'It is. About the only bit of me that's real,' she said provocatively.

'Oh, yeah?' He was intrigued.

'All this,' she said, waving a delicate hand in no particular direction, 'you and me, it's play-acting, isn't it?'

'Is it?' He wondered which bits.

She gave an embarrassed laugh. 'I guess I'm a frustrated actress at heart.'

'I suppose it would be uncool of me to ask about other jobs you've done.'

'This is my first time,' she said. 'Like I said, I'm only borrowed. You?'

'Lost my virginity a while ago, I'm afraid.'

'I'd never have guessed.' She smiled, nose cutely wrinkling.

They went through to the dining room to eat. He told her about his brief career in the army followed by a stint in the firearms unit as an undercover police officer, and his involvement in a fatal shooting following false intelligence before leaving West Midlands Police a disillusioned man. Lavender was an easy listener and whether it was wine or exhaustion, the need to talk to someone, anyone, Tallis found himself telling her about the terrible relationship he'd had with his father, the wonderful relationship he'd had with Belle.

'Sorry,' he said as the plates were cleared away. 'Not very cool of me.'

'Don't be so silly,' she said, resting her hand over his, the sudden warmth of her skin against his like a burn. 'It helps me understand.'

'Understand what?'

'Why you do what you do. It's easy to embrace loneliness when your heart's broken.'

'So what's your story?' he said, wanting to lighten the tone.

She shook her head and laughed. 'There's isn't one. After this, I'll probably return to my old stamping ground.'

'Shame,' he said, meaning it, sliding his fingers in between hers. 'Just when things were getting interesting.'

'I didn't think you were like that,' she said, playfully arching an eyebrow.

'I'm a bloke, Charlie. We're all like that.'

They booked the last available room for the night. The bed was enormous, demanding Olympic-league sex, Tallis thought, sitting down gingerly, bouncing a little, testing the mattress. Charlie came and sat on his lap, took his face in her hands, kissed him long and slow and whispered in his ear that she was going to take a shower. Tallis lay on the bed feeling heady with wine and lust and panic. Something in his chest suddenly froze. What if he saw Belle's face when he was making love? What if he couldn't do it? Jesus, couldn't get it up?

Charlie came out. She was wearing one of a pair of white towelling robes that hung on the back of the bathroom door. Her hair was loose and wet. Water glistened on her skin. He could see the neat curve of her collarbone, dark shadow at the top of her breasts. Her calves were smooth and lean. She wore deep-cherry nail polish on her toes. He felt an urgent stab of lust, as if he wanted to rip the robe off, crush her and do it there and then.

'Just taking a shower,' he said, bending down, his chest inches away from her, kissing her softly on the mouth, imagining her naked beneath the towelling. In the sanctity of the white-tiled bathroom, his panic assumed terrifying proportions. He stripped off, showered as best he could, trying to keep the cast on his left wrist dry. Next he turned his attention to his face. He really needed another shave. What was he thinking? She'd be flayed alive with this amount of stubble on his chin. As for his teeth, he flipped open a small complimentary tube of toothpaste and, using his index finger, cleaned them. By the time he returned, towel around his waist, he was dripping not with water but with something akin to dread. Then he saw her beautiful smile, the way she was lying on top of the bed facing him, the robe falling from one shoulder, one leg seductively turned towards him. He lay beside her, propped himself up on one elbow. 'Hello.' He smiled. 'Look, it's been a long—'

'Shut up, Tallis,' she said, pushing him down. Then, climbing astride him, she removed his towel and slipped off her robe.

35

HE DID not see Belle's face. He only saw Charlie's. As a
lover, she was everything he needed her to be. After the
first time he felt as if a weight had been lifted from him.

They were lying together, watching the light stream in
through the windows. She rolled over towards him. 'Want
me to take you home?'

'Soon,' he said, pulling her towards him again.

Afterwards, they showered and dressed and slipped downstairs. Tallis paid the bill while Charlie got the car. 'Everything to your satisfaction, sir?' The restaurant owner smiled.

'Definitely,' Tallis said, stepping out into a car park
flooded with September light.

'It's such a beautiful day,' Charlie said, gunning the
engine, 'I decided to drop the hood.'

They talked little mainly because the sound of the
engine was accentuated twentyfold with the top down. On
the outskirts of the city, she asked whether he thought it
safe to go back home.

'I'm not going back. At least, not yet.'

'Oh?' She flashed him an inquisitive sideways look.

'I want to check something out.'

He asked Charlie to take him to Walsall. He still had a set of keys to the premises. They arrived at the unit shortly after ten. Charlie waited outside while Tallis let himself in and found the vehicle he was looking for. He smiled. Kennedy hadn't got rid of it at all. Had he known that one day Tallis would come back for it? Making his way down to the bottom level, Tallis located the Rover and, unlocking it, jumped inside and drove round to meet Charlie. By comparison with the Vanquish, he felt as if he was driving a hairdryer.

'From the sublime to the ridiculous again.' He grinned, coming up alongside her.

'You'll be all right?' There was a reluctant note in her voice. He wasn't sure whether it was born of genuine worry for his safety or because they were saying goodbye.

'I'll be fine.'

'Great.' She smiled, awkward.

'Be in touch,' he added, then drove away, glancing in the rear-view mirror once.

The bungalow was as he had left it, apart from an extra layer of dust inside, calf-length grass and weeds outside. Both home and garden retained a mildly defeated air only lifted by the swanky presence of the Audi TT sitting in the carport. Cursory investigation told Tallis that it hadn't been keyed, windscreen wiper snapped off or any attempt made to steal it. Things were looking up in the neighbourhood.

Out of habit, he checked the bungalow for anything

untoward and was faintly surprised to find everything as he'd left it. Ignoring the urgent sound of his answering-machine telling him he had several messages, he changed into a clean pair of jeans and sweater then stood at the kitchen window for several minutes, waiting for the kettle to boil. The weather wasn't so great now. Sun, the colour of pale lemon, was shrinking against a sky blushing with red-tinged cloud. He immediately thought back over the past surreal twenty-four hours. Charlie was a brilliant woman and he felt a pang of guilt for leaving so abruptly. The truth was that, in spite of spending an exciting night with her, it felt marvellous to be solitary again. Alone, he knew where he was. Life was uncomplicated. Bottom line, he felt bleak about the possibility of forming another meaningful relationship. He never wanted to expose himself to the possibility of feeling such despair again.

After he made coffee, he settled down, feet up on the coffee-table, and listened to his messages: two from his mum, the latest asking if he would like to have lunch with her the following day; one from his sister, Hannah; one from Stu, his mate from the firearms days, which managed to be deeply interesting and uplifting. And two from Crow, the first informing him that she'd been up to her ears in work and hadn't been able to carry out his enquiries, the second that she'd found something out and needed to talk. He called her straight away. She wasn't simply pleased to hear from him. She was effusive. He glanced at his watch: noon. 'Where are you?' he said, as if he didn't know.

'A local hostelry, sitting outside having a fag and enjoying a rare moment of sunshine and peace.'

'What are you drinking?'

'V&T. My second, as it happens.'

'Only your second?'

'Cheeky sod. This is my first full weekend off in a month.'

'A policeman's lot and all that.'

'Police officer,' she corrected him, the rattly sound of her lungs expanding and contracting travelling down the phone line.

'Anyway,' he said, 'you called.'

'I did, indeed. Two snippets of information for you regarding Gayle Morello.'

'Yeah?' His gut sharpened.

'First husband, Bryn Gannon, killed in a road accident six years ago.'

'Yeah, I know.'

'Patience, Tallis.'

'Sorry, go on.'

'No witnesses, straight, fast bit of road, weather conditions fine, familiar route as Gannon used it each day to travel to and from work.' So what? Tallis thought. He knew the statistics. You were more likely to die in a road accident on home territory than miles away in a foreign county. 'According to the incident report, Gannon swerved off the road and hit a tree.'

'It happens. Maybe he was trying to avoid a bird or animal.'

'Except paint found on the wing of Gannon's car suggested it had come into contact with another vehicle, skid marks providing further evidence that another vehicle was present at the time of the accident.'

'What are you saying? That Gannon's car was forced off the road?'

'That's the opinion of the vehicle investigator.'

'Was the other car or driver ever traced?'

'No.'

Tallis scratched his head. Was it significant? He fully understood Gayle not wishing to talk about the death of her husband, but the fact that Garry had never mentioned it seemed odd. Garry was, after all, a crime correspondent. He would take an interest in such things. It was inconceivable he didn't know.

'Where did this take place?'

'Outskirts of York.' Of course, he remembered Gayle saying that she'd lived in Yorkshire for a time. Yes, that would explain her brother Stephen's accent.

'The second thing?'

'Gayle Morello's family. I checked them out. Mother still alive and living in Ireland. Sister resides in Canada. No record of Gayle Morello having a brother.'

'You're sure?' Tallis said. 'No half- or stepbrother?'

'No. All very curious, don't you think?'

Curious, yes, but hardly evidence.

'Think I'll keep a watching brief, if you don't mind.'

'You have the time?' He expressed surprise.

'I can always make time for people who interest me,' she said, a frisky note in her voice.

'Thanks, Micky. I owe you,' he said, cutting the call. He must have sounded glum. Crow had made no attempt to press home the advantage and call in the favour.

He phoned his mum and arranged to see her the following day for lunch. Fortunately, she was one of those rare women who didn't like to chatter for hours on the phone. Ten minutes after that he was on the road again. He slotted a newish CD into the player, *Shadows Fall*. Deciding to make a break with the past had been his sole reason for buying it, that and the weird cover of a screaming being with sewn-up eyes.

Skipping through the tracks, he homed in on 'Another Hero Lost', a poignant tribute to a young soldier who'd lost his life in the latest conflict in Iraq. Made Tallis think about Napier, made him wonder who or what the poor bastard was currently chasing.

Traffic for a Saturday was light. The TT felt a whole lot better than the Rover to drive but, up against the Aston, it was like driving a tank. The gear change, which he'd loved, felt tight and oversprung, steering uninvolving. Probably no more than a symptom of his rapid change in mood. Either way, he decided that when he got back to Birmingham, the TT had to go, returned to its rightful owner, except Kennedy would no longer be there or in a position to accept it. Probably already in a safe house, waiting to be flown halfway across the world to some unknown destination with a brand-new identity.

He pulled off the motorway and onto the A38 around

three-thirty in the afternoon. It took him another forty-five minutes to motor to the small popular holiday town of Kingsbridge, which lay situated at the head of an estuary. Simon Carroll, Kennedy's alleged victim, had fled there following the court case. Remembering Carroll's address from the file, he headed straight for the Tourist Information Centre, which was in the main part of the town in the middle of a car park. In front was a row of Georgian houses. To the left, a roundabout, and some shops off. Behind, a bar and restaurant with an outdoor eating and drinking area. It had the busy, bustly feel of a typical town near the seaside yet not quite near enough to fully qualify for full-blooded bucket-and-spade status. Beyond it, the road curved up to another roundabout then led straight up a hill.

Brief enquiry revealed Saffron Park to be a modern housing estate located on another hill off the main centre of the town five minutes' walk away. Putting a couple of hours' parking on the TT, Tallis decided to stretch his legs, the climb worth it. The weather was an improvement on the flaky, can't-make-your-mind-up stuff he'd experienced in the Midlands. The sun was warm and strong, blades of light bouncing off cream-coloured buildings and scenery. The sound of arguing seagulls rattled in his ears, the oystery smell of seaweed in his nostrils. The higher he went, the more outstanding the view. From the top, he glimpsed white sails cresting blue-green water. The estuary looked calm and tranquil and inviting. The houses were a mixture of small and larger builds, a few quite imposing.

After turning off into an avenue, he found Carroll's house, a large, double-fronted plain brick dwelling with a handsome porch and hanging baskets, a garage for two cars and a neat, well-tended front garden, mostly laid to lawn. He wondered how much such a place would cost. A small, dumpy woman was kneeling down on the grass, weeding a border. On his approach she looked up, her smile warm and friendly.

'Mrs Carroll?' he said.

She shook her head, struggled to her feet, wiping the dirt off her hands on the back of her ample denimed rear. 'Hasn't lived here for the past year.'

'Any idea where I can find her?'

'Sorry,' she said, the smile fading. Her brown hair was cut in a short soft bob. She had small eyes, small nose, small mouth. Even her head was small. Her body, by contrast, was out of all proportion. Tallis was reminded of an artist who regularly exhibited in the Halcyon Gallery in Birmingham. All her figures had pea heads and enormous bodies.

'I understand.' He smiled, nice and friendly with it.

'It's just that, well, you know, after what happened…' she said, dropping her voice as if frightened one of her neighbours might hear.

'Can't be too careful,' Tallis said. Especially not here, he thought. He'd been there five minutes yet at a guess it was the kind of place where everyone knew everyone else's business.

She agreed, small eyes fastening on him, clearly trying

to weigh him up and wondering whether she could trust him.

'Tell you what. Can you direct me to the nearest business park?' he said.

Again the cautious look. 'The one outside town?'

'The one where Mr Carroll worked? See, I'm planning to write a book about his abduction and murder.'

'Oh,' she said, small mouth falling slack. 'You're a writer.' She said it as if she'd never come across the breed before. Tallis was given the impression that he'd suddenly metamorphosed from foe to interesting and socially desirable friend.

'Uh-huh.'

'Come on in,' she said. 'I'm Verity Wintour, by the way,' she said, giving an odd little bob of her knees as if he were royalty. 'You look a bit warm after that climb up the hill. We can have a nice cold glass of homemade lemonade and I'll write it all down for you.'

Not only did Mrs Wintour draw a map and write down the address of the business unit used by Carroll before his unfortunate demise, she gave Tallis Wendy Carroll's telephone number. Cautious to the last, she declined to give the home address. 'Wouldn't be right,' she said, eyeing him.

'Always best to call first,' he agreed. 'Gives people a chance to decide whether they want to co-operate.'

Mrs Wintour nodded, the caution in her eyes still there, as if she was having second thoughts about entertaining a stranger. Silence filled the room. Unfazed, Tallis took the

opportunity to study his surroundings. The kitchen was all
fully fitted. The sitting room where she'd invited him to
sit down was plush and comfortable and led out to a huge
glass-domed conservatory. The back garden was a picture.
He reckoned it had to be four bedrooms minimum. The
pound signs that had been swivelling in his brain on first
viewing the house suddenly ratcheted up several-fold. He
wondered how the hell Carroll, a lowly council official,
had made the financial leap.

Finally, Verity Wintour broke. 'Locals reckoned he was
bumped off because he was in trouble with a crime lord.'

'Yeah,' Tallis said, noncommittal.

'Evidently that's why the Carrolls moved down this
way. Popular place for people on the run,' she sniffed,
taking another swig of lemonade.

'Right.' From his brief glimpse of Kingsbridge, he
didn't think it densely populated with crooks and nonces.
Refugees from the rat race, more like. He wondered if he
could settle in such a place. Doubted it.

'Wendy never spoke much about what happened. I think
she was too frightened. Mentioned a car accident Simon
was involved in.'

Tallis nodded.

'Never found the blokes that did it,' Mrs Wintour
chatted on. 'Think your research might provide a lead?'

'What?' Tallis said, his concentration jacking up a level.

'The blokes that did it.'

'Did what?'

'Killed Carroll,' she said, exasperated.

'Blokes?'

'There were two of them. At least, that's what I was told.'

'By whom?'

'One of the owners of a unit up there.'

'He saw them?'

Wintour shook her head vigorously. The soft bob of her hair rippled like a King Charles spaniel shaking its ears. 'Not exactly. He saw a couple of young men hanging round. Notice things like that, don't you? Evidently, they'd driven there on a motorbike. Anyway, he asked them if they were lost. One of them came up with an excuse and then they left, smartish, by all accounts. Well, as you'd imagine, after Mr Carroll went missing, he started to wonder.'

Yeah, Tallis thought, me, too.

Tallis called Mrs Carroll from his car. There was no reply and no answering-machine to take a message. By now, it was after five. Undeterred, he made his way to the business unit in Churchstowe some three miles or so out of the town. At once the surrounding countryside seemed to open out with banks on either side of the road, large fields beyond. He drove onto a bumpy bit of road and pulled into the industrial estate. There were several units, including computer supplies and services, a motor repair outfit and a place that supplied labels. A man with a buzz cut was locking up. Tallis didn't get to see what was inside. The man turned. He had the pinched expression of a bloke who worked long hard hours for little reward. There were too many people like him, Tallis thought.

'Help you?' the man said.

'Perhaps. I'm a journalist,' Tallis lied. 'Researching the murder of Simon Carroll.'

'Not local, then.'

Tallis threw him a quizzical look.

The man cracked a smile. Made him look younger. On first sight Tallis had had him down for mid-forties. Now he looked mid-thirties. 'I know all the local hacks.'

'Popular story, then.' Tallis smiled back.

'Don't have too many murders around here, at least not like that. We tend to go in more for domestics, somebody shagging somebody else's wife scenario.' He pulled out a packet of cigarettes, shook a couple out and offered one to Tallis, who declined.

'Know much about what happened?' Tallis said.

'Only hearsay. Before my time, thank God.'

'So what have you been told?'

'Carroll had a small business here repairing motor mowers, engines, bit of this bit of that. Lived in Kings-bridge after moving down from up country. Gather his missus moved to West Charleton after he disappeared,' the man said conversationally.

'Is that near here?'

'Back into Kingsbridge and it's the first village over the bridge at Bowcombe.'

'Right, sorry, you were saying.'

'Came to open up around six one morning and by the

time Steve over the way there...' he jerked his head vaguely in the direction of one of the other units '...arrived an hour later, he'd vanished.'

'Just like that?'

'Yup.' The man took a drag of his cigarette. 'One of the blokes here reckons that there were two fellas hanging round the day before. Whether or not they had anything to do with it, I don't know.'

'Don't suppose you know what those guys looked like?'

'Only that one of them had a tattoo on his hand—like half the population in the country.'

'Tattoo of a spider, by any chance?'

The man's jaw dropped open, his cigarette clinging tenaciously to his bottom lip. 'Yeah, that's right.'

Nathan Brass, Tallis thought, feeling as if a bitter wind had just blown over him, one of the two men responsible for Garry Morello's murder, the man who'd worked for Kennedy, the man whose name and activities had been blacked out in the file.

He arrived in West Charleton as the sun began to shed its last light. Still warm enough, Tallis thought, to sit outside.

A typical Devon village, West Charleton had a Church of England primary school, a post office and village shop, a church and pub, The Ashburton Arms. He parked in the tiny car park, and walked up into the beer garden, which was empty, the fine vantage point yielding an amazing view of the estuary and, more importantly, the rest of the village. Walking back down the steps, he went inside and ordered half a pint of lager. It wasn't especially busy for a Saturday night. From the flow of conversation, he judged that the four men and two women sitting and standing around the bar were local. Good.

Without preamble, Tallis asked the bartender where he could find Wendy Carroll. He might as well have asked for Rip Van Winkle. Seven pairs of suspicious eyes looked him up and down. 'No idea who or what you're talking about,' came back the stony reply. Tallis shrugged and took his drink to a table. Nobody moved a muscle. Nobody said a word. It was as if by mentioning the name he'd brought disease into the community. Fifteen minutes later, he finished his drink, and returned to the TT, moving it twenty-five metres away into the neighbouring road and parking it behind a large, ugly American-style Jeep, all balls no substance. Swiftly walking back to the pub, he shot up the steps to the rear of the building and waited in the shadows. A minute later, one of the men who'd been standing at the bar left the pub, turned left, crossed the road, walked three doors along, then with a shifty shake of his head recrossed to a row of tiny dwellings on the same side Tallis was standing. There followed the hollow sound of a door being rapped then opened. A rapid exchange took place. Tallis discerned a woman's voice though he couldn't see her face. Report of a door slamming shut. Tallis imagined the sound of a deadbolt and chain being slotted into place. It wouldn't be easy to get her attention, but at least he knew where Wendy Carroll lived.

* * *

That night, he found a small, comfortable bed and breakfast further along the road and paid up front. He also
enquired about the time of church services the following
morning. After checking into his room, he drove to the
next village of Frogmore and ate locally caught sea bass
at a pub called The Globe, returning to the guesthouse
shortly after ten. He slept badly, tossing and turning,
facing yet resisting the prospect that Kennedy had not
only ordered the murder of his friend Garry but had also
got away with it. More ugly still, he wondered who had
cut Nathan Brass such slack. The blacked-out section in
Kennedy's file intimated that someone had shopped
Kennedy, that someone might even have confessed to
being involved in Carroll's murder, and yet whoever it
was had not been brought to account but had been
released and gone on to kill again. Re-examining SOCA's
involvement, Tallis wondered whether Napier had taken
an earlier interest in Johnny Kennedy, whether he'd
believed that Kennedy was his route to recognition and
glory. No wonder he'd been less than impressed with
having the golden goose stolen from underneath his nose
by Asim.

Around six-thirty, Tallis got up, shivered in the cool
grey light and dressed. By seven-fifteen he was waiting
outside Wendy Carroll's house. At seven-twenty, the teal-
coloured door swung open and a woman, dressed in black,
hurried out, shutting the door behind her. She was small,
slim and hollow-eyed, looked as though she hadn't had a
decent night's sleep in years. She took off at a nervous

pace, heels clicking against the road. Tallis followed silently. As he suspected, she was heading for the church for early communion. He wondered whether she'd always believed in God, or felt driven to it as many were by life and the loss of it. She was descending the hill towards a complex of flats when he caught her up and put his hand on her elbow. She whipped round, eyes wide, mouth sagging then dropping, the scream inside trapped by terror, sheer and bright.

'Wendy,' he said quickly, 'I'm not here to hurt you.'

'N-no?' she stammered, bewilderment in her eyes.

'I want to talk to you about what happened to your husband.'

'You're a police officer?' She sounded dejected as if she had no trust in them.

'Used to be.' He looked over her head, spotted a bus shelter on the corner on the opposite side of the road. 'All right if we talk in there?' he said.

'Well, I don't…'

She looked back at the church as though some invisible voice was calling her. For a brief moment in time he wished he had her faith. 'If you like, we could do this afterwards.' Who was he to stand in the way of her weekly fix?

She continued to look back over her shoulder, hovering, confused about what to do, then suddenly and, with great clarity of purpose, turned back towards him. 'No,' she said. 'It's fine.'

Together they crossed the road and sat down. Tallis told her what he knew about her husband, what he knew, with edited highlights, about Johnny Kennedy. He also told her that a friend of his had been shot while investigating Kennedy.

Wendy Carroll shook her head sadly. 'They never proved he gave the order. He was questioned but never charged. But I knew. I knew he was responsible. I knew it in my bones.'

'Did the police ever tell you how they got wind of the information?'

She shook her head again. 'Some bloke, top man, apparently, Napier he was called, he came to talk to me, said they'd had a tip-off putting Kennedy in the frame, but without the evidence to prove it. Don't have to be a brain surgeon to work it out,' she said ruefully.

So, Tallis thought, he was right about what Napier had on Kennedy. 'But did he say who was responsible for Simon's abduction?'

She shook her head sadly. 'I don't think they ever found out.' Oh, yes, they did. Brass was the sprat to catch the mackerel, Tallis thought, stealing one of Napier's expressions.

'Anyway,' she said stoutly, 'Kennedy was the man who ordered the killing. He never forgave Simon for what happened.'

'What about you?' His voice was neutral.

'Me?'

He nodded slowly, didn't say another word, let it sink in. He watched her face change from shock to indignation. 'I don't understand.'

Tallis leant back, spread his legs out in front of him,

suggesting that he wasn't going anywhere in a hurry. 'Because of Simon you must have known that life, as you knew it, was over.'

She looked down, twisted her small hands in her lap. 'It's been wrecked,' she agreed sadly, her voice losing its sharp edge. 'Sometimes I feel as if I'm in a witness protection programme without the protection.'

A hook-beaked gull swooped down in the middle of the tarmac and walked along as if it owned the road.

'That's quite some house you had in town,' Tallis said, abruptly changing the direction of the conversation. 'Must have cost a bit.'

'We'd saved up.' The defensive note crept back.

'Right,' he said without conviction. The small hands twisted some more. 'The night of the accident,' he said, rolling the conversation again. 'How many people were in the car?'

Wendy Carroll swallowed hard. 'Four, I think.'

'You *think*?' he said, sharp.

'Four,' she murmured softly. 'Three were members of the same development team.'

'And the party was held for the great and good of Birmingham City Council, that right?'

'Yes,' she said uncertainly.

'And your husband was driving his car?'

She didn't reply. She was looking far away and into the distance.

'Wendy?'

'No,' she said quietly.

'No,' Tallis repeated.

A blade of sunshine popped out from behind a cloud illuminating the landscape.

'Not only wasn't he driving *his* car,' Tallis said softly. 'He wasn't driving the car at all.' Sure, he'd read the reports, seen the evidence, read the witness statements, all of them claiming Carroll to be the driver, but the grand house in Kingsbridge didn't compute with the lowly dwelling the Carrolls left behind in Birmingham. There had to be a different story. Carroll, as the junior member of the party, conscientious and eager to better himself, was an obvious fall guy.

'I didn't want him to do it,' she blurted out, turning to him with big, frightened eyes.

'To take the blame?'

She nodded, biting her lip.

'Who was really driving?'

Her small body shrank further into the bench. She reminded him of Orla, his niece, the way she hid and shut her eyes, believing that if she couldn't see, she couldn't be seen. 'The head of the team, bloke by the name of Finch, Cain Finch. He'd been drinking and when he hit that man, Billy Kennedy, he panicked and drove away. I'm not sure when or whether they realised how serious it was, and I don't know who exactly came up with the idea, but it was decided that they'd report to the nearest police station and say that Simon was driving. He hadn't been drinking because he was on a course of strong antibiotics for a bad tooth infection.'

'And he was happy to go along?' Tallis was incredulous.

She let out another weary sigh. 'Simon was a good man. Everything he had he'd worked hard for. He worked in an environment where you have to go along to get along.'

'Even so…'

'There was money.'

'He was bribed?'

'By Finch.'

'So that's how you could afford your house.'

'What nobody knew at the time was the identity of the victim. Had Simon known that it was Billy Kennedy, Johnny Kennedy's son, he'd never have agreed to go through with it.'

'Why didn't you tell the police this?'

She looked down at her hands once more. 'After what happened to Simon…' Her voice petered out.

'They bought you off, too.' Tallis could feel heat under his skin, a burning sensation in the pit of his stomach. It was really, really important that he receive a truthful answer to his next question. 'Wendy, does anyone else know?'

'About Finch? Only Simon, and he took that secret with him to his grave.'

Except, Tallis thought, he didn't.

36

ALL the way up the motorway Tallis was haunted by the chilling image of Simon Carroll pleading for his life. In the mistaken belief they'd spare him, he surely confessed the truth. Not that it had done the poor sod any good. What surprised Tallis was that no reprisals had been taken against Finch. Carroll's killers must have reported back to the boss. He found it inconceivable that Kennedy remained in the dark, even more inconceivable that he hadn't taken revenge. Unless, of course, he felt too hamstrung by his new police connections. But not too constrained to order a hit on Garry? Tallis shook his head. Something was off.

Checking in the mirror, Tallis clocked a Lexus bearing down on him. He pulled over into the middle lane, letting it pass. Returning to Kennedy, Tallis examined the man's motivation for removing Garry Morello. Garry must have witnessed Kennedy's conversation with Tardarti, but was that a reason for murder? What couldn't be denied was that Brass and Reid, both men who'd worked for Kennedy had killed Garry. It wasn't a coincidence and because of that fact alone he felt rage and shame, rage for being out smarted by Kennedy, shame for putting Gayle Morello under the spotlight, and drawing the wrong conclusions. Stephen was probably a lover, an old flame, perhaps. The most she could be charged with was indecent haste.

For the rest of the journey he ran over everything he knew, re-examining the evidence, finding Kennedy innocent of certain things, guilty of others then changing his mind, but sure he was missing something. He was pulling into his drive when his mobile went off. He picked it up. It was Asim.

'Thought you'd like to know we swooped on Ahmed at four yesterday morning and took him to Paddington Green. He's protesting his innocence like crazy but so far we've found an incriminating CD-ROM in one of his garages on the sourcing and manufacture of explosives, a document in his cab office with information likely to be useful to a person preparing to commit an act of terrorism, and a load of books and audio cassettes with radical and jihadi themes.'

'Careless of them,' Tallis said. Surely, all incriminating evidence would be painstakingly removed? Somehow he'd imagined lots of sterile-looking, empty rooms.

But Asim was in full flow. 'We've only started to take his premises apart but we're hopeful we'll find more in-formation. In the meantime, we're picking up targets already under surveillance at a number of addresses in Birmingham, and Manchester and Leeds, and various premises have been secured and sealed off, currently being searched. Don't be surprised if there's a heavy police presence in the city tomorrow.'

Tallis reckoned most of his old firearms colleagues would be deployed. 'And Kennedy?'

'Our conquering hero is currently under close protection.'

'Your conquering hero,' Tallis said bitterly, 'was responsible for Garry Morello's death.'

'Is that so?' No shock, no outrage.

'You knew?'

'We suspected. There's a difference.'

'No, there isn't.'

Asim let out a sigh. 'Paul, we've got a great result. Dozens of lives have been saved.'

'What about Garry Morello? What about his widow?' What about Simon Carroll and the poisoned chalice he'd been handed? What about the fat bastard with his dog who Kennedy had arranged to have killed? And what was the point of discussing such matters?

'I understand your feelings.'

Tallis felt his voice stoop to a low growl. 'You have no idea about my feelings.'

'Look, we couldn't have achieved any of this without you.'

'Spare me the congratulations,' Tallis said, icy, cutting the call.

He sat for a full five minutes, drumming his fingers in vexation on the steering-wheel, feeling the anger expand and lift inside him. Didn't matter a damn that he was under no illusions about the fucking horrible game he was caught up in, a game to be endured and lived with, to be sure, but not something he had to like. The only thing he'd been right about was that there were no good or bad guys, different degrees, different levels of, maybe, but basically they were all the same.

He went indoors, took a shower and tried to wash some of the bitterness out of his soul. He would go to his mother's home, share lunch with her and try and be a good son. After that, he would come back and reconsider his immediate future, work out what he wanted to do. Perhaps he'd go abroad, do some travelling, try and gain some life experiences.

Running insanely early, a novelty for him, he decided to leave and drive to his mother's anyway. He planned to pick up a bunch of flowers from one of the garden cum farm shops en route. He was about to make for the door when the doorbell rang. He peeked out of the spy-hole, saw his next-door neighbour's son slouching on the doorstep, bottle of milk in hand. Tallis opened the door.

'I've locked myself out,' Jimmy said, staring at his trainers. What was it about young people? Tallis thought. They only ever seemed to make statements, hoping someone would catch on and spot the problem then, with a bit of luck, solve it for them.

'That it?'

The trainers started scuffing the ground. 'Well, erm… thing is…' He tailed off.

'Yeah?' Tallis grinned.

'My parents are away, like.'

That was the other thing about them. Every sentence got punctuated by *like*.

'And I can't get in.'

'Yeah, you said.' It was cruel of him, he knew, but he found the lad's discomfiture mildly amusing.

Deep ridges started to appear in the gravel outside his front door. 'I was wondering, like.'

Progress, he supposed. 'Wondering what?' Tallis said with an encouraging smile.

'Whether you could help me get back inside.'

'Oh, right.' Tallis laughed. 'Wasn't so hard, was it, crafting an entire sentence all by yourself?'

Jimmy's stare from underneath the cover of his fringe was a mixture of embarrassment and belligerence.

'Let's have a look, then,' Tallis said, putting his own keys in his pocket, shutting the front door after him.

He did a quick circuit of the property, checking to see if doors were locked, windows secured, noting the sturdy Yale lock on the front door, deadlocks on the back and conservatory doors. The utility door, however, was warped with the recent rain.

'I'm fucked, aren't I?' Jimmy said, sullen with it.

'Not necessarily,' Tallis said, thinking it had been some time since he'd picked a lock.

'You're not going to break in, are you?' Jimmy said, sudden worry in his eyes. 'If there's any damage, my mom will kill me.'

Interesting balance of power, Tallis thought. Mother obviously wore the trousers. From what he'd observed, she wore the boots as well. 'Don't worry. If the worst comes to the worst there's a trick I learnt when I was in the army.'

It wasn't. It was something he'd learnt when he'd been with the police. 'Tell you what, while I think about it, come over to mine for bit.'

'Nah, s'all right. I'll stay here.' The morose expression didn't shift.

'How long have you been hanging around?'

'Couple of hours. Went out for some milk, didn't I?'

'Stay out much longer and it will go sour.' Bit like you, Tallis said. 'Had any breakfast yet?'

The lad shook his head.

'Bacon sarnie do you?'

'I'm all right.' He glanced away. He didn't look very comfortable, Tallis thought, remembering himself as a gawky fifteen-year-old, all raging hormones and a body doing weird things.

'Well, I'm going to have one.'

'Oh,' Jimmy said, perking up a bit. 'If it's no bother, like…'

'Come on,' Tallis said, walking back towards the bungalow, Jimmy shambling along behind. He'd had an idea. He didn't know where the hell it had come from, whether Jimmy had inspired it, but he knew he had to give it a shot.

They went inside. 'Kitchen's this way,' Tallis said, taking the pint and putting it in the fridge. 'Pull up a chair. I'll work out how we're going to get into your parents' house while you work out how I can best hack into a computer program.'

It was like inviting a Viking home for dinner. Tallis, even in his late teens and at his zenith for demolishing food, had never been able to eat like Jimmy. Three bacon sandwiches later, he started making serious inroads on a loaf of bread.

'So you're saying there's this bloke who is running a system within a system?' Jimmy was saying, spraying bits of toast onto the table.

'I don't know for certain. More of a hunch.'

'Bit like that Number Ten business, cash for honours, like? Police hacked into computers and found secret emails.'

Tallis felt genuine surprise. 'Didn't know you were that interested in current affairs and politics.'

'I'm not.' Jimmy scowled. 'My dad says politicians are a load of wankers, but anything techno—that's right inside my box.'

'So how would I go about taking a look?'

'You?' Jimmy looked at him as if Tallis had just announced he was going to have a sex change. He had a point. Tallis felt comfortable with finding his way around most computer systems but this was specialist stuff. Perhaps he should call up one of his mates in the force. Then again…

'Thing is, you can get round the password. Sometimes people put in a hint, like.'

'A hint?'

'Yeah, like a memory jogger. You'd be amazed how obvious they can be.' Tallis didn't think Kennedy dealt in the obvious. 'Failing that, you can go to the admin user and change the password, or log in via electronic mail.'

'Sounds simple.'

''Course, you might need more passwords to get further into the system, but sometimes you can get round that by running a program within the system's command files, giving you super-status.'

'Sounds ingenious.'

''Course, you might come up against beat the clock.'

'Beat the clock?'

'Systems that log out after a period of inactivity. Could be anything from sixty seconds to sixty minutes. Oh, yeah,' Jimmy said, as if he'd forgotten something crucial. 'This bloke might only use voice recognition.'

'To gain access.'

'Neat, huh?' Jimmy grinned.

Oh God, Tallis thought, baulking at the task ahead. The best he could expect was that he'd find out if Kennedy was hiding something.

'What kind of computer are we looking at?' Jimmy said, taking another enormous bite.

It depended. Most of the office used PCs. Kennedy had a flat-screen Mac, like him. He told Jimmy this.

'Could be using FireVault.'

'Contents will be encrypted,' Tallis said, glum. 'You're not making this any easier.'

'It's not supposed to be easy,' Jimmy scoffed. 'Who knows? Maybe he got lazy.'

Tallis didn't think so. 'Could you hack into it?'

'Maybe.'

Now that his stomach was full, Jimmy was reverting to *can't be arsed* mode, Tallis thought. Was he taking an unacceptable risk? Was he even putting Jimmy's life in danger? 'What are you doing later on?'

'Why?'

'Fancy a trip out?'

'Not especially.'

'Shame. Think it's going to rain.'

'What's that got to do with anything?'

'You're going to get wet.'

'But you said…' Jimmy burst out, indifference taking a sudden acrobatic leap to umbrage.

Tallis grinned. The lad had been outmanoeuvred and he knew it.

'Where?' Jimmy scowled.

'Nowhere scenic.'

They both knew what he was asking. Suddenly, Jimmy's demeanour seemed to alter. He sat up a bit, gave Tallis a shrewd look. 'You offering me a deal?'

'I am.' Tallis flashed a smile.

'Will money change hands?'

Tallis met Jimmy's crafty expression. What was it with kids today? From washing up to keeping their bedrooms tidy, they all expected filthy lucre. He'd even heard that schoolkids in higher education got paid a fat wedge, a bonus, if they consistently showed up. Ironic if the rise in binge drinking was directly connected to government handouts, he mused.

Jimmy continued to eye him. Tallis was beginning to feel like the parent whose every ideal and principle had crumbled under the weight of adolescent intractability.

'Could be arranged. In the meantime, you use my expertise in return for me using yours.'

Lock picked, and Jimmy safely installed back home again, Tallis arranged to collect him early evening, around six, and drove over to his mother's house in a backwater of Hereford.

'How lovely,' she said, taking the flowers he'd brought, looking pleased to see him. He followed her into the kitchen, watched as she filled a vase with water and carefully arranged them. She looked good, he thought. He'd expected her to lose weight, to look weary, yet she appeared more rested, fresher than she'd seemed in years. 'Sherry?' she said.

'Lovely. I'll fix it.'

He couldn't stand the stuff. Not that he'd ever admit it. It was one of those strange, harmless deceptions indulged in by families the world over. Trouble was, little deceptions led to bigger ones. Made him wonder how much parents really knew about their children. Probably about as much as children knew about their parents.

She'd gone to a lot of trouble: full roast with all the trimmings.

'And I've done your favourite,' she said happily, taking the potatoes out of the oven and turning them. 'Apple and blackberry crumble. Hope you're hungry.' He smiled, instantly regretting the late sandwich. 'About ten minutes then we can eat,' she said.

They went through to the conservatory, as his mother called it, a glass lean-to in which his father had grown geraniums. They talked of nothing important. Tallis found himself listening in stereo, one voice his mother's, the other Kennedy's.

'Hannah's coming up for half-term week with the children.'

I prize loyalty more highly than love.

'Says it will give Geoff a chance to catch up on some DIY.'

So you don't believe in punishment for wrongs?

'I thought I'd let the boys have your old room. Orla will sleep in Hannah's room on the Z-bed.'

Torture always guarantees the truth.

'Quite the little miss, isn't she?'

The deception, pretending you're someone you're not, becoming a bad guy to defeat people like me.

'Paul?'

Always reckoned you were special.

'Paul, you haven't been listening to a word I've said.'

'What?' He jolted. 'You were talking about the sleeping arrangements for the kids.'

She threw him an old-fashioned look, the same expression she'd reserved for him when he'd got away with lying to his father. After that he tried very hard to concentrate, to take an interest, to look animated. They had finished their main course when she asked him about his current employment.

'Still working for that lovely man?'

'No.'

'Oh, Paul,' she said, disappointed. 'Why ever not?'

'Things didn't work out.'

'What sort of things?' she said, eyeing him suspiciously.

'Business.'

'What will you do?'

'Good question.' He flashed a smile, trying to make light of it.

'It's the *only* question. You can't wander through life without purpose.'

He didn't react, didn't respond. The last thing he needed right now was a lecture from his mother.

'Sometimes…' she cleared her throat '…things don't work out the way you planned.' Either she meant Belle or his apparent lack of gainful employment. He felt a strange sullen kinship with Jimmy. 'That's when you have to be flexible,' she continued. 'You're still the same person with the same desires and ambitions. Nobody can change those. But you have to set about achieving those goals in a different, more imaginative way.'

He sat up, stared at her. 'Mum?'

'Yes, dear?'

'Will the crumble keep?'

'Why, yes, I sup—'

Tallis stood up. 'There's something I've got to do.'

'What, now?' she said, bewildered. 'I didn't mean—'

'No,' he said, striding over to her side of the table and kissing the top of her head. 'It's fine. You're absolutely right.'

He phoned Jimmy as soon as he hit the road. 'Change of plan. Should be able to pick you up around four.'

'We're not going in the crapmobile, are we?'

Materialistic little swine, Tallis thought, gunning the engine. 'If you mean the Rover, no.'

'Good. Wouldn't be seen dead in it.'

Tallis didn't notice the journey, the speed or road conditions. His thoughts were on Kennedy, his personality, his ingenuity, the way he'd double-crossed absolutely everyone, and played them all for fools.

Jimmy was outside waiting for him. He got into the car.

'Got your keys this time?' Tallis said, reversing hard into Jimmy's drive and haring back down the road.

'Ha-ha,' Jimmy said, slouching in the seat.

'Put your seat belt on,' Tallis said.

'What are you, my mother?'

'If I was your mother, I'd kick your arse into the next century. Now, put it on.'

He'd had to make a decision—Lye, Walsall, the haulage company or the brothel. It was also possible that Kennedy might have some form of incriminating evidence on his computer at Shakenbrook. His real problem was that he didn't know exactly what he was looking for. The only certainty he had was that Kennedy had not changed, had never changed. Revenge was programmed and in his hard drive.

He drove to Lye first. A Sunday, it was as quiet as a vault. He drove round the back, parked in Kennedy's private parking slot, automatically glancing up at the church belfry as he climbed out of the car. No flash of light, no sign of another. He felt relief seep out of him.

'This it?' Jimmy said with disdain.

''Fraid so.'

E.V. SEYMOUR   429

They went inside, Tallis taking care to disable the alarm.

'You want me to look at all those? We'll be here for days,' Jimmy said, eyeing the bank of PCs.

'Don't worry. We're going upstairs.' Where we can't be seen, Tallis thought.

'Fuckin' hell,' Jimmy said, gawping at the fridge in the corner, the expensive blinds at the windows, leather sofas, leather executive chair, leather-topped desk.

'Right, then. Can you see all right?' Tallis said.

'Can't we open the blinds?'

'Rather not.'

Jimmy shrugged. 'OK to put on the desk lamp?'

'Sure. Want a coffee?'

Jimmy nodded, switched on the Mac and rolled his sleeves up as if he were a concert pianist about to perform a Rachmaninoff piano concerto. Tallis smiled, scooted back downstairs to the tiny kitchen. Coffee made, he returned with it upstairs and, after putting Jimmy's on the desk beside him, retreated to the other end of the room. Five minutes passed then another five—the only sound the whirr and buzz of the computer, the tap of Jimmy's deft fingers across the keys. After another five minutes had passed, Tallis asked how the lad was getting on, was told to shut up.

Tallis picked up a trade journal, flicked through, put it back down, finished his coffee. Was he setting Jimmy off on a wild goose chase? Perhaps Kennedy, like his a-Q counterparts, was smart enough to ensure no trail was left behind. Perhaps all contact was made by word of mouth.

So what exactly was Kennedy planning? Sure, he'd delivered Ahmed, foiled a terrorist plot, but Tallis didn't believe that Kennedy had backed off from his real ambitions, not for a moment. Ahmed, the whole a-Q charade was a convenient smokescreen. While the security services were rushing around, their focus elsewhere, thanks to Kennedy's brand of information, he was going to unleash the fury he felt for Billy's disability and pull off something that would make them all shudder. Should he call Asim, tell him what he believed, and tell him that Finch—the real driver—and his cronies were in danger? Except he didn't know how exactly, or even when Kennedy would take his revenge, whether he was in it for the long haul.

'Found anything?' Tallis said once more.

'Lot of weird stuff on brain injuries.'

'To be expected. Anything else?'

'Nothing dodgy so far. I'm trying to work out the key password.'

Tallis drummed his fingers, thinking, thinking.

'Oh, fuck!'

'What?' Tallis started.

'I've just tried a password that's been rejected.'

'Try another one.'

'No, you don't understand. I only get two shots at this. If I screw up again, the whole system will close down.'

Great, Tallis thought, feeling a tic in his temple. He closed his eyes, and let his mind go blank. Suddenly, what had once been at the back of it flashed to the front. 'Mephisto,' he burst out.

'What?' Jimmy said, mouth going slack.

Tallis spelt it out for him, leant back, heard the leather creak, heard something else. He stood up, silently crossed the floor, peeked out from between the blinds, saw nothing. Imagination, he thought. Obviously getting jumpy.

'Who's Billy?' Jimmy said, out of the blue.

'Why?' Tallis walked away from the window towards him.

'You were right about the password. There's a list of names here, like this Billy's having a party.'

'What?' Tallis said, confused.

'See, Mephisto, it's in this secret folder.'

Tallis stared at the screen, looked at the names, people he'd never heard of, a hit list, for all he knew except that Finch wasn't on it. At the top of the ten-name list was a three-word heading entitled

BILLY'S BIG BANG.

'Jesus!' Tallis burst out. That was it. *Kennedy was going to plant a bomb.*

'You want to take a better look?' Jimmy said, standing up. 'I need to go for a piss.'

'Toilets are downstairs on the right,' Tallis said, sliding into the leather chair, still warm from where Jimmy had sat there.

Tallis stared some more then logged out of the program and followed an audit trail of orders that had come in over the past month, searching for items loosely described as fertiliser or chlorine, or any materials that could even remotely be used in the assembly of a bomb. Nothing leapt out at him. He trawled some more, mind bracing, thinking, forging connections. *Connections*—that was it, Kennedy's stock in trade. Christ, he thought, taking out his phone, glancing up as Jimmy, white-faced, sped across the carpet. Tallis looked at him sharply as Jimmy elbowed him out of the way, Jimmy's fingers zipping over the keyboard. When Tallis looked at the screen, he felt his blood run cold.

WE HAVE COMPANY—MEN WITH GUNS

Tallis looked at Jimmy, nodded silently, put a finger to his lips. He dragged the lad off the chair by his shoulder and thrust him underneath the deep recess of the desk, told him to wait for him there. Jimmy nodded back. Gone the swaggering manner, the *whatever* apathy of youth. His eyes were the frightened eyes of a child.

Tallis shut down the computer, slid open the top drawer, released the catch at the back, revealing a false compartment, took out the loaded gun Kennedy kept there for emergencies. It was a Heckler & Koch Universal Self-Loading pistol, USP for short. The model had ambidextrous controls, perfect for Kennedy as a left-hander. Tallis shifted the safety lever at the rear of the frame from S to F, crept with stealth across the carpet, the thickness of the pile muffling his footsteps. Opening the door a crack, he peered outside. Nobody in the stairwell. Nobody on the stairs. Yet.

He slid out of the door, closing it softly behind him and, with nimble speed, fled down the stairs to the ground floor. About to enter the toilets, a fair-haired man, the one he recognised from Lavender's photographs, opened the door, weapon raised. Tallis twisted and darted through to the main office, hurdled a desk and crashed down on the other side as shots fired over his head, slamming into and lodging in the wall. Returning fire, Tallis tried to work out how many there were. As if in answer, a shot from the kitchen confirmed that there was at least one other. Tallis tried to edge his way to the door. Every time he moved a fresh round of bullets sprayed the room, bouncing off furniture, splintering it, a stray smashing through the glass, shattering the window. The alarm should have gone off. Except, Tallis remembered bitterly, in his desire to protect himself, he'd disabled it. And Jimmy was still upstairs.

Another burst of fire broke over his head; he unleashed a volley of shots, one, he was sure, winging the fair-haired guy near the toilet block. He hunkered back down. Sweat was pouring off him then, without warning, he felt a flash of cold steel against his neck.

'Don't move,' the voice said.

Tallis half closed his eyes. He'd recognise that Brooklyn accent anywhere.

'Throw your weapon down. Nice and slow.'

Tallis obliged.

'Turn around.'

Tallis did. It was the man he knew as Koroglu. He wasn't smiling.

37

THEY frisked him, took his phone, cuffed him across the forearms, along the line where the cast on his left wrist finished, and put him in a car, a grey Lexus, the same Lexus he'd moved out of the way for on the motorway. Koroglu sat one side of him, fair-haired guy on the other. Bleeding from a flesh wound on his upper arm, blondie wasn't happy. A large-framed black man with a shaved head drove. He had big, steady hands and his eyes flicked constantly from the rear-view mirror to the road—on the lookout. Tallis wondered if he was the man who'd driven the Volvo and tailed him back to Solihull the day he'd been with Kennedy.

All four men were dressed casually, jeans and sweaters. All were armed to the teeth. Thank God, they hadn't found Jimmy, Tallis thought. It was him they had come for, him they wanted.

'You've made the biggest mistake of your life,' Tallis said, uncompromising.

'My line, buddy,' Koroglu snarled back.

Close up, he was even more imposing. Solid-jawed,

dark-skinned, porous-looking, he had a distinctly military bearing. The fair-haired guy seemed more of a thinker. Either that, or he was junior to Koroglu, which, come to think of it, Tallis realised, fitted the profile better.

'You've got the wrong man,' Tallis insisted.

'So you keep saying.'

'It's true.' He was looking out of the window, wondering where they were taking him. They were heading south down the M5. Baffling.

'For Chrissakes, you don't know what you're doing. There's a bomb in Birmingham. I've got to warn the authorities.'

'We *are* the authorities.' The fair-haired guy gave a low dry chuckle.

'Not in this country,' Tallis spat back, teeth grinding.

'Be surprised, pal.'

Tallis turned and gave him a withering look.

'This the bomb you set up?' Koroglu drawled.

'I'm not a terrorist.'

'Save it for the judge,' the fair-haired guy interposed again.

'Where's your evidence to charge me?' Tallis rounded on him.

'Don't worry about that,' Koroglu said. 'We've got plenty of dirt. We pay special attention to those who consort with individuals on our watch list.'

They meant Tardarti. 'I didn't cons—'

'You work for Johnny Kennedy, Mr Miller, or should I call you Paul?'

'Or Milton?' the fair-haired guy chipped in, derisive.

So the Turks had definitely been in the pockets of the Americans, Tallis thought. A cold metallic shiver rippled up his spine. He bet they'd also been right about Kennedy inciting the crime lords to terrorism. Undaunted, he stuck to his defence.

'Johnny Kennedy, for your information, is under the protection of MI5.'

Nobody spoke. The silence cut him.

'An organisation I work for.' Tallis didn't want to confess to it, but this was getting serious.

'We know that, too,' Koroglu said, dismissive. 'They told us.'

'What?' He was stunned.

'Asim vouched for you, Paul.'

Did he? Tallis thought. Surely that was a good thing? He said as much.

'Asim confirmed you were working alongside Kennedy,' Koroglu said testily, in the manner of a politician sticking stubbornly to his script, no deviation.

'And MI5,' Tallis insisted.

'Not what Asim told us,' the fair-haired guy cut in again.

Tallis stared at him. There'd been one hell of a mix-up. 'You've got the wrong idea. Kennedy is assisting MI5.' Except he wasn't, Tallis now knew. The only organisation Kennedy was assisting was his own, and Tallis had neither the time nor the confidence to try and convince the Americans. They wouldn't believe him anyway. 'I'm working for the security services,' he insisted.

Again, nobody said anything. Christ, Tallis thought,

Asim always maintained that he was working off the books, in a grey, unofficial capacity. But, surely, on this occasion, Asim had to come to his defence? Surely he wouldn't throw him to the other side and deny his existence? What would be the purpose? Then Tallis remembered the fragility of the relationship between the British and the Americans, the lack of trust, the need to build a new accord. What was it Asim had said? *Something that needs to be restored, and quickly.* Tallis also remembered how expendable he was. He was nothing more than a freelancer and as such outside the rules of the game. He felt a wave of despair rise up from deep in his soul. Asim's betrayal wasn't true, couldn't be.

'We've seen your file,' Koroglu added smugly.

No, no, no. He felt as if he was spiralling into madness. His file was confidential. They couldn't have unless—he spiked inside—it was all bluff. 'You're CIA, aren't you?'

'The one and only,' the fair-haired guy replied.

Tallis fell silent. He tried not to think the worst, yet couldn't help it. He'd been let go, sold out, whatever you wanted to call it.

'If you've seen my file, you'll know that what I say is true, that I want to prevent terrorism.'

Silence again.

Tallis stared down at his hands. Because of the cast on his wrist, they were free, mobile. Could he escape? But where would he go? And for what? 'Where are you taking me?' He tried hard to keep the desperation from his voice.

'You'll find out soon enough.'

The rest of the journey passed in a maze of confusion coupled with the very real terror that while MI5 and the police were tied up with Ahmed, Kennedy's plan would come to fruition.

Tallis made one more attempt to reason with them. 'All right,' he said. 'Forget about me, but you have to speak to Asim. You have to tell him that Kennedy is planning something big.'

'Thought you said he was assisting MI5,' Koroglu said, sarcastic.

'He was, but he has another agenda.' Tallis winced, realising that he was making things a whole lot worse for himself.

'So you are involved?' The fair-haired guy sneered.

'No, I—'

'When?' Koroglu barked.

'I don't know exactly.'

'Where?'

'Not sure.' The Mailbox, the train station, the Bullring had all been brought to MI5's attention. It had to be somewhere else.

Koroglu leaned forward, exchanged a look with the fair-haired guy, who shrugged. They weren't buying it, Tallis thought bleakly. They think I'm trying to deal.

They turned off towards Gloucester, bypassing the town and heading for open countryside, the sound of small aircraft noisy overhead. At last they came to a road with a wire mesh fence running alongside it. Notices announced that guard dogs regularly patrolled the place. CCTV cameras were in evidence.

Then it suddenly dawned on Tallis. They were heading for the longest runway in the United Kingdom: Fairfield. A defence facility, under threat of closure, it was reputed that the Queen often used the base for flying into the country. It was also alleged that the formidable Galaxy aircraft, a plane so enormous that it could transport another secret plane inside its hold, made frequent visits there. Tallis immediately thought of hoods, blindfolds, men wearing balaclavas, water torture. No doubt about it, they were going to spirit him out of the country.

After a short distance, they pulled off and stopped at a checkpoint. The guards—Ministry of Defence, Tallis reckoned from their uniforms—were armed with MP5s. They looked like they meant business. It occurred to him to try and get their attention but he swiftly realised that he wouldn't be believed. What was one man's testimony against the evidence of several? Koroglu handed over his pass and, after a brief exchange, was waved on through. Tallis craned forward slightly and saw ahead several large buildings, including aircraft hangars and a series of odd-looking domes. It was only hearsay, but he'd heard that they were used for secret testing, of what he wasn't certain.

The further they drove, the more obvious it was that the personnel were American. A number of skid cars were bumming around the area, the occupants creating mayhem out of boredom. The way those kids were driving the vehicles meant that they felt completely secure and safe, Tallis thought, spotting several military-looking bods strutting around the complex as if they owned it. This was good, Tallis thought. Arrogant people were often lazy in their thinking. Believing themselves to be invincible, they were more vulnerable to the element of surprise.

He was driven to one of the smaller buildings, manhandled out of the car where he was cuffed again with the more complicated kind of ancient-looking steel restraints he'd once seen in the police museum at Sparkhill, and pushed inside, the solid metal door swinging shut behind him. He heard the sounds of bolts being shot, locks turning. He was standing in what looked to be a hangar. There were no windows, a skylight in the roof the only source of illumination. Walls, twenty metres in length, were made of reinforced corrugated iron. He paced the dirt floor, looking for an escape route. Other than tunnelling with his bare hands, there was none. Might as well be buried back in his cell in the Basilica, he thought, laughter cold and bitter bursting out of him, ricocheting off the dull mercury-coloured walls. And if he did escape, what then?

He sat down, stretched out his legs, leaning against the solid metal. He imagined that they would come for him later, cram him into a Cessna, one of those specially adapted aircraft that flew quietly without alerting people on the ground. From there it would be a brief hop to a neighbouring country then a long-haul flight to who knew where. All he could do was wait and hope for rescue. From whom, he didn't know. In the meantime, he decided to rest and closed his eyes. His thoughts returned to Mephisto and the names on the list in the computer file. He hadn't really had time to process them until now. The names were all

British. Not one suggested a heritage that was remotely foreign. So who were they? Blokes who'd worked for Kennedy, perhaps, were willing to work for him or, more chillingly, people who were capable of designing and planting a bomb?

Must have drifted off to sleep. He woke with a start. Daylight had completely faded from the sky, replaced by the fake illumination of a circling searchlight. The temperature in the building had plummeted, the barren earth on which he lay cold and damp. That's when he caught sight of two items on the ground—a piece of crumpled paper that he hadn't seen there before and something next to it, glinting in the dirt, a five-inch blade sharp enough to cut a man's throat. He twisted round, studied the note and smiled.

Lavender's green dilly dilly.

Green, he thought, code for left, meaning that Lavender—God knew how she'd blagged her way in—was somewhere to the left of the building. Picking up the blade with both hands, he scrambled to his feet.

And to think he'd dismissed Lavender from his heart and from his mind.

They came for him after midnight. There were four of them, three heftily built soldiers with balaclavas, and Koroglu. They fanned out around Tallis like jackals circling prey. He took a step back, estimating his chances of scooting past them and running to freedom as a million to one. Not attractive odds. One of the soldiers shone a powerful torch into his eyes, temporarily blinding him. Another was rattling some kind of chain or shackle. Fuck, Tallis thought, they were going to strip and manacle him, trussing him up in the same way black slaves from the deep South had been treated centuries before, and drag him to a waiting plane. Where the hell was Lavender? Tallis blinked in despair as one of them made a grab for him.

'Hi, boys,' a sexy American female voice purred from the left of the entrance.

Four pairs of eyes turned and hooked onto an attractive brunette, dressed in a semblance of military uniform, cap at a jaunty angle, standing in front of them. The brunette smiled, raised her weapon. There followed the unmistakable popping sound of a gun firing with a silencer attached. Two men down, everything kicked off at once. At the same time as one of the soldier's heads disintegrated in front of him, Tallis acted with the speed of a viper. Bringing the blade up level with his assailant's throat, he sliced once, deep and across, the man collapsing where he stood clutching the remains of his windpipe.

Koroglu, temporarily transfixed, reached for his weapon with lightning speed. Using all of his weight, Tallis barged him, knocking the big man off balance, slicing the blade blindly across Koroglu's face and kicking him sprawling into the dirt. As Koroglu let out a howl of pain, Tallis felt Lavender's hand clamp on his arm and drag him forward.

'Bike's here,' she gasped, leaping on and gunning the engine as Tallis jumped on behind her.

With a squeal of tyres the bike tore off away from the buildings, a hail of random gunfire bursting over their heads.

'We'll never make it through the checkpoint,' Tallis yelled, hanging on as best he could.

'We're not going through the checkpoint,' Lavender screamed back.

Tallis glanced over his shoulder. The air base was lit up like a fairground attraction. Worse, heavy-duty search-lights scoured the perimeter. Men were running in every direction. Orders were being shouted. Vehicles comman-deered.

'Hold on,' Lavender bellowed as the bike suddenly careered off the runway and fishtailed across the scrub of land running alongside. The bike was leaping and bouncing over the ground, the suspension perfectly attuned to the terrain. Tallis clung on, the roar of the powerful engine in his head ear-bleedingly loud. As they headed straight for the chain-link fence, romantic images of Steve McQueen in the film *The Great Escape* flashed through his mind.

A burst of automatic fire exploded into the night behind them, shattering any illusions. Lavender leant forward, her glorious body in line with the bike, pulling Tallis down with her. By now, several military vehicles were in pursuit, sirens blazing, soldiers with automatics hanging out of Jeep windows, taking aim. Still Lavender revved the engine, the bike running parallel now with the road. Soon he feared they'd run out of fence—then what? He glanced behind, saw the flash and sparkle of automatic weaponry heading in their direction. They still had the lead but the gap was closing. All it would take was one shot, even a lucky shot, and they'd be finished. He wondered why their pursuers didn't simply shoot out the tyres.

'Brace yourself,' Lavender called out. 'Here we go.'

The fence was as pale as the moonlight illuminating it, but it was visible and, although Tallis prayed for a miracle akin to Jesus walking on water, he knew that there was no way they could go through, let alone make a leap over. Then he saw it, up ahead, a nick in the fence—no, more than a nick, a tear, a ragged hole, only big enough to get a bike through. Oh, my God, he thought, if Lavender didn't aim precisely, one or both of them were going to be caught and shredded on the wire. He felt the bike twist briefly to the left then right as, without losing power, she lined up the machine. Make or break, he thought, closing his eyes. He felt a rush of wind around him, a piercing pain as the skin on his left arm tore. Next he knew they were on solid road, the bike revving, blasting off into the distance. They were free.

Two hundred metres down the road, Lavender veered off into woodland to evade any roadblocks. She seemed to have an uncanny knowledge of the terrain, Tallis thought as she revved her way, earth and stones flying, down to a dirt track. At last, after several kilometres, they abandoned the bike and picked up the Land Rover Defender already parked on the other side of the woods. Tallis felt seriously impressed by her expertise and forward planning.

'How did you learn to shoot like that?'

'Firearms.'

'You never said before.'

'You never asked before. We'll need to get those re-straints removed,' she said, crisply uncoupling the trailer used for transporting the bike.

'Already got someone in mind.' Oz, his Aussie biker mate, he thought. He'd do the job—without asking questions.

'You're bleeding,' she said.

'It's nothing, a flesh wound. Mind if I ask who the Defender belongs to?'

'Me,' she said, scooping out some clothes from the back of the vehicle.

'Honest?'

'Along with my name, it's the second real fact you know about me,' she said, stripping off the uniform.

Look real enough, he thought, feeling an urgent stab of lust at the sight of her standing there in her bra and G-string. He idly wondered if she wanted any help with getting dressed. 'How the hell did you know where to find me?'

'Didn't think I'd give up that easily, did you?' she said, bending over, wriggling into a pair of jeans. He felt the blood fizz in his veins.

'A bit beyond the call of duty.'

'Who said anything about duty?' She smiled, pulling up the zip and taking hold of the sweater. 'Don't flatter yourself.' She flashed a cheeky grin. 'I was curious, that's all.'

'You saw me go to Kennedy's site?'

'Yup. I wondered what you were doing with that boy.'

'He's a trainee computer hacker,' Tallis said.

'Right.' She wrinkled her nose, not following him.

'Christ, Jimmy,' Tallis said. 'Is he all right?'

'Don't worry. I called a cab, put him in it. He got out seconds before the police arrived.'

'Thank God. You were saying?'

'While I was trying to suss that one out, I spotted our fair-haired friend.'

Tallis frowned. He was starting to remember things he wanted to forget, including the fact that they had just killed three American soldiers. 'Charlie, did you know that Asim sold me out?'

Her eyes widened in disbelief.

'You don't know?' he said.

'Of course I don't. Are you sure?'

'That's what our American friends said.'

'They would.'

'Think they were lying?' He really, really hoped so.

'Are you saying that Asim betrayed you?' She shook her head in disbelief.

He didn't know. Betrayal was such an emotive word. It was more a case of withholding the truth. Except why should he be surprised? Withholding the truth was the spook's stock in trade. 'Asim once told me never to accept the first-case scenario. I didn't realise he was being ironic.'

'Maybe he wasn't.'

'Whether he was or wasn't, there's a bigger issue than loyalty at stake. I need to get to Kennedy, and soon. Know where he's being held?'

'He isn't. He couldn't stand it, apparently, said he'd take his chances back in the real world. Last I heard he's back in Fort Shakenbrook. It would take an army to get inside.'

38

IT DIDN'T. It took two words.

First, they drove to Oz's place. He wasn't too pleased at being knocked up at four-thirty in the morning but once he saw the person responsible for breaking into his beauty sleep, he lightened up. Even in his dressing gown, Oz managed to look proud and imposing, Tallis thought.

'I don't want to know how you got into this mess,' Oz said, looking Tallis up and down before casting a mischievous glance in Lavender's direction.

'If you're thinking what I think you're thinking,' Tallis said, 'forget it.'

'If you say so.' Oz grinned. 'Going to introduce us?' he said, showing them inside.

Tallis did. 'Think you can get them off?' he said, lifting his arms and rattling the restraints. They were standing in Oz and Cheryl's living room. It was all hot colours, bleached-out backgrounds, a reminder, maybe, of the Australian outback.

'No prob. I'll drill the locks out. Want to clean up and get some shut-eye first? You could use the spare bedroom.'

Tallis looked at Lavender. For someone who'd been working round the clock she looked remarkably perky. 'I'd rather use some coffee,' she said.

Tallis agreed. 'Then I'd really like to get moving.'

'All right, give me five,' Oz said. 'Follow me to the kitchen, Charlie. Then you can tell me how you two met.' He winked back at Tallis.

Tallis sank down into the nearest easy chair. Lavender was quite a girl. On the drive to Oz's place, she'd told him how she'd watched the workings of the airbase, spotted the lax approach to security deep inside, timed the patrols protecting the perimeter, cut through the chain link with wire cutters and made her move. If it wasn't for Lavender, he'd be somewhere over the horizon, well outside British airspace, dressed in double-layer nappies, a tracksuit in excruciating taste and flat on his back shackled to a stretcher.

'Here,' Lavender said, putting a mug of coffee down in front of him. 'I got you a straw. Thought it was better than you trying to pick the mug up and spilling hot coffee down your trousers.'

He smiled thanks. It didn't suit him to feel so dependent, but he had no choice.

'How are you going to tackle Kennedy?' she said, giving him a level look. He'd already told her of his suspicions, how Kennedy had tricked everyone in order to carry out a bomb attack in some perverted act of revenge. She, like him, was aghast at the prospect of Britain's second major city suffering what would appear to be a terrorist attack just when the security services thought 'it was safe.

'No point in appealing to his better nature. He's planned this for a while.'

'Think you know where he'll strike?'

Not for certain, but there was a deadly logic to one location that sprang immediately to mind. Two criteria were needed: vulnerability and accessibility. Where else would Kennedy's enemies and those who'd denied Billy Kennedy gainful employment gather? When he'd tried to talk to Kennedy about possible terrorist locations, Kennedy had breezed on about all the main landmarks bar one.

'I've got a rough idea.'

'Kennedy will hardly confirm it.'

'Depends on the pressure I put on him.'

Lavender's expression turned thoughtful.

'What?' he said.

'You should be careful.'

'I'm always careful.' He laughed.

'I don't mean like that.' She was unsmiling. Her eyes, deep pools of green, looked troubled. 'Kennedy's dangerous but not for the reasons you think. He's a shrewd operator. You're vulnerable to a man like him because of the lousy relationship you had with your dad. The man's got under your skin.' Tallis opened his mouth in protest, even though he knew deep down that she spoke the truth. Lavender continued to talk. 'Equally, he's vulnerable to you because you represent the son he no longer has. He

E.V. SEYMOUR 451

sees you as a replacement. If push comes to shove, he'd make allowances for you.'

'For God's sake, are you a shrink, too?' It sounded harsh, testing, probably because, again, he knew she was right. Instantly regretting his flash of bad temper, he apologised straight away.

'Still think it wise to go in alone?' she said softly.

'Until I'm absolutely certain about Asim, I don't have much choice. Anyway.' He grinned. 'I won't be alone, will I?'

Lavender glanced up at him from beneath coal-black lashes and smiled.

Tallis was freed shortly before six-thirty that morning. Oz insisted they have breakfast to celebrate. Tallis looked at his watch. If he was correct, he had four hours to avert disaster so it made good sense to eat—bacon butties all round care of a carryout sandwich shop. Tallis was glad that Lavender wasn't one of those women who were picky about diet. Food was food—especially when expending the amount of calories she was.

'Here,' she said, handing him her weapon. 'Might come in handy.' It was a Beretta, a model 92, 9 mm, 8-round magazine, compact version.

He thanked her, took it. 'Don't suppose you've got a phone on you?'

She nodded, reached into her jacket pocket. 'Asim?'

'Not yet.'

'Bit early for a call,' she said, ruthlessly fishing.

It was. Crow was going to be none too happy, he thought, punching in her number, walking away a little. To his surprise she answered after the second ring, though he was right about her not being exactly thrilled to hear from him. Still, he'd soon change that.

'Right, Micky, might be worth you following up some names. Got a pen handy? I reckon they're all associates of Johnny Kennedy's. Once you've found out, let Gavin Shaw know at the Organised Crime Division, West Midlands.'

Aware that Shakenbrook might be under surveillance by both sides of the divide, Tallis borrowed Oz's work van. He also borrowed a pair of overalls. Even though he knew the code to open the electronic gates, he wanted Kennedy to know that he was playing things by the book, that he was showing due respect, that he didn't suspect him of hostile intent. It didn't occur to him that the man would refuse to let him in. Like Lavender had pointed out: Kennedy needed him.

Pulling up outside shortly before eight-thirty, he leant out of the van and activated the voice entry system. Two words were all it took: 'Johnny, Tallis.'

The gates swung open. Tallis felt as if he was seeing his surroundings for the first time, the slow, elegant curve of trees lining the block-paved drive, the vistas and terraces, the lawns and flower beds, the ha-ha and extensive grounds beyond. Then there was Shakenbrook rising up out of the landscape, defiant, proud. Kennedy, alone, stood at the entrance, a smile concealing the darkness in his eyes.

Tallis parked, jumped out, pulled off the overalls, throwing them into the back of the van.

'I knew you'd come back.' Kennedy smiled in greeting.

'Did you?' Tallis's voice was even. 'Where are Sam and Melissa?'

'Somewhere safe,' Kennedy said, closing the door behind them, letting Tallis walk ahead. 'I know it's early but you look as if you could do with a drink.'

'I could do with the truth.'

Kennedy didn't break step. 'What will it be?' he said, crossing the hall to the drawing room. 'Think I'm up for a Scotch and soda. That do you?'

'Johnny, can we stop playing games?'

Kennedy wheeled round. 'What's the matter?'

'I know what you're planning.'

'To stay alive.' Kennedy let out a dry laugh.

'To kill hundreds of innocent people.'

Kennedy said nothing, slowly helped himself to a drink from the cabinet. He had one of those old-fashioned soda siphons like the one Tallis's dad had used when he was a kid. His dad used to drink milk and soda, Tallis remembered, for when he'd had one of his frequent upset stomachs. After all these years, the thought still made him shudder.

Kennedy turned round, studied him with deep, distant eyes. 'Sure I can't tempt you?'

Tallis shook his head. 'You're using Ahmed and his crew as a smokescreen.'

'Am I?' A sly smile played on Kennedy's lips.

Tallis stared at him. Why did he look so triumphant? Then the truth suddenly hit Tallis with the same force as the Birmingham-to-Euston Intercity. He should have tumbled to it before. There *was* no smokescreen. Out of all the leading crime bosses, Ahmed simply fitted the profile best. Kennedy had set him up. He knew where to leave the evidence, how to incriminate his so-called brother in arms, and because he'd always come up with the goods before, why wouldn't he be believed this time? Even if Asim and his team found out that Ahmed was innocent, which was a moot point—people tended to believe what they wanted to believe in matters of terrorism—the real bombing would already have taken place by then.

'Wasn't difficult,' Kennedy murmured. 'To say that he was a sympathiser was an understatement.'

'The world is full of sympathisers. Doesn't mean to say they actively aid and abet terrorism.'

'True,' Kennedy conceded, as if it were a matter of no consequence.

'You want revenge for Billy's ruined life,' Tallis said simply.

'I took my revenge some time ago,' Kennedy said, snatching at his drink.

'On the wrong man.'

Kennedy gave Tallis a slow-eyed stare. No shock, no denial, Kennedy's failure to respond damning. 'The Turks were right,' Tallis continued slowly. 'You were even inciting your criminal chums, stirring them up, meanwhile playing the security services and law enforcement agencies, convincing them that you, and you alone, could deliver known criminals and unknown terrorists.' That's why Ahmed had looked so concerned after the first meeting, Tallis recalled. He knew that if anyone would be in the firing line for a link to fundamentalist nutters, he'd be first. Had he said as much to Kennedy? Was that the reason Kennedy had been in such a foul mood afterwards? 'Fuck, I reckon you even had Gabriel killed to build up your credibility.'

Kennedy said nothing.

Tallis felt his stomach give a queasy lurch. The man had died in agony. Kennedy had ordered it, supervised it. It was Kennedy who'd had his hand on the remote. 'He found out about your real agenda, didn't he?'

Kennedy didn't speak, his expression curiously inert.

'Everything you've said and done has been a blind so that you can take revenge.'

'What's wrong with that?'

'You're looking the wrong way.'

'Oh, yeah?' Kennedy smiled.

'You should be taking a good hard look at yourself.' Tallis's tone was uncompromising.

Kennedy's smile weakened. 'How do you work that out?'

'For your own dismal failures as a father.' And, my God, I should know, Tallis thought.

The smile vanished.

'Yeah,' Tallis jeered. 'Sam told me,' he said, driving home the emotional stake deep into Kennedy's heart. 'It was your fault Billy couldn't find work. It was your thuggish reputation that meant nobody wanted to touch him. Deep down, he was ashamed of you.'

'That's not true,' Kennedy burst out. 'It's a filthy lie.'

Time to give the stake a little twist. 'Why else do you think he stepped out in front of that car that night?'

'You bastard. He did no such thing.'

'How do you know? Did you speak to Carroll or his wife before you had him killed?'

'Stupid fucking man,' Kennedy cursed with savagery. 'He should never have covered for Finch.'

'Do you kill everyone who gets in your way? Is that why you had Garry Morello slotted?'

'Morello?' Kennedy railed. 'Who the fuck's Morello?'

'The journalist who was investigating you, who saw you with Tardarti.'

Kennedy gritted his teeth. 'I don't know what, or who, you're talking about.'

Tallis studied him. Kennedy looked genuinely clueless. Looked as if Crow was on the right trail after all. None of this was looking any prettier. He glanced at his watch and swallowed. 'I know the building you've targeted.'

'Really?' Kennedy shrugged.

'The Rotunda.' Tallis watched Kennedy with the same precision as a bird of prey.

'Why would I do that?' His voice was even but the glint in his eyes betrayed him.

'Because it will kill your enemies with one click of a button. Today's the day they're having their little party, remember?'

Kennedy stared at him, unblinking.

'Who's the bomber?' Tallis demanded.

A dark laugh trickled out between Kennedy's bloodless lips. 'There is no bomber.'

Christ, how can four and a half hours disappear to thirty-five minutes? Tallis thought, glancing at the grandfather clock in the drawing room. 'If you avert an attack, I'll do my best to put in a good word for you. The fact you've already helped should count for something.'

'Paul, you have this all wrong.'

'You want to spend the rest of your days banged up in Belmarsh?' Tallis burst out angrily. 'Never seeing your wife, or watching your daughter grow up, or holding Billy when he dies?'

'Like I said,' Kennedy said, eyes stormy. 'There is no bomber.'

Ten people on the list, Tallis thought frantically. Ten bombers? He pulled the Beretta.

'You won't shoot me.' Kennedy's voice was like honey dripping in his ear.

'The last man to say that didn't live to regret it.'

'We're family, you and me,' Kennedy schmoozed, taking a step backwards towards the drinks cabinet. 'First time I clapped eyes on you, I knew you could be like a son to me, like I could be a dad, a proper dad, to you. I know what you've been through.'

'Shut up.' Tallis tightened his grip. 'Contact the bombers. Call them off. Innocent people will be killed, children. You want blood on your conscience?'

But Kennedy was gone, lost in a monologue of self-justification. 'We've both suffered in life. We're cut from the same cloth, you and me, know what we want, how to get it. Both smart as razors.' Kennedy laughed. 'Both…'

Without warning, Kennedy produced a gun like a magician delivers a canary from the sleeve of his jacket. 'I never wanted it this way,' he said, eyes narrowed. 'And, for what it's worth, I never played you, Paul. Everything I said and believed about you was genuine, *is* genuine.'

'Don't be so bloody stupid,' Tallis said, steely. 'Look, in twenty minutes there will be a hole in the centre of Birmingham as big as a moon crater.'

'Shame.'

Tallis blinked. What the hell? His hand tightened on the gun. 'For Chrissakes, this is the city you love…'

'The city that fucked me over,' Kennedy growled.

Tallis stood his ground. 'You have to abort the attack.'

'Couldn't if I wanted to.'

'Yes, you can,' Tallis yelled in frustration. The big hand was ticking relentlessly round the clock.

'What are you waiting for?' Kennedy goaded Tallis. 'Shoot me.'

Tallis felt sweat break out across his brow. Somehow he had to keep things moving, keep Kennedy talking. If he took down Kennedy, he'd never find out the exact location of the strike and how to stop it. 'The meeting with Tardarti in Turkey,' he began.

'Nothing more than a ruse to prove I was a credible source of intelligence.' Kennedy smiled grimly. 'That prat,

Napier, fell for it sweet as a nut. Thought he was onto something really big. Didn't take much convincing, I can tell you, positively gagging for glory. Suppose that's what happens to people when they know they're screwed. They like the idea of one last roll of the dice. He really is a sick man, you know.' Then, for reasons beyond Tallis, Kennedy raised his weapon, left-handed. Two shots rang out simultaneously, one veering wide. Tallis leapt forward to Kennedy's crumpled form. 'Good shot,' Kennedy murmured, blood seeping from a wound in his chest. Tallis cursed. It should have been a clean shot to wing him, to disable his shooting arm, but instinct had prevailed. Either kill or be killed. Was that what Kennedy really wanted, a perverse desire for death by cop?

'Johnny, the bomber…'

Kennedy smiled. 'Told you, son. There's no bomber.'

'But, Johnny…'

'Look after my Billy for me, won't you?'

'Yes, Johnny, but, please, this is really important,' Tallis said, cradling the man in his arms, watching the light in his eyes waste and fade.

'You're a good man, Paul.' Kennedy smiled then he was gone.

Fuck, fuck, fuck, Tallis cursed, laying Kennedy down and reaching for his phone. Frantically trying to think. No bomber. Building about to blow. Instantly he thought about Demolition Dave, Griggsy, then, hell, yes, an idea as fragile as a butterfly was hovering at the back of his mind, and strangely he had Napier to thank for shining a light in a most unlikely corner. Tallis punched in a number. 'Listen, Asim, you son of a bitch. You've got exactly fourteen and a half minutes to evacuate the Rotunda.'

39

IT STARTED as a whisper, a murmur, eventually a word followed by phrases, the odd sentence until the ripple effect of the news spread like wildfire throughout the assembly. The mayor, together with the chairman of the development company, took the lead, moving swiftly, without panic, without fuss.

They were British, for God's sake. Dignitaries and worthies, the great and the good of Birmingham City Council headed silently after them for the nearest exits. Among their number was a man called Cain Finch and two others who'd travelled in the car with him that fateful night; they didn't yet realise that they were the reason behind the evacuation. They didn't catch on that they were about to be interviewed by West Midlands police.

Outside, media personnel, the communications men, television and camera crews hung around, trying to get the story, before being moved on briskly by police officers, some armed, to a designated place of safety. Ironically, Kennedy's diversionary tactics had ensured a heavy police presence already in the city so that shoppers in the nearby

Bullring and commuters from New Street Station were also quickly evacuated from the scene. As the bomb disposal team moved in, confirming that another terrorist attack was in the process of being thwarted, smartly dressed men, some wearing sunglasses, all with ear-pieces, talked into their cuffs. A tall Egyptian-looking fellow was taking command. He had one hand clamped to his ear, his wrist to his mouth near the transmitter embedded in his sleeve.

'Yes, I've passed on the information to the bomb squad. I've got all that. Yes, they know to look in the walls and ceilings, around the windows, all the weakest spots in the structure. They've already uncovered and spotted detonation wires and dismantled them. Picked up a bloke in the vicinity, Justin Stathers... What...? Right, one of Kennedy's men. You've done a terrific job, Paul. We'll talk later and I'll explain more fully.'

Tallis closed his phone. He was standing outside Shakenbrook. Sun was pouring through silvery-tipped cloud. The sky looked like a sea of mercury. He took a deep breath, knowing that to try to stop the shaking of his limbs, the sickness he felt was a waste of time. You could only go with it, let it run its course. He smiled to himself. Nobody mentioned the nausea that followed the taking of a life in movies or books. Wasn't cool.

Exhaling and gulping down another lungful of wet air, he realised how sheer luck had prevented disaster that morning. Luck, that Kennedy by his stout denial of bombers had pointed him in a different, less obvious direction. Luck, that Napier's association with the First Gulf War had led Tallis off on a random yet no less calculated train of thought. He'd heard of insurgents who, by bribing construction workers, planted artillery shells and explosives into the fabric of newly constructed schools and hospitals in an attempt to inflict massive casualties. Kennedy was not only perfectly placed as a supplier to access the Rotunda, but Tallis wagered he'd also illicitly supplied men—ten men exactly and probably under assumed names—to build the explosives into the ceilings, the walls, the windows. For all his charm and charisma, he was a cold-blooded murderer at heart. Any blurred feelings he'd had for the man disappeared.

Napier, however, was a tough one. Came down to heroes and crooks, Tallis decided. Napier reminded him of a football player who, ducking and weaving down the pitch, twisting his way through a whole tranche of defenders, avoiding every single tackle, finally passed the ball heroically to a striker, only to watch his teammate cock it up and pass to the opposite side. His illness probably contributed to his mental state, Tallis thought sadly, watching as a familiar figure walked towards him.

'What did Asim say?'

'Thanks very much.'

'I meant about you.' Lavender flicked an engaging smile.

'That the Americans were playing outside the box. He claimed the service had sent caveats with all communications to them insisting that I was working undercover with Kennedy and that no action should be taken against me.'

'Which they ignored.'

'So it seems.'

'You don't believe him?'

Tallis flashed a weary smile. 'I'm not sure who to believe.'

'Well, as long as we're not in the dock for murder, I guess all's well that ends well. You look as if you need a drink.'

Tallis smiled, remembering Kennedy saying the same, his words and voice a haunting refrain in his ear. 'You're probably right.'

'I'll treat you,' she said, brightening. 'Bar Estilo?' A Spanish-themed tapas bar near the Mailbox, Tallis remembered. He used to visit it with Belle, whose flat had been nearby.

'I'd prefer somewhere more central.'

'Somewhere chic and minimalist?'

'Anywhere where they serve a decent pint.' Tallis laughed, taking her hand.

40

TALLIS looked out of the window and watched the world slow as the train pulled into Euston station. He felt glad that the sun was shining, glad it was uncommonly warm for the time of year. It meant the plan should work like clockwork.

It was two weeks later, ten days since he'd received the strangest of phone calls, a week since he'd hooked up with Gayle Morello and agreed to meet, the destination a newly opened café opposite Kentish Town Tube station. Alighting from the train early, he went in search of a double-shot espresso. He needed the caffeine fix. He wanted to be alert.

Twenty minutes later and suitably hot-wired, he was boarding a tube on the Northern line, the compartment filled with the babble of foreign voices. Tallis tuned in, tuned out. He had other, more pressing, matters on his mind.

As anticipated, Gayle was already there. She'd taken a seat outside on the pavement below a green-and-white striped awning, the café behind her full of light, modern, with prints on the walls, wholesome looking. A fair number of people were inside, eating and drinking.

On his approach, she rose, kissed him on both cheeks and asked what she could get him. He ordered a coffee he knew he'd never drink, watched as she moved smoothly inside, a roll in her hips. He took out his sunglasses and put them on, looked the busy street up and down, picked up the menu, clocked his fellow diners, exchanged a glance with a fat woman sitting at the next-door table. For a second he flashed back to the café in Turkey.

After a few moments Gayle reappeared, a smile on her face.

'You look good,' he said. He meant it. She glowed. A strange state for a new widow, he thought, until he remembered his mum. That was different, he told himself sharply. His mother had said goodbye to his father a long time ago. There was a big contrast between sudden, violent death, or death before time, and someone old fading painfully away. Made a big difference to those left behind. He should know.

'Thanks,' she said, gracefully crossing her legs. 'Sorry I didn't inform you about the funeral. Kathleen was supposed to be in charge of contacting everyone. She obviously slipped up.'

'Kathleen's your sister, right?'

She agreed with her eyes and raised the cup to her lips.

'What about Stephen?'

She took a slow sip. 'What about him?'

'Wasn't he involved in the funeral arrangements? I'd have thought he remembered talking to me.'

Her expression was apologetic. 'Sorry, Paul. Like I said,

there was a lot to organise. There was quite a turnout, as you'd imagine. I left Stephen in charge of catering.'

'Makes sense. What with his experience,' Tallis said, stretching out his legs.

'Experience?' She frowned.

'I guess he must have done it before—when Bryn was killed.'

'Oh, yes, I see,' she said, flicking him a quick smile.

'Garry mentioned it last time I saw him.'

'Mentioned what?' Her grey-blue eyes flicked from him to the street and back again. It took less than a second.

'That Bryn died in suspicious circumstances. You know, with there being a mystery car involved.'

'I don't know where you got that idea.' She stiffened.

'It wasn't true?'

'It was never proved.'

'No,' he said mildly, picking up his cup. 'It's nice here, isn't it?' He smiled.

'It is,' she said, her mouth a short frozen line.

He watched as she picked up the cup again. At this rate she was going to run out of coffee.

'I'm surprised Garry mentioned the car,' she said, trying to sound as if it was a matter of curiosity rather than suspicion.

'Why?'

'We never really talked about it.'

Tallis shrugged. 'Garry was an investigative journalist. He had an enquiring mind.'

'You're right there,' she said with a sudden smile.

'That's why we hit it off. Both got the same nose for intrigue. Both of us sticklers for the truth,' he said, sweeping his sunglasses off, giving her the full force of his glaring expression.

Again, the lift of the cup to the mouth. Unhurried. Very cool. Her eyes did that funny thing again. Flick. Flick.

'When I came to your flat after Garry was killed,' Tallis said, 'a couple of things jarred—like the toilet seat.'

'The what?' She half smiled, half frowned.

'I wondered why a woman living alone would leave it up, but then I thought you'd probably had a male visitor, maybe one of the coppers.'

'And you'd be right,' she said.

'But when I searched Garry's room, I noticed some-thing odd.'

'Oh?'

'A passbook in your old married name. It was dated several months after Bryn died. Lot of money in it.'

'Like most husbands, Bryn had life insurance,' she said harshly.

Tallis nodded. His tone was even. 'Like I said, only got me thinking. I'm guessing, because of the nature of his job, Garry's insurance was particularly high.'

'So what? And you had no business going through my stuff,' she added, indignant.

'Quite right. But you see I'm starting to find patterns here. Like Bryn, Garry was an only son.'

'Your point?' she said, a haughty note in her voice.

'Both inherited from their surviving parent a year

before they were killed.' He knew that Crow had done her research well.

'Coincidence.' Flick. Flick.

'Making you a very wealthy woman.'

'You think money matters a damn to me?' she snarled. 'I've lost two of the most important men in my life.'

'That's right, but you never really loved either of them. That role was reserved for Stephen.'

'My brother?' She burst out laughing.

'Your lover. You don't have a brother.'

A white van sped past. Tallis turned his head. Where Highgate Road filtered into Kentish Town Road, he saw a bike weaving through the traffic, hacking towards them. Good.

'Dead easy, wasn't it? You were the only person who could exploit Garry's contacts, who could delve into Garry's murky little world, a world where anyone might bear him a grudge. You knew of his trips to Turkey. Was it Stephen who mugged him and took his wallet, or did you pay someone else to do your dirty work? And what about Reid and Brass, the men who killed him? Nice choice, going to Kennedy's old employees. Did Stephen approach them, or did you? And then you paid to have them killed, didn't you?'

The sound of the bike was deafening.

'I don't have to listen to this,' she said, angrily standing up to leave, as he'd known she would. Kicking the chair back, he made a grab for her. Twisting and turning, she yelled a stream of obscenities, appealing to the fat woman sitting at the next-door table, who sat as implacable as statuary. At the sight of the two masked figures speeding towards them Gayle's screams grew louder and more desperate. People were looking. People were rising from their chairs.

'What is it, Gayle?' Tallis shouted in her ear. 'Afraid of being caught in the crossfire?'

On seeing the bike speed to a halt, people instinctively screamed and dived for cover. Only Tallis and the fat woman remained mute. The pillion passenger got off the bike, strode towards them, reaching into his jacket with menacing ease. Gayle was shouting and struggling, doing everything in her power to twist away from Tallis, to let him take the bullet. Tallis stood, stubborn and resolute, grip on the straining woman vice-like. He wasn't afraid. He'd been in worse situations than this. Far worse.

'Not me, you fool,' Gayle Morello cried out. 'Him!'

The figure hesitated, withdrew his hand from his jacket empty, and removed the helmet. Tallis took the strain as Gayle's knees buckled.

'Remember me, Mrs Morello? I'm the bloke you tried to recruit to kill Mr Tallis here? All right, Paul?' The man winked.

'Good to see you, Stu. Nice bit of undercover work. Glad you're back in the fold. Lovely to see you again, too,' Tallis said, glancing appreciatively across at Charlie Lavender, who was sitting smiling broadly.

The fat woman at the neighbouring table stood up and trundled towards them. 'Gayle Morello,' Crow said, 'I'm arresting you for conspiracy to murder.'

* * *

'I guess this is it,' Lavender said. They were standing outside the police station. 'Playtime over. You go your way. I go mine.'

'Charlie…'

'It's cool, Tallis.' She smiled, pressing a finger lightly to his lips. 'I'll come to the rescue again some day.'

'Promise?' He grinned.

'You bet,' she said, turning and walking away with a laugh.

'Charlie?' he called after her.

'Yeah?' She turned.

'Thanks.'

'The pleasure was all mine.' She winked.

He watched as she swung onto the bike, started the engine and drove away. She didn't look back.

'Enough, Romeo,' Crow said, emerging from the entrance to the nick. She was looking particularly florid, Tallis thought. 'Once I've sorted Mrs Morello out, you can take me for a large drink.'

'Can't. Got a previous engagement.'

'I thought the previous engagement just disappeared down the road.'

'Well, you were wrong.' Tallis laughed, walking away.

'I'll be in touch,' she called after him, a little desperately, he thought.

'Can't wait,' he called back.

He caught a tube to South Kensington, went to the usual hotel, asked for the usual reservation and went to his room. There he showered, shaved and exchanged his jeans, T-shirt and trainers for a pale blue tailored shirt, dark trousers and jacket and Oxford loafers. After brief deliberation, he chose a navy tie with a gold stripe. Leaving the hotel, he walked over the road to where several taxis were waiting. Jumping inside, he asked the driver to take him to the Ritz Hotel in Piccadilly. The journey was spectacularly uneventful. The cabbie was one of those rare, silent types. Tallis felt glad.

Nodding to the doorman, Tallis made his way to the Palm Court dining room where afternoon tea was being served. What a very civilised venue, he thought, glancing across the sumptuously decorated room, for such uncivilised business.

'May I help you, sir?' a waiter enquired.

'It's fine, thank you,' he said, gesturing to a corner table where Asim was waiting for him.

'Very good, sir. This way.'

Tallis slowly crossed the room, standing back as a chair was pulled out for him. He sat down, looked at Asim, who was smiling.

'Glad you could join me,' Asim said. 'Tea?'

Tallis nodded. As soon as the waiter disappeared, he leant forward. 'Has that Yank—Koroglu, or whatever the hell he's called—been put back in his box?'

'Most definitely. Probably on a literacy course even as we speak.'

'Ah, the mysterious caveats,' Tallis said.

'Nothing mysterious about them, Paul. They were plain as day.'

'So no suggestion of you selling me out?' Tallis watched Asim's face very carefully, listened closely to the answer.

'You're too valuable to us. We wouldn't want to lose you.'

Ten steps ahead, Asim, Tallis thought, studying the man's normally unreadable face. If he was a betting man, he'd say, this time, Asim was telling the truth. However, Tallis didn't allow himself to get too carried away. Quite simply, Asim was protecting his asset, his decision based on sound commercial sense. 'So he won't be pressing charges?'

'For what?' Asim said, offering him a teeny thinly sliced sandwich.

'The three American soldiers who died,' Tallis said, declining.

'Unfortunate accident. Happens all the time.'

'So the next time I visit the States, I won't be arrested, deported or clapped in irons—that right?'

Asim's smile was broad. 'Funny you should say that.'

'Why?' Tallis said, suspicious. 'Oh, no,' he said, spotting the mischief in Asim's eyes. 'I didn't mean I planned to go there.'

'No?' Asim laughed playfully.

'No,' Tallis insisted, reaching grumpily for a scone.

'Tell you what,' Asim said, taking a pound coin from his pocket. 'Let's toss for it.'

'Fuck's sake, is this how you normally select an operative for a job?'

'You're not an operative, remember.' Asim's eyes gleamed.

Hired hand, more like. 'What happens if it goes the other way?'

'You get to travel somewhere else.'

Tallis glanced away, watched his fellow diners and listened to the chink of china, thinking what protected lives these people had because of people like him. 'Go on, then, flip the coin,' he dared Asim. He never could resist a challenge.

Asim did. The coin went high, spinning and spinning, somersaulting through the air until gravity took over and it started its final descent. Asim's smooth hand shot out ready, his other hand poised to capture the coin, which it did with a resounding slap. 'What's it to be?' he asked.

Tallis closed his eyes tight, made a wish like he used to do as a kid and, opening them, cried, 'Heads!'

Then, like the showman he was, Asim slid his hand away and smiled.

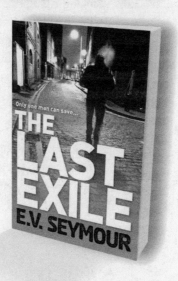